Alexandra Joel is the author of *Bes*
in Australia and *Parade: The Story*
books detail the development of
identity.

She is a former editor of the Australian edition of *Harper's Bazaar* and of *Portfolio,* Australia's first magazine for working women. She has also been a regular contributor of feature articles, interviews and reviews to a number of national and metropolitan publications.

More recently, Alexandra has been a practising counsellor and psychotherapist. She is an honours graduate from the University of Sydney.

ROSETTA

ALEXANDRA JOEL

VINTAGE BOOKS
Australia

A Vintage book
Published by Random House Australia Pty Ltd
Level 3, 100 Pacific Highway, North Sydney NSW 2060
www.randomhouse.com.au

First published by Vintage in 2016

Random House Books is part of the Penguin Random House group of companies whose addresses can be found at global.penguinrandomhouse.com/offices.

National Library of Australia
Cataloguing-in-Publication entry

Joel, Alexandra, 1953– author
Rosetta: a scandalous true story/Alexandra Joel

ISBN 978 0 14378 047 2 (paperback)

Solomon, Rosetta
Women – Australia – Biography
Runaway wives – Australia – Biography
Family secrets

920.72

Cover image © Sarah Jarrett, courtesy of Arcangel
Cover design by Sandy Cull, gogoGingko
Typeset in 12/15.5 Minion Pro by Midland Typesetters, Australia
Printed in Australia by Griffin Press, an accredited ISO AS/NZS 14001:2004 Environmental Management System printer

Random House Australia uses papers that are natural, renewable and recyclable products and made from wood grown in sustainable forests. The logging and manufacturing processes are expected to conform to the environmental regulations of the country of origin.

To my children

Rosetta stone

'A key to some previously indecipherable mystery ...'

Oxford English Dictionary

PART ONE

AUSTRALIA

ONE

MELBOURNE, 1905

She is filled with anguish and uncertainty. Her future is opaque. The dreadful step she is contemplating torments her during endless troubled nights. The action she considers is both irrevocable and forbidden; the consequences grave. For a wife to leave her husband is, at best, unwise. But to leave her child? She is aware that condemnation will rain down upon her from all sides.

What will happen to her if she does this thing? How will her life unfold? And yet if she does nothing, stays exactly as she is, can she tolerate an eternity spent existing in a void? These questions gnaw at her until she feels she is quite mad.

It is in this turbulent condition Rosetta recalls that some time ago she heard of a talented fortune teller who could be found near Melbourne's mysterious Chinatown. It may well have been her aristocratic Irish friend, Lilian Pakenham, who told her – yes, that was it – during one of their intimate exchanges over cups of Lapsang Souchong tea.

'There is a man,' Lilian had said, smoothing her yellow dress. 'He is part Chinese but very handsome. He has special gifts …'

Momentarily, Rosetta closes her dark eyes. She cannot recall the seer's name – something exotic, she thinks, and vaguely improbable. It doesn't matter. She remembers the address; it is enough for now. She decides that if in one week's time she is no closer to a resolution she will seek the oriental fortune teller out.

Rosetta hopes this plan will afford her a measure of tranquillity. It does not. During the hours that follow, while she shops for bread and milk and cheese, returns home, attempts to write a letter to one of her younger sisters, her unrest seems only to increase.

She tries to sew. It is impossible; the needle slips. She pricks her finger, sees a bead of crimson blood and feels squeamish. Finally, she throws the child's dress and its unfinished hem onto a chair and starts to pace about the room. It seems unnaturally confining, as if the very walls, the timber beams and lintels are conspiring to trap and restrain. Surely this distress cannot be endured for another seven days.

Yet still Rosetta hesitates. She forces herself to be still, to think. The man will surely prove a charlatan; to seek his counsel is a foolish escapade. Rosetta resolves that she must remain exactly where she is. 'It is the wisest course,' she thinks.

Slowly, she sits down again. She regards the small, crumpled dress that has been cast aside. Then, suddenly, Rosetta rises to her feet. She reaches for her coat and reticule, crams her beribboned hat onto her thick, bronze-coloured hair and flies out of the door.

TWO

Rosetta is not an invention. She lived. She created an extraordinary life, took risks, transcended all manner of circumstances that might have constrained her from inhabiting the world of international glamour and desire which she embraced and which in turn embraced her.

I see her, vividly alive, at twenty-five: an arresting beauty with thick chestnut hair and restless, toffee-coloured eyes. She has been married since the age of eighteen. Her husband is a respectable man of means. She is a mother, too. The year is 1905, the place is Melbourne, capital of gold-rush enriched Victoria, a thriving state in the new nation of Australia. All seems well.

But this is the year when – abruptly, scandalously – everything changes. Rosetta leaves, and not just her husband, though this is bad enough. No, she does something far worse than that. She abandons little Frances Catherine, aged just five; runs away with a man self-styled Zeno the Magnificent. Shockingly, Zeno is half Chinese. He is also a mesmerising schemer, a fortune teller and seducer of souls. With wit, charm and wile, Rosetta and Zeno first enchant the inhabitants of Sydney. Next, with their sights set on more distant horizons and grander goals, they conquer British and European society. Princes, duchesses, lords and ladies – all find themselves helplessly beguiled.

There will be no more children for Rosetta. Yet, even after her triumphant return to Australia, she has no contact with her daughter. She never meets her granddaughter (my mother, Sybil), or her great-granddaughter – me. On 28 July 1958, just five days before my fifth birthday, Rosetta dies. But none of us, neither daughter, granddaughter nor great-granddaughter, is aware this has transpired.

I have always known that my great-grandmother did a dreadful thing. It must have been when I was very young that I was first told she deserted her only child. This alarming knowledge – some mothers simply choose to disappear – became a part of the child I was, my identity.

Where had my errant great-grandmother gone, and why?

No doubt even in the far-off 1950s, when children were not encouraged to be forthcoming but, rather, to know their place, many were braver than I was, asked more questions, demanded answers in response. I did not.

I don't believe it was simple timidity that caused my questions to remain unspoken; it had something more to do with the risk I sensed. I suppose that every family has its painful, bruised places to which one journeys at one's peril. Even as a child I understood the way in which a misplaced query might disturb these tender realms.

Abandonment by the one who gave you life; the loss is both vast and elemental. I knew, on some unconscious, visceral level, that beneath my grandmother's and mother's glamorous facades, behind their lacquered hairstyles and bright, carefully lipsticked mouths, lay the shadows of hurt and turmoil.

Words can be avoided, thoughts suppressed, but feelings work their way through the line and texture of one's being. None of us escaped though, not surprisingly, Rosetta's daughter, Frances, my Nana Billie, was the most deeply affected by her mother's flight. Billie was not an easy woman, being mercurial in mood and acutely sensitive to any act or comment that she perceived could be a slight. Even minor incidents were likely to evoke a furious response. Though tender-hearted, a kind of madness would erupt.

'She'd get upset and throw cups and saucers,' my mother confessed one morning over tea.

'At what?' I asked.

'At me.'

A child has no trouble knowing damage when she lives with it each day.

Over the years my curiosity did not wane. It stayed hovering at the furthest edges of sentience, unsaid. The truth is, whether talked about or not, it would have made no difference. Nobody knew anything.

'I wasn't even told her name,' I remember my mother saying not so very long ago while we sat together in the sterile comfort of her dentist's waiting room. A moment later, her own name was called.

'Sybil? Sybil Joel?'

'Yes.' And then she rose, was escorted by a nurse with a professional smile towards a gleaming, equipment-filled room that could be glimpsed behind a screen of synthetic plant life.

I followed but, despite the glare of the fluorescent lights, found that I'd become disorientated – the brief exchange had unsettled me. Names are quotidian, simple things yet have great power. When they are lost, that loss is beyond what can be calculated.

It was only after Billie's death, in 1988, that the first vital scrap of information was uncovered. Strangely, it was my father, Asher, who made the initial discovery and even then it was by accident. In his seventies, after a life spent largely on the public stage (Dad was best known for the organisation of royal visits and other state occasions), he was seeking an activity that would provide meaning to his days. Perhaps it was because 1988 was the year Australia marked two centuries of European settlement. When he was younger, my father might have expected to mastermind the celebrations.

'I need a challenge,' he proclaimed. This was a call to arms with which I was familiar, for he thrived on grand undertakings and intense activity, becoming melancholic when they ceased.

Dad's attention turned inward. He became absorbed by the private pursuit of family history, devoted to finding out all he could, not only about his ancestors, but almost anybody and anything connected to his rich past. It was only natural: my father had begun his career as a newspaperman back in the glory days of the 1920s and had lost neither his passion for unearthing facts nor for running what might prove a compelling tale to ground.

Evidence of his dedication to this new-found enterprise abounded. Files bulged with correspondence. Typists and research assistants came and went. Meanwhile my mother, all too aware of the enormous amount of time and attention her husband was devoting to this endeavour, began to grow peevish.

'What about me?' she said to him one day, with an expression that made it clear she did not enjoy being overlooked. 'I hardly know a thing about *my* family, and as for my grandmother, the one who took off – well, there's never been a trace.'

A secret story, waiting to be uncovered and disclosed; it was all that was required to pique Dad's curiosity.

My father had a special gleam in his eye, a buoyancy of step whenever he had come across a lead that might prove fruitful.

This must have been the way he looked on the day he announced to my mother, 'I've got it.'

'Got what?'

'Billie's death certificate.' I suppose Dad's eagerness seemed at odds with the nature of his find. 'I know her name!'

My mother, taken unawares, had been about to dial a number on the telephone. 'Whose name? What?' She turned and looked quizzically at him, the fingers of her hand still poised mid-air.

'Your grandmother's. She was called Rosetta. I'm going to find out more.'

And so Pandora's box was breached.

My father's small discovery re-ignited those old reporter's instincts honed so many years before. Galvanised, he sought out documents, found sources, looked in unexpected places. Startling details began to emerge.

I can recall the day he met me at the door of his office where, fired up with the exhilaration of the chase, he exclaimed, 'Al, Rosetta's life was incredible. There's the makings of a book here. You should write it.'

It was a brief remark, but my father's excited words – part suggestion, part command – stayed with me long after he passed away. I could not tell if they would prove to be a legacy or a burden.

THREE

I did not start seeking my great-grandmother until I had become a mother myself, and known tragedy. My life was ruptured, ripped apart. I had a child who died. It was a cataclysm that broke all the natural laws of the universe. How could it be that I would not spend another precious moment with her, that I would never, ever see her navy eyes or feathery hair, the sweet bow of her mouth again? As impossible as the sun setting in the east or rising in the west, it was beyond my imagination.

I tried not to scan the faces of other little girls in parks, on trains, in cars, on streets. Knowing the quest was hopeless, I did my best to resist. Come nightfall, though, my resolve evaporated. In my dreams I searched for her. And I began to wonder, did Rosetta ever look for her child, too?

Much later, with the balm of my son and another daughter, my world settled. By then I was aware that my great-grandmother had lived a passionate, daring life. Yet all the while she hid her secret shame, the little girl she left behind.

I was torn. Despite my growing fascination with Rosetta, I wondered: could I come or even want to know a woman I half thought a kind of monster? Despite my struggle, I found Rosetta irresistible. I went in search of her.

It was in the garage of my brother, Michael, that I first saw the results of my father's labours; tangible evidence of Rosetta's life.

'Here it is,' Michael said, running a protective hand over a brown cardboard filing box and three thick spiral binders, one black, one red and one blue.

'I've photocopied the family tree, but don't take anything else away,' he instructed. 'It can't be lost.'

She was his great-grandmother, too. But I did take it. I took everything.

When I arrived home I turned the contents out onto the smooth plane of my dining-room table and spread out what there was: a variety of ageing documents that had been assembled in shiny plastic sleeves, photocopies from the pages of old newspapers, the recollections of several people who knew Rosetta at first hand and a few short pieces of prose that Dad had written himself, typed up in pre-computer days on a machine that over-inked the e's and smudged the d's. Best of all was a folder of fading photographs and an intriguing bundle of handwritten letters, a number of them bearing crests and coronets. But would this trove be enough to re-create the woman whom I sought? I wasn't sure.

In the end, it didn't matter. Even with the gaps and the omissions, Rosetta became so real to me that not only could I picture her, I felt a kind of insistence, as if she were demanding to be brought back to life.

I did wonder if by embarking on this process of re-creation I might be guilty of committing a transgression. Though I made a promise to myself that I would not change any known facts, there was some anxiety. I asked myself if it would be wrong to lay claim to what Rosetta thought, felt or said, as if these things were grounded in the pure reality of truth. But then I reflected, even were a hundred people to provide a hundred memories of my great-grandmother, would any one of them have really known the contents of her mind, her heart?

It was then that I became a conjurer, calling forth a phantom with the name Rosetta.

FOUR

MELBOURNE, 1905

There is a sign on the first-floor entrance of 238 Swanston Street that reads '*Zeno the Magnificent*'; it is picked out in shimmering silver and gold. Rosetta, though her thoughts are whirling and she is out of breath, notes as she passes that it is not a gaudy thing, but a rather beautiful hand-painted arrangement of swirls and lines. A moment later the door opens – she wonders afterwards how he knew that she was there – and Rosetta steps inside.

She finds that she is looking at the great Zeno himself but, with a hot wave of shock, she realises that she has seen this man before.

In an instant images flood Rosetta's mind.

She is in a Carlton grocery on the corner of Lygon and Faraday streets. She sees herself struggling to keep hold of her three-year-old daughter, Frances, and the shopping; her long skirts tangle and the package of tea she carries goes flying. Then a handsome, dark, distinguished man with high cheekbones and faintly slanting eyes moves towards her and says, 'Please, allow me.'

The shop, its sacks of sugar, flour and spices, fades. Other customers, the grocer, her own child dissolve into a blur. The sounds of people talking and the carriages in the street are hardly heard. For Rosetta, only she and this man remain.

Rosetta finds she cannot look away. It isn't just his foreign countenance that draws her, but the way that he regards her, with a stillness. There is something in his gaze that speaks of danger. And something else, a feeling that he sees not just who she is but the woman she could be.

Afterwards, Rosetta would sometimes catch a glimpse of him, perhaps in the distance, or disappearing around the corner of a Carlton street. Always, he was just out of reach. Except at night, when he came to her in dreams.

With a jolt she emerges from her reverie, becomes aware that Zeno is waiting. He is in possession of the same quality of stillness that she recalls. His almond eyes retain their frank appraisal. There is, however, something she has not noticed previously, some new quality. Though the room is dim, Zeno appears to have about him a faint luminosity.

Nothing seems quite real. Mysterious images appear to twist and hover before her eyes; on one wall she can make out paintings of a lion, a scorpion and a rearing bull. There are other pictures, too, of red suns and yellow stars and moons.

Rosetta takes her place opposite Zeno at a small, round table covered with a cloth of dull gold. The only other source of illumination, the flickering candle in the brass lantern that sits between them, casts shadows on his face, emphasising its planes and angles, shallow surfaces and smooth hollows. Next to the lantern is a bronze statuette, its exotic appearance echoing the man. There are also cards adorned with occult symbols, a chart of some kind and what looks like a human skull.

A strong aroma pervades the room. In one corner, Rosetta sees a number of long tapers in a lotus-patterned vase that burn with an intense cinnamon perfume. Some other fragrance also imbues the air, more difficult to identify. It has a bitter note yet at the same time an intoxicating sweetness. Rosetta breathes deeply, feels her head begin to swim.

'Mr Zeno, I think we may have encountered each other once before,' she begins.

'That is true.' His voice is low and mesmerising. 'Many times, in fact, over many years.'

'No, I don't think . . .'

'I know that it is so. I believe, Mrs Raphael, we knew each other long before we entered this life. In another time, in another place, perhaps in the Celestial Empire, or the Kingdom of Judaea, or in ancient Greece.'

As Zeno speaks, he weaves a spell. His words take flight, swirl about the room and make dreams seem real. Zeno has many ways to tell the future and see into the past. He reads palms, consults joss sticks, runs his hands over a client's scalp. Zeno is practised in the arcane art of phrenology. He searches for a skull's depressions and resistance, for the dips and furrows that he reads like an inner map. They tell him what may ail a man or what can cause a woman to feel wounded, sad or raw. For Rosetta, however, he need only hold her hand and sense the energy that flows from her to know what lies in store.

As Zeno clasps her, palm to palm, she feels both soothed and at the same time undeniably aroused. It is his gaze, his voice, but most of all that touch.

Afterwards, as she makes her way home to Carlton, Rosetta has the sensation that she is inhabiting a dream. Somehow she buys a ticket for the tram, takes her seat, alights at the correct stop. But Melbourne, the Melbourne that Rosetta knows, with its familiar grid of streets, its solid buildings and well-mannered parks, has disappeared. Images of more exotic lands dance before her eyes and, in her ears, Zeno's alluring prophecies sing of adventure and desire.

That night Rosetta thinks over what has transpired. Away from the cinnamon-scented smoke, the suns and moons, she suspects that Zeno is not all he claims to be. She doesn't care. He is rendered all the more attractive because of his dishonesty. Zeno breaks rules. He is cloaked in danger. Rosetta thinks of little else but this man and the feeling of his hand pressed against her own. A white heat is coiling in her belly. She might do anything.

FIVE

I find my family tree, the one my brother had copied, on an unprepossessing single sheet of paper at the very front of the blue binder. It begins in England, in the eighteenth century: the 'Age of Enlightenment', they called it, even while thousands of hapless men, women and children were banished to a distant land and deprived of their liberty.

As I look at the straight, ruled lines, I imagine other, invisible links, a multitude of them that become a great tangle of interconnected vines. It strikes me then that, though this is just one family's history, it is also part of a greater narrative, always moving over time.

The document I hold in my hand is not elaborate but neat and workmanlike, setting out eight generations of births, deaths and marriages in small type. At the top is Reuben Rheuben, broker, of Whitechapel. Below him comes Rosetta's grandfather, my great, great, great-grandfather Abraham, who arrived in Hobart on the *Bengal Merchant* in 1828.

According to the original Session Papers I find, he'd been arrested for the theft of a sovereign and half a crown the year before and then tried before a judge in London's Old Bailey.

'I followed him and collared him,' a Bow Street patrol officer testified.

'I picked it up,' was all the young defendant replied. At just sixteen, transportation to Australia was the punishment for his small crime.

How was it for that poor boy, alone in the great London court, at the moment he was told he would be locked in a ship for months upon the seas, sailing for a place beyond the terror of his dreams? I can only speculate. What I do know is that his life changed dramatically. It took seven hard years to regain his freedom, a further four before he married a girl called Rosetta Marks (now I know from where the name Rosetta came). The couple had ten children, all listed in a row across the page, culminating with the youngest, Frances, and then, below her, Frances' own brood of nine. The name of Frances' first born, my great-grandmother, is written out in full – Rosetta Esther Sarah Solomon – together with some brief details.

At first it is difficult to glean a great deal about Rosetta from this impenetrable network of names and dates. And yet, as I look at the meagre facts set down on the page, I find that the other documents I have, the legal papers, newspaper reports and the half-remembered stories and memories that my father recorded, all begin, rather like magic, to fall into place.

MELBOURNE, 31 MAY 1899

Time unwinds much like a spool of flickering film, alive with vivid images.

It is my great-grandmother's wedding night. She is very young, just eighteen years old, with all the vanity that youth bestows together with its innocence. She stands, quite still, before a long, sparkling mirror, examines herself, is pleased by what she sees. Tall, blessed with thick, dark-red hair, full breasts and creamy skin, she has a rare, strong beauty.

Rosetta is in Melbourne's Hotel Windsor, an establishment fabled for its luxury. It is a place in which any traveller would find comfort, but it is also more than that. Situated opposite the imposing classical facades of the Parliament of Victoria and the Treasury, the hotel is known to play host to those with wealth, power and influence. The very constitution of a new nation called Australia was drafted just the year before in one of its exclusive suites.

The serried rows of pediments that arc along the walls, the great stone sculptures of a reclining Peace and Plenty above the entrance and the soaring, cupola-capped twin towers; all these things invite comparison with a Renaissance palace. Rosetta is captivated by its grandeur and its elegance.

The room in which the mirror hangs envelops her with richness. Midnight-blue curtains embellished with golden tassels and thick braid caress the windows, while a chandelier of glittering crystal floods the scene with light. Together they give Rosetta the sensation that she is inhabiting a particularly opulent theatre, though she is unaware as to the part that she will be required to play or, indeed, what drama will unfold that night.

Competing with the heightened illumination are two small candles on a table covered by fine damask. The cloth shows evidence of the first supper she shared with Louis as a married woman – a single smear acquired when a fork of sliced mutton dropped from her unsteady hand, a scatter of breadcrumbs from the tearing of a soft white roll.

She has had little appetite, even though since the moment her mother, Frances (who everyone calls Fanny), woke her just after dawn, there has barely been time to eat. Indeed, there was such an urgency about her preparations that, following her bath, the usual languor with which she smoothed oil scented with almonds and oranges along her warm, receptive limbs had been replaced with a brisk efficiency. Next, her dark auburn hair was elaborately dressed in an upswept pompadour. Finally, her complicated clothing was put on in layer after layer, until Rosetta felt herself almost extinguished beneath the weight of so much artifice.

This sense of unreality persisted. The ceremony had been followed by the wedding breakfast, though almost all the details escape her now. A perturbing sense of disconnection had accompanied her as she moved through the festivities, greeting her guests, thanking them for their gifts, listening to speeches and to toasts.

Rosetta felt as she did when, as a child, she had ridden high upon the rearing horse of a merry-go-round. She was unstable, had lost the fixed points that anchored her small world. As the carousel turned, familiar people, trees and houses had become formless, whirling by in a fast-moving, amorphous stream. This was how the day just past had seemed. Only a few, odd moments remain sharp. One was when she signed the marriage register. Rosetta remembers looking down and, as if seeing something belonging to quite a different woman, noting the gold band upon her finger, her trembling hand.

Now Rosetta is breathless. Beneath her gown she wears the unforgiving bones of whales and lacing that grips her tightly round the waist – but this is not the only cause. The knowledge that it is her wedding night, the first as Mrs Louis Raphael, is sufficient reason to make the hotel room and all its elaborate furnishings appear to sway. Or perhaps it is because she is unaccustomed to drinking champagne. Rosetta can taste it still, its syrupy sharpness. She swallows, wincing, has the sensation of a scratch inside her throat, decides it would be better to focus on what she sees before her in the gilt-edged frame instead.

Rosetta's wedding dress had been a sweeping, ivory-coloured confection. It had a scalloped collar that sat high upon her slender neck and narrow sleeves that concluded at her wrists with a foam of lace. Save for her hands and face, Rosetta had been completely covered. She was decorous, sedate.

The low-cut gown she wears now is significantly less demure. Above the bodice she is quite exposed, save for a wisp of pale-blue tulle about her shoulders and a pair of long suede gloves, grey and soft as pigeon's down. During their meal Rosetta had noted with satisfaction the way that Louis' eyes had been drawn to her uncovered upper arms, the wide spaced bones beneath her throat and the swelling smoothness below.

She is familiar with observation. Men first began to notice her at fourteen. Her sinuous form, though always discreetly attired, provoked attention. A slight turn of the head by a man passing by in his trap, a quick glance or a movement, was enough for her to realise she created awareness, enough to cause a flicker of excitement to lick at her within.

She enjoys this admiration, the sense of power it bestows. But, despite appearances, she is not worldly. Her sophistication is fragile, eggshell thin.

Rosetta is uninformed. Those things Fanny does with her children's father occur in darkness and in silence. She will not speak of them, not even to her eldest child.

Fanny, a careful mother, had other priorities. She made sure to tell Rosetta that appearance was of keen importance. But she also warned her daughter that the impression a person might choose to make contained the potential to be wreathed in deceit. 'Not everyone you meet is who they seem to be,' she said, with an air of someone whose caution was based on personal experience.

In surging Victoria the most unlikely people might suddenly acquire undreamt-of wealth and, as a consequence, astounding transformations could be made. Fanny told her daughter stories of men such as Sir William Clarke, Australia's first baronet, who had built 'Rupertswood', a palatial mansion equipped with a personal squad of soldiers and a private railway station. Sir William dominated what was deemed Victorian society, entertaining as lavishly as an Eastern prince. But only the clever land speculation of his modest butcher father had enabled him to play the part of this Antipodean potentate.

Rosetta was aware, too, that although her grandfather, Abraham Rheuben, had arrived in wild Van Diemen's Land wearing manacles and chains, he had enjoyed a considerable rise in station. No longer the boy driven by his poverty to steal purses in the backstreets of Whitechapel, he became, despite this unpromising beginning, a wealthy ship owner, a coal and wood merchant and, most astonishing of all, a prominent justice of the peace and alderman.

Indeed, such was the former convict's renown that upon his death in 1876 Hobart's leading newspaper, *The Mercury*, described him as 'one of our most respected citizens'. Rosetta had seen the newspaper clipping, for her mother kept it in a frame.

Having been born four years after he passed away, she never knew her grandfather. But her knowledge of his triumphant reinvention led her to feel proud of him.

Fanny's own feelings were more complex. She felt as if her daughter trod upon a precipice. A single misstep on her behalf, and all that Abraham Rheuben had attained – financial security, position and respect – could disappear. Above all, she must keep Rosetta from this fate.

Late at night beside the fire, her chocolate-coloured hair smooth in its tight knot, Fanny would murmur to her, 'Only men can make their fortune. We women have but two currencies. Purity is paramount – you must live a life above reproach. But do not forget beauty, the way you present yourself to the world.' Fanny had observed more than one woman possessed of aspirations who had, by the careful cultivation of her attributes and the adoption of impeccable attire, entered into realms that she would otherwise have been denied.

What else had Rosetta's mother told her in the stillness of the night?

'A woman is always vulnerable. She lives in danger. Marriage to a steady man provides the only real security. To take any other path is folly. Darling girl, it can only lead to grief.'

Her daughter listened carefully. She knew nothing of the way in which a less certain life could heighten every appetite, make the senses sing.

SIX

It was at a musical evening that took place in the home of an old friend of her Uncle Edward that Rosetta first encountered her future husband. She hadn't noticed him immediately, but during a short interlude between the playing of some rather pretty folk songs and the more serious matter of a Mozart prelude she had looked across the room and seen a vigorous-looking, broad-shouldered fellow engaged in conversation with a group of other guests. There was something discordant about the man that captured her attention: he was quick to smile and amiable, yet his grey-blue eyes contained a hint of steel. She found the combination intriguing.

Rosetta sought her uncle out, inclined her head in the man's direction, then turned back to Edward with a raised eyebrow. 'Ah, yes, that's Louis,' Edward said. 'By the way, his last name's written like the painter, but pronounced Ray-ful.'

'You mean, like something filled with light?' The image, a product of the more romantic aspect of Rosetta's nature, made her smile.

'If you like. Anyway, I believe he's from New Zealand, Dunedin I think, though he's established himself rather well here in Melbourne. He's a commission agent,' Edward added, then, seeing his niece's puzzled look, explained, 'he buys and sells commodities like cattle or wheat or wool, horses as well, on behalf of others. He's a knack for it, too, makes good money.' He looked at her more closely. 'My dear, am I right in detecting a certain interest on your behalf?'

Rosetta nodded.

'Well then, I'd say you could do a great deal worse than Louis Raphael. Why don't you come with me and I'll introduce you? Just remember that he's keen on politics, and then there's cricket and golf, of course. Oh, and he's damnably good at picking winners when it comes to racing.'

Edward did not mention that his acquaintance might also have a taste for other, more clandestine, forms of recreation.

'Melbourne's most refined brothel' was discreetly located in Lonsdale Street, at number 32. Lavishly decorated in red plush, alabaster and gilt, it was run with efficiency and style by the formidable Prussian-born Madame Brussels – the 'queen of harlotry', according to *The Truth*; 'Caroline' to her intimate friends.

The vice she administered was 'vice in kid gloves and broadcloth; vice with plenty of money at its command'. Her girls were particularly obliging and, more important, knew that Louis Raphael was a busy man.

While some clients liked to chat, to talk about their wives or their professions, even their hopes and dreams, this was not a service Mr Raphael required. Businessman that he was, he sought an uncomplicated transaction; fair work for fair money paid.

Frankly, it was a relief. After exhausting days spent using whatever powers he had to convince his clients that either the price they were demanding for their goods was too high or, alternatively, the amount being offered by prospective purchasers was laughably inadequate, Louis found such a straightforward arrangement soothing. That suited the girls, too; being quick and efficient, it relieved them of the burden of sympathy that was the invariable requirement of so many needy men.

'Mr Raphael,' they would say to each other, 'might be a man in a hurry, but at least you know where you are with him.'

Louis, however, had recently decided that this hitherto satisfactory arrangement no longer sufficed. Being possessed of some ambition, it had occurred to him that, at the relatively mature age of thirty-two, if he were to make his way further in the world nothing less than a wife was required. Hence, when Edward introduced his striking niece, Louis was in a receptive frame of mind.

Mindful of her uncle's advice, Rosetta embarked upon what she felt might be a suitable opening gambit. 'Mr Raphael, what do you think of the plans for Federation?' she enquired.

'Come now, Miss Solomon,' Louis replied. 'Surely a young lady as lovely as you does not really wish to discuss politics.'

Rosetta could not help but enjoy the compliment. It was only later, when she recalled Mr Raphael's quick assumption, that she experienced a faint annoyance.

Louis was decisive. 'Rosetta would be an asset to any man,' he thought. He did not acknowledge, even to himself, how much he wanted her in his bed. Lonsdale Street's pouting harlots would not be so easily deceived. In the weeks to come, they noted the increased frequency of his visits, heard him cry her name at that moment when all men's defences cease.

His mind made up, he began to woo Rosetta with earnest dedication. Picnic lunches were consumed, concerts attended and walks by the river took place, all properly chaperoned. An aunt or a married cousin was co-opted for the task; the courtship was a chaste, well-ordered process.

It was unusual then, when, one sunny Sunday afternoon, Rosetta found herself in her parents' parlour with her admirer, quite alone. She knew, of course, of his interest in her and, feeling both nervous and excited, wondered what he might say or do. She did not have to wait long. Rather suddenly, Louis bent down on one knee, brought out a small diamond and sapphire ring and asked her to marry him.

Rosetta hesitated, a little flustered. Louis' rapid courtship had barely allowed her time to contemplate a future spent in his company. She was so young; might there be more life to live before she took this step, perhaps even some other, more thrilling man for her, one she had not yet had the opportunity to meet?

But she knew her mother and father wanted the union to proceed.

'He would do nicely, Rosie,' had been the way her father, Lewis, had summed up Louis Raphael just a few days earlier. Her father had delivered this opinion a moment after he had finished playing a cheerful air on the piano; she remembered the way he had hummed along to the melody with an expression of contented satisfaction. It was not just that Louis was an acquaintance of Edward's and thus known to the family. He was reputable, respectable and, like them, Jewish.

Neither Fanny nor Lewis considered their faith to be central to their identity. Though they observed the traditional Jewish rituals associated with birth, death and marriage, together with most colonists they considered themselves British above all else. They knew, however, that there were others who considered that their religion set people like them apart; perhaps it did. It was far better for their daughter to share a common faith with her husband. They thought it would help to protect her from harm.

So it was that Rosetta, who at least for now was dutiful, regained her composure and responded, 'Yes,' then added, 'thank you, Louis.' Her parents wished it, she understood their reasons, and she did like him. In any case, it was what young women did: they married.

The couple celebrated with her parents and drank sherry. Louis, constrained by his formal black suit, reached awkwardly for the decanter. As he poured, Rosetta regarded him, noted the white, scar-like line that lay between his sunburnt skin and shorn hair. 'He has made sure to visit the barber,' she thought. 'He has prepared.'

That night, after Louis had left for his St Kilda home, Rosetta, thoughtful, stood alone in her parents' garden, inhaling the fading perfume of late roses mixed with the headier fragrances of frangipani and jasmine. In the quiet, scented stillness, she considered her future husband. He was a man of practicalities; there was nothing fanciful about him. Rosetta was aware that life with Louis was likely to be conventional. But no doubt this was the best, the safest way to live.

SEVEN

The thought that something intensely physical, highly intimate and almost certainly painful will take place on her wedding night has not crossed Rosetta's mind. She knows, of course, that children are the inevitable consequence of marriage. However, in the absence of maternal enlightenment she has developed her own idiosyncratic theory for the way in which the process of creating progeny might transpire.

Rosetta has observed that the world is filled with new and inexplicable phenomena, such as the telegraph, or electricity, whereby one unlikely thing emerges from quite a different entity. Words and heat and light are, she knows, produced by way of unseen emanations that exist somewhere in the atmosphere. From this she has determined that babies are most likely to be conceived in a similarly abstract fashion.

A woman retires to bed with her husband. She sleeps next to him. Invisible pulses fly through the air. This is the way in which it happens.

Secure in the confidence of these conclusions, Rosetta waits for Louis. She glances at the brass clock beside the bed, sees that a half-hour has passed since he announced he was going to the bar for whiskey. Rosetta puzzles over this prolonged absence. Suddenly lonely, she longs for his company.

When she hears the rasp of the key turning in the lock, she looks up eagerly. She has no doubt what a new husband's customary expressions of devotion might be. Rosetta anticipates a charming compliment and the type of romantic gesture described in the novels she borrows from the library. (They make much of eyes meeting eyes and lips other lips, say little of greater familiarity.)

The door swings open. She sees Louis frowning. He is terse, says only, 'I left you long enough. Yet I see that you have chosen not to prepare yourself for me.'

Rosetta is confused. What does he want? Why are his lips so narrow, his jaw so tight? Her husband's arms are folded high upon his chest. His hands are clenched in a way that reminds her of the men she has seen outside factories when there is no work to be had. She hasn't seen him look like this before, frustrated and annoyed and grim. He has always seemed reasonable and moderate. Rosetta does not know what she has or hasn't done to bring about this change of temperament.

She looks away, finds herself confronted by the ruby coverlet upon the bed, the amber and the gold of its embellished trim. This lavishness, so recently admired, now cloys. She feels uncomfortable.

Louis steps forward. He holds her shoulders, hard, looks at her and says, 'I expected you to be ready in the manner in which a wife should be. Take off your clothes now, Rosetta.' He does not like women to toy with him.

She does not like his voice. She hears a razored edge. It brings out the wilfulness within her. She may be just eighteen but, as an eldest child of many children, Rosetta is used to commanding some authority.

She does not try to struggle from his grip, not yet, but merely says, 'What right have you to speak to me like this?' The tone she strains for is imperious, but a tremor in her voice betrays a lack of certainty.

'Rosetta, I am your husband.'

It is not the words – they are innocuous – but the way in which he speaks them that penetrates. There is no tenderness, no warmth. Even anger would be better. At least that would provide some evidence of feeling. Often Rosetta's own emotions bubble over – the younger children know when to avoid her quick tirades. But she has always been filled with life and when she swings them high or plans some adventure they soon forget her hot temper, the sudden slap.

Louis' tone is cold. Cold and hard as metal railings on a freezing day. He is a strong man with muscled arms and a fierce grip acquired by heaving bails of wool and lifting bags of wheat. He hoists them in the air to feel their weight, trusting instinct more than the scales of other men. He will not be taken for a fool.

Now his strength is used against Rosetta. He spins her around, forcing her down until she is pinned to the bed. Rosetta's face is buried in that treacherous coverlet. It seems to rise up about her so that she gasps for air. One of Louis' hands moves from her shoulder. It clamps a flailing, pale-skinned arm. His other hand claws at the silken undergarments beneath her petticoats and gown. The sound as they tear and give way is like a sea bird's cry, a sharp lament.

She has misjudged him. He is not passionless and cold. His manner masks the fury of a man who, thwarted, feels humiliated. Rosetta tries to stop him, tries to strike out with the hand she still has free. He doesn't notice, immersed in a ruthless mission all his own. Face still down, struggling for breath, Rosetta is blinded. It is impossible to see or know what is taking place. Possession, when it comes, is short and brutal. Any softness she has felt for him has been replaced by something poisonous and molten. Her sightlessness intensifies the pain. Robbed of one sense, those that remain are so heightened that all her being is inhabited by violation. She is engulfed by it.

EIGHT

The events that took place on her wedding night, on that troubled bed in the Hotel Windsor suite, were the key to much that happened afterwards. As Rosetta lay back the next morning amid the twisted sheets, she vowed that she would never forgive her husband for what he had done.

Louis had already risen, dressed swiftly and, with barely a word to his wife, removed himself downstairs for breakfast. Rosetta, grateful for her solitude, reflected upon the circumstances that led up to the horror of the night. She recalled her pride when she had stood with Louis by her side beneath the richly embroidered wedding canopy, or *chupa*, a vestige of the tents occupied by their desert-dwelling ancestors in ancient times. The rabbi had presented them with two silver cups of ruby-coloured wine. One cup stood for sorrow, the other joy, a symbol of all a couple might encounter in their life. Rosetta, struggling to contain her fierce dismay, knew that the contents of the first cup had already prevailed.

~

I see her, as the wedding ceremony drew to a close, watching Louis raise one polished boot then stamp down hard upon the crystal glass that lay before him on a marble tile. This, too, was an act that harked back to a different time. Twelfth-century Kabbalists believed that there were demons intent upon ruining the newlyweds' peace of mind. I wonder, when Rosetta saw the splinters fly, if she imagined, as did those medieval mystics, that this small act of destruction would be enough to keep the evil spirits satisfied.

She could not avoid it: her gaze continued to turn to the tangle of torn tulle that lay on the floor in disarray. Her pretty gown was now a distasteful, mocking reminder of her shame.

'No, I will not have it!' Rosetta exclaimed, tearing her eyes away. She leapt from her bed and went to bathe; tried to eliminate both her bruised and bloodied soreness and her profound agitation. The warm water of the deep bath calmed her and, as her body relaxed, her mind floated free. In that liquid moment, when her anger commenced its bitter journey towards disdain, she began to formulate a plan.

Fanny must be told of the attack – how shocked she would be! Rosetta felt certain that once her mother was informed, her own extrication from this intolerable situation would be imminent. With this conclusion came a modest recovery.

To become swept away by strong emotions was a part of Rosetta's nature. But, conversely, there existed that quality of mind that allowed her to detach, to coolly weigh up options and act upon them. It was strange, this trait, which permitted calculation to replace passion. In the years ahead, perhaps it was this ability that enabled her to do the unthinkable things she did.

As Louis sat wincing in the sunlight that flooded into the Windsor's breakfast room, he contemplated, with an aching head, the disaster of the previous evening. In a moment of unusual introspection, he realised that too much champagne followed by claret and whiskey and the allure of Rosetta herself – why, she'd looked nearly naked in that gown – had only added to his desire; he suspected it might have made him vile.

Feeling irritable, he put this thought aside. After all, he was not to blame. Having paid a large sum for the hotel's hospitality he had naturally expected that Rosetta would be, if not eager exactly, then at least grateful.

After several steaming cups of coffee and, as a consequence, a clearer head, it occurred to Louis for the first time that he had made the wrong assumptions about the nature of his bride. He'd thought her anxious to please, a sweet, biddable girl, not the furious creature he had encountered on their wedding night.

Rosetta had fought him, when all that he demanded was his right. True, his needs had been satisfied – even now the memory of her violent possession stirred him – but even so, he could not help wondering if his marriage had been unwise.

Rosetta appeared at her parents' house in Fitzroy that afternoon. She had concocted an excuse, as ridiculous as it was hasty, which had to do with the need to collect a particular wedding present from her mother, a fine china tea service without which, she claimed, it was not possible to properly begin married life.

She wasted little time after her arrival, pausing only to throw herself upon an overstuffed, patterned sofa before tearfully revealing the dreadful nature of her assault. She did not, however, receive the response she had expected. Rosetta heard only a small, uncomfortable cough, then silence.

'But Rosie,' her mother said finally, 'did you really never anticipate something like this?'

Fanny's strained expression only intensified when she saw Rosetta's face. It was marked with an anger that she knew could overtake her daughter in an instant. She had observed it many times before; the flashing eyes and jutting jaw.

'How could I,' Rosetta retorted, springing to her feet, 'as you told me only about pretty frocks and charming conversation and a thousand other things but nothing about this, this violation!' With that, she picked up a small embroidered cushion and flung it across the room. The thunderous crash heard when the Coalport china dish it collided with hurtled to the floor seemed to echo Rosetta's stormy mood.

Fanny, appalled by this display, took a large breath. Grappling now with the reluctance to speak of intimate matters that had left her daughter so ill prepared, she gripped the arms of the straight-backed velvet chair in which she sat before explaining, as briefly as was possible, those acts – she called them 'physical congress' – that customarily took place between man and wife.

'Of course, this is the way in which babies are made,' she added, as an afterthought. 'That is, after all, the purpose of marriage.'

Rosetta felt the burn of mortification. How stupid, how ignorant she had been. She did not want her husband or his babies. Rosetta wished to go home, back to safety, to a world where if not completely unfettered she would at least not be bound to Louis for all eternity. 'Let me return,' she begged. Fanny ignored her daughter's plea.

'At first it is a shock, of course I understand that. But that is what a wife must do. She must obey. Marriage is forever. You must make the best of it. You can never leave. You would be disgraced.'

This painful conversation occurred as Rosetta sat in Fanny's parlour, an ordered room of stiff mahogany furniture and precise botanical prints. It was the beginning of June, a cold month in Melbourne, but there was no coolness in Rosetta. For the first time the enormity of what marriage meant struck her like a blow. Her breath came quickly as she felt the weight of realisation press against her chest.

'I will never be free again.' The thought was appalling.

NINE

MELBOURNE, 7 NOVEMBER 1899

Rosetta has no idea it will be at the Melbourne Cup, the colony's premier racing event and prime occasion for ostentatious display, that she will meet a woman whose destiny will be intimately interwoven with her own. Nor does she know that one day she will, like this same woman, be on the closest terms with some of the most celebrated inhabitants of Europe and Great Britain.

On the morning of the Cup, a day of clear skies and brilliant sunshine, Rosetta's chief preoccupation is the challenge of accommodating her stays. Though she is still only nineteen and it has taken some time for her pregnancy – the result of her disastrous wedding night – to show, still she struggles with the lacing and the many hooks and eyes.

There has been at least one redeeming feature of being with child. 'Louis, you really cannot expect me to share a bed with you in my condition,' she said sharply when her fears were confirmed. 'It would be unwise.' Her husband, now conscious of Rosetta's quick temper, has retired to another room. Though he desires her still, he is prepared to wait. That he seeks comfort in the arms of other, more acquiescent women, is inevitable. As Louis says, though only to himself, 'What is a man, with a man's needs, to do?'

While Rosetta wrestles with her undergarments she, too, contemplates the consequences that birth will bring, though she is less sanguine. More than the fact that she will be tied to Louis forever, it seems to her that becoming a mother spells the end of . . . possibilities. The possibilities for what, exactly, she isn't sure, but something beyond the safe, circumspect world of provincial Melbourne. She wants more than that.

Rosetta's fashionable wasp-waisted dress has been a considered choice, for she knows that the Cup is likely to be the last occasion on which she can go easily about in public dressed in such an unforgiving style. Its colour is known as *eau-de-Nil*; she whispers the words to herself, enjoys the fluid, foreign way they sound and the exotic images they bring to mind. The cool mint colour flatters Rosetta's pale complexion, enhances her dark russet hair. On her head she places a fantastical wide-brimmed hat trimmed with black net, white silk flowers and swooping feathers dyed forest green. When Louis sees her he exclaims, 'Rosetta, you look most attractive.' She permits him a brief smile.

By the time Rosetta reaches Flemington racecourse she feels unwell. It is too hot, her dress too tight, her pretty hat now weighs heavily upon her head. She does not speak of her discomfort, however, for she is determined to enjoy this last chance for amusement. Rosetta observes the ladies of society as they greet friends and move about the banks of golden roses and fern-filled urns. She notes with a tiny stab of envy that several women wear the unmistakable ensembles from the Paris-based house of Worth: their fabrics are more sumptuous, the trimmings more lavish than any others, and their cut is conspicuously refined.

Unhappily, the tranquil conditions, so beneficial for seeing and being seen, change suddenly. Indeed, even *The Australasian*'s seasoned reporter is observed to scribble in his moist notebook that 'never on Cup Day' has it rained as it does from noon.

While the heavens open and monsoonal torrents of water pour from murderous skies, frantic racegoers, valuing the preservation of finery rather more highly than the safeguarding of dignity, rush and scramble for whatever shelter they can find. The sodden lawn, so recently the venue for much pleasant preening, is now unapproachable and the enclosure has become an oozing black quagmire.

Fortunately for Louis and Rosetta, the members' stand is nearby. By two o'clock the rain has stopped. As a fierce sun begins to emerge from behind the clouds they are beckoned over by a well-turned-out man wearing a sleek top hat.

'Ah, Mr Raphael,' he says, 'just the man I need. I've trained my colt Merriwee hard, but do you think he has a chance on such a slow track?'

'Mr Powell,' Louis replies, shaking his hand. 'I think he has. He's young but has a certain gait I like. I've placed a good wager on him, anyway.'

'Well then, why don't you and Mrs Raphael join me here?' Powell asks. 'Your wife may bring me luck.'

The air within the overcrowded stand is close. Rosetta feels giddy and a slick of sweat forms on her brow. As the race draws nearer, the temperature rises and racegoers crowd ever closer. She fears she will be crushed. Rosetta hears a sudden noise and, as the barrier jerks up, she turns her head sharply towards the track.

The horses spring away, their jockeys already riding high and straining forward. Now all is streaming colour, flashing silk, flying whips and noise. There is a deep rumble as hooves strike the churning ground, a thudding felt in limbs and bellies and a ringing in the ears as a hundred thousand voices cry out 'Faster!' and urge their favourites on. Louis is absorbed, his knuckles clench and tighten. Rosetta sees a piece of earth and grass fly through the air and, after that, nothing more.

~

'This was a mistake,' Louis says gravely as he bends over his wife. Rosetta has fainted. She doesn't know that Merriwee has won. Her head is being cradled by a woman she has never seen before, a woman whose hair reminds Rosetta of wind-rippled wheat fields and whose clear blue eyes seem like pieces of the sky.

'I am Mrs Pakenham,' the woman says, her heart-shaped face creased with concern. 'My husband and I were with His Excellency Lord Brassey in the Vice-Regal party, just across the aisle. I saw you faint.'

The two women regard each other. Something passes between them, a kind of recognition though they have never met before. In that brief moment an understanding is established and Rosetta knows that Louis is quite wrong. Coming to the Cup has not been a mistake at all.

I discover the detailed web of connections that wind themselves about Lilian Blanche Georgina Pakenham buried in the dense type of some photocopied pages from that definitive guide to the British aristocracy, *Debrett's Illustrated Peerage*. There is obviously some skill in reading *Debrett's*, and it is one in which I am not practised – untangling who, exactly, was related to whom is a challenge. One fact, however, quickly becomes clear: the daughter of Privy Counsellor the Right Honourable (Anthony) Evelyn Ashley and granddaughter of the Earl of Shaftesbury, Lilian was born in Ireland in 1875 into a world of undeniable privilege.

As I note the plethora of elaborate titles, it occurs to me that in this elevated realm marriage was not so much a matter of romance as of advantage. Occasionally, there was an irregular liaison such as in the case of Lilian's brother, the future Wilfred Lord Mount Temple, who *Debrett's* informs me was destined to wed a young woman by the name of Maud Cassel. Although Maud was the daughter of a German-born Jewish financier, Sir Ernest

Cassel, these drawbacks were clearly overlooked; Sir Ernest was, after all, an intimate friend of Edward, Prince of Wales, and fabulously rich.

After Maud sadly succumbed to consumption at the age of thirty-two, Sir Ernest declared that her daughter – Lilian's niece, Edwina – would be, upon his death, the principal beneficiary of his enormous fortune. It meant that, following her grandfather's demise, the twenty-year-old girl inherited not only millions of pounds, but Brook House, his palatial Mayfair mansion. Overnight, Edwina Ashley had become, in the words of *The World's News*, 'the greatest heiress in the kingdom'.

Apart from fantastic wealth and a distinctly racy, well-publicised reputation, what was to distinguish the blue-eyed Edwina was her marriage to Lord Louis Mountbatten, Earl Mountbatten of Burma and cousin of the King. Their union is, of course, also documented in *Debrett's*, though not its unusual nature. Lord Mountbatten admitted to his friends that he and his wife 'spent all our married lives getting into other people's beds'.

One day Edwina Mountbatten would concern herself with my great-grandmother's own unorthodox liaisons.

By contrast, Lilian's marriage promised, at least at first, to be conventional. At the age of twenty she wed Hercules Arthur Pakenham, an eligible young captain in the 2nd Grenadier Guards. A charming account of the marriage, which took place at the Guards' Chapel, Wellington Barracks, appeared on 20 November 1895 in the columns of the *Hampshire Advertiser.*

The report made the point that the bride was attended by nine bridesmaids attired in pink 'flesh-tinted' dresses and black velvet hats with black plumes; I note that their names (there were two Violets, an Evelyn and a Sybil among them) were uniformly preceded by a rarefied prefix – each one of the nine was a Lady or Hon.

The newspaper next painted a glorious picture: against a backdrop of palms, banks of chrysanthemums and white arum lilies, the satin- and chiffon-clad bride made her way, on the arm of her father, down an aisle lined with crisply saluting red-coated Guardsmen.

Was it possible, as the bevy of bridesmaids passed by, that one soldier winked and an Hon, in response, could have fluttered her lashes? And did Lilian, when she heard the choir break into a rendition of 'Lead Us Heavenly Father Lead Us' accompanied by 'a string quartette, a piano and a harmonium', have a moment's concern as to what life might be like as the next Mrs Pakenham?

Hercules, or Arthur as he was usually addressed, was a man of distinguished family. Not only had his grandfather, General Ned Pakenham, fought alongside the Duke of Wellington at the Battle of Waterloo, Ned's sister, Kitty, had married the revered hero. With both Miss Ashley and Captain Pakenham in possession of such illustrious relations, it was generally thought by all concerned that their marriage was not merely suitable but destined for success.

Arthur, though a soldier, was attracted to a political career. As a minor member of the aristocracy (albeit with an impeccable pedigree), a position of service in a distant colony was deemed by his father's well-placed friends to be the most efficacious way in which to further these ambitions. A brandy taken at the right club, a word in the appropriate ear, and Arthur was duly appointed private secretary to the Governor of Victoria, Lord Brassey.

Lilian was not consulted about whether she wished to come to this remote land. Her husband simply announced one day, shortly before a regimental dinner (from which, due to her sex, she was naturally excluded), that this was the course of action on which he had decided. So it was that in 1899, and with the Pakenham motto, *Glory is the Shadow of Virtue*, firmly fixed in her husband's mind, Lilian found herself in Melbourne.

TEN

The Pakenhams inhabit vast Government House. So grand is it in size that it exceeds any other of the Empire's Vice-Regal mansions. The Governor's splendid ballroom, much to the sovereign's chagrin, is larger even than her own at Buckingham Palace. Rumour has it that Her Majesty tried to stop it being built, so envious was she of its emphatic scale, but word came back too late; construction had begun.

Lilian is kept busy in this magnificent edifice by a round of receptions and official engagements. She helps her husband to entertain Melbourne's *nouveau riche*, visiting dignitaries and their wives. She greets and meets and talks and smiles. She feels constrained.

Just a few miles to the east, across the Yarra River, Rosetta's life is quiet. As her pregnancy advances, she ceases to go about in society. Sometimes she visits her mother or younger sisters, perhaps strolls in the park with them. Most days she stays in her new home, a white-painted cottage in Waltham Street, Richmond. Rosetta walks about her small lavender-filled garden or rests on a silk-draped day bed beneath a lemon tree. It is a lonely, sequestered way of being.

A note from her new acquaintance enquiring if she may call upon Mrs Raphael for tea provides the promise of a welcome diversion. Rosetta, delighted, responds with alacrity.

When the two women meet they exchange the usual pleasantries. One praises her guest's primrose dress, the other her hostess's charming house. But beneath this polite social intercourse both feel the same connection they did previously.

Rosetta does not want anything to cast a shadow over this incipient friendship. 'Mrs Pakenham,' she begins.

'Please, I would like you to call me Lilian. And, if I may, I will address you as Rosetta.'

'Lilian.' A little more at ease now, Rosetta starts again. 'As you know, our society is young and those who came here first were not always of fortunate circumstance.' She looks down, examines the oriental pattern of her cup. 'I myself am the granddaughter of a former convict. I feel it best you know that.'

Lilian is composed. She says that she has met others – even in Government House – possessed of a similar background. She adds that, in any case, she does not care. Then, with a wry smile, she remarks, 'Still, my grandfather the Earl and, who knows, perhaps yours too, might have had something to say about it.'

Despite the marked differences in lineage, both women enjoy a rare harmony. After this first visit Lilian comes often, and as their friendship deepens it occurs to Rosetta that her companion seems as distanced from her own husband as she herself is from Louis. One day, while strolling with Rosetta in her garden, Lilian breaks off a stem of lavender, inhales its scent and then confesses, 'My husband and I ...' She hesitates before adding, 'There is an arrangement ...'

Her friend moves in circles more exalted than Rosetta's own. They make their own rules, have their own discreet ways of observing society's conventions while, in private, they conduct their lives precisely as they choose.

Rosetta, at first a little taken aback by Lilian's revelations, finds herself intrigued. She begins to see that relations between men and women are not fixed within the immutability of marriage but allow for unexpected variations.

The people Lilian knows are the kind whom the Melbourne newspaper *The Argus* reports on in a regular column headed 'Personal', which chronicles the lives of the socially well connected. Reports are constructed within a pyramid of status, always commencing with Vice-Regal activities before moving on to matters concerning lesser men and women. It is in one of these columns that Rosetta discovers that Captain Pakenham 'had the misfortune to break his collar-bone when playing tennis at Mr. R. Power's residence, Toorak'.

'Yes, of course,' Rosetta thinks. This must be the reason that is given for Mrs Pakenham's frequent appearance at official engagements in the company of the Governor's handsome *aide-de-camp*, Lord Richard Plantagenet Neville. *The Argus* says she also hunts with him.

Rosetta, alone and heavy with child, lies upon her day bed and dreams that it is she who hunts with Lilian riding at her side.

On the morning of 22 February 1900, the first pains strike. They are as sharp and as hard as punishment, and for what? Rosetta, furious and wild, slams her hand down, hard, upon the mantelpiece and cries, 'Why should I suffer in this way when it is Louis, Louis who is to blame?'

Her distress rapidly heightening, she calls out to the tow-haired girl who helps her in the house. 'Dear God, Ivy! Go straight away – fetch my mother and the midwife.'

Now the pain is far worse. It wracks her and torments her; there is nothing else. When Fanny arrives she finds her daughter walking back and forward across the parlour. Every few minutes Rosetta stops, clings to a marble-topped table, gasps and writhes. Mrs Wainwright, the midwife, comes in moments later, takes in the scene and insists that Mrs Raphael retire to her bed. 'It is happening very quickly,' she says to Fanny. 'You wouldn't think it was her first.' Rosetta is feverish. She feels she is surely being consumed by fire. As the fierce urge to bear down consumes her she thinks only, 'Let me survive.'

At last a little girl, red and bewildered, is born. Her translucent eyes open briefly to meet those of her mother, then close as she makes a soft, mewing sound. Rosetta turns her head away. Fanny, anxious, is with child herself and birth is only weeks away. There is little she can do to help her daughter now.

'Rosie, what will you call her?' she asks.

'Frances. After you.'

The baby's second name, Catherine, is decided upon later. Louis insists; it is his mother's name. It is all the same to Rosetta. Ever since the birth a listlessness has come upon her. The future looks grey and formless, and though she knows she has what most women crave – a home, a husband with property and a good income, a child – it doesn't seem enough. In the long hours of the night, when the baby cries to be suckled, Rosetta feels as if a thick sack has been pulled over her head, a sack that invisible hands are tightening so she can neither see nor breathe nor think. She merely feels the suffocation as the thought 'This is forever' whirrs about her mind and is repeated, again and again.

'It's strange,' Ivy says to her mother one night after she has returned home to their tiny Collingwood terrace, 'but Mrs Raphael doesn't seem quite right with Frances.' The girl looks up from the stockings she is mending. 'She isn't sharp with her, I don't mean that.'

'Well, she rounds on you quickly enough,' Ivy's mother says.

‘That’s what makes it so hard to understand,’ Ivy replies. ‘I like Mrs Raphael, even though she’s the type to give you a piece of her mind.’ She shakes her head. ‘But I don’t know, with Frances, well, she just doesn’t seem herself.’

The baby wants Rosetta, always. She reminds her of Louis; his insistent demands upon her flesh are now shared by his infant daughter. Rosetta suffers. She finds she cannot love the child.

Another blow is struck. *The Argus* announces that the following month the Governor, Lord Brassey, will return to England. There is no choice; Lilian and her husband must depart with them. One final meeting between the two friends takes place in Rosetta’s garden. ‘Dearest, I will miss you so,’ Lilian says. ‘Look, I have brought you these.’ At that time there exists a singular language, consisting not of words but blooms; careful nuances lie behind each variety and type. The golden pansies that she holds have a special meaning: ‘Think of me as I will think of you’. In the sunlit garden the two women, one fair, one dark, shed tears as they embrace.

Lilian leaves Melbourne just a few days afterwards. The door that has been briefly opened has shut abruptly on Rosetta’s dreams and hopes.

Months later a parcel arrives for her. Ivy calls out, ‘Mrs Raphael, come and look! You’ll never guess – something’s been sent from London.’

The box is on the hall table next to a vase of lavender, not large but sturdy, tied securely with string and bearing several stamps. The address is written in a sloping hand which, with a rare wave of excitement, Rosetta recognises. Eagerly, she begins to untie knots, to tear at the wrapping so that shreds of paper fly through the air like parchment wings.

Inside the box, carefully enclosed in a soft, lemon-coloured cloth, she finds a gift. Rosetta takes it out. She runs her fingers over its length, first the slender, plaited leather shaft, then the carved bone of its ridged handle. Next she sees the initials *L.P.*, the words *From R.P.N.* and *Melbourne, June 1899* engraved on two circles of polished brass. And then she smiles. It is Lilian's riding crop, the whip that she took with her when she hunted.

Now that gift belongs to me. I see it on my desk and, just like Rosetta, I too touch the bone, the leather and the brass. I pick it up and hold it in my hand, this conjurer's talisman.

ELEVEN

Carlton is very smart these days. Its renovated Victorian architecture has been painted in fashionable twenty-first-century colours such as charcoal and pale grey. The streets are lined with interesting bars and restaurants and boutiques selling designer clothes, mostly black. There are wonderful food shops; some offer dozens of different kinds of olive oils that glimmer on crowded shelves, others display ribbons of freshly made pasta or tempt with fragrant, sultana-studded pastries. In cafes where a multitude of coffee blends, grinds and flavours are on offer, patrons sit and sip and smile. When not consulting their smartphones or laptops, they watch other, similar people going by.

After this introduction to slick and thriving Carlton, arriving at Frances Villa is a shock. This was where, in December 1901, legal records show my great-grandparents and their infant daughter next took up residence.

Presumably, Louis had determined that the house be called after their child, though the name is no longer on display. I see only a modest cottage, the last of a row of six in Faraday Street. All are in varying states of dilapidation, several are enveloped by graffiti and a couple look frankly uninhabitable. The house in which Rosetta lived with Louis and Frances is in better condition than the others, though still poor. The wounded roof bears red streaks of rust and the corrugated-iron awning above the veranda slopes at an alarming angle.

Feeling awkward, I ring the doorbell and explain the reason for my interest to Leanne, a friendly blonde woman who, though anxious to leave for work, generously invites me inside. 'These are the last unrenovated places in Carlton,' she says. From the look of the house, the years have not been kind.

I step inside and am instantly transported to another time, in the very place where my great-grandparents with their new baby tried to go about their lives. I see the bedroom in which Rosetta spent long, troubled nights beneath the white plaster ceiling rose, the kitchen with its modern shiny stove placed in the same arched alcove where Ivy helped her to produce cakes and puddings, bread and roasts.

I want to believe that in those first few years at least my great-grandmother found space for Frances in her heart. So I stand before the empty hearth and picture her, sitting by the fire, her child nearby. Perhaps Rosetta invited Frances to play with the silky scraps of fabric that fell from her sewing box, or took her into the garden, pointing out bright rosellas flashing blue and green between thick clusters of scarlet gum blossom and sun-dappled leaves. It seems possible to me.

I thank Leanne who, with a flick of her ponytail, takes off down the street. As I watch her go I feel a shiver. No doubt it is the result of the cool Melbourne breeze whipping down the side lane, but as the door slammed shut I'd felt a sort of presence. It was as if Rosetta had just slipped by, as if she too desired to see where she had been.

JANUARY 1901

A restless energy pervades Melbourne's quiet tree-lined streets. Though the old Queen still sits upon the throne, her loyal subjects in even this distant dominion know it will not be for long. Change hovers in the air and, with it, the promise of transformation.

First comes Federation: six mismatched colonies are forged into a new nation. On the first day of January, beneath a fierce sun, Australia's inaugural Governor-General, the vainglorious Lord Hopetoun, mounts a grand dais in Sydney's Centennial Park and reads the Proclamation of the Commonwealth.

Louis, studying the newspaper at breakfast the next morning, turns to his wife and says, 'I do not understand why it wasn't done in Melbourne. Everyone knows this is the superior place. What was it that writer Richard Twopeny said about Melbourne? "The people dress better, talk better, are better." He was right.'

Louis puts the paper down, then pushes his toast and marmalade away in an exasperated fashion. 'Honestly, it's enough to make a man choke.'

Glaring, he opens the pages once again. 'Rosetta, listen, there's more. *The Age* says there was an enormous crowd, more than 250,000 strong, and a vast procession. Five thousand shearers led the way and, apparently, two women with long, flowing hair displayed themselves on a sort of float. One stood on the shoulders of the other, who was seated on a chair of gold.' He looks over at his wife. 'What do you say to that?'

Rosetta does not say anything. But she wonders how it felt to be one of those women and what it might have been like to be there, with them.

Just a few weeks later Ivy arrives at Faraday Street, excited and distraught. She has passed by the freckle-faced paperboy on the corner, yelling the most extraordinary news, as she made her way to work. 'Oh, Mrs Raphael,' she cries, 'have you heard? Our dear sovereign is dead!'

Life pauses. Victoria was queen for sixty years; what will the future hold now? A shocked, grey pall is cast across the land. The inhabitants of Frances Villa, in the midst of their own disquiet, respond each in their own way. Louis ensures that, at least as far as he is concerned, correct mourning will be assumed. He draws comfort from the outward observation of form. Every morning, as he readies himself for the day's work, he puts on black crepe armbands over the sleeves of his dark suit. Before he leaves he checks they are secure. He knows that they, if nothing else, will stay just as they should.

Rosetta, by contrast, feels rebellious. She is secretly pleased when she discovers that her usual dressmaker has been overwhelmed with orders for sooty dresses and that even the dependable department store Buckley & Nunn has sold out of black veils.

'I will wear my violet and grey,' Rosetta announces with a toss of her head when her mother pays a call. 'Anything else is simply too depressing.'

Fanny is used to Rosetta's moods. Still, she is puzzled by the cause of her daughter's lack of ease, cannot understand why this is not the life, with all its certainties, that she wants to lead.

'What is wrong with you, my dear?' she asks. 'I know you are distressed.'

'I cannot tell you that for I hardly know myself,' is all Rosetta says. She walks over to the dresser, begins rearranging the long-stemmed crimson roses she placed there in a vase only that morning. A moment later she starts adjusting picture frames that are already level. How to explain this agitation? Like an unruly genie, she feels her dormant spirit, contained for far too long, begin to press against life's boundaries.

Then in August, Prince Edward is crowned King and the world seems to shift on its axis; become more vivid, faster, brighter. Unlike his late mother, who lived a life of largely secluded gloom, confident, charming Edward adores fashionable society. The new sovereign is a man of great good humour with a knack for *bonhomie*. Edward is known to conduct a number of amorous liaisons with voluptuous beauties. He sets trends; wears tweed suits and homburg hats; embraces extravagance.

Constraint seems to melt away. The twentieth century beckons and, with it, all manner of tempting possibilities.

By the following November, in 1902, my great-grandparents had left Frances Villa for another, grander Carlton home. Louis must have kept it, though, as they were to return there twice more. That year's electoral roll describes Louis as a man 'of independent means', while his wife's name is listed as Rose. Neither one was quite as they had been.

I find their new house on a day of dense cloud and bruised, rain-filled skies. As I seek shelter beneath the silver-grey leaves of a dripping eucalypt I note that, unlike the ailing Frances Villa, number 66 Elgin Street is in pristine condition. It is equipped with an impeccable wrought-iron balustrade on its first-floor veranda and a front fence consisting of a row of perfectly aligned metal spears. Like its neighbours, the house is painted mint green, though it is distinguished from them by the presence of a single, sentry-like tree.

I begin taking photographs – probably I look suspicious – and a tall man stops and speaks to me. He explains that it is no longer a home, but a showroom for a fashionable clothing brand; little will be gained from venturing inside. Feeling damp and cold I tell myself that it is just another house in which Rosetta lived and, therefore, only a small piece for me to puzzle over as I try to solve the mystery of her life. Yet something still draws me to the place.

After consulting my damp map it strikes me just how close I am to Station Street, and all at once I understand. Here is one of the secrets that my father had unearthed. For in a small cottage at number 55 lived the mysterious man who would transform my great-grandmother's life.

TWELVE

His name, William Norman, was good and plain and, unlike the person who bore it, quintessentially British. Perhaps his Chinese father thought that like William, the Norman duke best known for his victory at the Battle of Hastings, his son might in time conquer the English.

I expect all William felt was that his historic appellation didn't seem to bestow a single discernible advantage. No doubt this was one reason why he chose to style himself Carl Zeno. The name 'Carl' has a certain distinguished European sound, while 'Zeno' hints at mysterious Eastern origins. 'The Magnificent' would come later, a title calculated to evoke potent images of other-worldly powers.

In fact, Zeno of Elea was an ancient Greek sage. He was most famous for his nine paradoxes, particularly the one in which, impossibly, a tortoise continuously outruns Achilles, swift-footed hero of the Trojan War. An article I found in the academic journal *Science* said that this paradox 'gives the feeling that you're perpetually on the verge of solving it without ever doing so'. I know this sensation well. Being near to unravelling a mystery but never quite managing to do so is very often the way I feel about Zeno and my great-grandmother. At times they seem to come just into view before moving, ever-tantalisingly, further away.

The original Zeno maintained that time and motion are but illusions. His latter reincarnation, whose stock-in-trade was artifice wrapped in a vaporous cloak of scientific mystique, also seemed fond of this idea. Carl Zeno had barely any education. But he was a master of invention with a magnificence, albeit entirely self-created, all his own. He had his books and charts, had learnt something of Chinese herbs and medicines, but not much more than this. Zeno did, however, have one precious gift, and that was his uncanny ability to divine an anxious supplicant's dearest, most heartfelt wish.

Born in 1875 in Tuena, a small town that lay in a picturesque valley between Goulburn and Bathurst in New South Wales, Zeno was the son of a Chinese immigrant from the plague- and rebellion-wracked province of Guangdong. China's emperor referred to himself as the 'Son of Heaven'; he called the vast realm over which he ruled the 'Celestial Empire'. As a consequence 'Celestials' was the term that English speakers bestowed upon those tens of thousands of Chinese labourers who arrived at Australia's goldfields during the 1850s. Suggestive of an ethereal race who dwelt in a heavenly world of clouds, the term was not one of approbation, nor was the place from which they came benign. Despite the Emperor's title, it was more hell than paradise.

Zeno's mother, Elizabeth, known as Eliza, was the Australian-born daughter of a stonemason and illiterate; she could not even sign her name. Marriages like hers – Eliza was of British descent – were highly unusual for racism was rife.

'Alarming' was the way in which the Reverend William Young summed up the phenomena in 1868. I find this pronouncement, displayed in close proximity to a selection of dazzling opera costumes and a red and yellow dragon of tremendous size, in Melbourne's Chinese Museum. There is worse to come in the Museum of Sydney – one wall displays in oversized bold type an even blunter opinion belonging to no lesser person than Sir Henry Parkes, the father of Federation. 'There can be no ... intermarriage or social communion between the British and the Chinese,' thunders his proclamation. I begin to understand just how shocking the attraction that Rosetta felt for Zeno really was.

As the nineteenth century drew to a close, prejudice increased. Reports circulated about youths with flaming torches attacking Chinese miners at Lambing Flat. Angry men were seen pouring into public halls to protest against future arrivals. Next, ships with Chinese passengers on board were turned away from Sydney Harbour. Finally, in 1901, one of the first acts of the new Federal Parliament was the effective ban of Asian immigration. Dubbed the White Australia Policy, this notorious legislation was enforced by a dictation test, deliberately chosen in an improbable European language – it might be Romanian or Danish or Czech – that would ensure failure.

Growing up, the position William Norman found himself in would have been at best uncomfortable; at worst, dangerous. Carrying as he did the burden of his Chinese race yet also feeling strongly that he was his mother's son, it must have seemed as if there were no safe place in which he felt he belonged. By trade he was a tinsmith. I wonder if, as he beat upon that insubstantial metal with his workman's tools, it was then he decided he would fashion a new persona, one based on magical words and wishes that would protect him like a charm.

I make my way down Elgin Street with the rain now increasing in intensity, pulling up the hood of my raincoat as I turn left into Canning and take a quick right into Palmerston. It is easy to imagine the way it was, in 1903, when both Rosetta and Zeno lived in the neighbourhood. The small Victorian villas and dignified terraces all remain, save for the occasional contemporary block of flats, multicoloured and with odd angles asserting a vaguely post-modernist aesthetic.

A sudden left again, this time into Station Street, and there it is. I stand before a modest red-brick cottage with a white fence and, above its awning, a glossy dark-green trim. The walk between Rosetta's house and Zeno's has taken only a few minutes to complete.

Though the couple are not officially recorded as meeting for at least another two years, their proximity suggests that it was here in Carlton that they initially encountered each other. I imagine that it might have been in the grocer's King & Godfree, established in 1874 and still serving customers today, that Rosetta dropped a parcel containing her favourite Lapsang Souchong tea.

THIRTEEN

DECEMBER 1903

Rosetta has long since left her innocence behind. She is a woman of twenty-three and resolute. Unhappy since her wedding night, she has made half-hearted attempts to play the part of wife and mother. They do not suit. She has submitted to Louis' desires, learnt that by allowing her mind to disengage it is possible to provide him with the physical satisfaction he seeks while some more essential part of her remains quite separate from him.

But there comes a time when she can do this no longer. A man she doesn't know, a man with honey-coloured skin and almond eyes, has intervened.

It is during one hot summer's night in Frances Villa, beneath clammy linen sheets, that Louis reaches for her and she stiffens. There is no struggle, nor are there cries. Rosetta merely says, with a new composure, 'I will never lie with you in that way again. Do you understand? I feel nothing. It doesn't matter what you say or do. I will not, I refuse.'

Louis goes to speak, then stops. His desire for her has never waned. But his wife's moods, her temper and her tantrums are exhausting. He has other, more accommodating women.

'I know you do not love me, Rosetta,' he says wearily. 'What is it you want?'

What does she want? It is a question Rosetta has been asking herself for months, no, years. And in this room, at this moment, her first step is taken.

'I want to go from here, from you.' There, it is said.

'I won't fight you, Rosetta. Go. I will support you. But I want Frances to stay with me.'

Rosetta objects. She takes the child with her. It is what she thinks she should do.

Louis bides his time. It is not until Christmas and New Year have passed that he dons his black suit and visits his solicitor. Louis is a man of precise habits, methodical, and intent on doing even this unpleasant task in the proper fashion. He discusses what he needs with Mr W.B.R. Blair, a young man who has recently inherited his practice from his father. Mr Blair is tall and thin and kind. He regards his client with sympathetic eyes.

'I apologise for any embarrassment, Mr Raphael,' Blair says, 'but it simply can't be helped. I must ask you to make a candid declaration regarding the state of your and Mrs Raphael's conjugal relations. Just tell my clerk about the situation; he'll put it into the correct legal language and read it back.'

'*On or about the twentieth day of December (1903) … cohabitation finally ceased between us owing to the Respondent (Rosetta) refusing to allow me to have intercourse with her …*' The clerk, old and gnarled, recites these shocking words in his reedy voice, bows his head and then retires.

Mr Blair draws up the Deed of Separation. The sum of '*one pound and five shillings per week*' is fixed upon as a reasonable income to support Mr Raphael's wife and child. He will also '*give and deliver . . . her wearing apparel, jewellery, trinkets and personal ornaments*'. Louis signs the deed and, later, so does Rosetta. The date is 7 January 1904. It is done.

Rosetta takes up residence in a small house in St Kilda, begins what she believes her new life will be. She does what is needed; she shops, she sews, she cares for her daughter, but these tasks seem only to add to her dissatisfaction. Leaving Louis has not brought the fulfilment she expected. As one day fades into another she starts to feel as if she is fading, too, becoming insubstantial, a wraith she barely recognises.

Often, Rosetta goes walking, holds her daughter's hand in her own. She finds it difficult to focus on Frances' chatter. Instead, she ponders what might lie ahead for both of them.

Life changes in unexpected ways. On a particularly bleak, grey afternoon while she strolls with Frances along St Kilda pier, Rosetta is approached by a girl with alabaster skin and coils of shining black hair. The girl remarks on a great flock of gulls that have just swooped by, and as she does so Rosetta sees that the diminutive stature of this tiny, animated being has deceived her. She is not so very young, but of a similar age to herself.

As Frances skips ahead, preoccupied with a game of her own devising, the two women fall into easy conversation. Rosetta's new acquaintance is fascinating. She speaks with a marked, throaty accent, comes from Poland and has all kinds of original ideas. The young woman is staying with a family in St Kilda, says something about helping with the children, though she is vague when asked what has brought her so far from home. Rosetta chooses not to pursue the matter. 'We all have our secrets,' she thinks.

After that, they meet often, always at the pier. They begin exchanging confidences, to speak of their lives and dreams.

'I want to tell you about something, something important,' Rosetta's friend says one misty day as both gaze at the long grey waves rolling in across Port Phillip Bay.

'I have an extraordinary cream that can perform miracles – truly. It's based on an old family recipe using essence of pine bark and water lilies. The main ingredient is wool fat – what you Australians call lanolin – something that is very rich and good here, only the smell is awful.' She wrinkles her arched nose. 'So I have made up my mind to produce it and to sell it, but with a fragrance. That has never been done before!' She flings her arms wide in an exuberant gesture. Rosetta, watching, thinks, 'How certain, how confident she is.'

'I considered using oil of lavender, but I believe now that is too old-fashioned. Anyway, you have given me another idea.'

'Me? What?'

'I'm going to use rose.'

Rosetta's new friend continues to confide. 'I know a man – his name is John Thompson. Mr Thompson manages the Robur Tea Company, you must have heard of it. He is very kind to me.'

Rosetta, a little more worldly now, has some idea of what this kindness might entail.

'Don't tell anyone as his wife cannot know, but John is lending me some money.'

'Whatever for?'

'I'm sorry, truly, to say this, but women here have dreadful skin, burnt and coarse and dry.' Rosetta gives her friend a quick look and raises her eyebrows.

'Yes, alright, your own is not so bad. I see you go out when it is hot with your straw boater and your little parasol. But Rosetta, it is not enough.

'My plan is that, with John's help, I will open a wonderful salon devoted to improving the complexions of Australian ladies. I want to sell my beautiful rose Valaze cream and teach them all about how to care for themselves – everything! And, my dear, if that succeeds it will only be the beginning. One little shop will not be enough for me – I want to build an empire of beauty.'

Rosetta only half believes her friend but is impressed nonetheless by such a grand ambition. 'And what will this marvellous place be called?' she asks.

'Oh, that is easy. It will be my own name, of course. Helena Rubinstein.'

Rosetta's first visit to the newly opened salon is on a particularly blustery morning. She stumbles inside, clutching at her flying skirts, her cheeks whipped pink by the furious wind that swirls up Collins Street. 'Oh, this weather!' she says to Helena. 'I must look completely dishevelled.'

Helena, in her neatly buttoned peach-coloured uniform, moves back a step and studies her, taking in Rosetta's long cream skirt and blue striped blouse, her glowing face and lustrous hair. She can see that several bronze tendrils are beginning to escape the boater Rosetta has endeavoured to anchor against the wind with a silver hatpin. 'Actually, you look wonderful,' she pronounces in her distinctive tones, 'rather like a woman in a painting by Manet or Renoir. You could be strolling down a Parisian boulevard.'

'A Parisian boulevard,' Rosetta repeats to herself. She perches on one of the salon's bamboo chairs and imagines a world where a lady might wander a cobblestoned street, catch an artist's eye and be captured forever in glowing tints.

Suddenly, the curtains at the windows billow in the breeze before drifting back down into white, airy clouds. 'They're lovely,' Rosetta murmurs. Helena winks, then whispers that they were made from the dresses – 'you know, darling, with those enormous skirts' – that she brought in her suitcase from Poland.

The filmy curtains rise and swell again as the salon door opens and a woman of remarkable appearance steps inside. Her enormous hat, adorned with a quivering ostrich feather, her richly embroidered gown and long row of gleaming pearls only serve to heighten the imposing effect she makes. Rosetta's dark eyes widen as she realises who the woman is. 'She has come home, of course, it is the tour,' Rosetta thinks. 'But what can Nellie Melba want?'

Helena, with her usual aplomb, swiftly moves towards the resplendent diva's side. Even so, she is surprised when, without preamble, Melba announces: 'I desire that you give me a complexion to match my voice – like this.' And then she sings.

As the captivating, crystalline sound soars and fills the salon Rosetta feels an immense longing. She thinks about the oriental man that she encountered and the promise in his eyes. She thinks of Paris, of Lilian and London, of Helena's plans, of artists and of opera. She imagines what it might be like to live a life rich in experience and pleasure.

Rosetta knows that Nellie Melba was once young Helen Mitchell of Mackay, yet this had not stopped the girl from achieving her dreams. She can now see, too, that Helena Rubinstein's own ambitions would very likely come to fruition. Yes, it is true, women face impossible constraints. But perhaps her mother is wrong. At least a few might dare to forge their own paths, make their fortunes, create an extraordinary life. That is, once some deft reinvention has taken place.

Rosetta begins to wonder if she, too, can transcend her present circumstances. She is not foolish, knows that she possesses neither Melba's talent nor Rubinstein's unique skills. But perhaps there may be some other way to embark on her own, glittering journey, create her own version of success.

This diverting meditation comes to an abrupt end with the conclusion of Melba's brief burst of song. It is as if a spell has been broken. Rosetta catches a glimpse of herself in one of the salon's mirrors, considers her reflection, her hat, her hair, her flushed cheeks. Even if Helena is right and she does look like a woman in a painting, what difference does it make? 'I am still married, and there is Frances,' she thinks, and sighs. 'I am marooned in Melbourne. That is my reality.'

FOURTEEN

It is possible for me to follow the tumultuous route that Rosetta's life now takes due to a large document headed 'Divorce Papers *Raphael vs Raphael* 1905'. The papers detail the legal proceedings that occurred in the Supreme Court of Victoria. Like the other official records, they are written in an ordered hand, though their contents reflect a situation that had become frankly chaotic.

The documents tell me that on 15 September 1904 Rosetta returned to her husband. It could have been at the urging of her mother, or because she feared the loss of security, the protection afforded by Louis Raphael's good name. Maybe the pursuit of an alternative seemed hopeless, impossible to contemplate. Whatever the reason, she was back.

They moved again. Louis found a house in Hoddle Street, East Melbourne, but within six months the family returned to Frances Villa. What was it they were looking for? Were they trying to outrun their unhappiness? They seemed unable to settle anywhere.

~

It appears the novelty of another house won't be enough. A new city is required, and though Louis has always considered Sydney a trifle raffish, the people a shade too loud, the Raphaels embark upon a visit in August 1905. Perhaps, this time, Rosetta will be satisfied.

Sydney has a special light caused by winter's drenching sun. It is so bright that Rosetta's dresses of pale mauve and pink look instead to be bleached, bone white. She finds herself attracted to the city and its sights. She admires the sparkling harbour and the effervescence of the foaming, turquoise surf. They stay in Paddington, in Glenmore Road, and this is pleasing, too. Rosetta enjoys the erratic, narrow streets, the way they twist and turn, dip and fall, revealing an unexpected glimpse of shimmering water, a window-box crammed with brick-red geraniums, a lush vine draping a garden wall. Melbourne, by contrast, is mainly flat, its roads do not diverge. Rather like its citizens, it is sensible and disciplined; a more polite terrain.

Sydney seduces Rosetta's senses. It has an edge of savagery. As she moves beneath the city's bright blue skies she feels its throbbing beat; it awakens something wild within her, a fierce energy. She decides it is a place where she could make all manner of discoveries.

But not with Louis. Rosetta's return to him has required that, once more, she must submit to his physical demands; she finds his brisk brutality hard to endure. Even setting this burden to one side, she sees before her only a future of frustration, colourless and empty. 'Life – it is happening somewhere else,' she thinks, 'and I am trapped, trapped in a prison of banality.' She waits a day, a week and then, after a month, she runs away again.

Rosetta returns to Melbourne, stays the night with Mrs Dowall, a friend of Fanny's. 'Don't worry, dear. You go and rest, I'll happily take care of little Frances,' the woman says. Though she is grateful, Rosetta is not interested in her mother's friend, barely notices her surroundings. Consumed by a tempest of emotions, her pulse races with excitement. But she is also frightened.

That night, exhausted and troubled, she claws at her sheets, twists and turns in her narrow bed. It is the same dilemma that first drove her to the fortune teller. 'Should I return again to Louis,' she asks herself, repeatedly, 'or dare I leave forever?' This time, she knows, there can be no turning back. Whatever her decision, it will bind her for eternity.

She wakes the next morning, surprised that she has been asleep. She feels quite different. It is as if, during those hours of slumber, something fundamental has altered. Those wild, disparate parts of herself have rearranged themselves, becoming whole and cogent.

Rosetta stretches, the echo of a dream, a dream where something important was said, playing on her mind. Then she remembers; the dream was about Zeno, of course. 'Both in the stars and on your palm,' he'd said, 'are written all the events that will in time unfold.'

But Rosetta doesn't want to wait; she has been waiting all her life. She wants her future now.

That day she returns to the fortune teller's rooms in Swanston Street. According to a report in *The Age* newspaper, Rosetta claims the reason for her visit is to undertake 'lessons in painting'. It isn't true. Though among Zeno's diverse and curious talents he is, in fact, an artist, her purpose is not to learn how to master watercolours or oils.

Rosetta enters Zeno's room. She wears a slim black skirt and a black lace, high-buttoned blouse. She closes the door firmly behind her, turns, unbuttons her gloves, takes off her coat and hat and lets them fall. She does not sit down. Rosetta goes to Zeno. He is silent, betrays no surprise at her sudden appearance. They are so close that she can smell his breath; it is a mixture of aniseed and mint. The fortune teller pauses, as if some distant music only he can hear has ceased. He waits a beat, then two, regards Rosetta with his panther eyes. Then he guides her to a low divan draped with fringed crimson silk and gestures for her to recline. His murmured question to her is really more a statement of intent.

'This is what you desire.'

'Yes.'

Only one word yet, once spoken, her life will never be the same.

Immaculate and composed, Zeno remains in his usual attire – a dark suit, crisp white shirt and tie – as he slowly parts Rosetta from her clothes. He removes her black lace blouse, her skirt, her petticoats and, finally, her satin corset. As each garment slides towards the floor Zeno whispers to her, shocking, thrilling words. When Rosetta's voluptuous, milky body is finally revealed he begins to touch her lightly, tracing the outline of her face, her lips, her throat, her breasts. Zeno taunts Rosetta's nipples with his fingertips; it makes her gasp with pleasure and arch her back.

Zeno asks for nothing. His demeanour does not change; perhaps his black eyes are just a little more opaque. Only a slight huskiness in his voice betrays the effort of restraint.

The fortune teller has much experience. Zeno knows how best to stroke and tease and please. His hands and mouth search out hidden, tender places, commit small, indecent acts. The things he does have never been done to Rosetta before. How long it lasts, this abandoned pleasure, she doesn't know. But then a moment comes when she has never felt so alive, so powerful.

Zeno has no scruples; Rosetta has no shame. It is all too easy to believe that the stars are right and she is not to blame.

'It is my destiny,' she tells herself, her mouth curving into a jubilant smile, 'to live a different life.' Her decision made, she feels a sense of wild exhilaration, as if she were falling with reckless speed through space.

~

According to the records of the court, Rosetta next appears on 23 October. She goes with Frances to Fanny's house in Johnston Street, Fitzroy. Louis has been living there: confused about his wife's intentions, he has been hoping she might visit. The papers state that Rosetta stayed for just one night. The next day she received her weekly allowance from her husband. Then she went. She never spent another night under the same roof with Louis again and, this time, she left her child behind.

These things are all set down in official legal proceedings and personal statements. I know they are merely a collection of old documents, but still I find the contents so affecting that I can't continue reading. It is not difficult to comprehend the temptations of desire. Coming to terms with the abandonment of a child is infinitely more challenging.

I think about what it might have been like to be a young woman living in Australia in 1905, how narrow and circumscribed life was, how hard it must have been. I try to imagine how it felt for Rosetta to crave the freedom to become the person she felt driven to be.

My friend Robert, a gifted psychiatrist, believes that it is entirely possible for a person to arrange his or her mind so that any action, no matter how unthinkable or how much it contravenes social and moral codes, becomes the natural, the obvious step to take. 'Some human beings are like that,' he says. 'If they want something badly enough they will find a way to justify anything.'

Desire for Zeno and the promise of a world of passion, a life lived on a bigger stage where anything might happen; these things held Rosetta in their thrall.

Guilt, remorse, compassion; such unquiet spirits had the power to rise unbidden and drag her down into the depths. Rosetta would be manacled just as surely as had her convict grandfather. She would not allow it.

I was to learn, much later, that she embraced a different narrative, a rationalisation that made it possible to live with what she'd done. Rosetta maintained it was the violent events that took place on her wedding night that excused everything. She clung to this defence throughout her life as a woman in danger of drowning might grasp at a single, flimsy plank in a treacherous sea. It was necessary.

If she permitted herself a moment's softness she might waver. Only Frances had the potential to undo her. Like Achilles' mortal heel, she was Rosetta's greatest danger. It caused the exile of the child. Not only did Rosetta refuse to see her daughter, her very name was banned. She would not permit it to be uttered by a soul.

I think about my own lost child, the way I never hear her name, then think more about Rosetta and her dreadful, desperate decision. The fact is, we all carry our children within us: it doesn't matter if they are here or gone. All mothers learn this lesson.

FIFTEEN

Frances, Nana Billie to me, always claimed that she didn't remember her mother. She maintained that Rosetta abandoned her when she was just a few months old.

'My mother didn't want me. She left when I was still a baby,' she would say to me, rejection hanging like dust suspended in the air. 'I never knew her at all.'

It wasn't true. Rosetta didn't leave her daughter until she was well over five. This puzzles me. It is not unusual for there to be no memories up to two or three years of age. But at five, something as cataclysmic as her mother walking out, surely she would remember that.

In an effort to comprehend, I fall back on theories I read years ago when I was studying psychotherapy. In doing so, I recall the term that the old master Sigmund Freud devised in his Viennese study, with its collection of small pagan gods and famous couch, less than a decade before these traumatic events occurred. 'Repressed memory': it seems to me that, though so much of what Freud wrote is now dismissed, called ill conceived or out of date, this concept is neither of these things. It makes sense, gives me a way to understand why it was essential that the five-year-old Frances forgot everything to do with her mother – how Rosetta spoke, her chestnut hair and dark, toffee eyes – but most of all, her act of desertion. Erasing her memory of Rosetta was not only a means to reduce suffering. I think it was the way in which my grandmother survived.

24 OCTOBER 1905

The day it happens is like many others. Frances and her mother have spent the night at Grandma Fanny's house. She eats a breakfast of hot oats and milk, then dresses in new boots and a blue smock. Her long-limbed Aunt Daisy, just fifteen herself, walks with her to the nearby school. Little brown-haired, blue-eyed Frances lines up with the other children, rubbing her new boots together to produce a pleasing, squeaky sound. This minor misdeed is masked by energetic singing of 'God Save the King'. There is a photograph of His Majesty on the schoolroom wall. Close by is a chart of letters and, opposite that, a map with many countries coloured pink, like sweets.

Just an ordinary day, in fact somewhat more regular, more certain than most. During Frances' short life the family has shifted about a lot; sometimes she and her mother move to another house even when her father does not. Sometimes Ivy looks after her, sometimes it is Grandma. Frances has grown used to it, just as she has become familiar with the sound of her parents arguing or, strangely worse, the sudden silences. But that day, after school when she returns to Fanny's house with Daisy, is the first time she hears her father shout in pain.

'Go into the back room with Daisy,' her father insists. 'And don't come out!'

Frances goes where she is told and, as the door begins to shut, hears her father bellow like an injured beast in a desperate, wounded way. 'It's his fault, that devil Zeno – I don't care what you say!'

Now her mother is crying. Frances thinks she hears a crash. She pushes open the door, runs past her parents and out into the street. So immersed are Rosetta and Louis in this dreadful scene that they fail to see her. It is Daisy who has the wit to follow close behind.

The tears that fill Frances' eyes and the noise inside her head make her oblivious to the baker's cart and his blinkered horse thundering by. The driver, bent on making good time, is not aware of the distraught child rushing towards the street. Daisy leaps from the pavement, pulls Frances aside. The two girls fall back into the gutter. Both are trembling and Frances begins to weep.

'Come back inside,' says Daisy, once she has caught her breath.

'No, I can't.' Frances knows that, inside the house, something fearful waits.

Kind, good Aunt Daisy, with her tumble of black curls, puts her arm around Frances while they sit side by side. Time passes. Eventually she is coaxed back. The first thing she sees is Father. He looks angrier than Frances has ever seen him but somehow more miserable as well. But where is Mother? No response.

She screams now, 'Where is my mother?'

No one says a word. It is as if she hasn't said anything at all.

Frances is in a state of unutterable misery. She waits for her mother for hours, then days, then weeks. She grieves.

The longing for her mother's return does not diminish. Only hope begins to fade. One day Frances overhears someone say that Rosetta has gone to Sydney, but if she did what made her go and why hasn't she come back? She wonders if the reason Mother left was something she had done. Perhaps she had not been pretty, or good, or sweet enough; dirtied her dress, forgotten her lessons, squeaked the boots she now regards with nothing but reproach.

Finally, one freezing day as all the days feel now, her heavy-eyed father sits her down. He says, 'Your mother is gone. You will never see her again.'

Only that.

'Never' is a place vaster than any ocean. It is not something that a five-year-old can hope to fathom.

There are some beautiful birds, Frances has seen them in the park, that fly away and don't come back. Her mother has become one of those birds, a glossy creature with flashing eyes and strong, soft wings. Rosetta has soared up into the sky, far, far beyond reach, until there is no part of her that can be seen. Frances' memories of her mother simply disappear, like that.

SIXTEEN

The 'Divorce Papers *Raphael vs Raphael*' provide a surprisingly unrestrained if inconsistent account of the collapse of Rosetta's marriage. Louis' sworn affidavit of 3 November 1905 takes up the tale ten days after Rosetta's flight:

> *I first suspected improper adulterous intercourse between the Respondent and the said Co-Respondent on or about the 26th day of October last when the Respondent informed me that she had during the previous six weeks been improperly intimate with a man whom she loved . . . and whose name she positively refused to disclose.*

Curiously, Louis also states that Rosetta told him that it was as recently as 15 October that she first '*called at the shop of (William Norman) . . . to have her fortune told*'.

This is bewildering. If the affair had begun six weeks prior to her purported 26 October confession, then the 15 October date cannot be correct. That pivotal, initial visit amid the painted suns and moons must have taken place earlier in 1905, perhaps in June or July and certainly before the ill-fated Sydney sojourn.

Next, Louis reports:

> *I then made enquiries and found that the Respondent was in the habit of visiting the Co-Respondent at his shop in Swanston Street Melbourne. On the following day, namely the 27th day of October 1905 I received a letter from my wife dated 26th October 1905 in which she confessed that she lived with another man as his wife but she declined to reveal his name.*

'*Lived with another man as his wife*'; the phrase is coy, barely gives a hint of the illicit passion that engulfed my great-grandmother and her lover. As for the account itself, it seems questionable to me, a tale confected for the benefit of the court. It doesn't matter what Rosetta tried to hide or to withhold, or what dates were flung about; I think that when she walked out on 24 October Louis knew, knew only too well, who it was that had seduced his wife.

I determine this, and much else besides, not from the legal documents contained in my father's files but from other places. The same fascination with the chase my father had has overtaken me as well. Now I seek out experts, books and journals and, of course, delve into the internet. It is there that I discover an intriguing report from what at first appears a most unlikely source. Under the heading 'A Melbourne Divorce Case', *The North Western Advocate and the Emu Bay Times* reveals that, ominously, Louis had already 'been advised to watch his wife'. Furthermore, he had 'remonstrated with her for returning home late . . .'.

The newspaper continues, 'He traced her to the shop of William Norman, trading as Carl Zeno, in Swanston Street.' It says that Louis went to see the man, that he told Mr Norman 'he would not permit his wife's visits to his place'.

This intervention does not meet with success; the affair continues. The next step is inevitable.

Subpoenas are issued for a number of witnesses; they are to testify to Rosetta's wickedness. The roll call includes a domestic servant, a plain-clothes constable, a dealer, a clerk, a commission agent and a cab driver. No defence is mounted. The case is heard before a judge. Apparently, in a situation like this, a jury is superfluous.

On 3 April 1906, Louis Raphael of Johnston Street, Fitzroy, is granted a divorce from Rosetta Raphael, of Fitzroy Street, St Kilda.

The shameful findings are all included on the public record. Rosetta is found '*guilty of adultery*' at Swanston Street on each of five days, from 27 to 31 October 1905. Carl Zeno, seducer, Celestial son and seer, is named the Co-Respondent.

The last step of the legal process, a *decree nisi*, is issued in the Supreme Court of Victoria by Mr Justice Hood.

It is now 22 June 1906. My great-grandmother's troubled marriage is over. It has ended in disgrace.

'Rosetta has done what?' Fanny's horrified friend, Mrs Dowall, exclaims. Her brow is furrowed and on her face is an expression of the utmost repugnance.

'Run away from Louis, you say, and left Frances? For a *Chinaman*?' Mrs Dowall shakes her head. 'I can't believe I took her in.

'Fanny, you know she will be shunned. Nobody will receive her, not now. A Chinaman!'

Rosetta's grave transgression is the very thing that cautious Fanny has most dreaded. Then there is the future of her five other daughters: Florence, Ivy, Winifred, Daisy and Evelyn. How to ensure they will not fall as has their sister?

She doesn't know, is certain of only one thing. 'I will not abandon Rosetta,' she says to her friend.

Mrs Dowall expresses the more common attitude. Beautiful Rosetta with all her charming manners and her style has broken every social convention current in Australia at the time. No, worse than broken: they have been defiled. Rosetta is a bad wife, a wicked mother and, most shocking, an oriental fortune teller's concubine.

Rosetta and Zeno, Mrs Raphael and Mr Norman; whichever way their names are said in Melbourne's shocked drawing rooms and parlours, it is invariably with one word attached and that word is 'scandal'.

Doors close. Some people go so far as to cross the road when they see Mrs Raphael walking towards them, casting their eyes down and averting their faces. When Rosetta approaches two fashionably dressed women she knows in Flinders Street there is no word of greeting: they simply engage each other from beneath their elaborate wide-brimmed hats in increasingly determined conversation. It is a shock. Rosetta had been prepared for gossip, hadn't imagined the severity of the penalty imposed by notoriety.

What can she do, where can she go for comfort? There are her parents and her sisters, yes, but Fanny and Lewis are old, her sisters so much younger and still innocent. Who else?

Helena can do nothing: she is on the other side of the world, studying beauty treatments in Krakow, mixing creams and lotions in Wiesbaden, revelling in the great cities of Paris and London. While her friend's world is expanding, Rosetta's is growing smaller. This is not what she yearned for. And every day, wherever she goes, she is reminded of what she has done; the absence she has caused. The sparrow sounds made by a little girl are missing; there is no trilling laughter, nor are there small cries, but only silence by her side.

'Darling, look towards me. No, turn your head this way.' Zeno is sketching Rosetta. He tries to capture the fullness of her mouth, the way she lifts her chin, with quick, sure strokes of his pencil. Something, though, is wrong, something in her eyes. Their golden lights are veiled. He studies her. She is preoccupied.

'You are unhappy,' Zeno says. 'I hardly need to be a mind reader to know that.' He goes to Rosetta, kneels in front of the striped, green velvet chair in which she sits, takes her hands in his.

She leans forward, looks at her lover. 'I simply cannot continue in this fashion,' she says. 'You have seen it, the way people behave.' She pulls her hands away, looks towards the open window, the hard silver sky. 'Melbourne is too much to bear!' she cries.

On her cheek, a single tear and then another trace a path. But Rosetta makes no mention of her heart, the way it flutters with unexpected pain. She says nothing about what it is like to live in the same city as a child who now bears a forbidden name.

SEVENTEEN

SYDNEY, 1906

Sydney promised Rosetta and Zeno a clean slate, a way to start again. It wasn't just that the city was six hundred miles away from Melbourne and in the new state of New South Wales; a siren song of possibility whispered in its balmy breeze. Built around the sapphire waters of Sydney Harbour, one of the finest sea ports ever known, it was a place of arrivals and departures, of great vessels carrying sailors, merchants and travellers between the New World and the Old.

All kinds of people came to Sydney, famous, infamous, respectable or not, some seeking its beauty and vitality, some wanting only to disappear and be lost. In 1906 it was a bright, brash, thriving and, most important, forgiving city. A couple with ambition like Rosetta and Zeno could chance their luck there among citizens who had a taste for novelty and a willingness to be impressed.

~

On 28 June, just six days after the *decree nisi* has been granted, Rosetta and Zeno arrive at Chancery Square in Macquarie Street. This elegant precinct is presided over by a commanding statue of the late Queen Victoria who looks, in all her stony splendour, to be the epitome of imperial power. She stands high above the multitude of lesser mortals who pass beneath her elevated gaze, with the royal orb and sceptre in her hands, a singularly forbidding expression on her face and what looks like one faintly raised eyebrow.

Although the honey-coloured St Mary's Cathedral and the dual colonial facades of The Mint and the Parliament of New South Wales are nearby, that part of Chancery Square where Rosetta and Zeno are to be found is neither sacred nor profane. A place of temporal authority, its modesty is at odds with the more splendid edifices on each side. In just a few years' time it will be transformed into a sandstone-faced Gothic fantasy, equipped with the crenellated parapets of fairytales. It will become the Lands Titles Office, otherwise known as the 'Office of the Damned'. But for now it is in this rather plain rectangular building, in a civil wedding ceremony conducted by the Deputy Registrar-General, Mr Ridley, that the marriage between Rosetta Raphael nee Solomon and her second husband, William Norman (though now becoming rather better known as Zeno the Magnificent), takes place.

Rosetta is not the adolescent bride she was in 1899. She is a twenty-five-year-old woman in her prime. There will be no demure lace dress and veil today. She wears a tightly fitted cream gabardine ensemble, its well-cut skirt and jacket flattering to womanly curves. Setting off Rosetta's burnished hair is one of the fantastic hats she favours; it is trimmed with white camellias and very wide. For the first time in her life Rosetta is in love. She turns to her new husband, touches his arm, smiles.

Beside Rosetta, Zeno wears his customary dark suit but somehow, whereas other men look stiff and uncomfortable in this attire, he seems, as ever, utterly relaxed. It is apparent in every one of his photographs. Considering the way in which the inhabitants of his world regard men of mixed race, it is a particularly surprising quality, this sense of being completely at home wherever he is.

For his part, Zeno recognises that the woman he has wed is a rare, like-minded soul. She is a natural risk-taker, an adventurer unintimidated by other people's rules. He feels, and he is nothing if not perceptive, an invigorating sense of possibilities waiting to unfold.

The Marriage Certificate, written in the tight, bureaucratic hand of a servant of the state, reveals many things, not the least being the couple's increasing penchant for invention. It notes the groom's profession as 'Artist', with the word 'Painter' added in brackets, just in case there is some doubt. So, no longer a tinsmith and not a teller of fortunes, either, at least not officially.

The profession of everyone else appearing on that Certificate appears also to have changed. Zeno's father, the Cantonese labourer that was, is now a Mechanical Engineer. Even more unlikely, Rosetta herself is described as a 'Physical Culturalist'.

I suppose it seemed so easy. All it needed was a stroke of the pen and you could be anyone you wished.

Number 29 Queen Street, the Woollahra terrace into which the newlywed Mr and Mrs Norman moved, continues to exist. Painted a startling combination of buttercup and vivid blue, its first-floor balcony sags vertiginously towards the right and, in place of the original wrought-iron fence, there is a clumsy wall of exposed brick. Compared with its genteel neighbours, the house looks eccentric to me. It doesn't seem to fit.

By contrast, most Queen Street residences exhibit well-maintained restraint. A number of the most imposing are

Victorian villas that display the names of ancient battle sites. *Libya*, *Arbela*, *Marathon*; they are like calls to arms. These references to antique wars are located high up near the roof lines, framed by urns and scrolls, a silent tribute to a lost, more heroic world. I wander up and down, gazing at all the homes, and think about who Rosetta and Zeno might have encountered, the people who lived inside.

Alexander Alston, a master stonemason whose deft hands chiselled gargoyles at the University of Sydney, lived at number 115 in a grand, free-standing Georgian house. This was of course years before his granddaughter, the future opera singer Dame Joan Sutherland, became a resident. Dr Patrick Collins was next door in St Kevin's, though he too was to be superseded by a more famous inhabitant when many decades later the former Prime Minister Paul Keating moved in. (Keating announced that, though the mansion would undergo restoration, he would eschew any changes that might conform to 'passing infatuations with fashionable configuration'.)

There was also a mayor, several politicians and a number of writers living in Queen Street in 1906, with the most renowned of these undoubtedly Andrew Barton 'Banjo' Paterson; solicitor, journalist, war correspondent and widely admired poet of the bush. I can see that some of his most famous works, *Waltzing Matilda*, *The Man from Snowy River* and *Clancy of the Overflow*, have been commemorated by latter-day residents with a literary bent in the form of shiny, round bronze plaques sunk into the pavement.

Paterson moved into number 135 not long after marrying his wife, Alice, in Tenterfield three years previously. By the time my great-grandmother arrived they had a daughter, Grace, and another child on the way.

Despite Paterson's country origins and the themes of much of his verse, he was an urbane, sophisticated man of the world. The painter Norman Lindsay, known best for his depiction of erotic nymphs and nudes, described his poet friend with an artist's acuity: 'Black hair, dark eyes, a long, finely articulated nose, an ironic mouth, a dark pigmentation of the skin … His eyes, as eyes must be, were his most distinctive feature, slightly hooded, with a glance that looked beyond one as he talked.'

I picture him, with those distinctive features and distant gaze. He has chanced upon Zeno at the Lord Dudley, then as now a well-patronised local watering hole, and struck up a conversation with the Chinese tinsmith turned artist.

'Yes, I've seen quite a lot of the world by now,' Banjo says to Zeno as he leans against the bar.

'That is something to which I aspire,' Zeno replies.

'Mr Norman, you must go away. You can't imagine what you'll do or see. Do you know, during the Boer War I was in South Africa at the surrender of Bloemfontein – the first correspondent to ride into town with General French. And I saw the capture of Pretoria and the relief of Kimberley … they were unforgettable experiences.'

Paterson nods at the barman, then gestures towards his unlikely companion. The barman frowns, then shrugs his shoulders and sets new glasses of foaming ale in front of the two men.

'I was only back for a year before *The Sydney Morning Herald* sent me sailing off to China: extraordinary place. Next it was London, now there's a marvellous city. You know of the writer Rudyard Kipling? Fine fellow: I stayed with him.'

Zeno is heartened by Paterson's pleasant manner. The times are not kind to those of mixed race. A man only has to leaf through the pages of a popular paper like *The Bulletin* to be struck by a barrage of ferocious prejudice. It adopts a savage anti-Aboriginal, anti-semitic and, above all, anti-Chinese stance. In every issue the exhortation 'Australia for the White Man' appears on the front page.

Though Zeno's finely etched features have about them a European cast, he knows that his tilted eyes and cheekbones betray his past. Whether he calls himself William or Carl or Zeno makes no difference; he is familiar with remarks that sting, with exclusion, stares. Marriage to Rosetta has only caused this to intensify.

Zeno turns over what Paterson has said ... *You must go away. You can't imagine what you'll do or see.*

Though in truth Zeno cannot see into the future, he divines then and there that Paterson is right. If he and Rosetta are to make their way in the world, one day they must leave Australia, venture far away. 'London might be best,' he thinks. 'That sounds like a city with opportunities for a man like me.'

For now, Zeno has other matters that occupy his mind. He checks the time, sees the late hour and makes a hurried goodbye.

'Thank you, sir,' he says to Paterson. 'I won't forget your advice.'

There is an unusual sense of urgency about Zeno as he turns away. For, each evening just as night begins to fall, he must leave the well-ordered terraces of Queen Street behind. His destination is a place of dreams and nightmares, shadow and illusion. It is called Wonderland City.

EIGHTEEN

Its Fame and Glory Extolled by Thousands ...
You Cannot Picture its Magnitude.
IT HAS TO BE SEEN.
The Sydney Morning Herald, 22 December 1906

A constant succession of novelties keeps interest in Wonderland fresh. The latest is a lady who used to be 'The Human Firefly,' but at Wonderland is 'The Lady Comet.' She nightly makes ineffectual and sensational efforts to get burnt to death.

Chefalo, the reckless, will loop the death loop, and Signorina Chefalo will also do something hair-raising. Baker's Circus will be on tap at the King's Theatre. In addition Katzenjammer, Topsy-turvey, and all the rest of the side-shows are in full blast. But for the man who has found someone ideal there is nothing better than the shaded seats besides the cool fountains in the luminous darkness.

The Bulletin, 10 January and 14 February 1907

What was this strange and dangerous realm?

Intrigued, I sit for hours under bright strip lighting in a modern municipal library, turning page after page of old newspapers that describe a lost world of marvels and imagination. Wonderland City was the brainchild of the flamboyant entrepreneur William Anderson. It was the culmination of all his theatrical ambitions, first sparked in Bendigo at the age of eight when he formed a plan to run away and join a visiting circus. Anderson's lifelong attachment to greasepaint and the suspension of disbelief led him to produce all kinds of shows across Australia, but never anything on such a scale as this.

The Indigenous tribes that lived beside the fierce currents of a small treacherous bay just a few kilometres south of what is now called Sydney Heads are said to have called it Gamma Gamma, or 'storm'. Thousands of years before Europeans took it for themselves, these peoples lived along its coastline in natural shelters chiselled by the wind. They left behind mysterious rock carvings made from punching holes with stones and then joining them together by way of grooves made in the rock. It is hard to tell exactly what they represent: something marine, perhaps, a whale or possibly two fish.

Today, the area is called Tamarama. The waves that claw the sand upon its beach are just as treacherous as ever, but now surfboard riders in wetsuits glide in among them like sleek black seals.

It was here that in 1906 William Anderson decided to lease Tamarama Glen plus the land formerly occupied by The Royal Aquarium and Pleasure Grounds. The old amusement park had swings, a shooting gallery, water boats and Punch and Judy shows. The Aquarium was inhabited by stingrays, lobsters, turtles, porcupine-fish, a tiger shark and a wobbegong.

These attractions, charming but limited, were insufficient to satisfy Anderson's ambitions. He wanted to build something that would be sensational, extraordinary. The result, at least at first, fulfilled all his dreams. Twenty-thousand people flocked to the opening night; Wonderland caused transports of delight.

~

'So, Mrs Norman, how do you think I should address your husband, then – is he to be William, Carl, Zeno or just The Magnificent?' Anderson has a cigar clenched firmly between his teeth, a twirling ringmaster's moustache and a yellow rose in his buttonhole, fresh and dewy despite the heat. He strides about energetically, proudly shows the Normans his domain.

Down past the Katzenjammer Castle they go, with its weird noises and shrieks, past screaming people flying around the Helter Skelter, and on to the Topsy-turvy where excited fans are thrown upside down. Pleasure seekers rush and swirl about them, uncertain where to turn next. That they wear their customary attire, long skirts and large hats on the women, high-buttoned suits for men, does not deter them from the experience. Whether it is at the Imperial Menagerie of Wild Beasts, the Hall of Laughter, the Box Ball Alley, the Maze, the Haunted House or Ice-skating Rink, inhibitions disappear. They embrace abandonment.

'Call him what you will' is Rosetta's laughing reply as the astonishing scenes unfold.

Anderson turns towards his new magician. 'I think I'll call you William. But in public it will of course be Zeno the Magnificent.'

The febrile atmosphere of bewitchment is further enhanced by countless coloured lamps glowing ruby, gold, azure blue and emerald green among the rides and on the cliffs. People cluster on the embankment just to marvel at the display. Anderson has ensured that, while city streets are still lit by subdued gas light, his world is ablaze, illuminated by electricity, that marvel of the age. He has his own steam plant.

The three arrive at their destination, the Palace of Illusions. Though painted ebony, its name is picked out in yet more dazzling light. This is the place where Zeno is to see the future, tell fortunes and mesmerise.

'Well, here it is,' says Anderson with a flamboyant gesture. 'You start tonight.'

Zeno understands the world of artifice. He discards his customary suit and tie in favour of a black silk robe with a scarlet dragon embroidered down one side. This is not the time to shrink from an oriental heritage. He assumes an air of impenetrable mystery, even elongates his eyes with a little charcoal from the fire. He knows what his audience wants and plays to type.

'Beware,' he says, if a customer who is visiting his stall looks anxious. 'I see great riches,' if his coat is new and of good cloth. 'You have an admirer,' this for a woman of a certain age, not quite sure about her looks. All are amazed.

'How does he know,' they ask their friends, 'the secrets of my heart?'

Zeno is elegant. Always courteous, he delivers his pronouncements in his beautiful, low voice in a way that leaves no room for doubt. He is particularly popular with ladies, a cause of great satisfaction for Anderson who watches greedily as the queues outside the sparkling black building grow. Rosetta notices them too. She remembers how she and Zeno met and feels, just for a moment, a faint disquiet. But Zeno is attentive. All is well. She brushes it aside.

So delighted is Anderson with the way his latest employee has turned out that he soon invites him to perform in the splendid King's Theatre of Varieties.

'You're made for bigger things, my friend,' he says, ashing his cigar.

Zeno thinks so, too. He is more than ready for this step. That night, when the theatre's deep blue curtains part, he appears spotlit, alone on stage. The Acrobatic Marvels, Morris and Wilson, have already thrilled by flying through the air. The extraordinary contortions executed by the Eight Sunbeams are complete. After so much excitement it takes a moment for the crowd to become settled and quiet.

Zeno is still and silent. He waits. There is the sound of low drumming and soft clouds of smoke steal across the stage. Cymbals clash, the smoke clears, Zeno holds his arms out wide and in a thrilling voice he says: 'Who among you has lost a precious object? What is it that you seek? Your wallet, perhaps? Your spectacles, a necklace?

'No, ladies and gentlemen, do not tell me. Let Zeno the Magnificent guess. With the powers I have at my command I will divine your need. Not only that, I will reveal where the object that you seek can be retrieved.'

One by one, as if by magic, Zeno correctly identifies a man with a tall hat who has mysteriously lost his pen, a plump woman sick with worry over her missing golden bracelet and a young, ungainly fellow who blushes over a letter from his sweetheart that has unexpectedly gone astray. The crowd murmurs its approval, but Zeno hasn't finished yet. He invites a young lady up on stage, a small boy and a large, well-built man. Approval turns to wild applause when the pen, the bracelet and the letter are all found inside, respectively, the astonished young lady's reticule, the small boy's pocket and the large man's coat.

Next Zeno asks the crowd, 'Who wants to be transported, to become a bird or beast? Unbelievers are welcome. Only step up and join me on stage.'

Two young men oblige, obviously friends. They wear three-piece suits and a superior air. Zeno gestures to the first young man to take a chair at the right of where he stands. His subject can see only Zeno's wizard eyes in the stage lights' glare. Zeno mutters a string of foreign-sounding words. He encourages the young man to focus on a curious golden medallion he holds before him, spinning on a chain.

Zeno is practised in this art. It doesn't take long for the young man to fall under his spell. All roar with amusement as he is directed to bray like a donkey and roar like a bull. Next it is the other fellow's turn. He has laughed as hard as anyone and announces, 'You won't have the same luck with me.' Zeno only smiles. He is really very good at what he does. Within moments the audience is entertained by an impersonation of a rooster, a duck and finally a hen.

During the thunderous applause that follows, Zeno slips away to settle up with the light-fingered boy he has earlier engaged to redistribute certain objects from unsuspecting people waiting to come in. So much for magic. But Zeno's hypnotic skills are real: to resist his will is as unlikely as turning back the sea.

Hurrying, Zeno joins Rosetta in the wings. 'My wicked, clever darling, you really are quite dazzling – or should I say, magnificent,' she says, and kisses him on the lips. The two then turn towards the stage. They watch the debonair master of ceremonies in his white tie, top hat and tails as, standing in the spotlight, he announces, 'Professor Godfrey's sensational Dog and Monkey Circus!' to the crowd.

Terriers in red jackets and curly-tailed marmosets with green fez hats begin to waltz. Next, a Professor West inches his way down a narrow plank placed at an alarming angle. 'Think of it, ladies and gentlemen,' the ringmaster cries, 'it is at least one hundred feet in length!' Finally, the last member of this professorial trio, a man by the name of Cormack who is 'capable of extraordinary feats', dives from an enormous height into a small tank that Anderson vows is filled with sharks. But Zeno is no longer watching. 'Professor,' he reflects. 'What a good idea that title is.'

Other readers come and go but I remain in the library. I am transfixed by one tale after another, each more astonishing than the last.

It seems that Wonderland City is filled with perilous things to see and do.

A man called Jack Lewis rollerskates down a ramp and through a loop of fire. Another daredevil, an American with the unlikely name of Alphonse Stewart, sets off in an enormous balloon called the *President Roosevelt* and flies to the dizzying altitude of three thousand feet before stepping out into thin air. At the last moment a blue parachute opens. Now a tiny, flailing figure suspended above the sea, he soars past and is lost to view. Miraculously, Alphonse lands without injury on a cliff-top grave in nearby Waverley Cemetery. 'I would have preferred to come down on a more cheerful spot,' he remarks to a reporter from *The Daily Telegraph* and grins insouciantly.

Next, eager patrons climb aboard a blimp-like airship. It travels in a precarious fashion just above the waves on a cable strung between the cliffs. Inevitably, it breaks down, and with rough seas sweeping the beach below, disgruntled lifesavers have to rescue the stranded thrill-seekers, lest they be lost at sea.

No one knows what to expect next.

NINETEEN

Despite Wonderland's extraordinary diversions, among fickle Sydney-siders a certain ennui begins creeping in. Anderson rises to the occasion. He stages fireworks displays, then mock battles between the army and the navy on the beach. There are flame throwers and explosions and cannons going off. At night he re-creates Ned Kelly's last stand at Glenrowan. Still, it is not enough. The stakes rise.

One evening Rosetta strolls along the cliffs. There is a wind, and a long strand of russet hair blows free as she holds her straw hat. A shout goes up. She turns, together with a thousand others, towards the roaring surf. 'Someone, help!' a desperate voice cries out. All eyes are fixed on a small ship heading towards the rocks. But nothing can be done. An awful silence falls. Waves whipping jagged rocks is the single sound. Rosetta is terrified. Didn't Zeno say this morning he was going out to sea? She begins to shake as, horror-stricken, she watches helplessly.

But what is this? With a tremendous jolt the small ship hits a hidden, sandy reef. It is safe. The crew emerge on deck and take their bows; Zeno waves, another man grins at the crowd, then blows a kiss. The spectators' gasps of horror turn into wild applause. It has been an illusion, after all. Annoyed that Zeno has allowed her to think the worst, still Rosetta is exhilarated. She is a risk-taker, and jeopardy has its appeal.

The next day Rosetta finds Mr Anderson on the beach. He is dealing with problems caused by the eight-foot wire fence he has had erected across his land. The fence stops anyone trying to gain entry to Wonderland without a ticket, but it keeps out swimmers, too. This has infuriated the swimmers who, once again, have cut the wire despite threats to call the police.

Rosetta, in a filmy long white dress, waits patiently, half closing her eyes against the sun. She watches Alice, Wonderland's famous elephant, as the great beast makes her way along the beach. The children in the crimson and gold howdah on top of her are screaming with delight but Alice is unbothered. It has become her life.

'Mr Anderson,' Rosetta says, smiling.

'Why, Mrs Norman. You are looking particularly charming today. How can I help?'

'I am most intrigued by your entertaining spectacles,' she says. 'Might I make a suggestion of my own?'

Rosetta's plans are enthusiastically received. 'My dear, what a perfectly splendid idea!' he says. 'We'll do it on Saturday; it's our biggest night of the week.'

Rosetta has felt just a little unsure of late. Everything is so uncertain, so different from the way it used to be. It is good to be occupied with this new project. It stops her thinking of all she has left behind as well as what may lie ahead.

She moves away from the beach and onto the adjoining grass. It is quiet now. Most rides will not operate until after sunset. The Palace of Illusions is also closed, but she knows Zeno is somewhere inside. He has told her he is needed to help another performer rehearse an act. That is all.

It is very dark within the black walls of the Palace. The sparkling lights are not turned on. The space is cavernous and none of the stalls seem to be in the right place anymore. Rosetta stumbles ahead blindly. She hits her shin on something sharp and hidden. Wincing, she stops. Then she hears a voice she knows. There is only one person who has that low and thrilling tone.

Limping a little, Rosetta walks towards the sound. She wants to tell Zeno about her conversation with Mr Anderson, anticipates the way her ingenuity will delight her husband. A heavy curtain blocks her way, ash coloured in the gloom. Impatient now, she pulls it aside, and as she does so sees by candlelight the figure of a showgirl wearing a small silver-spangled slip and little else. The girl has her back towards her. She is entwined with a man against a wall. He looks over the girl's shoulder. Abruptly, he lets his arms fall.

It is too late. Rosetta has turned and gone.

Reeling into the sunshine, Rosetta is distraught. She has given up everything; security, her reputation, a life spent with her child, for this?

'I should have known!' she tells herself. 'With Zeno, nothing is ever as it seems.'

Rosetta rushes away, furious and wounded. By the time she reaches her Queen Street home her eyes are filled with angry, stinging tears. 'It is intolerable,' she thinks, as she pushes open the front door. 'I would like nothing better than to, to … hurt him as horribly as he's hurt me.'

Burning with rage she tears off her clothes, throws herself onto the bed. A feverish pulse beats in her naked limbs and breasts; there is a hot, splintering feeling inside her head. Yet, even as her mind replays the shocking intimacy she's seen, she becomes aware of other passions being stirred. Zeno in the arms of another woman. Vivid images arise. Does he do the same things to that woman as he does to her? Against her will, she is aroused.

Later, when he comes to her, when he slides silently into her bed, it is she who takes him, demands that she be satisfied. She has never been so fierce, so uninhibited. Only afterwards, when she is still and her passion sated, does Zeno conjure up the words he knows must now be said in order to placate. 'My darling, I am sorry,' he murmurs. 'I have caused you pain and there is no excuse for that. I took what was offered. It is the life that I have always led. But you know that I adore you. Believe me when I say that you won't have to worry again.'

By now, Rosetta has learnt to interpret the spaces between Zeno's caressing words, the things he doesn't say. '*You won't have to worry again.*' What kind of assurance is that? Perhaps it means only that he now knows he must be discreet. The part of her that detaches from her strong emotions coolly assesses the way she feels. He adores her. She believes him. But might he stray from her again? She can't be sure.

Zeno, despite their closeness, has within him hidden things, secrets that she will never know. He is neither safe nor simple. It is a part of the attraction he has for her, this edge of danger. Like stepping from a balloon mid-air, not knowing if you will land or crash, it is addictive. She doesn't want to live without that.

It is Saturday night at Wonderland City. So many people have come to see the new attraction, rumoured to be the most breathtaking ever conceived, that local trams have proven inadequate for the task. Some people have travelled in carriages or ridden on ponies. Many more have chosen to walk, despite the good suits, the silks and satins they wear. All that matters is that they are present.

The atmosphere is taut. Spectators are consumed by anticipation. This is how *The Daily Telegraph*'s reporter will describe the unfolding drama:

> About 9 o'clock the great crowd congregated above the beach. Down on the sand there had been erected a three-storey building, which represented a terrace of houses. It was Christmas Eve, and the street was thronged with people of all classes.
>
> Here went wealth in arrogance of oblivion of other members of the human family, who passed in rags, or fought on the sidewalks, or lurched off to the prison in the clutch of the police; there went comfort and yonder skulked misery.
>
> The central figures were a fireman with his wife and child.

Rosetta's idea has resulted in this amazing sight. Not wishing to be merely the author of the production, with what seems a certain irony she has also chosen to play the mother. She wears a simple blue muslin dress that flutters around her form. The younger brother of the light-fingered boy who assisted Zeno in his act is the child. The versatile Professor Cormack's head for heights has qualified him for the role of her husband and fireman.

The festive purchases having been completed, the family turn homeward, where the father takes leave of his loved ones to attend to his duty. The wife and child wave farewell and go inside. All is quiet. Then, moments later, the darkened house is illuminated by the first red blush of fire. Cries rise from windows and a balcony just as, with a raucous clanging of bells, the firefighters arrive. The hoses are soon at work and the ladders are raised to the top floors, where the frenzied inmates are calling for help. Despite the firemen's energetic efforts, the inferno spreads.

Suddenly, the ground trembles. That tremendous elephant, Alice, in her draperies of crimson and gold, thunders in. She lifts her long grey trunk and emits a noise that chills the bone. Alice trumpets wildly. She stamps her great feet. Next she dips that mighty trunk into a tank that has miraculously appeared. Again and again Alice sprays a fantastic torrent of water onto the fire, but still the flames burn on.

The first man up the ladder is the father. Time is short. Now fear seizes the crowd. The elephant might charge. Someone is sure to burn. Long moments pass. There is a terrible scorching smell and glowing cinders rain down. Just as all seems lost the fireman father reappears, triumphant. From the blazing house he is carrying the child. A great cheer breaks out from the thousands on the banks above and from the beach below.

But not everyone has been rescued. Where is the saintly mother? The crowd's cheers turn to cries of panic and alarm. The fire begins licking at the second storey when, on the rooftop, there appears the slim figure of a woman clad in blue. She is trapped. There is no escape. A shout goes up for her to jump. A net is quickly spread. But the woman cannot. She shakes her head. 'Jump, jump!' the crowd begins to cry. Many are sobbing in distress when, with an unexpected grace considering the dire circumstances, the figure abruptly hurls herself through space.

A moment later a triumphant if soot-covered Rosetta is receiving the congratulations of a delighted Mr Anderson, the Eight Sunbeams, the Acrobatic Marvels, Ben Hur the strongman, Alphonse and all three of the professors. Only Zeno holds back. Finally, when Rosetta has changed her dress and been toasted on her success with a great deal of fine champagne, he takes her aside.

'You are an extraordinary woman,' he says. 'Unlike any other I have met. You are beautiful and fearless. But you are also very precious. Tonight I was terrified that I might lose you forever.' He clasps her so close that she can feel the bones and muscles under his shirt, feel his heart as it beats within.

During the coming months the fire breaks out with unfailing regularity. Mrs Norman, however, chooses not to take part again.

TWENTY

18 June 1910

My dear Rosetta,

I hardly know where to start. Dermot is nearly nine years old, Esther turned six in February and little Beatrix will soon be seven months. They are all well, yes, but I have a sense of great disquiet. In fact, I am able to confess – though only to you – that I feel most unsure with regard to my entire situation. But what am I to do? It is the way in which women like me live.

I cannot say my life is harsh. That would be absurd. Our home is lovely. We have the servants. Arthur and I take our part in society; it is, of course, rather grand. There are so many balls and dinners and country house parties that my head begins to swim. And yet something – perhaps I should say, someone – is absent, rather like a puzzle that has lost a piece.

I think so often of the happy times we spent together in Melbourne. How long ago it was! Yet I remember it just as if it were yesterday, especially you, dear friend. There you are, your gleaming hair piled up high, pouring tea surrounded by bunches of lavender in your pretty house. How much we shared, and how we laughed together. I can still see the curve of your lovely mouth and the way your dark eyes would light up when we indulged in one of our heavenly afternoons. How good it was to dream our dreams and imagine what lay in store. I have never had a more intimate friend than you. Rosetta, truly, I miss you more and more.

My dearest wish is that you should come to Britain. My husband's duties as High Sheriff of County Antrim divert his attention constantly. This year, as you know, he contested North St Pancras for Parliament and now he speaks of running for London County Council. In fact, I'm sure he will. He is devoted to politics and public life. As for me? It sounds foolish, but sometimes I feel I no longer know who I am.

Do come, come with your dear husband. He is quite the extraordinary man. I adore your letters, Rosetta, how daring you have been! I am sure that if you come here, to me, you will both be able to achieve a great deal. Of course, I would help you in any way I can.

Think on it, dearest Rosetta, and, as always, think of me.

Your loving friend,

Lilian.

Rosetta, thoughtful, is holding the letter in her Queen Street parlour when her husband walks into the room. He doesn't notice when she puts it to one side, seems to have his own preoccupations on his mind.

'What is it, William?' she asks. She always calls him that when they are alone. 'Is all not well?'

'I have concerns,' he says. 'They have been building for some time. It is Wonderland. Something is not right. I haven't been able to determine exactly what it is. But have you noticed, when you visit, that the crowds are not what they were at night?'

Rosetta reflects upon what he says. It is true, the queues for the performances no longer snake around the tent. There are fewer eager visitors on rides or taking in the sights. The atmosphere has changed as well. The difference has been subtle, but now that she considers it, she realises that what was once a mood of joyous astonishment has become somehow stale.

That night Rosetta visits Wonderland. While Zeno is busy with his act she wanders the embankment and casts her eyes across the grand amusement park. The thousand lights continue to glitter as before and the Switchback Railway still snakes across the cliffs, but for the first time she sees the peeling paint on Katzenjammer Castle and pools of water from rusting leaks around the skating rink.

It is while gazing at the Imperial Menagerie of Wild Beasts that Rosetta's concern changes to alarm. She has always felt a little sad when visiting the lion and the tigers, the camels, donkeys and the chimpanzees. They are confined in very little space. Now, as she watches the beasts pace restlessly, she is frankly horrified. The tigers' coats are dull and in places the lion's mane is bare. The zebra looks particularly poor. The animal is lying down, listless, and Rosetta can see its ribs. It views her with dull, glassy eyes. The poor beast has about it a look of death.

Those visitors who have come to the Menagerie seem similarly concerned. There is unrest in the small crowd and Rosetta hears one woman say, 'It shouldn't be allowed.'

Next Rosetta visits the Airem Scarem airship down on the beach. There are few people about here, too, and those who are shake their heads and complain. The airship hangs forlornly, listing in the breeze. As Rosetta is puzzling over the cause of this calamity she sees William Anderson just ahead.

'Mrs Norman,' he says. Anderson attempts to arrange his features into his customary jaunty smile but the effect is more like a grimace. 'What a pleasure it is to see you. Will you walk with me for a while?'

They stroll about Anderson's creation, his grand domain, and as they do Rosetta sees behind his usual bombast a worried man. The posturing is all there, the same grandiloquence, but the words come just a shade too quickly. They seem forced. For the first time she notices lines running down the showman's cheeks and grey in his slick, black hair.

'Why, whatever is the matter, Mr Anderson?' she gently enquires. 'Please don't tell me all is well. I know that it is not.'

'Ah, Mrs Norman, you seem to be acquiring some of your husband's mind-reading skills. You are right. Just now I am beset with worries.

'You think those wild animals in the cages are dangerous? Let me tell you about the public. There is the truly savage beast. Oh, they will allow themselves to be dazzled, let you think you can do no wrong. But be warned. They have no loyalty. Once they turn on you, you're gone.'

Anderson, his shoulders sagging, shares his problems with the sympathetic, beguiling Mrs Norman. He finds it is a relief. By now the two of them are sitting in his office, next to the old Aquarium. He pours them both a brandy, quickly downs his own then pours himself a second. Thus fortified, he explains that for the past eighteen months Wonderland City has been struggling.

'At first I thought it was because the damned airship – begging your pardon, Mrs Norman – kept breaking down. The papers started saying it was too dangerous and somebody would drown. But then I began to receive complaints about the animals. People claimed I was mistreating them and they were poorly housed – me!' Anderson, much aggrieved, shakes his head in disbelief.

'But it's those wretched so-called swimmers who have been the last straw. They're just a lot of wealthy, influential businessmen who live around here and don't want their precious sleep disturbed. It's all politics, you know. They went to see James Ashton, the Minister for Lands at the Parliament of New South Wales. Ashton has no spine.

'So that's it, then.' Anderson groans. 'Ashton has given them exactly what they want. I have the order here somewhere.' He rummages on his desk.

'Yes, look, it says "free access for all time to the beach at Tamarama Bay". It's clear they want to ruin me! I can't stop anyone from coming in without paying now.'

Wonderland's proprietor downs a third brandy, puts his head in his hands and falls silent.

'What are you saying, Mr Anderson? How bad are things really? Might Wonderland have to close?'

'It's not come to that, Mrs Norman. No, I'll find a way to fight on.'

Later, when she thinks over this conversation and the things she has observed, Rosetta is less than certain that Anderson is right. Bad publicity and poor crowds is a fatal recipe. Wonderland is teetering and will more than likely fail. Then what will she and William do? Her thoughts return to Lilian's letter waiting in the bureau.

TWENTY-ONE

It took Rosetta a full three days to make up her mind. She'd planned to tell Zeno that night when he returned home after his performance, but her husband was in the excitable mood that sometimes came upon him after he'd been on stage, so she said nothing. At moments like these, she knew, he was filled with tensile energy and thought only of erotic pleasure. She was surprised, then, when he joined her in their bed and, instead of reaching for her, said abruptly, 'Rosetta, what have you been up to? Anderson said you'd been to see him. What is it I should know?'

She sat up, pushed back the tangled strands of her long hair, and began to speak. Rosetta revealed all the sad details of Anderson's current difficulties, the unsafe rides and sick animals, the diminishing financial returns and the machinations of the politicians. 'The outlook seems hopeless,' she said finally. 'I think it means the end.'

'I never suspected things were so bad,' her husband said, a darkening expression on his face. 'Why on earth didn't you tell me as soon as you found out?'

'Because of this.' Rosetta slipped out of bed, went over to the bureau and returned bearing Lilian's letter.

Zeno scanned the pages quickly, frowning as he read. 'I see she's asked us both to come,' he said.

'I didn't want to say anything until I was sure. But now, considering what Mr Anderson has told me, well, I can't see an alternative. It's a big step, my sweetheart, but don't you remember what the poet Mr Paterson advised? I think he's right. We must go to London and, considering what's going on here, as soon as possible.'

Suddenly, Zeno laughed. 'What a little minx you are, Rosetta, plotting and planning behind my back. Yes, you're right of course. We'll go. Why ever not?'

The reality was that, putting any misgivings they might have had about Anderson's teetering venture to one side, Rosetta and Zeno were both ready for something new. Like Wonderland's audiences, they had grown a little jaded. By now the acts, performances and spectacles were a familiar part of life. As for Zeno, turning local upstarts into ducks or hens held little challenge. A certain fatigue had set in, rather too close to boredom for either's liking. It wasn't merely that the two of them craved excitement, though this was true enough. Each in their own way desired a grander stage.

Then there was the problem of Zeno's race. By night, his exotic appearance worked in his favour; audiences embraced his oriental mystique. But by day, when Zeno the Magnificent was replaced by plain William Norman, life was quite different. That was when he became aware of muttered comments and jostling in queues. Only recently a boy had called out, 'Hey Chinaman, where's your pigtail?' when he was walking in the street. It was worse when he was out with Rosetta. Men looked at her with admiration, then scowled at him.

~

The next morning Zeno hands in his notice. It is a clear day but so blustery that the windows in Anderson's office rattle mournfully in the wind. Despite the early hour, the ringmaster pours them both a tumbler of apple brandy. Zeno, glancing down, observes the small tremor in his employer's outstretched hand.

'I'll miss you, William,' the showman says. 'You're quite sure you won't reconsider?'

'I am sorry, Mr Anderson, but no. Our minds are made up.'

When it becomes known that Zeno the Magnificent will be at Wonderland City for only another month, there is a surge of visitors anxious for one last session with the seer. A whimsical newspaper correspondent who writes a weekly column entitled *Sydney Gossip: The Idle letter of an Idle Woman* observes that 'he is being overrun … by all the important barristers, lawyers and doctors'.

Suddenly, it seems that Sydney is filled with people seized with a desire to discover what their future has in store. With few exceptions, Zeno tells them much the same. Love, happiness and good fortune will be showered upon them, he claims. It is what they want to hear, after all. He knows that few would welcome the visions that sometimes come to him; he has seen a woman weeping, a man lying in a grave.

On the final evening, after the last member of the audience has left, Mr Anderson puts away his worries for the night. He is irrepressible by nature and has convinced himself that, somehow, the books will balance and everything will once more be alright. 'I'm throwing a party in Zeno and Rosetta's honour,' he announces through a megaphone. 'Everyone, follow me down to the beach.'

At midnight, beneath a star-filled obsidian sky, the showman in his grey frock coat rises unsteadily to his feet. 'A speech!' the cry goes up. Everybody waits. Anderson is used to occupying centre stage and doesn't disappoint. The great man is eloquent, his voice magnificent and soaring. Yet, as the showman's address draws to a close, he begins to falter. Finally, a catch in his throat, he can manage only a single, quiet word, 'Farewell.'

There is a moment's silence, then Anderson appears to rally. He lifts his head, opens his arms wide and, with a sudden joyful return of his familiar verve and energy, cries out, 'A toast to our guests of honour!

'To a glorious future,' he says expansively, 'for two of the most extraordinary people I have ever met. Ladies and gentlemen, would you be so kind as to raise your glasses to our divine Rosetta and the incomparable Zeno the Magnificent!'

Chilled champagne is poured from magnums and a cake in the shape of a dragon appears, iced a brilliant red. As a full, lantern-like moon rises over Tamarama Bay, that strange, eccentric band of souls who work at Wonderland laugh and talk long into the night.

There are jokes, more toasts and promises of undying friendship given and received from Alphonse the High Flyer, the acrobatic duo Wilson and Morris, the three professors, The Tattooed Songstress, mighty Ben Hur the strongman, the reckless Signor Chefalo and Mexican Jack the Card King. Then two handsome Spaniards, better known as The Sharpshooters Carlos and José, produce guitars and start strumming earthy Catalonian melodies.

One of the Eight Sunbeams begins beating on a drum and Signorina Chefalo, her hips and arms swaying, takes up a tambourine. Next Anderson ignites a towering bonfire with the end of his cigar. Orange flames leap and flare; Zeno tears off his shirt, then pulls Rosetta to his side. Her dress is crimson, his skin is golden in the light. As they begin to dance, twisting and turning, twirling and spinning, they seem like spirits conjured by the fire.

~

It is nearly dawn when the revelry comes to an end. As the first pale fingers of apricot light breach Tamarama's cliffs and steal across the sand, Zeno turns to Rosetta.

'It has all been a grand adventure, hasn't it, my darling?'

Rosetta replies that the adventure has only just begun.

PART TWO

EUROPE

TWENTY-TWO

THE MEDITERRANEAN SEA, 1910

On a dark, tempestuous night somewhere between Port Said and Marseille, Zeno the Magnificent is lost at sea.

Rosetta insists it is necessary.

'The circus tricks, the conjuring and fortune telling must end,' she says to her husband. Rosetta has a firmness about her jaw and the dark gold in her eyes flashes as she looks at him, hard, in the dim light. It is the expression that customarily comes upon her whenever she has arrived at a decision of significance; she is by nature determined and her unconventional life of the past four years has, if anything, made her more resolute. 'At least, they must appear to do so,' she continues. 'This is our new opportunity. We will be respectable. We start again.'

It is early spring, a cool time of the year even in the balmy Mediterranean. Rosetta and Zeno – recorded in the ship's registry as Mr and Mrs William Norman – are making their way, with some difficulty, along the narrow internal corridor that leads to the wood-panelled dining room of the SS *Omrah*. They are sailing for London.

Progress is slow, for a remorseless wind whips the Mediterranean into great watery cliffs that break repeatedly against the ship's steel hull. In response, the *Omrah* pitches and rolls in a way that proves challenging to even the most sure-footed passengers. There is no rhythm to the ship's movements. A sudden, squally gust forces its bow to dip abruptly between the towering waves, renders what a moment before was a dependably horizontal deck suddenly untrustworthy, oblique.

Due to the weather, the Captain is on the bridge struggling at the wheel of his vessel instead of at his regular table entertaining his favoured guests. His absence has been explained by way of a note, personally signed by him and hand-delivered by a nervous junior steward to the first-class cabins of his usual privileged dinner companions. Sincere regrets are expressed; the Captain hopes that on this occasion all will understand his duties prevent him from joining them.

Most are too indisposed to care, even fewer bother to attend the evening meal. Nevertheless, the elderly Egyptian-born magnate Farouk El Fadez braves the unpleasant conditions and assumes his place, accompanied by his attentive secretaries. The two young Arabs are very much alike. They have Oxbridge accents, wear immaculate dinner suits and, on their chiselled features, expressions of faint contempt. Also at the table sits a scrupulously elegant silver-haired older woman, as always dressed in black, who is referred to only as Madame: it will take more than a storm at sea to deter her. Accompanying Madame, albeit on this occasion reluctantly, is her young, sweet-faced companion Mademoiselle Elise.

Despite the scarcity of other passengers in the dining room it is as sumptuously appointed as usual. The pristine linen cloths resting lightly on the thirty round tables are of such extreme whiteness that they resemble drifts of snow. Polished silver, crystal tumblers and goblets wait, unused, beside arrangements of fragrant tangerine roses, acquired by the purser after spirited haggling in the steamy markets of Port Said.

On this difficult night such things as roses and linen, artfully arrayed though they might be, are largely ignored. Many of the passengers who have managed to make their way to the dining room look perturbed. With each new gust of wind the ship judders and several half rise, as if preparing to flee. Most think better of it and resume their seats, in the knowledge that the confines of their cabins promise an even less agreeable alternative.

Rosetta and Zeno also exhibit a lack of enthusiasm for their repast, though neither is bothered by the wild night. The couple have discovered that they are excellent sailors, unaffected by the ship's unpredictable motion. Perhaps it is because both are familiar with uncertainty. They are at ease in the grand dining room, occupying a table at which they are the only guests. The fact that they speak little and that their meals – a roast guinea fowl for Zeno and for Rosetta, a grilled trout – sit neglected before them, cooling on gold-edged monogrammed plates, has nothing to do with the inclement conditions outside. Zeno's and Rosetta's appetites, like their conversation, are limited only because each is deep in thought.

It is afterwards, in the more intimate surroundings of the saloon lounge, that the two begin to speak in earnest. They arrange themselves in the comfort of maroon leather chairs by the flickering light of brass lamps. Rosetta, in a simple black gown embroidered with gleaming jet, wraps her coral cashmere stole a little closer in the coolness of the night. Zeno lights a Cuban cigar; it is a habit he has recently acquired. Then, as the wind's roar drops from its former thunderous pitch and the sea begins to calm, they set about their clandestine task; devising Zeno's new persona.

It is essential that they succeed if they are to have any hope of achieving their hearts' desires.

TWENTY-THREE

I open my folder of fading photographs frequently. Then I pick up the images and scrutinise each one, searching avidly for revealing details. There is handsome Zeno with all his poise, and Rosetta, so confident and self-possessed. I wonder if these expressions were assumed for the benefit of the camera, but I rather think that they were not. There is nothing forced or inauthentic that I can detect.

The problem is, the photographs cannot speak. No matter what insights they provide and as precious as they are, they're not helping me progress. It is in this uncertain state that I contemplate the demoralising possibility that, after travelling this far in my quest, my journey may have come to an end. I need to discover what happened to Rosetta and Zeno during that glittering period I have come to think of as 'The Great London Adventure', which spanned the years 1910 to 1914. Suddenly, I feel adrift.

There was another folder I had not bothered with. I'd given it only cursory attention, assuming it contained merely photocopies of the same pictures that so fascinated me, but in this I was deceived. The first page was the only photocopy there. In fact, tucked safely behind that single sheet, lay hidden treasure.

A simple, lined piece of paper constitutes the first breakthrough. Yellowed and with a jagged edge, it appears to have been torn from an accounts book of some kind. At the top of the long, rectangular sheet are written the words *List of Patrons*. Not clients, or patients, but *Patrons*: a word with very particular connotations. It suggests a distinguished form of protection, encompassing both advocacy and reward. Beneath this heading are noted, in no particular order, thirty-one names. To my astonishment, they include:

Lady Archibald Campbell
The Princess of Pless
Lord Victor Paget
Prince Min of Korea
Lady Lilian Bagot
Her Grace the Duchess of Rutland
Lady Diana Manners
The Hon Diana Lister
The Duchess of Westminster
Lady Juliet Duff
The Right Honourable the Countess of Glasgow.

The list continues in this vein. It is not only comprised of titled members of the aristocracy. There are other luminaries: the eminent physicist Sir Oliver Lodge, the celebrated actress Miss Gertie Miller (who later became the Countess of Dudley), Mrs Marconi ('wife of the inventor' is added helpfully in parentheses) and the renowned conductor, Sir Thomas Beecham. It is an extraordinary cast.

If my great-grandparents were both to make their fortune and live the life they dreamt of, it was necessary to win the confidence, indeed, devotion of some of the greatest men and women of the age. The list tells me that they succeeded, perhaps beyond even their own improbable fantasies.

What intrigues me most is the way in which this feat was achieved. In 1910 Edwardian society was dominated by the Court.

Class and position were everything unless, and then usually grudgingly, one had vast wealth. There can have been few individuals less likely than Rosetta and Zeno to attain acceptance, let alone wild success.

Rosetta was a highly attractive woman, but her dark-eyed looks were strong and striking; she was not by any means endowed with the doll-faced prettiness of the typical Edwardian beauty. Even had Rosetta the appearance of a blonde-haired, blue-eyed goddess, acceptance by Edwardian society was an impossibility. Rosetta was Australian. She was not rich. She had no particular talent nor, save for Lilian Pakenham, whom she had not set eyes on for a decade, did she have a single aristocratic connection. Then there was the matter of her religion. Amid the upper classes Jews – even if one were a Rothschild – were frequently tolerated at best. And worst of all by far, Rosetta was the granddaughter of a convict. These deficiencies alone should have proven disastrous.

Poor as Rosetta's prospects were, my step-great-grandfather Zeno's were even worse. Looked at coolly, with all the romance stripped aside, he was nothing but a trickster, a sideshow performer who'd fled a failing enterprise. Then there was the additional burden that he carried. This could never be ignored. At least Rosetta was a Caucasian. She could hide both her religion and her penal origins. But Zeno, son of a goldfields Celestial, was Chinese. How could he possibly obscure that fact?

The truth was, he could not. But then, truth was of little use to Zeno or Rosetta. It is likely that, on the storm-tossed seas of the Mediterranean, they devised a perfect solution to their dilemma. In future, Carl Zeno would be Japanese. As for Rosetta, she had always thought it would be amusing to be an American.

I learn of these ingenious fabrications by way of a document entitled 'Census of England and Wales, 1911'. It is a facsimile of the very card that my great-grandmother and her husband filled out, by hand, while living in the United Kingdom. Under 'Birthplace' Zeno makes the blithe declaration that he comes from

Japan. Rosetta writes that 'America' is her own country of origin, then adds that she is a 'British subject by parentage'. She is also no longer thirty-one years of age but, instead, just twenty-eight. Entirely unintimidated by the official nature of the government's enquiries, all these outrageous lies are written down and there, for posterity, they remain.

Zeno's reinvention showed a particular flair. After beginning slowly in the middle of the nineteenth century, a mania for Japan swept through the cultured circles of Paris and London. This unfathomable land had remained isolated until the American Commodore Matthew Perry sailed into its waters in 1853. Perry's delegation, in their frock coats and military uniforms, entered into long negotiations with the Shogun's stern, purple-robed men. Eventually, it was agreed. Japan's 216-year-old Policy of Seclusion was at an end.

Though trade started hesitantly, it was not long before a reckless desire for all things Japanese came to exist. To jaded Europeans, the unfamiliar items that reached their shores held the promise of escape from the banal, the everyday. The acquisition of these exotic objects was as addictive as a drug.

In Paris and in London seductive exchanges were conducted behind trembling apricot and cherry blossom painted fans. Enthusiasts drank fragrant jasmine tea from fragile blue and white ceramic cups while indulging in the secret pleasure of a silk kimono gliding against bare skin. They bought black lacquer boxes and cloisonné enamels depicting cerise water lilies and golden chrysanthemums.

The fascination continued for decades, unchecked. The striking wood-block prints spoke a particularly vivid language to artists such as van Gogh. He collected hundreds of these images, embracing their surprising viewpoints, bold outlines and pure colours of emerald, vermilion and cobalt. Van Gogh was not alone; the most daring painters including Monet, Degas, Gauguin, Toulouse-Lautrec and Matisse, together with a host of others – poets, authors, connoisseurs and *bon vivants* – succumbed.

Well, perhaps not all. 'There is no such country, there are no such people,' wrote Oscar Wilde. Following his own initial infatuation, it seems that Wilde alone perceived this oriental utopia of refinement and nuance was but a European's fantasy. 'The whole of Japan is pure invention,' he said, definitively.

'Pure invention': it really is a perfect description for what Zeno and Rosetta carried off with such élan. I wonder if they ever read Wilde's views.

Zeno needed a country, and not any country would do. He required a land so remote and so little known that almost any assertion as to his origins could be made with impunity. Given his appearance, it had to be somewhere in Asia and, preferably, a place shrouded in irresistible mystique. In all these respects, The Land of the Rising Sun provided an ideal fit.

The fabrication did not, could not, end there. Something more was needed if Zeno was to earn a handsome living doing what he knew best: spinning tales, stealing souls, soothing troubled hearts and minds. An additional invention, the more audacious the better, was required.

In the end, it was as easy as bewitchment. Magically, Zeno attained the distinguished qualifications that a former wizard was unlikely to possess. They are all there, printed on the front page of my next, unexpected discovery, one that can only be described as fantastic in the truest sense. Nestled next to the *List of Patrons* I find a small, two-page black and white pamphlet with, on the front cover, a series of entirely fraudulent claims of breathtaking magnitude.

The Master Science – Radium – Therapeutics.

PROFESSOR CARL ZENO

(Erstwhile of the Ku-Mari Hospital and Medical Schools, Japan)

The title of Professor was a marvellously useful affectation, one that had the power to endow its bearer with instant gravitas. Presumably, the honorific was inspired by the three 'professors' Zeno worked with at Wonderland. If Mr Anderson could confer academic credentials upon the director of a dog and monkey circus, a man who threw himself into small tanks and another whose sole claim to fame was walking on steep planks, then the former William Norman would follow suit. In any case, it was Wonderland City, with all its magic and its madness, that had provided him with his most important higher education. The beachside pleasure palace was where, over four thrilling years, he learnt the value of true showmanship, grandness of vision and the importance of absolute self-belief.

That Zeno, son of a Chinese immigrant and an illiterate mother, had barely been to school did not bother him at all. The fact that he never graduated from a university, nor was on the staff of a hospital in Japan or anywhere else, was an irrelevant detail. Zeno would now not merely look into the future. He would heal the sick and make them well again.

There is a photograph of Zeno on the front of the pamphlet. His hair is thick, as black as onyx and carefully brushed to one side. Light falls on his high cheekbones and smooth forehead, heightening the expression of intense concentration on his face. His almond eyes look down: he is conducting an experiment. Zeno pours liquid from a silver cup into a transparent beaker he grasps in his left hand. I can see that his fingers are supple and elegant. Behind him is a small square table on which stand dark-coloured bottles, various lenses and a gleaming microscope. Zeno is beautifully dressed in a white high-collared shirt, cutaway jacket, striped trousers, a discreet patterned tie and pearl cufflinks. He still looks like a sorcerer to me, even though there is neither a black robe nor red dragon in sight.

~

Once Rosetta had convinced her husband that the creation of a new identity was essential, he embraced the process with so much enthusiasm that it was she who began to have some doubts. Would London's great and good really be so easily duped?

The two had been talking for some time when she exclaimed, 'Honestly, William!' Rosetta smoothed her coral stole with a tense movement of her hand. 'A Japanese medical professor – that can't be wise.'

'Why, whatever is the matter, dearest?' Zeno responded, while drawing back eagerly on one more cigar. 'You don't think that people will believe?

'Let me tell you, if there is one thing I have learnt during my years of fortune telling it is that what people really want, indeed yearn for, is another reality.'

'Yes, but don't you think that this time you have gone too far?' Rosetta asked.

Zeno smiled, shook his head. 'That is the beauty of it. It is well known by every showman. The greater, the more far-fetched the artifice, the higher one's credibility will soar! It is really rather like the story of the emperor's new clothes. A small lapse of truth and people will be merciless. But an enormous illusion? Nobody wants to let that go.

'Professor Zeno will be regarded as an expert in his field by the highest in the land. Why, I will be a man beyond reproach. Do not make the mistake of underestimating me, my dear.'

Despite all she now knew of him, once more Rosetta found herself falling under Zeno's spell.

'Now, as soon as we leave the ship in Southampton, you must start to call me Carl. William Norman no longer exists. And as for Zeno the Magnificent? You are quite right. There can be no hint of vaudeville. From now on, we will be legitimate.'

Zeno laughed heartily and, a moment later, Rosetta, too, joined in.

TWENTY-FOUR

Bond Street, Mayfair, in the heart of London's West End, represents the apotheosis of style and class. Developed in 1683 by the royal Comptroller Sir Thomas Bond – a man whose personal motto, *The World is Not Enough*, seems particulary prescient – it has been a playground for society's wealthiest and most influential individuals ever since. Among the street's better known inhabitants have been Admiral Horatio Nelson, the one-armed, one-eyed hero of Trafalgar, and his notorious mistress Lady Emma Hamilton. In *Sense and Sensibility* Jane Austen wryly describes the impoverished Dashwood sisters' visit to Bond Street with the smiling Mrs Palmer, 'whose eye was caught by everything pretty, expensive or new; who was wild to buy all, could determine on none, and dawdled away her time in rapture and indecision'.

Bond Street's reputation for luxurious diversion remains. Today the two- and three-storey Georgian and Victorian buildings that line this elite road flaunt exclusive brands such as Bvlgari, Hermès, Cartier and Chanel. The street has another distinction, this one of rather more importance to me. According to the pamphlet, in its northern reaches (dubbed New Bond Street), at number 118, stands the former consultation rooms of the eminent Japanese specialist Professor Carl Zeno. The address is very, very good.

The day is chilly and, hurrying down the street, I feel my skin prickle as I glance at the small scraps of leopard-patterned satin and black lace in the windows of Victoria's Secret. Number 118 is just two doors away from this jungle of exotic lingerie, next to the more sober Swiss shoemaker Bally. A neat white rectangle, it is bisected by three rows of slim Georgian windows that stand above the handbag designer Anya Hindmarch's boutique. A blonde woman points at something in expensive grey suede in the window and I overhear her say, 'You would keep that one forever.' Her equally blonde friend nods as both slip eagerly inside.

In Zeno's time it might have been a shop purveying something medical, perhaps an oculist selling pince-nez and spectacles. Zeno would have utilised the upper floor; his illustrious patrons would prefer the privacy.

Her Grace the Duchess of Rutland enters 118 New Bond Street via the discreet door that is positioned on the left. Violet, christened Marion Margaret but always known by her third, more romantic name, is with her exquisite daughter, the much admired Lady Diana Manners. Diana will become the celebrated if unconventional actress wife of the British ambassador Duff Cooper, though this lies in the future.

The two women make their way up a flight of stairs that leads them to the Professor's rooms. They have heard about his unusual abilities, anticipate a small adventure.

'How delightful to meet you,' Rosetta says as both walk in through the door. She invites them to sit in pretty brocade-covered walnut chairs. 'May I offer you a mint tisane?' she asks and, with their assent, busies herself. The ladies find themselves enchanted by Madame Zeno's warmth and grace. Already they begin to feel that, compared with their usual medical appointments, this will be a quite different experience.

Dominating the room is a sumptuous oriental rug in shades of blue and, on the table in front of the Duchess and her daughter, a white porcelain vase is filled with vivid delphiniums.

'Do you know, Mama, I feel a little better already,' says Diana. 'It is so very soothing here. But Madame Zeno, whatever is that delicious smell?'

Rosetta barely has time to respond, 'A little cinnamon mixed with a touch of rare Eastern spice,' before the door to Zeno's room opens and the man himself appears.

'I believe it would be preferable to see Lady Diana alone,' Zeno says.

'She is only eighteen,' the Duchess protests.

'Oh Mama, don't be silly,' Diana replies quickly. 'We must do as the Professor says.'

Diana is a great beauty. She has fair hair and limpid, jewel-like eyes. She is also, as her mother has always been, a determined bohemian. As a child she was dressed in black velvet when the other children wore sweet-pea coloured smocks. Later she wore a black picture hat at Ascot decorated with sheaves of gold and silver wheat; when she was photographed in a group of girls dressed for a pageant as white swans she was the single black-feathered debutante. Loved, admired and envied, she is deemed by *Vogue* magazine to be 'the loveliest young Englishwoman of her generation'.

Diana belongs to a group of well-connected young people with the kind of surnames that fill the newspapers: Asquith, Cunard and Curzon. They call themselves The Corrupt Coterie. Diana adores this moderate rebellion.

The Duchess and Zeno exchange careful looks. Slender and with a cloud of pale auburn hair, Violet gives the impression of fey soulfulness. But reflected in her deep-set eyes Zeno sees a woman of some experience.

'Perhaps, Duchess, you would like to step in first,' he says. Violet accedes, inclines her head.

Zeno's room is very quiet. The heady cinnamon aroma is more intense. On the polished floorboards is a fringed square of carpet, ruby red. There is a wide mahogany desk, but Zeno does not sit at it, nor does he offer Violet a chair. Instead, he suggests that she may be more comfortable on the black velvet-covered divan. Next he invites her to remove her sweeping hat, loosen the top few buttons of her pale-pink silk dress.

Violet is a little startled but does as Zeno asks. As ever, he finds it easy to exert his will. Zeno knows the most effective way to do so is to commence with a modest demand; it is only when compliance has been achieved that he will begin increasing his requests by carefully calibrated intervals. He is still surprised at times to what acts a woman, or a man, will be prepared to consent.

Zeno places a chair for himself beside Violet and they begin to speak. He explains that before treatment can progress it is important he attains a complete sense of her being. 'After all,' he says, 'we are much more than flesh and blood, are we not?'

Violet discovers that she and this elegant oriental practitioner have much in common. Both draw and paint; they have artistic tastes. Despite the sophisticated world in which she lives, she finds him as fascinating as he is sympathetic. 'Lilian Pakenham was right,' she thinks. 'I believe this man has special gifts.'

Zeno knows the status of his patron; Rosetta makes certain he is well prepared for each new patient. 'Violet Manners is not only a duchess,' she had told him after scanning the list of the day's appointments that morning. 'She is a queen of sorts, at least of that section of society who see themselves as forward thinkers; the *avant-garde*, I think they call it.

'They're a group of aristocrats who frequent one another's salons. Scholarly endeavour appears to constitute their principal passion – they like to talk about the latest book or play or work of art. Although…' Rosetta pauses, an arch expression playing across her face, 'I believe they are not averse to directing their attention towards less intellectual matters, with the pursuit of each other principal among them. The Souls, they're known as.'

Zeno, too, has the ability to obtain information, though of a different type. The reputation he has acquired as a reader of minds is not in fact unfounded, for his uncanny powers of observation coupled with an extensive if jaded knowledge of human nature allow him unusual access to the thoughts of others. It is in this way that he assesses Violet, sees beneath the practised charm a soul that is unquiet. Of all people, Zeno is aware when another hides behind a carefully constructed carapace.

'Duchess, why not confide in me what it is that disturbs you so,' he murmurs in his low voice. 'I am here to help you in any way I can.'

Zeno's words are so filled with concern that, unexpectedly, Violet begins to weep. 'But however did you know?' she asks finally, when she is more composed.

'I am trained to see what others cannot,' is Zeno's confident response. 'I can help you shed this dreadful burden that weighs on you so heavily. Only tell me what it is and I will use all my powers, from this world and the next, to assist.'

Afterwards, Violet was never sure whether it was that hypnotic voice, the scented air or the fragrant tisane she drank that banished her inhibitions so quickly and made her frank. As soon as Zeno intoned, 'I see a darkness in your life,' she began to confide.

'Professor, I believe I have committed a dreadful sin. You see, my husband the Duke and I have very little in common. He prefers the hunt and the company of chorus girls to me. You can imagine how that makes me feel.

'Some years ago my vulnerability was such that I became entangled with a most handsome man. Oh, he was witty and charming and made me feel adored. I will refer to him as Henry; that is all. Henry is a poet and a gifted editor. He pursued me ardently and eventually his silken words turned my head. They led me to his bed.'

Zeno keeps his counsel. He knows Violet is not naïve; she is fashioning her tale in a way that makes it easier for her to live with the consequences of what she did.

'I discovered I was carrying his child. Nobody can ever know that Lady Diana is Henry's daughter. She is not the Duke's.

'You must have noticed how little she resembles my husband or, for that matter, me. Diana looks just like her true father; she has his divine face and brilliant eyes.'

Still Zeno is silent. He allows the words to flow unchecked.

'But dear Professor, that is not the worst; there is more.' Violet weeps again and this time Zeno holds her hand.

'Duchess,' he says. 'Have courage! You must tell me all.' He offers Violet a curious green beverage, promising her it is his own herbal elixir and will help to calm her jagged nerves.

Violet sips the drink, which has a pleasant licorice taste. She does not understand what impulse compels her to confess. All she knows is that she no longer wishes to resist.

'The Duke's son and mine, darling Robert, died two years after Diana was born. The dear lamb was only nine.' Violet's slim shoulders begin to shake. After years of control, emotions sweep through her like storms. 'Tell me, Professor, do you believe it was divine punishment for my faithlessness? Was precious Robert's death my fault?'

'Duchess,' Zeno responds in a soothing tone, now lightly stroking her fingers with his own. With his other hand he removes from a coat pocket his golden medallion on its glistening chain. 'Watch this carefully with all the concentration that you have,' he says, 'and all will become clear.'

Violet falls into a trance. She lies back on the smooth velvet and feels herself becoming as light and fine as mist. Curling deliciously through her body is the sensation of great happiness, of bliss. From far away a mesmerising voice whispers that all is as it should be. It says that the gleam of light that is Diana was destined to come into existence in the very way she did. Violet is not to blame for Robert's death. Robert was too perfect for this world of woe. The angels claimed him for their own.

When Violet wakens she stretches, sighs. Zeno's hand is still in hers. She feels quite different now. Peace has descended upon her. The Duchess looks at Zeno and thinks, 'He really is most remarkable.'

Seduction, Zeno knows, takes many forms. It is not always carnal, not at all.

TWENTY-FIVE

There is more in the folder, forty-eight letters, three postcards and three telegrams; it is a thrilling discovery. Most of the correspondence is written on ageing paper in varying shades of cream; a few are light blue. I place them before me, in date order, on my desk. At first I don't try to read, but only look. There are torn edges, the tiny piercings of industrious insects and deep, discoloured folds and creases. As I begin to read, I realise that they contain a wealth of personal remarks together with occasional tantalising references to history-changing events. The letters seem to live.

Just three are addressed to Rosetta. A further forty-five have been written to her husband. Some display crown-topped crests and grand addresses; each one is a testament to Rosetta and Zeno's awesome success. Some of Zeno's correspondents have penned multiple letters; five are from the Earl of Sandwich. There is no mention of illness. Instead, Sandwich, as he signs his name, seems more anxious to entertain Zeno at lunch.

Fourteen are simply signed '*Charlotte*'. She, too, must be a grand personage for her letters bear an embossed crest consisting of a red and gold coronet surmounting four interlocking purple C's, the whole contained within a golden disc. Even a quick browse reveals how frequently Charlotte refers to a host of princes and princesses, yet so far I have no idea who the enigmatic Charlotte is.

One telegram is from a certain Danilo. Despatched from the town of Jena, in Germany, it beseeches Zeno to assist. In this case, the identity of the author becomes clear: it is Danilo of Montenegro, a dashing, romantically handsome Balkan prince. But the nature of their relationship remains a puzzle, as does how they came to meet.

The three postcards take the form of photographs. The first, by W.A. Smith of Stratford-upon-Avon, is of the pretty American actress Marjorie Patterson (who, curiously, was the great-niece of Napoleon I) dressed as Viola from Shakespeare's *Twelfth Night*. The card has been enclosed with a letter to Zeno from Marjorie's mother, Mrs Wilson Patterson, inviting him to come to Apartment 26 Curzon Hotel, Curzon Street. Waiting with anticipation will be seven women including her daughter, another well-known performer, Rosina Filippi (she claimed descent from the great actress Eleonora Duse), and Mrs Simpson, the wife of the naval attaché to the American Embassy. Mrs Patterson addresses Zeno as '*My dear*' and writes: '*Can you come at half after two o'clock? And what would be the fee? – I would arrange that you should see each one …*'

The second card is more obscure. The image it bears shows Zeno at the bedside of a distinguished-looking bearded man. Zeno bends towards him, looks concerned. The third card sports an image of Prince Victor Napoleon. On the back is an announcement of the birth of his son and heir. The questions of who the bearded man is, and why Zeno has been sent a picture of the Pretender to the throne of France, are, like Charlotte's identity, just two more mysteries.

Several letters to Zeno refer to matters of physical intimacy. There is one from the Lady Archibald Campbell, wife of the eighth Duke of Argyll's son. It is not difficult to discover the details of her life, for her beauty is so renowned that she attracts admiration even from Oscar Wilde, who writes of her incomparable eyes of 'beryl'.

Lady Campbell is also the subject of one of Whistler's most controversial portraits, painted in his Tite Street studio against a black velvet backdrop.

In the picture she glances over her left shoulder with arresting eyes; both a challenge and a promise are reflected in her penetrating gaze. Her left sleeve lies open, exposing her slender wrist. In her hand she holds a yellow glove – she seems about to drop it at her feet. Though Lady Campbell is swathed in dark fabric and plush fur, the painting has a disturbing aura of temptation heightened by Whistler's decisions to reveal her slim black-stockinged ankle, to highlight her pointed yellow shoe. When the portrait was placed on public display, Sir Archibald and his father the Duke were shocked: they thought it made her look like a streetwalker, a common prostitute.

Such knowledge provides context for the letter that Lady Campbell has written to Zeno from her home at Rutland Gate, SW, in which she enquires: '*Could you let me have a box of the red douche powder which you formerly recommended me for injecting into the Vagina ...?*' After referring to other matters of equal delicacy, she finishes with, '*Believe me, yours faithfully, Janey.*'

Two letters, written by Zeno himself, provide new insights into this complicated man. There is no copperplate to be seen, no scrolls or unnecessary embellishments. The writing is strong and clear and, like the author's character, the signature is bold. I consider the meaning that an expert graphologist might extract from this unique hand; the t's that are always slashed with wide strokes, the capital letters that are never linked with the words that they initiate, but always stand alone.

Aug 24th 1912

My Very Dear Patient,

You seem like a little cloud that has wandered far away in the distance and I trust you are not permitting too many dark ones to surround you, as you need all the light and sunshine nature can give you.

You must not let your cherry lips and sweet smiles plunge too deep into gloom or oppression. I want the little flower to bud and develop, to strengthen and to succeed in all sorts of weather be it sunshine or storm.

I am often thinking about you and sending my influence to you.

If you are ... too much alone and sad you must return to have your usual treatment.

Write and let me know when you are returning.

Wishing you all that mind and thought can wish.

Yours very sincerely

C. Zeno

Even if one makes allowances for the florid Edwardian prose, '*your cherry lips and sweet smiles*' seems remarkably personal language for an exchange between a doctor and a patient. It sounds to me more like a letter from a lover.

Did Rosetta feel the same way? Did she eye this inflamed correspondence, toss her head, drum her fingers on her *escritoire* in annoyance? Or perhaps I am wrong. Perhaps she smiled indulgently, amused by how easy it was to win over these bored rich women, to woo them with honeyed words dripping with devotion.

The nature of the '*usual treatment*' to which Zeno refers, like the services he provided in the Curzon Hotel, can only be imagined, though considering the content of the pamphlet and of some of the letters I have read I suspect it could be almost anything from the merely bizarre to the outright dangerous. Zeno's second letter indicates that communication with the spirit world is a distinct possibility.

Oct 21st 1912

My dear Patient,

… [I] did not feel surprised to hear of some 'black cloud' come to pass. In fact after you left here I felt death near your friend. She has been very upset and worried in fact she has felt like sharing the same fate. I have been using every force to keep up her strength …

Zeno's arsenal of witchcraft included hypnotic trances, the ingestion of his own 'drugless' medications, aromatherapy and various forms of massage. This last treatment was a particular speciality: it seems Zeno's clever fingers were able to minister to a body's hidden needs with an unusual blend of force and tenderness.

TWENTY-SIX

It is dangerous for me, this *List of Patrons* and the letters with their esteemed signatures. I feel as if I have succumbed to that most classic of the magician's techniques: my attention has been diverted elsewhere by all the glamour and mystique. I'm not looking closely enough at the mechanics of the trick. The challenges Zeno and Rosetta confronted in their new life should not be minimised. Despite their abundant confidence and the evidence I have seen, I have to remind myself that attracting the type of devoted clients who flocked to their door was a not inconsiderable task.

London in 1910 was the hub of a vast Empire. It boasted great public squares and classical monuments, palatial hotels and marble temples of commerce, bustling docks, thriving markets and gilded theatres, music halls, shops, restaurants and treasure-filled museums. Money was London's lifeblood; it ran through the city's streets and lanes as if through arteries and veins.

There were parts of the metropolis that had never experienced displays of such extravagance and wealth. The mansions were more splendid, jewels and gowns more opulent, the balls and dinners more magnificent than anyone had ever seen.

That the man at the very centre of this brilliance, King Edward VII, died in May and was replaced by his sober son, George V, made no difference. The indulgent, gorgeous, carefree life of the upper classes whirled on, for now safe and secure. It was admission to this world of unparalleled excess for which Zeno and Rosetta yearned.

The acquisition of suitable countries of origin was but the first step. In order to penetrate the upper echelons of Edwardian society, my great-grandparents had to be seen as not just respectable, which, all things considered, was challenging enough. Wild popularity depended on being perceived as stylish and smart. It was a high-stakes balancing act.

Zeno and Rosetta trod a line as fine and fraught with risk as any that Wonderland's most daring tightrope walkers ever had, requiring infinite finesse. If they stumbled, if in an unguarded moment or by some inopportune circumstance their former lives were discovered, descent into a world of louche outcasts would be the unspeakable result. Only someone not just clever, but *au fait* with the arcane habits of society, would have been able to advise Zeno and Rosetta on the way to prevent this fatal fall from grace.

There was just one such person who possessed the necessary flair for publicity and presentation, in addition to the right connections, just one who could help them light the flame necessary to ignite their bonfire of success.

'Don't worry, my dear, from you I have no secrets; well, perhaps just a few.'

Rosetta has been reunited with her good friend Helena Rubinstein who, hungry for success, has cultivated all the right people and done extremely well for herself. The former impoverished Polish émigrée who once looked after other people's children in suburban St Kilda now revels in her international popularity. She is brilliant, and driven.

The two women are in the upper drawing room of the elegant Georgian mansion at 24 Grafton Street that once belonged to the former British Prime Minister Lord Salisbury. Decorated with select antiques mixed with finds from flea markets, it has a modern quality of witty elegance.

'The salon is of course at street level. Clients who happen to be visiting the Royal Academy of Arts, Fortnum & Mason or Berkeley Square find it most convenient,' Helena remarks, then asks her maid to bring them cups of hot chocolate. 'There is even a telephone. You must ring me – the number is Mayfair 4611.

'Now, down to business. First, I have always believed one should go where the customer is most comfortable. It is the reason why I established my salon in Melbourne's Collins Street and then in Paris on the rue Saint-Honoré. You must open your doors at precisely that place where all the best people want to be. I see that you have chosen Mayfair, just like me. So, you have made an excellent beginning.'

Helena turns to Rosetta, once more studies her friend's appearance. The simple boater, blouse and skirt she would wear to visit the Melbourne salon have been exchanged for something more impressive. Now she is dressed elaborately in a tremendous black hat with a large feather. Wrapped in fur, she flaunts a brace of grey fox with heads and tails intact. At thirty, she personifies the late King Edward's ideal woman: voluptuous and rather grand.

Though possessed of an equally full figure, Madame Rubinstein is dressed in quite a different style, simpler, yet with an exotic quality. Helena's innate theatricality is heightened by the vivid green silk tunic she wears over a slim, dark purple skirt, by the glistening pearls and emeralds hanging from her ears and looping around her throat.

'Ah Rosetta, I see you are admiring these.' Helena's fingertips caress her matchless jewels. 'They are my vice. Each time my husband, Titus, and I argue, I indulge myself.

'Strictly between the two of us, for, after all, we have known each other for so long, I left Titus when we were in France.'

'Helena, whatever for?'

'Because I discovered my charming husband engaged in an act of unfaithfulness when we were in Nice. After lunch one day I returned to our hotel suite. I hadn't planned to, but I needed my parasol – and there he was. He simply adores beautiful, alluring women. But honestly, Rosetta, it was our honeymoon!' She shook her head, her earrings swinging furiously.

'Ah, I should have more sense. As you see, I have taken him back. I love the man, so what else can I do? It was after the French debacle that I acquired my first important string of pearls. The experience was quite uplifting. You know, I have discovered that shopping is a marvellous antidote for the absence of many other things.

'And speaking of shopping, naturally you look very well in your clothes but something a little less complicated, more *au courant*, would be better, I feel. Do let me introduce you to my favourite couturier, Paul Poiret. His new designs are really the *dernier cri*. He has been inspired by the costumes – you should see the colours – from the Ballets Russes. Simply everyone is talking about the company's divine dancers, Nijinsky especially. He has this wonderful, athletic grace.'

She takes Rosetta's hand. 'You must not, of course, dress like me. I am in the beauty business where it is essential to wear the latest fashion. That would not be appropriate for you, but as the wife of an eminent Professor,' Helena winks, 'you must still look chic. It inspires confidence. In my experience, important clothes impress important people.'

During a pause in Helena's rapid, accented instructions, she takes the opportunity to sip from the delicate cup of rich, steaming chocolate that her maid has placed on a small gilt table.

'Which brings me to the last important matter. I will refer clients, of course, but you yourself must come to know the right, fashionable people. Study them, their habits, interests and families, as I have done. Always be ready to oblige and, take it from me, the rich adore a little special treatment, you know what I mean? Waive the occasional account, give them a small gift, some bibelot or other, and they will think you quite marvellous. Before long, you will find they recommend you to all their friends.

'Oh, and one more thing. Do not forget the benefits of publicity. Zeno needs something to prove his credentials, his – now what is the word, yes – *veracity*. Let me see … I would advise that he writes an article for a respected journal; it doesn't have to be very long. But it should sound scientific and talk about all the latest techniques. Then you simply need to make sure it is circulated. It is extraordinary, I know, but it seems one only has to see a thing in print for it to be believed.'

Helena stops in mid-flow. She consults a jade and onyx clock. It is not one of her flea-market finds but has been purchased quite recently at some expense from Sotheby's, a nearby auction house. Between Helena's well-groomed brows, as finely etched and dark as swallows' wings, a small frown appears, a tiny flaw in her otherwise perfect, porcelain skin.

'Rosetta, I have been enjoying such a splendid conversation with you, my dear, that the time has completely run away. I must be on my way to Dover to catch the boat for Calais. Colette, my writer friend, is having a soiree for me in Paris.

'Colette is quite wicked, you know, but she's been such a help to me. Did you read what she told the French reporters after she had one of my salon massages, the ones we offer with special extra, ah, how shall I put it … enhancements? She said that without them a French woman had no hope of keeping her lover! It was in all the newspapers, the publicity was wonderful. You must try the same massage, darling – we use those little electromechanical machines. They vibrate beautifully – anyway, when you come in you will see exactly what I mean.

'Now I must say goodbye. And Rosetta, do just as I advise. Don't forget a thing!'

TWENTY-SEVEN

There are no letters from Rosetta. I do know what her writing looks like, though, because it is on the back of several photographs that she sent from London to her sister Florence. Rosetta's hand is neither small nor neat. Like her character, it is a touch flamboyant, has a certain flourish. She addresses her sister by her pet name, Florrie, and signs with her own diminutive '*best love & wishes, Rose xxx*'.

I wonder what Rosetta thought of the extraordinary new world in which she lived, how it felt to be sought by so many famous and important people; scientists, actresses, writers, a host of aristocrats and a brace of princes and princesses. At first it must have seemed as if she were inhabiting a fairytale, a kingdom imagined only in her dreams. Now this is the medium through which I reach out to Rosetta: she lives within my reveries.

In all the letters to Zeno, apart from the inclusion by grateful patients of such greetings as '*Fond remembrances to Madame*', there is barely a word about Rosetta. This may well have been because most of his female clients – not just in London but from half a dozen cities scattered across the Continent – were at least half in love with him.

'*I think of you constantly,*' wrote Baroness Ernesta Stern, dear friend of Proust and a cache of European royalty, from her magnificent villa on the French Riviera's Cap Martin.

Another devotee, this one from the Paris address of 65 Boulevard de Clichy, near the Moulin Rouge, exclaimed: '*I will never forget the moment I met you, it was Light for me.*'

A Hungarian noblewoman from Vas Megye, her letterhead among those bearing crowns, was equally entranced, confessing '*You interest me more than I can say …*'

Only a man of mesmerising, charismatic charm could have attracted this kind of adoration from such sophisticated women of the world. One can sense Zeno's irresistible magnetism reflected in his admirers' ardent words. Given this surfeit of adoring protestations, Rosetta could hardly be looked at askance for failing to dissuade an admirer of her own.

He is among the new men who stroll across London's squares with such distinctive nonchalance. Slender and graceful, with brilliant black hair and sleek moustaches, they wear their suits cut close to their taut bodies and their hats at an angle just a little more acute than those of other men. Their skin is smooth and their dark eyes have a tendency to linger a moment longer than strictly necessary when they pass a beautiful woman. They are rich, have divine manners and practised charm. They ride superbly and dance in a disturbing, dazzling way that no one before has ever seen. They are from the Argentine.

It is likely that these are the men for whom the word 'playboy' has been invented, for they appear to have no purpose in life other than the ardent pursuit of pleasure. They are notorious for their womanising, though curiously few of their conquests ever seem to complain. Bearing names such as Vincente, Carlos and Eduardo, they are the pampered, well-born scions of South American families who have made vast fortunes from their herds of cattle and endless fields of grain.

With a life of luxury at their disposal, they seek indulgence far beyond the safe confines of Buenos Aires' upper classes. First they sail for Paris, where these men and the dance they bring with them cause a sensation. After this triumph, they come to London.

Rosetta watches Lilian from the other side of an elegant panelled room. Since her arrival in London they have had few opportunities to enjoy each other's company, for Arthur's pursuit of a political career has required his wife to make a myriad of smiling, dutiful appearances, first in the electorate of North St Pancras and then in Marylebone East.

Now, at last, the two women are together once again. Lilian is just as beautiful as Rosetta remembers, though with a new quality. It isn't just that her blonde hair is a shade deeper, has become more a burnished gold, or that motherhood has led to a more womanly figure. Behind Lilian's customary poise, so artfully reinforced by years of training and control, Rosetta senses a vulnerability, a heightened need she has not noticed previously. It renders Lilian more appealing, less contained, a little more reckless than when she lived within the walls of Victoria's Government House so many years ago. Rosetta observes that her friend's attractions are not wasted on her dancing partner. This is not the staid Arthur Pakenham but a particularly stylish dark-eyed man.

Never before has Rosetta seen a gentleman hold his partner as closely as this stranger holds Lilian. It would be cause for scandal if not for the fact that this is exactly the way in which every other couple at Lady Diana's *thé dansant* is entwined. The couples move together, twirling and turning to a pulsating rhythm that makes Rosetta's senses sing.

~

'Madame Zeno, I do adore your gown. Poiret, if I'm not wrong?' It is Lady Diana herself; together with her mother, the Duchess of Rutland, she is hosting this soiree at their palatial Mayfair home. 'How good of you to come. And Mrs Pakenham, too, I see. I say, she does seem to be having quite a good time, doesn't she?

'Now, as the Professor sadly cannot join us, you must have a dancing partner, too. Ah, perfect. Here is Senor Alberto Rivero.'

A tall man, a little younger than Rosetta, approaches bearing two sparkling glasses of champagne. He is not dressed as an Englishman would be. The shoulders of his coat are sharper, his trousers narrower on the leg. He holds himself differently, too, with formal elegance. There is none of the Englishman's customary slouch.

Diana makes the necessary introductions. Her sapphire eyes are dancing with delight. 'Take good care of Madame Zeno,' she says. 'She is a new and quite marvellous acquaintance of mine.' With that, Diana, just a little pleased with herself, departs.

'Madame Zeno, how fortunate I am that Lady Diana has been kind enough to introduce me to you.' Alberto, despite his youth, has a considerable quantity of polished charm. 'I would regard it a rare honour if a woman as beautiful as you would consent to be my partner for this dance.'

As Alberto smiles, Rosetta sees his lips part to show his teeth, white against his tanned skin. She catches herself wondering what it would be like to taste the champagne on those lips, how it might be to press her own mouth to his.

Alberto is not always sincere. But on this occasion he is not resorting to false flattery. Rosetta has taken Helena's advice to heart; she no longer wears the voluminous, padded clothing deemed essential during King Edward's reign. Her simple Poiret dress drapes across the fullness of her breasts, glides smoothly over her hips. It has restored to Rosetta a youthful suppleness.

The skirt, designed to resemble a tulip, curves at the front in two arcs. When she walks, the petal-like shapes part, daring to reveal the line of her long, slim legs. Rosetta's gown is in a shade of orange customarily found only in a sunset. Heightening the amber in her hair and the gold within her eyes, it makes her radiant. Rosetta has the scintillating sensation that inhabits a woman when she knows she looks her best. It has bestowed a special confidence, made her more vivacious and more likely to take risks. Yet she declines Alberto's invitation.

'I am very flattered, Senor, but you see I am not familiar with the steps.' Rosetta's words are cool, almost dismissive. She is unwilling to betray her interest.

Alberto's dark gaze is unusually direct. Rich, young and far from his home in Buenos Aires, he is accountable to no one. There is nothing to be lost by allowing the attraction in his eyes to show.

'If that is your only objection, Madame,' he responds silkily, 'then that can be easily overcome. I will teach you everything.'

Rosetta's resistance to Alberto's charm is rapidly diminishing. 'Well, if you are to be my teacher, the first thing I must learn is this dance's name,' she says. Alberto smiles once more as he responds. 'Tango, Madame Zeno. It is called tango.'

The fashionable drawing rooms of Mayfair are a long way from the more dissolute brothels of Argentina. It might surprise the Duchess of Rutland and her daughter, should they realise the truth, that these wild, disreputable places are well known to their handsome foreign guests.

In Buenos Aires these men are bored, seek the stimulation of forbidden pleasure. Alberto and his friends leave the comfort of their palatial *casas*, ride recklessly into the night. They go to the *barrios* to find the danger missing from their lives. This is the place where they discover the icy white powder that makes life sharper, more intense; find hard women and harder men who do not hesitate to draw a sudden flashing blade. It is in this decadent domain that the most passionate dancing takes place.

Alberto knows that tango is many things. It is a dance of proud walks and of two bodies entwined in intimate embrace. It belongs to the night. Tango is a vehicle devised solely for the purpose of showing off the control of high pleasure. Like an intensely erotic encounter, it is a blend of giving and withholding, of surrender and restraint.

To have the undivided interest of an attractive young man is not merely gratifying. Just at this moment, it is exactly what Rosetta needs. She has observed that Zeno enjoys much success. This is what she wants for him, for both of them. She has even grown accustomed to the fact that she, his wife, is not the only object of his attention. But the realm in which they live has changed. The women who spend time with Zeno behind the closed doors of New Bond Street or in hotel suites are not simple showgirls. Duchesses and their like wield true power, the kind that comes with titles, wealth and position. If disappointed or dismayed, these privileged women can be dangerous, vicious. They will close ranks and a careless interloper will soon know the damage their authority can wreak, what a fall from grace can mean.

Of late Rosetta has been considering a solution to Zeno's incautious behaviour. It is not because she fears for her relationship with him. She knows that, no matter what the nature of his proclivities, he adores her, will never leave. Rosetta is frightened that something Zeno might do or say could bring them both undone. She fears this more than anything. Rosetta shakes her head, clears her mind. 'I will deal with this at another time,' she thinks. Instead, she meets Alberto's gaze and, with that, gives way to a diversion of her own.

'*El tango no est en los pies. Est en el corazen,*' Alberto murmurs as he looks into Rosetta's questioning eyes. 'Madame Zeno, all you need to know before we begin is that tango is not in the feet. It is in the heart.' With that, this handsome man takes Rosetta in his arms.

Alberto's right arm encircles Rosetta's waist; she feels its heat. The long fingers of his left hand hold her right hand's fingertips. He stands absolutely erect. Rosetta feels his strength as his body presses against her waiting form. Then he marches forward, clasping her firmly as she matches him, step for step.

Alberto is sure and certain; it is not difficult for Rosetta to follow him. She is sensuous by nature and not inhibited. This is, after all, the same woman who once danced at midnight on Tamarama Beach. Her body still remembers the way it felt to move to a driving Latin beat. Still, Rosetta is shrewd. She has retained her ability to detach her mind from her fiercer instincts. Aware she now plays a different role, no longer a magician's consort but a Professor's wife, she exercises discipline. No one must notice how deeply affected she really is. For an instant she longs for Wonderland, for a less prudent life.

Alberto stops, tips Rosetta back and swoops over her before bringing her upright, pausing, right leg thrust against her left, then does the same again. It is an image of exquisite conquest. Though Alberto's steps are executed with absolute precision, this control only serves to enhance Rosetta's mounting pleasure. The music's insistent beat echoes her quickened pulse as, together, 'they dance cheek to cheek, thigh to thigh, in a poem of attraction'.

I came upon these words by Robert Farris Thompson in his book *Tango: The Art History of Love* and could not help thinking that it was as if he were describing Rosetta and Alberto, on that day in 1912, in the Duchess of Rutland's drawing room.

TWENTY-EIGHT

MELBOURNE, 1910

The clock of time turns back its face. Rosetta's daughter, Frances Catherine, is living with her father in Melbourne. She has neither seen nor heard from her mother for four years. Rosetta's name is never spoken. She might have ceased to exist. Frances has a stepmother now; Louis married again only months after Rosetta left. He was nearly thirty-nine. Minnie Isaacs, his new bride, was aged just nineteen. She could have been his child.

The date is 22 February, Frances' tenth birthday. At the same time as the ship that bears the magnificent magician and her lost mother is carving its way through the sparkling water of Sydney Harbour en route to distant shores, Frances is playing beside the sea at St Kilda. She is a pretty child, if somewhat small for her age, with her father's grey-blue eyes and fine, light-brown hair. On this warm, late summer day, with a wind gusting from the west, she has been taken out by her grandmother for a treat. Her strawberry ice cream is finished, leaving a delicious, sweet stickiness around her mouth and on her teeth. Now it is time for the beach. With joy, Frances kicks off her soft kid shoes, removes her silk socks and runs barefoot along the sand. The child laughs delightedly as she feels the hot wind whip across her cheeks and through her hair. Then she stops abruptly as seagulls begin to shriek.

When Frances turns to watch the gulls she experiences a strange sensation; the sand seems to shift beneath her feet. She runs from it, escapes into the shallows. Frances feels the swirling water spread across her toes. The wavelets are cold and topped with foam, like the icy milk that is delivered on winter mornings to her home.

Suddenly, the air about her is disturbed by dozens of beating wings. She can feel the changed atmosphere press against her face, the sound throb inside her ears. With this, a vivid image of a woman comes into Frances' mind. The woman has long, dark-red hair and her mouth is curved into a smile that, strangely, makes Frances feel unexpectedly alone.

A moment later the seagulls wheel across the sky, turning in a great arc before flying straight across the water and on towards the sun. As she watches their flight, the image of the woman, so sharp only a moment before, is, like the gulls, just as quickly gone.

It is two years later, 1912. While Rosetta learns to tango, for Frances there are other lessons to absorb. Desertion by her mother is followed, after a fashion, by that of her father. This year, Louis turns forty-five. His young wife has babies of her own now, two little boys to bring up. Frances is at a difficult age; no longer a girl, she is not yet a woman. Louis wonders, 'What am I to do with Rosetta's child?'

The solution is to deposit the twelve-year-old at a convent. Genazzano is a grand boarding school. Founded by the Faithful Companions of Jesus in 1895, it is located on a hill in Kew.

The Annals of Genazzano describe the property's sweeping view of Melbourne 'with its domes, majestic pillars and cathedral spires, the many step-like villages, pretty villas half hidden among the trees, clumps of fir trees and eucalyptus, and vast fields traversed by the winding waters of the Yarra Yarra . . .'.

Our Lady of Good Counsel is Genazzano's patron. I am not certain of the wise counsel my grandmother might have received while in her care.

The school was established by the Companions for the daughters of the country-dwelling Catholic well-to-do. That Frances Catherine Raphael is city-born and of a quite different faith seems not to be a problem. Perhaps it is because she bears the names of two fine saints. Save for occasional holidays at home, Frances spends years within the convent's austere Gothic walls. I try to imagine what it was like for this lonely child, losing all she knew. How did that child feel as she walked through the great arched entrance surmounted by the cross of Christ; did she realise that this would be the place she was to stay? The nuns were stern in those days but even if they had been saints themselves, who could have expected life in a convent to replace a mother, a father, a home?

Genazzano has thoughtfully provided me with a book that describes its history. I find just one mention of my grandmother there: it notes her singular religion. The school's 'Hymn to Our Lady of Good Counsel' also captures my attention, particularly the third verse. I hope Frances found more solace than she felt sorrow when its words were sung.

By the love within thy dear eyes dwelling,
By the tears that dim their lustre too;
By the story that these tears are telling,
Mother, tell me what am I to do?

TWENTY-NINE

Press Extract from "Scientific News."

After many experimental researches the notable successes recently reported from the use of radium as a curative power by PROFESSOR CARL ZENO have led to a greatly increased interest in the subject matter; even amongst the great experts in pathological and scientific circles.

He has contributed, the result of deep study, bacteriological investigations, electrical and other experiments on the origin of human suffering both as affecting body and mind, and has achieved great success in the discovery of remedies of high therapeutic value.

Of late years the Japanese have come very much to the fore in medical science, and their experiments, having evolved the best methods of remedial treatment, have commanded the appreciation and respect of the entire medical world. And here in regard to PROFESSOR ZENO we have a case in point of a Japanese Specialist of to-day, and one, who by great perseverance, theoretical, scientific and practical experiments, has attained an extraordinary proficiency. He has successfully traced the *via media* invasion of certain specific germs known as "coma bacillus" and others of a Saprophythic and Pathogenic species.

The wonders of radium have revolutionised the modern methods of healing, and indeed holds out the promise of bringing about cures undreamt of and impossible a few years ago.

A special and unique method of the Zeno treatment in connection with radium and radio-active liquids is the emanations and gases used in conjunction with the concentrated essence of certain sensitised, re-vitalising, efficacious herbs specially cultured and imported from the East.

The number of cases, chronic and otherwise, already treated and successfully cured by radium emanations and drugless systems prove, beyond doubt, that this miraculous but natural and simple method of healing is

THE LAST WORD

in the eradication and final conquest of all ailments and diseases.

Botanical and Bacteriological Laboratory.

145, EDGWARE ROAD, W.

Consultation Rooms:

118, NEW BOND STREET, W.

Like Rosetta, Zeno had taken Helena Rubinstein's advice to heart and with equal finesse. But whereas his wife changed her attire, Zeno embraced the uniquely successful Rubinstein publicity formula. She had advised Rosetta to ensure that Zeno wrote an article for a respected journal and to make certain it was circulated. And so, just such an article was produced. Distributed in the form of a pamphlet, it was a *tour de force* of wild claims and invention, filled with references to improbable medical techniques and claims of unparalleled success.

I suspect Zeno then added one more layer of illusion. Rather than have it appear that he was merely boasting about his own achievements, his intention was that the publication itself would appear to be endorsing his prowess. After all, 'Press Extract from "Scientific News"' is not a very precise description. He might have hoodwinked the journal's editors into thinking that his were reputable claims, or even paid for the article's inclusion in its pages. Perhaps the extract never appeared in *Scientific News* at all. For Zeno, sleight of hand was second nature. His and Rosetta's lives were an inversion of that Ciceronian exhortation *Esse Quam Videri* – To Be Rather Than To Seem To Be. What was important, they knew only too well, was not substance: it was the appearance of a thing.

The fact that Zeno had his own laboratory is interesting. Many of the letters indicate that his custom-made medications were wildly popular: it was not only Lady Archibald Campbell who wrote to Zeno with anxious requests for additional supplies. But what ingredients went into the pills, the powders and the potions he concocted remain a matter about which I can only speculate. Just what were those 'sensitised, re-vitalising, efficacious herbs'?

Ginseng, wolfberry, red peony, dog spine and ginger, cinnamon and licorice, astragalus root, white wood ear, devil's trumpet and ephedra stem: there must have been rows of wooden shelves in the Edgware Road laboratory lined with these exotic substances, the glass containers in which they lay carefully labelled, their aromas combining to produce a bitter-sweet, pungent fragrance that hung heavy in the air. It would have been easy for Zeno to become familiar with the herbs and their healing properties when he occupied the rooms in Swanston Street, so close to Melbourne's Chinatown. Considering the popularity of his products, though, I imagine that at least some of these imported 'efficacious herbs' might now come under the legal heading of 'Controlled Substances'. They could have included opium from China and quite possibly South American cocaine.

I have no sense of what the building that housed the laboratory looked like, for the original structure is no longer there. Its place has been taken by a modern shop that sells a brand of clothing called High and Mighty, designed to be worn by substantial men. I suppose that the laboratory must have been a busy place, one in which Bunsen burners flared and test tubes bubbled, where assorted elixirs were distilled by an elderly Chinese man who had spent a lifetime studying the herbs' many secrets. No doubt others assisted, men well versed in the dream-like effects or, alternatively, the stimulation afforded by the ingredients employed in the manufacture of more potent remedies.

Whenever the demands of his patients allowed it, the mixing of these 'medicines', the pressing of tablets and the compounding of powders would have been overseen by the master, Zeno himself. I see him standing, wizard-like, directing this welter of activity, breathing in the heavy, scented air that very likely induced visions of his own. Perhaps a part of him had come to believe he really was a distinguished professor, that his powers were not imaginary but real.

I read the pamphlet, and read it again, several times. It is oddly reminiscent of something else I have seen. What strikes me first is the way in which its claims are so similar to the multitude of cosmetic advertisements that now appear in glossy magazines, many of which adopt scientific terms like 'pH factor' and 'cellular renewal', 'powerful new formula', 'synchronised recovery' and the ubiquitous 'clinically proven'.

Such scientific jargon, initiated by Helena Rubinstein, has now become the contemporary language of incantation, replacing more ancient invocations. How quickly Zeno understood the force such words would have, how easily he cast his spell and left fashionable society entranced.

It was only natural that the newly minted Japanese Professor should insert all those references to radium into his text, for, in an age of boiling scientific revelation, its discovery was arguably the most exciting. Ever since 1903, when Marie Curie first identified this startling element, a new industry based entirely on radio-active quackery had emerged. After Madame Curie won the Nobel Prize in 1911, it gathered additional momentum.

Zeno was not slow to seize upon radium's 'wonders' and potential – for his own commercial gain, if not for medical accomplishment. The wording of the pamphlet shows that he was well aware of the allure of this new substance. The opportunity for him to tout it as a magic panacea for almost any ailment was a godsend.

Of course, if Zeno did actually utilise radium there is no doubt it would have caused a great deal more harm than good. Radiation poisoning was to prove lethal, though, to be fair, at that stage no one was aware of its effects. Even Marie Curie herself, who died from complications caused by her exposure to the deadly substance (she was said to have carried about glowing fragments in her pocket), knew very little of its dangers. In the absence of evidence to the contrary, its use must have seemed to Zeno a splendid way in which to convince his clients that he had a profound mastery of science.

Something else about the pamphlet occurs to me, which is how very like William Anderson's advertisements for Wonder-land its language is. The phrasing has the same rolling cadences of the ringmaster; the claims reflect an equivalent delight in the use of superlatives. As I read the words I can almost hear Anderson's persuasive voice proclaiming, 'Roll up, roll up for the Greatest Show on Earth,' the single difference being that the show in this instance was taking place in Professor Carl Zeno's New Bond Street suite rather than in the Palace of Illusions, in an amusement park by the sea.

~

The pamphlet worked magnificently. Consider the patronage of Zeno by none other than Sir Oliver Lodge, knighted by King Edward for his exceptional contribution to science, recipient of the prestigious Rumford Medal from the Royal Society for 'an outstandingly important scientific discovery', and first Principal of the University of Birmingham. Sir Oliver developed the key patents that led to the Nobel Prize-winning Marconi's invention of that miracle of the age, the wireless. Consider also Marconi's wife, the former Honourable Beatrice O'Brien, daughter of the 14th Baron of Inchiquin, who was, like Sir Oliver, another of Professor Zeno's loyal patrons.

Lodge and Marconi were men of the highest scientific probity. They devoted their professional lives to the study of electromagnetic waves. Yet, despite the fact that one was a brilliant physicist and the other an equally gifted electrical engineer, Zeno's outrageous claim that '*electrical and other experiments*' had resulted in he alone becoming the possessor of 'the last word in the eradication and final conquest of all ailments and diseases' was apparently accepted at face value. I suppose it does prove Zeno's thesis: the more immense and fabulous the lie, the more likely it is to be believed.

Sir Oliver, it seems, was completely taken in. Standing as he did at the very pinnacle of Britain's scientific community, this seems extraordinary to me. That is, until I discover that Sir Oliver, despite all his scientific prowess and academic eminence, was an ardent believer in the existence of another world inhabited by spirits.

At first I was bewildered by such naïvety. How could this imminent man of science – and he was but one of many – succumb to such absurd flights of fancy? Yet, upon reflection, I began to see not just the sense but also the logic behind Sir Oliver's conviction.

In this exciting age of scientific innovation it sometimes seemed that breakthroughs were made on a near daily basis. X-rays and cathode rays and electromagnetism, light waves and sound waves and the power of radiation: a veritable tidal wave of discoveries swept away what had for centuries been thought immutable and unchanging. As early as 1884, Sir Oliver Lodge wrote, 'Things hitherto held impossible do actually occur.' They did, and proof abounded.

This phenomena was, perhaps, expressed most evocatively in 1913 by the writer Edith Nesbit, who posed what must have seemed a reasonable question: 'If electricity can move through the air unseen, why not carpets?'

Why not indeed? Embedded in this wondrous supposition was a thrilling *plausibility.*

Possessed by a desire to communicate with those who lived beyond the grave, Sir Oliver, the former president of the Physical Society, became president of the Psychical Society, instead. This exchange, heralding so much more than merely the rearrangement of a few letters, led him into the realm of seers, mediums and clairvoyants.

It was inevitable that the esteemed Professor Zeno, erstwhile of the Ku-Mari Hospital and Medical Schools, Japan, would come to his attention. For, though Zeno may have appeared to embrace the latest scientific advances, he was, in fact, never to relinquish his former professional practices. Seeing the future, sensing emanations, foretelling death, joyous events and terrible disasters; these arcane skills remained his stock in trade. Rather than dispensing with his tricks, the magician merely utilised the semblance of current, scientific breakthroughs in order to remain fashionably pertinent or, as Helena Rubinstein would have said, *au courant.*

THIRTY

The room is dim. Deep shadows are cast by two bronze lamps, which rest in alcoves in the walls. A fire has been lit, its flames creating a golden warmth that, together with liberal amounts of fine cognac, creates a sense of languor among the guests. The scents of lilies and tuberoses perfume the air with an aroma that, though lovely, contains within it a hint of sweet decay, of decadence.

In the centre of the room is a large, round table covered with a plush velvet cloth, soft and black as a raven's wing. Around it sit a collection of individuals, all distinguished in their way, either by wealth, intellect, beauty or sheer daring. Zeno is there, of course. Though dressed just like the other men in white tie and tails, his shirt starched and crisp with its row of pearly studs, there is no doubt that he is the evening's maestro. It is he who has called this group together, grand puppeteer that he is, a sorcerer professor with unusual abilities. Or so he says.

Rosetta, his striking consort, sits opposite. She wears a gown of amethyst silk, cut low to enhance her décolletage. Faceted jet earrings hang from her ears; a wide cuff of black jet encircles her wrist. The effect is a perfect combination of elegance and seduction. This is not mere coincidence. It is important that the tone of this *mise en scène* is precise. Rosetta and Zeno have considered, examined and resolved each detail, in order that every person who attends is not just drawn in by the evening's promise and allure – that part is relatively easy – but convinced of the proceedings' integrity. This is essential if the next stage of the couple's journey is to be accomplished.

Rosetta looks at Zeno. It is just a glance, but enough for him to understand her meaning. All is ready. It is nearly midnight, a strange time to commence an evening's entertainment, if indeed that is what it can be termed, but this, too, has been carefully estimated. The witching hour has always had a certain unholy quality. Now it is time to call their guests to order and allow the evening's purpose to unfold.

Sir Oliver, tall and slim, is, naturally, present. The lure of a seance, for this is what has been planned, is impossible to resist. Strangely, despite his outstanding scientific work on electromagnetic radiation, he is convinced that there exists a massless, incompressible *ether* wherein not only do the planets swim but in which the spirit world exists. Sir Oliver has come to know Zeno quite well over recent months, is delighted by the knowledgeable way in which this distinguished professor is not only able to discuss paranormal phenomena, but is apparently in possession of the means for unearthly communication.

Lodge has brought two others with him, a man and a woman. They are not a couple – indeed, neither has met before – though both share his fervour for the spirit world. The first is, like Sir Oliver, a man of science. He is a towering, rather serious Scottish doctor whose specialisation is ophthalmology. This is not, however, the profession that has made him celebrated throughout the land. Sir Oliver's friend is renowned for writing books about a brilliant if troubled detective who likes to play the violin and from time to time indulges in cocaine. He is Sir Arthur Conan Doyle.

Lodge and Conan Doyle have known each other for many years. Both are members of The Ghost Club, a select organisation created for those believers who wish to further their investigation of the spirit world. By coincidence, each man's knighthood was proclaimed in King Edward's Coronation Honours List of 1902. After both had knelt before their sovereign, they fell into discussion, not of science or of literature or indeed the relative merits of the King's most recent mistress, but of their mutual fascination with the afterlife. Their animated conversation ranged over telekinesis, telepathy, and the efficacy of mediums, celebrated and otherwise. The most intriguing topic, however, was what becomes of the eternal souls of the departed.

Lodge introduces Conan Doyle to those not yet acquainted with him, though he makes no mention of the famous character long associated with the author's name. He is aware of the frustrations his friend experiences, the way he feels dogged by his own invention, a sort of monster to his Frankenstein. Sir Oliver says merely that his companion is a medical specialist and distinguished author; he trusts the others will take his lead and refrain from mentioning clues or deerstalkers. Next he turns to his female friend and, gesturing at the assemblage, says, 'May I now introduce the renowned Baroness Ernesta Stern?'

Ernesta is a writer, too. Under her *nom de plume*, Maria Star, she produces novels, travel journals, comedies and books of aphorisms. Critical response is mixed: it matters little. She is the extraordinarily wealthy widow of the French banker Baron Louis Stern and has only recently finished building her elaborate Venetian palazzo on the Grand Canal. She also has a spectacular home in Paris on the Rue du Faubourg Saint-Honoré, though increasingly she spends her time at her enormous neo-Romanesque villa in the south of France at Cap Martin.

Madame Stern is a large woman. Her gown is a dark burgundy and with it she wears a heavy rock crystal and pyrite pendant around her neck. She is rather pale, somewhat imperious, but has a friendly manner for all that. Indeed, she tells the other guests that she believes she is the reincarnation of Semiramis, Queen of Babylon. She also mentions that she is something of a medium herself. The others listen politely, for though here with open minds they are not yet ready for the wholesale suspension of disbelief.

Zeno and Rosetta are already aware that Ernesta presides over an exclusive Parisian *salon*, that she is a close friend of the celebrated writer Marcel Proust. She numbers, too, a clutch of royal princes and princesses and even a former empress among her most intimate acquaintances. All are fiercely loyal. When that debauched poet Comte Robert de Montesquiou makes a number of waspish comments as to the literary value of her work, her son, Jean, challenges him to a duel. They fence at dawn in Neuilly where, according to *Le Figaro*, Jean's victory is 'overwhelming'. The incident adds to her reputation a certain piquant notoriety.

This small scandal is the kind of detail Rosetta has made it her business to discover. She has used a private detective, perhaps not so brilliant as the fictive Sherlock Holmes but useful nonetheless. He has helped her thoroughly research her illustrious guests, in preparation for what is to come on this most significant of nights.

In a short time Baroness Stern will play an important role in Zeno and Rosetta's life, bringing them into contact with a strata of society even more elevated than the one which they have already entered with such apparent ease. But that lies in the future. For now Ernesta, like the others, waits to see what the evening will reveal.

Senor Rivero is seated next to Rosetta. He watches her with fervent eyes. Though his manners are as refined as ever, he gives the other guests only the minimum of attention in order not to cause offence. It is clear that there is just one person whose company he desires. Since arriving in London Alberto has enjoyed the charms of many women, from chambermaids to, it is rumoured, a royal princess. Only Rosetta seems immune to his appeal. She fascinates him. Neither European nor English, neither titled nor rich, there is an elusive, sensual quality about her he has found captivating.

It is not that Rosetta hasn't wondered, when they dance, what it would be like to place her hands upon the long, lean muscles she has felt beneath Alberto's close-cut coat. She is tempted. But she is determined to remain in control, will allow Alberto to take just sufficient liberties so that his ardour, rather than lessen, only grows. She has learnt the power of what it means to withhold.

Alberto is useful. He makes a perfect escort for the ballet or the opera when Zeno is too busy with his patrons to attend. Alberto's devotion leads Zeno to feel uncertain. He is unused to this. Though Rosetta has laughed, assured her husband that it is but a harmless flirtation, Zeno's customary composure is, she knows, no longer quite so complete. It is something that has made his love-making more passionate, drives him to require from her things that she has not done before. She complies, aroused by these novelties, but still Zeno is not reassured. He watches Alberto watching her.

Lilian Pakenham, who sits beside Zeno, is the remaining guest. Zeno has come to know her well. She is by now almost as much his friend as she is Rosetta's. Lilian is charming and intelligent. She is not as compelling as his wife, but he finds her company to be relaxing. Lilian is that rare woman he feels he has no need to impress: he can be completely himself with her. Tonight she wears a slender silver gown, its flowing drapery reminiscent of the ancient world. Zeno recognises that she is exceptionally pretty. He also knows she is forbidden.

After completing the introductions and making some brief welcoming remarks, the Professor begins to speak. He has a spell to weave.

'My friends, tonight I believe that we will witness a mystery. It is one that we may not understand. But then, as you gentlemen of science know only too well, our human knowledge is but a fraction of what is left to be discovered. We remain at the very cusp of comprehension.'

Zeno's low voice has adopted a rhythmical cadence that induces calm. Each word he chooses ensures that his listeners feel special, unique, singled out for a journey of high purpose that they alone are equipped to undertake. Soon, he will provide them with reason to believe. It will be what they most want to embrace.

'There are seven in our company of venturers tonight, for venturers we surely are. Our intention is to enter into realms to which mortals rarely go.'

While Zeno speaks Rosetta remains silent. She sees the rapt faces of her guests, the way they look towards the master; their helplessness.

'Seven is a number of immense mystical significance. There are seven pillars in the House of Wisdom. In the Book of Revelations we find seven golden stars, seven torches of burning fire, seven angels and their trumpets, seven diadems and kings.

'We should not forget, either, that there are seven deadly sins. Or that the gateways traversed by the goddess Inanna during her descent into the Underworld number seven, too.

'Tonight we follow the goddess into that spirit world.'

Zeno takes his gold medallion from his breast pocket and begins to swing it slowly back and forth. 'Friends,' his voice is even lower; his guests strain to hear each word. 'It is necessary for you to gaze upon this ancient coin. Give it all your attention, for this is the means by which Inanna is invoked. Do not look away. Concentrate with every fibre of your being so that she may draw upon your energy. Only then can Inanna transmit the thoughts of those who dwell within a realm we cannot know. Watch, watch this ancient coin. It is the means to bring the goddess into our midst.'

The mesmerist is deft. His hypnotic powers have only heightened over time.

'Now you must all place your hands in one another's,' he says. 'Be peaceful. Allow the continuum of moments to alter space and time, to reform their particles into a different reality.'

His guests are still. This is the meaning of enchantment.

THIRTY-ONE

'I have a message.' Zeno speaks, yet in another's voice. His customary low tone is exchanged for something higher, softer, though no less commanding. By some alchemy Inanna has taken Zeno's place; she communicates through him.

Sir Oliver's heart beats quickly. Madame Stern feels a chill run down her spine. Sir Arthur's broad shoulders tense and Senor Rivero is wide-eyed. Anticipation has built to near fever pitch, but clever Zeno waits. There is in men and women an acute hunger that is strongest in the moment just before desire becomes fulfilled. He knows that moment has arrived.

He begins to tell them things about themselves that they believe no mortal could ever know. Secret wishes and hidden needs are revealed to gasps and cries. Next there are messages from the departed for each guest.

Lilian's grandmother, the Countess, tells her of a man whose initials are RPN, speaks of encounters in a far-off place, of two riders on horses who gallop together across dark hills and through shadowed glades. Then she says Lilian will return to that distant land one day, that it is there her destiny will be fulfilled. Though Lilian is well aware of the frankly fraudulent nature of the proceedings, still she is taken by surprise.

Now it is Alberto's turn. A long-dead Jesuit priest, his much-loved tutor when he was a child in Buenos Aires, admonishes his former acolyte with stern authority. 'My boy, my boy,' he says. 'Why have you wandered so far from the paths of righteousness? There is debauchery in your life and it endangers your immortal soul. I have strived to watch over you from afar, but should you persist in wanton immorality's embrace, I will be unable to prevent the hellish judgement that awaits.'

Alberto's face is white beneath his tan, his hand quite suddenly cold to Rosetta's touch. She smiles inwardly, secretly pleased that her husband seems bent on ensuring that, between herself and Senor Rivero, nothing untoward will come to pass.

Sir Oliver is next. As the great man leans forward he hears the words, 'I am Menelaus of Alexandria.'

Lodge recognises the name at once. Menelaus, revered mathematician of antiquity, known for astronomical measurement and the study of the spheres. 'The past and the future collapse into new realities beyond human expression or understanding,' Menelaus intones. 'You must continue on the spirit path; only in this way can you solve the great and complex mysteries that taunt you so. Time moves through space in a world composed not just of matter but of spirit. We ancients knew this. Fellow seeker after truth, do not lay down the torch that has been passed to you.'

Sir Oliver nods gravely, an expression of resolve upon his face. A few details of his life are revealed, just enough to confirm that he is in the presence of one who has the gift of second sight. Then a final, chilling warning comes. 'Beware. There is a great conflagration on the horizon, the like of which has not been seen before. You and another who is present will know suffering, I caution you.'

What this can mean nobody knows, though each guest has his or her own fears. There is not one, however, who envisages the inferno that waits to engulf them. They breathe the perfumed air and wonder at the disturbing prophecy.

'Arthur, Arthur ...' A new sweetness enters Zeno's voice. 'It is Touie, I am here.' A revealing portrait of Conan Doyle has been provided to Rosetta by the sleuth she has engaged; the man, not immune to the irony of this particular commission, has applied himself with special rigour to the case.

Touie was the author's pet name for Louisa, his first wife: consumption rendered her an invalid for a dozen years before she died. During her long illness Sir Arthur conducted a passionate liaison with Jean Leckie, the young, attractive woman who is now his wife. Although the relationship was chaste while Louisa was alive, Sir Arthur was tormented by the notion that his desperately ill wife might have guessed where his affections truly lay. He was a man of honour – had this knowledge caused her pain? That thought enveloped him with anguish. Indeed, though seven years have passed since Louisa's sad demise, it continues to torment him to this day.

Now Conan Doyle hears what purports to be his first wife murmuring, 'Dearest Arthur, do not be distressed. I know all, have always known. You and Jean have my blessing.' When she adds, fainter now, 'I have only ever wished for your happiness,' a sound, much like a strangled sob, is heard to emanate from this large, bluff man.

There is a reason Zeno has left the Baroness until the last. She is his target. The evening's elaborate performance has been designed with one overarching objective. It is quite simple: Madame Stern is the key to what he hopes will be his and Rosetta's increasingly brilliant future. They must entrance her, win her ardent support, her unqualified affection.

Zeno has chosen Ernesta's mother to communicate with her from beyond the grave. There are certain particulars stated pertaining to her childhood in Trieste, the name of her lapdog and so on, intended to build trust and confidence. Following that, some astute observations about her marriage to the banker Louis Stern are made. She nods. Yes, it is all true.

Suddenly, there is a rupture. The fire flares and the very air seems heavy, charged. Then Zeno speaks in yet a different voice: tonight his versatility has full reign. In an accent redolent of the East he says, 'I am Semiramis, warrior queen of Babylon.' Ernesta leans forward, a look of the most intense excitement on her face. 'I have conquered many lands; the Persians and the Assyrians called me sovereign. For centuries my spirit has imbued remarkable women. I spoke through Boudicca and Joan of Arc. Now, Ernesta, I choose to speak through you.'

Ernesta slumps, appears limp and faint. Rosetta frowns. Madame Stern is infinitely suggestible. Perhaps Zeno has gone too far?

But then, recovering, the Baroness lifts her head, adjusts her posture until that ungainly body does indeed adopt a regal air. Next she proclaims, 'I have a message for one who is present in this room. It is from a young woman, still half girl. She is not from my time but your own. Neither is this woman-child from the afterlife. She dwells in a distant place, across vast oceans and burning continents.

'I hear this half girl's voice cry out, "Mother, mother mine. I saw your great bird wings beat against the sky. I could not call you back. You would not return to me, to be by my side."' With that, Ernesta falls forward, spent.

The gathering is by turns shocked, perplexed and, finally, bemused. There is just one person whose heart lurches in her chest, only one for whom this strange message has a terrible resonance. Rosetta, using all of her self-discipline, wills herself to move, to bring Ernesta smelling salts and brandy, then takes a little for herself. She has come too far, sacrificed too much, to allow that sealed part of her heart to crack and break.

With that, the seance is brought to a close. The guests remain a little dazed, their trance-like state persisting until Professor

Zeno gently leads them back to safety; to the tangible, the world they know. In doing so he reinforces his hypnotic claims, ensures that the memories will be as lasting as words chiselled on a tomb.

'Tonight we seven have been graced by manifestations from the spirit realm. We have seen the past and future collapse in time,' he says. 'None of us will ever forget what we have heard and witnessed here inside this room.'

THIRTY-TWO

I return to the letters, Ernesta's three, of course, but also those penned by the mysterious Charlotte, she of the copious crown-topped correspondence with the interlinking purple C's. There are fourteen of these, which means that on average she took up her pen, composed her thoughts and wrote to Zeno once every fortnight over a period of seven months. It speaks of dedication.

The warm, intimate communications from Ernesta and Charlotte provide me with the richest clues to the life Rosetta and Zeno led during the still-splendid days that stretched from the end of 1913 until midway through 1914. The letters show me that, against a backdrop of simmering international tension, my great-grandmother and her magnetic husband revelled in the splendour of what was to be the final, precious moments of that gloriously indulgent, lost time, now forever known as *La Belle Époque*.

Charlotte's writing is impenetrable. With the appearance of a series of single, bold straight lines, broken up at intervals by long diagonal strokes and shorter, heavier marks, it looks as if rows of millipedes have colonised the pages. It is a hand unlike any

I have seen before. My father must have been equally confounded, for I can see that, fortunately, he arranged for transcriptions to be made.

I look at them, an enticing small pile. They have been neatly typed on a manual machine and then numbered by hand from 1 to 14. I have other letters, from a range of correspondents, but no other writer is represented in such abundance. I can only speculate as to their significance because, maddeningly, I still don't know who Charlotte is. I can tell that she is a close friend of Madame Stern, as both refer to each other fondly. It is also clear, from the very first of Charlotte's letters, that she, too, has succumbed to Zeno's unique appeal.

Villa La Fôret,
Cannes,
20 December 1913

I spent a charming afternoon on Wednesday with M. Stern and we spoke so much about you …

My 2 interviews with you will ever remain the most interesting and pleasant recollections of my hitherto sad and hard life …

As yet, I have no idea what Charlotte's '*sad and hard*' life might have been like. The second letter, written from her friend Ernesta's fabled villa by the Mediterranean Sea, provides no further insights. It does, however, reveal the two women's growing infatuation.

Torre Clementina,
Cap Martin, Par Cabbé Roquebrune,
Menton, Alpes-Maritimes,
29 January 1914

We constantly talk of you and long for you to join in our conversations …

All my grateful love forever … Charlotte.

Should Charlotte have continued in this vein, her letters would have provided me with just more proof, though in truth by now none is needed, of Zeno's singular ability to gain the devotion of yet another rich, well-connected woman. I have grown used to, even a little bored with, these adoring protestations. They begin to cloy.

As I read on, however, I notice that something a good deal more interesting occurs. Charlotte begins to mention international affairs. Her second letter refers to:

> *The great unrest in political circles all over the world, also at home … it makes me very uneasy …*

By the fourth letter her comments not only reveal a deteriorating situation; they provide an insight into Zeno's remarkable prescience.

> *Monterey,*
> *Cannes,*
> *4 April 1914*
>
> *The fire of unrest has indeed commenced, and your sad predictions I feel must be true, slaughter and bloodshed and revolutions and other troubles must come on …*

Zeno's '*sad predictions*' had been made months before the commencement of the Great War. This was at a time when almost no one – premiers, prime ministers or their sovereigns – imagined the catastrophic events that would come to pass. How was it that my step-great-grandfather knew these things? I catch myself beginning to wonder if he really had the power to foretell the future, after all. Perhaps, as was the case for so many, many women and not a few men, the explanation is all too simple. I, too, am falling under Zeno's spell.

Charlotte's letters, with their increasingly fascinating content, have only added to my bewilderment. In the face of my confusion, I decide that, by necessity, she must wait. I will deal with Ernesta Stern's correspondence first.

Her hand is nothing like that of Charlotte. She writes with a clear precision, in very dark ink on small cards. These cards are topped not only with her address: they bear a curious sea-green insignia, its elements confined within a neat rectangle so that it looks something like a seal. There are her initials, ES, but also two blooms on each side. They look to me like lotus flowers, ancient emblem of Egypt and the Nile. A looping line connects these motifs with, at their centre, a five-pointed star. It is a centuries-old occult sign believed to drive away evil spirits and prove inviting to the benign; a pentagram.

Each one of Ernesta's letters reveals in what rarefied circles Zeno and Rosetta have now begun to move. In a few short paragraphs one undated despatch, written from her grand home, includes a plethora of royal references.

Torre Clementina,
Cap Martin, Par Cabbé Roquebrune,
Menton, Alpes-Maritimes

Dear Friend

The charming Princess came to luncheon today. We talked the whole time of you. She loves you and admires you – so do I.

I am sending you the photos I took of you and those of the Princess, of Prince Louis of Monaco, of Prince Ismail.

. . . You are my protection and my blessing.

Don't you think it was sweet of the Princess to meet you at the station? She deserves being happy. You must try to impress the Emperor's mind, to wish to know you. I will send you in a few days his photograph that I took and my children's too.

I am very anxious to receive news from you.

God bless you.

Ernesta

My love to Mrs. Zeno.

I imagine Rosetta holding this letter in her hand. She is smiling a little, nodding her head. If ever she had doubts about her husband's unusual abilities, here is proof that his immense self-confidence has been more than justified. A princess, two princes and an emperor, all mentioned in the space of one letter! The Princess already '*loves*' and '*admires*' him, Her Royal Highness going so far as to meet his train. Professor Carl Zeno's journey, presumably by railway from Paris to smart seaside Nice, would not have been so very long. The former William Norman, tinsmith, son of a goldfields Celestial and sometime fortune teller, has travelled a great deal further in his life.

A second letter, also written from Torre Clementina but this time dated 27 December 1913, reveals Ernesta's growing affection for Rosetta.

First, Ernesta mentions that she has not received Rosetta's presents, a jade heart and carved shell. I can see why Rosetta selected these particular objects: they are exotic, possess a certain oriental flair. The Baroness is worried that these baubles may have been lost en route. '*They have not yet reached me and I felt rather anxious about it.*' Considering her fabulous riches and extensive jewellery collection, this concern over the arrival of two comparatively modest gifts serves to demonstrate that, once again, Helena Rubinstein was right: the wealthy can be beguiled by such well-chosen tokens.

Ernesta becomes effusive, writing:

> *Will you kindly accept my heartiest wishes for the New Year? One of these wishes is to see you here next March with dear Professor. You are both in my heart always.*

Finally, she signs the letter '*Your affectionate spiritual sister, Ernesta*'. This is how I know that Rosetta has also practised enchantment.

The third communication from Ernesta is dated 31 December, the last day of the final year of peace, 1913. Zeno is no longer addressed as '*Dear Friend*' but '*My adored Brother*'. He is as close to her as if they shared the same womb.

> *I won't be happy quite, until I get a little thinner. My flesh makes me feel sad. Since my soul has developed and all my aspirations are heavenly, I cannot stand my huge body.*
>
> *Help me dear friend, please help me . . .*

Whether Ernesta wishes Zeno to assist in the reduction of her earthly bulk or in the realisation of more ethereal ambitions is not made clear. Perhaps it is both. But then her attention turns to more political concerns.

> *I am sending you the photograph of the Prince who could save our country. But he wants energy and resolution.*

This 'Prince' is surely Napoleon Victor Jérôme Frédéric Bonaparte, Pretender to the throne of France, though always referred to by his more fervent supporters as Napoleon V. I have already discovered the postcard that bears his photograph. It shows a balding, unprepossessing man of around forty with an enormous black moustache and a faintly troubled air. He does not look like a saviour to me. Pasted on the back is a newspaper clipping, dated

23 January 1914, which announces that the Prince's son, Louis Napoleon, 'heir of the greatest name with which the nation can be honoured', has been born.

Victor will prove unable to protect his homeland, though it will not be merely insufficiency of '*energy and resolution*' to blame.

There is a final allusion to another royal, Prince Bahram of Persia, '*who has been photographed with you*'. This solves one more, albeit small, mystery; it is the distinguished-looking bearded man in the photograph I have found who looks sadly from the bed in which he lies, with Zeno, immaculate in suit and tie, tending to his needs while by his side.

Ernesta's letter demonstrates that Rosetta and Zeno's plan met with wild success. Their goal – to win Madame Stern's favour and, by doing so, gain entry into an elite, glittering world – had been achieved. The Baroness, on intimate terms with the era's most famous writers, painters and poets, crowned heads of state and princes of the church, had come to love Rosetta. But she treasured Zeno.

'*Tell the divine Master please that I feel quite happy and most serene; I wish only to please Him*,' she implored. By now Ernesta had not only concluded that her '*adored Brother*' was capable of influencing the destiny of rulers. She believed that he possessed the singular ability to communicate with the very greatest of divinities.

THIRTY-THREE

I know who Charlotte is. I have spread all fourteen of her letters out and isolated names and dates and places, references to Charlotte's residence *Meiningen*, to her father-in-law the Duke and the date of his death. I wrote all these facts down, searched, checked and checked again. Suddenly, it all made sense. My father always wondered who she was. But then he didn't have the benefit of the internet. After decades in which the letters' author remained a mystery, solving this riddle turns out to be as easy as tapping the right sequence of keys.

I am amazed by what I find. No wonder Zeno's most frequent correspondent began to comment increasingly on the turbulent state of world affairs; the fourteen highly personal, handwritten letters were penned by none other than the formidable Princess Charlotte of Prussia, daughter of the German Emperor, Frederick III, granddaughter of Queen Victoria and sister of Kaiser Wilhelm II, last Emperor of Germany.

From 20 December 1913 to 15 July 1914, the princess who was described in an article carried by *The New York Times* just four days after her final missive as 'the Kaiser's most brilliant, gifted, and fascinating sister' wrote from the very centre of the dramatic events that were to lead to a war that engulfed the world.

Now Ernesta's undated letter makes sense. The Princess who came to luncheon, talked of nothing but Zeno, who loves and admires him, was Charlotte. It was Princess Charlotte who sweetly met Zeno at the station. And when Ernesta wrote, '*You must try to impress the Emperor's mind, to wish to know you*', she was referring to none other than Charlotte's brother, Emperor Wilhelm, supreme sovereign of Europe's greatest power.

For thirty-three-year-old Rosetta, granddaughter of a convict, mother of an abandoned child, wife of a fairground charlatan, the devoted friendship of the Emperor's sister must surely have amounted to the very summit of success. It was a triumph.

LONDON, 1914

The knock on the door is hesitant. Rosetta, preoccupied with the accounts, looks up, frowns. There are no patients scheduled; she thinks Zeno is at his laboratory, though she acknowledges that she cannot be absolutely certain of his whereabouts. She chooses never to question him about that.

Rosetta does not welcome this disturbance, for she has been busy adding columns of figures, assessing the revenue from Zeno's increasingly lucrative practice and the sale of his custom-made medicines. The results are most satisfactory, so much so that lately she has commenced purchasing property, particularly in Ireland, where Lilian is able not only to effect useful introductions but to provide certain information on who has lost his fortune due to his addiction to the race track, or whose habit of supporting expensive mistresses has caused his marriage to collapse. Rosetta seems to know, innately, how best to take advantage of these helpful details. She has grown shrewd, discovered that she has an aptitude for business. Rosetta has learnt a great deal since she came to London.

It is with some impatience, then, that she moves towards the door. Behind it is a boy of about twelve, a little nervous, a little out of breath. She gives him a couple of pennies, he hands her a telegram. After the boy is gone, after she has opened and read the message, all sign of Rosetta's irritation disappears.

The date is 29 January 1914. The telegram has been sent to Professor Zeno at 118 New Bond Street London from Cap Martin, despatched at precisely 11.35 am, and is of just sixteen words in length.

ERNESTA DELIGHTED TO HAVE YOU FEBRUARY 20
WITH MRS ZENO
BEG OF YOU TO COME CHARLOTTE

How extraordinary, Rosetta thinks. They have arrived in London, two vagabonds with nothing. Now a royal princess, sister of Europe's most powerful emperor, does not simply ask her and her beloved to come and visit. The Princess begs.

February is bleak in London and so cold that, in the streets, a single breath feels like a stab of steel. The days stretch on with only a deepening monochrome – silver in the morning, iron-grey by afternoon and then, too soon, the bitter black of night – to indicate that time is passing. Rosetta thinks of Australia, of the steamy tropical days that late summer brings, when the kookaburras call throatily from gum trees at dawn and a sea breeze curls its way through open windows, bringing with it the scent of eucalypts and lilly pillies as the day's bright, clear light begins to dim.

It is fortunate, Rosetta reflects as she contemplates another sunless London day, that soon they will be leaving for the south of France. It will offer respite from this relentless English winter and, of course, the pleasant prospect of staying in sumptuous surroundings while being waited on by Ernesta's coven of attentive servants. Putting up with Madame Stern and the Princess as they simper over her husband can be tedious, but this is a small price to pay in exchange for an escape from ice and gales.

Zeno interrupts her thoughts. 'Darling, I have heard from the Princess again,' he says. 'I must say, she is dreadfully keen to spend time with me.' He grins and Rosetta thinks he has a wolfish look.

'Listen, I'll read it to you.

> *'My dear Professor*
>
> *Be thanked so much for your very kind ended letter, far too flattering for me . . .'*

Zeno looks up. 'Yes of course, that's what she *says*, but you know as well as I do that it is quite impossible to flatter these women too much. Their appetite for compliments is insatiable. Anyway, then she writes:

> *'. . . but specially for the great pleasure caused by your telegram and our being together in the garden of Eden: for I've arranged with M. Stern to come and spend 2 days at Torre Clementina, while you are there, so that we can have a few undisturbed hours.'*

The Professor's eyes meet those of his wife as he exclaims, 'Thank heaven you're coming with me.'

'Surely you're not complaining?' Rosetta smiles impishly. 'Just think, there you'll be with the Princess and the Baroness, a trio of kindred spirits communing, or healing or whatever it is you will be doing, all in the lap of luxury – by the way, what *do* you have planned?'

'We can come to that later. In any case mostly, you know, they just want to be listened to. But it is strange, Rosetta, I do seem to be, well, developing a heightened awareness.'

Rosetta raises an arched eyebrow.

'No, really. I have the strongest feeling that the way things are, for the world, for us, well ... it cannot last.'

Zeno continues. 'Anyway, that is not what I wanted to tell you about, or at least, not right now. Hear what Charlotte says at the end of the letter. It seems there will be one more guest.'

As Zeno reads on, Rosetta notes an unusual tremor of excitement in her husband's voice.

> *'I'm so looking forward to your meeting that rare, charming and fine Empress Eugenie, whom we told all we could about you and your coming on the 20th.*

'The Empress, Rosetta. Just think, we are meeting with the Empress! Ah, my darling, I am beginning to believe this visit may prove rather special, after all.'

Zeno seizes his wife and kisses her passionately. He presses her ripe body against his own, conscious not just of desire but of an overwhelming sense of exhilaration. The showman in him has been roused. There is nothing like the thought of putting on a really spectacular display before a new audience – and such an elevated one, at that – for stimulating this strange man.

THIRTY-FOUR

The French Riviera: it is a place whose name still evokes an image of glamorous abandon; a location made for sybarites where the restraint imposed by other lives lived far away can be set aside under a balmy sun and soft blue skies. Ever since the 1920s, when Coco Chanel deemed suntans to be smart and the fabulous doomed Americans Scott and Zelda Fitzgerald spent months there in the wild pursuit of pleasure, it has been a site for summer revelry. But during the affluent, indulgent years of the late nineteenth and early twentieth centuries, it was in the winter months that the Riviera functioned as an enticing playground for the rich, the famous and the titled.

From the beginning of January until precisely the first of May, they flocked to the sparkling strip that lies between Saint Tropez and Menton. Initially, they were drawn by winters that, in 1834, Britain's former Lord Chancellor Lord Henry Brougham declared to be 'as mild as Cairo'. But there was so much more than fine weather to be had.

There were the sheltered bays and sweeping headlands, opulent hotels that had the appearance of lavishly decorated wedding cakes and, increasingly, flamboyant villas, boating on the turquoise sea, gambling in Monte Carlo, parties, balls and receptions everywhere. And, always, there was a certain permissiveness that enabled these important people to act in a manner that would be considered rather shocking in the palaces and stately homes they had, for a few gratifying months, left behind.

Elegant men and women travelled south in their luxurious private railway carriages with enormous quantities of monogrammed luggage and retinues of servants: maids and valets, footmen and drivers. They motored through the pretty villages and chic towns in gleaming Daimlers and Bugattis, driven by liveried chauffeurs valued as much for their discretion as their skill behind a wheel, for private assignations were not uncommon. Some came by sea, sailing into Cannes in sleek yachts with swan-white sails, sipping champagne as their eyes scanned the shore in anticipation of the agreeable diversions that awaited them.

More than any other traveller, it was that renowned pleasure seeker Edward, Prince of Wales, who created the vogue for this resort. During the 1880s and 1890s Edward regularly embarked upon three-week visits, timing his stay for the annual Pre-Lenten Battle of the Flowers at Nice. There, his carriage was bombarded with blossoms – roses and peonies, hyacinths, tulips and freesias – until layers of fragrant petals lay thick upon its roof. Stray blooms lined the corners of the carriage windows and adorned its doors so that the vehicle was quite transformed. No longer a staid conveyance suitable for a future king, it resembled a travelling fairy bower. Prince Edward delighted in the experience. As he proceeded along the parade route he laughed and waved, basking in the energetic approval of the cheering crowds while the vibrant floral tributes continued to fly, arcing their way across a brilliant sky.

The philandering prince chose not to bring Alexandra, his wife of more than two decades, instead enjoying the company of famous actresses and courtesans when not attending to more publicly documented duties such as unveiling monuments and laying cornerstones.

The French Riviera (or *Côte d'Azur* as, since the writer Stéphen Liégeard coined the term in 1887, it was also known) had become the winter destination for, not just the British, but the members of a dozen other royal families. In 1905 King Leopold of the Belgians bought twenty-six hectares on Cap Ferrat, building sumptuous residences for an unholy trinity consisting of himself, his young mistress and his chaplain. Despite opposition from her German Emperor brother who had no love for the French, Princess Charlotte purchased a grand villa at Cannes, La Fôret, where she entertained with enthusiasm.

France's last Empress, the indomitable Eugenie, widow of the deposed Emperor Napoleon III, was also in residence. She occupied a luxurious mansion, Villa Cyrnos, at Cap Martin.

A pride of prowling Teutonic princes indulged in baccarat, roulette and cards, though none matched the Russian grand dukes' voracious appetite for games of chance. They gambled with fierce carelessness. Fortunes were lost and won, and lost again. These extraordinarily rich men (for now, at least) kept their mistresses in Monte Carlo. There, elegant in their homburgs and pin-striped suits, they could be seen strolling down the sea-front promenades with the most beautiful of the *demi-mondaines*. Such pretty women: they wore long, white dresses and large hats trimmed with drifting veils. From behind this filmy protection they regarded their imperial patrons with lovely, knowing eyes.

So marked was the torrent of royalty that the Empress Eugenie herself exclaimed, in a letter to her niece, '*All the crowned heads of Europe are rendezvousing on the Riviera.*'

The dishevelled British Prime Minister Lord Salisbury, enjoying the delights of what he referred to as 'the cottage' (in fact a vast, square villa named La Bastide at Beaulieu), made the more acerbic though nonetheless accurate observation, '*Flies in summer; royalty in winter.*'

The jaded senses of millionaires and kings were roused by captivating performances. In 1913 the Ballets Russes' greatest dancer, Nijinsky, caused a sensation in Cannes with his soaring leap at the conclusion of a performance of *The Afternoon of a Faun*. The following year, in 1914, after Nijinsky had made the unpardonable error of marrying, the impresario Diaghilev's new paramour, the eighteen-year-old Léonide Massine, astounded audiences with his own athletic feats. It was not only dancers who were drawn to the Riviera. The composer Richard Strauss roared in from Munich on his motorbike to see his ballet *The Legend of Joseph* being rehearsed. Famous opera singers such as Feodor Chaliapin and renowned musicians, including the brilliant young pianist Arthur Rubinstein, came to entertain the statesmen, the industrialists and the aristocrats who continued to flock south.

There were also two others – without traditional talents, yet undoubtedly gifted in other less conventional ways, neither born to greatness nor to wealth though adored by many who were – who arrived at this happy, sun-dappled coast. The year was 1914 and, after that, nothing was the same.

THIRTY-FIVE

CAP MARTIN, FEBRUARY 1914

The Empress is old now, so very old. Her head is encircled not by a diadem of diamonds as in her youth but by a cloud of white hair; arthritis cripples her ageing limbs but still she takes the most intense interest in all around her. Eugenie is nearing ninety. She has known terrible grief, burying her beloved only child, his father's heir, when the boy was just twenty-three. Eugenie has watched great states rise and fall. She has ruled an empire only to see her husband, Louis Napoleon, deposed. Escaping France, the country in which once she basked in all the gilded glory that the Second Empire could bestow, she fled to England, into exile. She waited there.

Years passed until her return to France was possible. The Riviera was the perfect place to build an impressive villa in which she could reside. Far from the capital where, even now, her presence might prove a dangerous provocation, she settled on the wooded peninsula of Cap Martin. This is where, in 1892, the imposing Villa Cyrnos was constructed in an Italianate style. The villa's name is ancient Greek for Corsica, that rugged island where the most illustrious of all the Bonapartes was born. It is fortuitously close to her confidante, Madame Ernesta Stern.

Eugenie holds court in her great white mansion, surrounded by elderly retainers and elaborately arranged flowers. Crowned heads, royal dukes and princelings all come to pay her their respects. Even Eugenie's old friend, Queen Victoria, would visit her there during her final years. It was the Queen's top-hatted coachman, a kilted Highlander by his side, who drove the dear sovereign through the high double-crowned gates and on to Eugenie's home. The two monarchs, one past, one present, walked beneath the palms and cypress trees in her pine-scented grounds, the Queen tiny beneath a black parasol, the Empress leaning heavily on her gold-topped cane. They talked of life, though prudently avoided politics. There were lingering goodbyes.

Unlike the late English Queen, Zeno is not invited to call upon the Empress. Eugenie is wary, sceptical for, despite the fact that he has won the approval of the Princess and the Baroness, she has known too many frauds and tricksters in her time to feel quite certain that the Professor should be allowed to breach her privacy. Instead she comes to Torre Clementina to assess him for herself, this man who, although spoken of so warmly by her friends, she still refers to as 'that Japanese'.

The romantic gardens, lovingly designed by Madame Stern's great favourite, the Italian landscape painter Raffaele Mainella, contain a remarkable swooping marble staircase slashed at its core by a terraced waterfall. As Rosetta strolls through Torre Clementina's extensive grounds she sees this curious feature gleaming, white and somehow eerie, despite the clear Mediterranean light. She touches Zeno's arm, about to comment but, seeing he is deep in thought, drops her hand. He looks neither left nor right. They pass stone columns and ancient statuary yet he remains withdrawn, unusually preoccupied. As they continue, it is as if he does not see the rose-entwined pergolas, the terracotta archways or cascading fountains but another world, one to which he alone has access.

In Rosetta's view Torre Clementina, beautiful but strange, is the product of a very rich woman's surfeit of imagination. A mixture of the Gothic, the Venetian and the Byzantine, it looks to her much like an overwrought setting for a self-styled Scheherazade. Despite its fanciful facade, the villa's exterior does little to prepare Rosetta for what lies inside. It is an Aladdin's cave of sorts, a spiritualist's treasure trove.

Wherever Rosetta looks, be it on an ebony table or marble plinth, in an alabaster niche or engraved cabinet, she sees an eruption of arcane artefacts, a testament to her hostess's ecumenical inclinations. Jewel-encrusted Coptic icons jostle ancient Hebrew candelabra on a sideboard. Across the room, a Byzantine crucifix rests in close proximity to an immense bronze Buddha tinged green with time while, grouped together on a desk of ormolu, statues of Gothic saints peer from lidless eyes at Egyptian gods and dancing Hindu divinities. It is a riot of religious reference.

Surrounded by this barbarous confusion, Rosetta sips sweet, strong Turkish coffee. It is served to her beneath a cathedral-like ceiling in the villa's large central room by a young Nubian attendant, his snowy jacket a stark contrast to the dark gleam of his skin. Before her, on a low table, lies a lacquered plate of Arabian sweetmeats; Rosetta inhales their tantalising aroma of honey, almond and cardamom.

Savouring the moment, she reflects upon her first meeting with Zeno – how long ago it seems – in the now distant Antipodes. 'It is this life,' she thinks as she considers her august company, 'that is the destiny he revealed to me.'

Madame Stern interrupts her thoughts. 'Divine, aren't they?' she says, discreetly patting small flakes of golden pastry from the corners of her lips. 'I find these confections quite impossible to resist.'

For the sake of politeness Rosetta takes one, smiles. She plays her part, for like these others she, too, is an experienced consort. Her role is not to rule either kingdom or salon. She charms, keeps Charlotte and Ernesta suitably diverted while her husband is occupied with the Empress in one of the adjoining rooms.

The Princess is addicted to gossip. 'Did you know,' she remarks in her alluring voice, 'they say the very first place Diaghilev took his new little dancer – that beautiful Massine – after his audition was to look at Catherine the Great's paintings in the Hermitage? What is your view of this, Madame Zeno?'

Rosetta, smiling, responds airily, 'As I believe his next stop was the maestro's hotel room, I would say it was the beginning of a rather rapid education.' The grand ladies laugh in appreciation; the Professor's wife is never less than amusing.

For all their sophisticated *sang-froid*, Madame Stern and the Princess have proven to be, in the presence of their beloved Professor, quite overcome. Ernesta is fifty-nine, Charlotte nearly fifty-three, but when in his company they conduct themselves with a coquettish demeanour that belies both their station and their years.

Zeno has spent time with the two women earlier that day. Rosetta does not yet know what has been discussed in these intimate sessions, nor will she enquire. Zeno will reveal these confidences to her in his own time. She assumes, however, by the flushed appearance of the ladies as they have, by turn, emerged from their individual consultations, that at the conclusion of their sessions each has enjoyed one of the Professor's uniquely beneficial massages. They are reputed to transfer psychic energy and are popular with women of a certain age, particularly widows or those with inattentive husbands.

My great-grandmother, Rosetta, known in London as Madame Zeno, c. 1913. By age thirty-three and as stylish as she was arresting, Rosetta had beguiled society both in Europe and Great Britain.

Rosetta holds one of her exquisite tea cups while her nonchalant paramour looks on. Melbourne, c. 1905.

Wonderland City with, among its thrilling attractions, the Switchback Railway (foreground) and an airship perilously suspended above the sea. Tamarama Beach, Sydney, c. 1907. *Waverley Library Local History Image Collection*

Rosetta, pictured at Sydney's Government House with a chauffeur and her splendid Packard limousine, c.1928.

The distinguished Professor Carl Zeno, 'erstwhile of Japan'. In reality, William Norman, son of a Chinese immigrant who came to Australia to work on the goldfields. London, c. 1910.

Rosetta's daughter, my grandmother Frances Catherine Raphael, age two, Melbourne, 1902. Only three years later, her mother ran away.

The aristocratic Lilian Pakenham developed a unique relationship with Zeno and Rosetta. Photographed by T. Humphrey, *Table Talk*, Melbourne, 13 October 1899. *National Library of Australia*

'A figure, white as alabaster, in a dark, sylvan glade.' Zeno is thought to have created this portrait of Rosetta during the early 1930s.

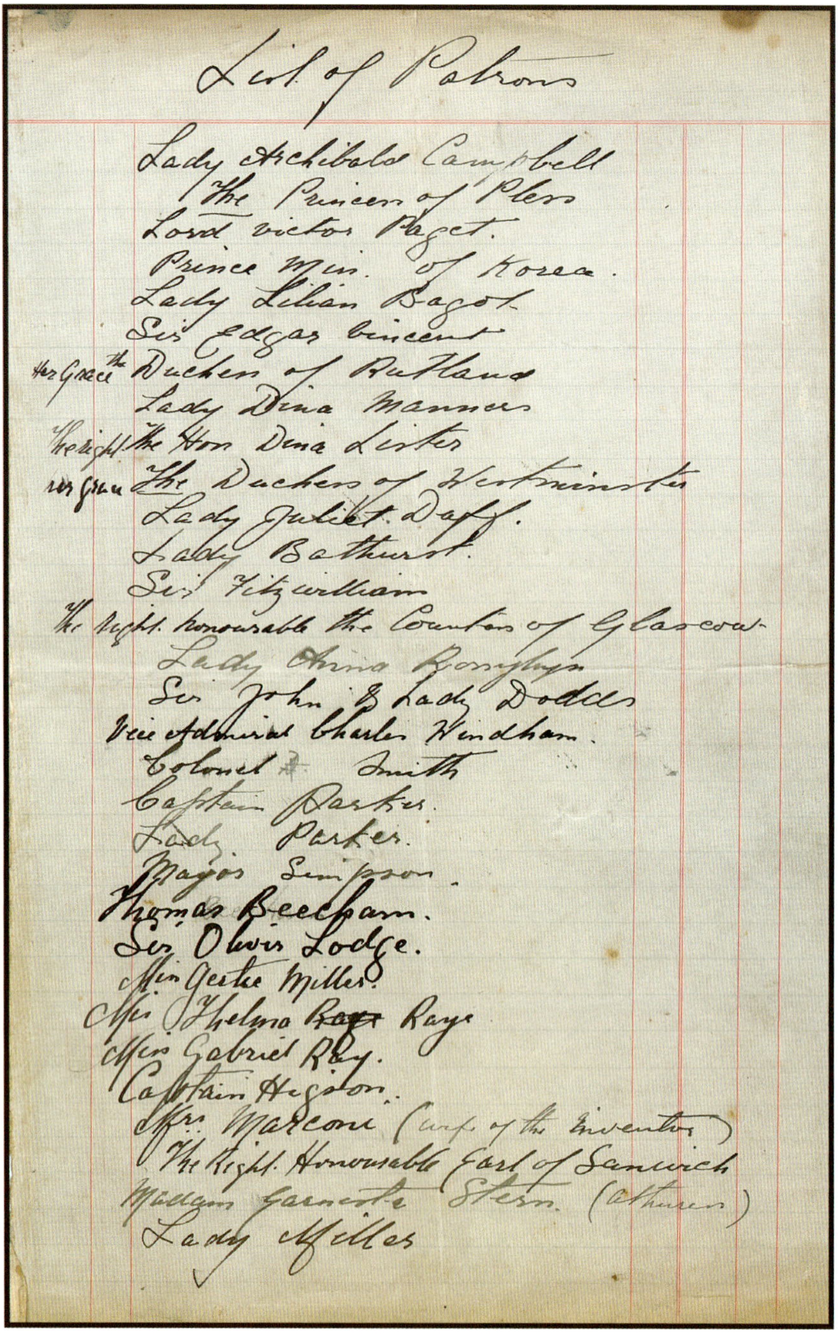
List of Patrons

Lady Archibald Campbell
The Princess of Pless
Lord Victor Paget.
Prince Min. of Korea.
Lady Lilian Bagot.
Sir Edgar Vincent
Her Grace the Duchess of Rutland
Lady Diana Manners
The Right the Hon Diana Lister
Her Grace The Duchess of Westminster
Lady Juliet Duff.
Lady Bathurst.
Sir Fitzwilliam
The Right honourable the Countess of Glascow
Lady Anna Rossylyn
Sir John & Lady Dodds
Vice Admiral Charles Windham.
Colonel P. Smith
Captain Parker.
Lady Parker.
Major Simpson.
Thomas Beecham.
Sir Oliver Lodge.
Miss Gertie Millar.
Miss Thelma ~~Raye~~ Raye
Miss Gabriel Ray.
Captain Hegson.
Mrs Marconi (wife of the inventor)
The Right Honourable Earl of Sandwich
Madame Garnett Stern. (authoress)
Lady Miller

Professor Zeno's astonishing *List of Patrons*.

My parents, Asher and Sybil – later the Hon. Sir Asher and Lady Joel – attending a state banquet held in honour of Queen Elizabeth II, Sydney, 1954. My mother doesn't know she has a grandmother living in the same city.

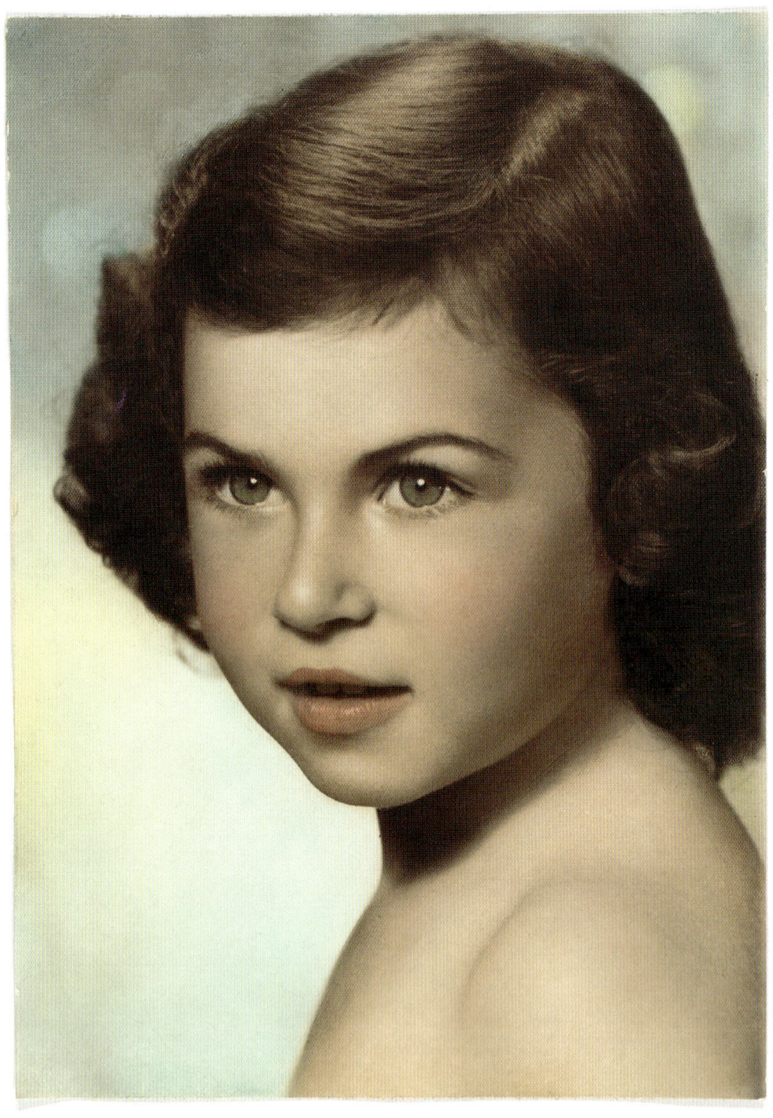

This photograph of me, age five, was taken in 1958. It was the same year that Rosetta, my unknown and unseen great-grandmother, died.

Rosetta has grown used to rank, to majesty. She sees that, beneath the thin distinction of wealth and caste, a person's wants and needs are very much alike. She has learnt that the same terror of the night, the same longing for another's touch, are shared by all humanity. Death is feared and love desired. Absolution for past wrongs is sought. And always, there is that primeval longing for revelation, a key that will unlock the secrets of one's life. Rosetta knows this need well: after all, it is what first drew her to the magician who now sits in seclusion, sharing his visions of the future with an Empress by his side.

Rosetta hears a small, soft sound and looks towards it. It is Eugenie, shuffling across the marble floor in her pale-blue silken slippers, the only footwear that her poor twisted feet can bear. Zeno has been with her for no more than an hour, yet she is obviously exhausted. Princess Charlotte, worried, moves to her old friend's side while Madame Stern rings for a servant, calling, 'Hurry, brandy for the Empress!'

But Eugenie stills them with a single wave of her frail, bejewelled hand.

'My dears, do not concern yourselves about me. It is only that I am very, very tired. The Professor and I have had discussions of the greatest importance.

'This man,' she gestures at Zeno, following behind, 'sees butchery and bloodshed. I may seem old and foolish, but I know much of violence and loss of life. My own dear son was cut down, massacred in Africa during the war between the English and the Zulus.'

The Empress looks even older now, and very pale.

'Already, trouble begins to ferment in half a dozen places. But what do our statesmen do? They make empty gestures, speak in platitudes. The Professor predicts conflagration of a magnitude that we have never seen. He says there will be slaughter and carnage. I wish I did not believe him.'

With the last of her strength Eugenie turns to Zeno and says, 'Professor, I thank you for your revelations. I came here expecting shallow entertainment. But you have paid me the compliment of honesty, something an empress rarely sees. I pray to God the turmoil of your prophecy will never come to pass, but I fear that what you say is true.

'I doubt we will meet again. It seems that circumstances are unlikely to permit this taking place.

'I am retiring to my villa now, to rest and think. Certain people must be warned that there is danger. Whether they will listen … well, I don't imagine that they will.' She sighs deeply, steadies herself.

'Professor, Madame Zeno, travel safely. *Adieu*.'

THIRTY-SIX

I cannot go to Torre Clementina.

This is not because the villa has been destroyed – it remains intact, perched above the azure waters of the Mediterranean at Cap Martin, just as it was a century ago when Rosetta went there with Zeno and exchanged confidences with Baroness Stern, Princess Charlotte and Empress Eugenie. Unfortunately, unlike a number of other, nearby Belle Époque villas, such as the great flamingo-pink mansion at Cap Ferrat that Béatrice Ephrussi de Rothschild donated to the French nation, Torre Clementina is privately owned. Members of the public are not welcome.

Worse, for me at least, the proprietor, Frederick Robinson Koch, is a man described by *Vanity Fair* magazine as 'notoriously private'. Like his three younger brothers, Frederick Koch is an American billionaire. Unlike them, he is not known to be enamoured with conservative political causes – two have famously pledged a billion dollars to support the Republican candidate in the 2016 US presidential election. Frederick seems not to be politically inclined, nor does he seek publicity. Rather, he 'conducts his life as if striving for obscurity'.

Despite this passionate discretion, however, Frederick has a reputation for philanthropy. He is the man who, it was much later revealed, underwrote the multimillion-dollar reconstruction of the Swan Theatre at Shakespeare's Stratford-upon-Avon in 1986. He has endowed the Frick Museum in New York, the Carnegie Institute in Pittsburgh and libraries at Yale and Harvard universities with priceless historic documents. Among them are handwritten scores by Mozart and Schubert, letters by Baudelaire and Proust, poems by Cocteau and Victor Hugo, the drafts of manuscripts by Henry Miller and Oscar Wilde.

Frederick Koch is also known to have extraordinary objects that remain in his possession. There are pictures by Fragonard, fine wood panelling from the palace of Versailles, a bed that the Mayor of Paris gave to Marie Antoinette when she married Louis XVI, a marble head of Antinous that once belonged to his lover, the Emperor Hadrian. Frederick is a discerning, avid collector of stained glass and mosaics, of bronze statuary, of carpets, paintings and tapestries and, most relevant to my preoccupations, of historic properties. He bought Sutton Place in England, the legendary seven-hundred-acre estate where Henry VIII met Anne Boleyn (though now it is in the possession of an oligarch from Russia). He owns an enormous royal hunting lodge in Austria, and the Woolworth mansion in Manhattan. And, since purchasing it from the granddaughter of Ernesta Stern three decades ago, among his stellar accumulation is Torre Clementina.

Discovering who owns the villa has not been difficult. Gaining entry is quite a different matter. Mr Koch has many faithful retainers in his employ. They protect him and his interests with zeal. Layers of security surround him, ensuring the maintenance of not only his personal safety, but his privacy. *Esquire* magazine says that he is 'impossible to contact'. Mr Koch is unreachable.

This is a great disappointment to me. I become possessed with the thought of seeing Torre Clementina, this place which, arguably, represents the pinnacle of my great-grandmother's conquest of a near-Olympian world. For me, it has an almost mythic quality. I desire to inhabit the same rooms, walk in the gardens, stand as Rosetta did when, flanked by a princess and an empress, she sipped Turkish coffee and looked out upon a foreign sea. I can read about the villa's appearance in various accounts, and of course I have the letters, but it is not enough. I dream of being where she has been.

I sit in my garden on a sultry Sydney day and share my discouragement with a dear childhood friend who is visiting from his home in the United States. We are catching up, exchanging the details of our lives, our families. Martin is remarkable. A former Australian academic, he moved to Washington many years ago and became a US citizen. Martin's unique skills and exceptional intellect saw him become Deputy Secretary of State and an American ambassador – the only one, as has often been remarked, with an Australian accent. Martin is on familiar terms with presidents and prime ministers and the princes who rule Middle Eastern kingdoms. Nevertheless, I am surprised when, as we sip lime juice and bite into ripe strawberries, he laughs and says, 'Frederick Koch? I know him.'

It takes a moment or two to absorb this piece of news. Here I am in Sydney, with my old friend who lives in America, and he is telling me that I just might be able to go to this particular, impossible-to-visit French villa. I realise it is a foolish notion but, still, I cannot help believing that, once more, unseen forces may be intervening.

Martin advises me that Frederick Koch is 'old school'. I will have to supply credentials, provide information about myself, my family. There will be an assessment. Naturally, I comply as best I can. Emails are sent. Correspondence flies across the globe. I wait impatiently.

Then Mr Koch writes back and I discover that the margins of possibility have once more been erased. Just like my great-grandmother before me, I, too, have been invited to Torre Clementina. Call it happenstance, coincidence, good fortune – it seems like alchemy.

The villa's permanent staff keep it in a state of perfect readiness. Should its owner make one of his rare visits, he will see trees laden with tangerines and lemons. Rare pink Japanese wisteria and creamy rhododendrons will be in bloom and the bougainvillea, heavy with cerise blossoms, will be flourishing. Mr Koch will find that the pillows on the sun-beds by the swimming pool are plumped, the limestone terraces are swept, the brass taps and handrails and doorknobs gleam. The villa waits for him. Yet, as I walk through its rustic brick and stone portals, I have the distinct feeling that it also waits for me.

Here, at last, I stand in that soaring, central room, the same place in which Rosetta met Empress Eugenie, where she gossiped with Princess Charlotte and nibbled fragrant pastries alongside Baroness Stern. There is now barely a trace of Ernesta's eccentric collection of religious artefacts. They have been replaced by Frederick's exquisite possessions. To divulge the details of these priceless works would be to violate the trust of my absent host. It is enough to say that they are marvellous and of rare quality; I am surrounded by sculpture and furniture and paintings, an array of *objets d'art* that any number of museums would be eager to possess.

As I wander from one object to another, marvelling at these things, I hear an exclamation. It comes from Mark Ryan, the urbane man whom Mr Koch entrusts with the principal care of this unique property and who is accompanying me.

'I have been here for fifteen years and I have never seen that before,' Mark says, excitedly. I follow his gaze, look to see what, among all these treasures, could possibly have attracted his attention.

A single magnificent pheasant has alighted on the vivid green lawn outside. I leave the artfully arranged objects behind and follow Mark out onto the limestone terrace in order to observe it more closely. Beneath the Mediterranean sun the creature's iridescent plumage shines like bronze. Its glossy head, small and elegant, is held at a slight angle; there is a faint movement, a barely palpable pulse, beating in its throat. Its long tail feathers flicker, one wing is unfurled. In this place of memories and spirits, it casts its yellow eyes on me.

THIRTY-SEVEN

LONDON, APRIL 1914

Zeno has not been his usual self of late. He is restless, highly strung. There is a certain wildness in his eyes. Rosetta thinks that, if she had to put a date on it, it would be ever since their return from Cap Martin. But the more she considers, the more she begins to believe that the changes started earlier. Rosetta reflects on the feverish excitement that consumed him on the day he discovered he would be meeting the Empress Eugenie. It was out of character for this most self-contained of men. Now there is the repeated talk of war, the blood-soaked visions that come to him at night. Perhaps it is all the time spent in his laboratory, she thinks, inhaling God knows what poisonous substances shipped in from the East.

His practice is busier than ever. Zeno is at the beck and call of a dozen famous men. And the women; it seems they cannot get enough of him, of his predictions and his medicines, his massages and special treatments. She frowns. The fact is, beneath his carefully groomed exterior, his calm facade, Zeno is a man of restless, burning appetites. As the pressures in his life begin to mount, it has become more difficult to keep his needs confined. More than ever, she worries that he is entangled with a titled woman, a viscount's wife or, worse, a duke's – several possible candidates come to mind – who, if disappointed by his fecklessness, will not hesitate to strike.

It is too much; it is frenetic. The work, the intimate encounters, the dinners and the entertaining and, always, the constant need to ensure that their true identities remain buried, the ever-present requirement to sustain this new, distinguished life. Zeno has reached so high and yet he seems to want to soar higher still. Like Icarus, he tempts fate. His wings may singe and burn.

Rosetta knows that if Zeno falls she will plummet with him. She must prevent this catastrophe from happening at any cost. Retribution will be swift and bitter. She does not shrink from divine judgement; the kind that humans pass is terrible enough. Rosetta is well aware that she is vulnerable. She carries with her the awful sin, desertion of her flesh and blood, hidden in her heart.

She shakes herself. The iron shutter that has allowed her to come this far is put back in its place. She will not dwell on what is over, past. Her mind turns instead to the only person in England, apart from her husband, for whom she cares deeply. Now that Helena Rubinstein is spending so much time building her cosmetic empire in other parts of the world, there is just one soul with whom Rosetta and Zeno can relax their guard, who knows both who they really are and from where they come: Lilian Pakenham. But Rosetta is troubled about her, too, her deep unhappiness. Lilian has a loveless marriage to a soldier politician from whom she dreams only of escape.

Not quite an idea, but the merest whisper of a notion begins to spin a web of possibility. Rosetta is secure. Her husband worships her. But she knows he likes … variety. Perhaps, perhaps, why not? Lilian and Zeno are already very close. He talks with her in a way he does no other woman. Strangely, despite Lilian's blonde beauty, the rounded figure Rosetta has noticed other men admire, she has never detected in her husband the smallest sign of attraction for her friend. She supposes Zeno must have lines that even he will not cross. He knows that Lilian and Rosetta share a passionate friendship: he will not wound his wife. But if Rosetta were to give such a liaison her blessing – no, what is she thinking?

She busies herself with orders and accounts. But her attention wanders. She makes small arithmetical mistakes. Distracted, Rosetta lets her pencil drop. She decides instead to walk in Hyde Park. The early spring has brought a haze of new green leaves to trees whose branches were bare a week ago, and jonquil buds push through fresh grass. As she walks, her light coat wrapped about her, Rosetta finds herself returning to her earlier thoughts. Somehow, the idea does not seem so very shocking now. Zeno could make Lilian happy. She knows her friend has always found her husband to be attractive; what woman does not?

Rosetta is struck by how simple, indeed, how useful a suitable arrangement between the three of them would be. Her friend would receive the attention she deserves and the risks attached to Zeno's aristocratic dalliances might be reduced. And Lilian will keep their secrets. They will be safe with her.

While Rosetta starts her journey homeward, still pondering this unconventional strategy, Zeno, at his desk in New Bond Street, is opening yet another letter. Princess Charlotte is in near constant contact; she has one matter that dominates her thoughts. When will her father-in-law, the Grand Duke, die? It is an issue that consumes her day and night.

At seventeen, on an unusually mild Berlin day in February 1878, Charlotte married her brother's scholarly friend, the Hereditary Prince his Highness, Bernhard, Duke of Saxe-Meiningen. Soon after, she became the leader of Berlin society, or at least that part of it regarded as smart, dissolute. Widely celebrated for her style and wit, she bought clothes only from Paris, smoked and drank, spread gossip and made outrageous comments. There were intrigues; scandalous rumours of wild promiscuity began to circulate. Although in the words of her cousin, Queen Marie of Romania, Charlotte 'could have disarmed an ogre', and each of her cat-like movements resembled 'a caress', these attributes failed to impress her brother, Kaiser Wilhelm. Instead, with Charlotte under something of a cloud, in 1892 he insisted that she and Bernhard vacate Berlin.

The couple have remained more or less in exile in the dreary German town of Breslau ever since. It is little wonder that in 1898 Charlotte built her Cannes villa, La Fôret. But life on the Riviera provides only diversion: it cannot satisfy Charlotte's ambition.

The strained relations with her Emperor brother mean that, although as a Princess of Prussia she receives an income, it is insufficient, at least in her opinion. Until Bernhard can succeed his father, Georg II of Saxe-Meiningen, the royal couple must endure relative impoverishment and, what is worse, a status that is annoyingly inconsequential.

To Charlotte's regret, and despite her long-felt anticipation, Georg II has declined to pass away. Exasperated, she is of the opinion that, due to her royal father-in-law's stubborn determination to remain alive, her husband has been denied his rightful inheritance. It is, then, with a sense of some desperation, that she has turned to the only man she feels certain is able to expedite the matter, who can bring it to a rapid, ardently wished for, irrevocable conclusion.

Professor Zeno advises Charlotte to be calm. He holds her hand and says in his most soothing tone, 'Patience, my dear Princess. I see his death. It is not far away.'

It is too distant for Charlotte. That the principality of Saxe-Meiningen is one of the smallest of the states that make up the confederation of the German Empire is unimportant. She has been a princess long enough. Now she desires a throne.

THIRTY-EIGHT

Charlotte's letters chart her European peregrinations; she writes from half a dozen salubrious resorts and palaces. I read each one, see her hunger, and think of what it must have been like for Zeno to be the recipient of this singular woman's innermost hopes and dreams. It is all there, captured for eternity in her peculiar, glyphic handwriting; Charlotte's frustration and despair, her appalling longing for the ageing Duke's demise.

Cannes,
4 April 1914

I feel sure that the Duke's death must be close at hand for I found him so feeble, shrunk and low spirited that he cannot last much longer … It was most pathetic watching him on Thursday, his 88th birthday …

I have faith in your transmissions, therefore I hope for the best, and should the long wished death occur soon, I shall let you know of it at once.

Grand Hotel Frankfurter-Hof,
Frankfurt,
16 April

The Duke has stood his journey to Italy wonderfully well and fear!? 'the hovering death' can't mean him, as I so hoped for.

Hotel Marienbad,
Munich,
26 April 1914

I am so grateful to you for sending your thoughts all the stronger for the Force and Strength you wish me to possess; in time they must be of some avail and help to undo the rejuvenating of the old gentleman … the obstinacy beyond belief!

In the midst of Charlotte's bulletins there is another crisis. Ernesta sends an urgent telegram from Cap Martin.

> PLEASE DEAR FRIEND DO TELEGRAPH TO PRINCE DANILO CETINJE MONTENEGRO GIVING HIM COURAGE PRINCESS WORSE

Charlotte, too, mentions the Princess Jutta, Duchess of Mecklenburg, in her letter of April the 26th.

I wonder what's up with her! Is not something wrong with her inside, or has she had some mental shock?

Next there is a cable from the dashing, moustachioed Crown Prince of Montenegro himself. Despite an international reputation for profligate womanising, the playboy prince is desperately concerned about his wife.

I AM AT JENA AND THE PRINCESS HERE IN A SANATORIUM I BEG YOU TO THINK OF US KINDEST REGARDS DANILO

It is little wonder that Zeno is disturbed. In constant demand by a litter of troubled individuals upon whose heads rest so many European crowns, he feels besieged on all sides. Now he is expected to save the life of one royal personage while, at the same time, hastening another towards an untimely end.

If this were not enough cause for consternation, it is at this point Charlotte's letters begin to delve into international matters of concern.

The wars and bloodshed in Mexico looks very bad and [I] don't see any way out of this stupidly managed affair.

Then, after her signature, comes the intriguing line: '*Did you see anything of the King and Queen since their French visit?*'

I am not sure to which King and Queen Charlotte is referring. So many spring to mind; perhaps her brother-in-law Constantine and sister Sophie, the King and Queen of Greece, or possibly her cousins, King George and Queen Mary of Great Britain. It is not important. What strikes me most is the casual assumption this chatty postscript contains. These days, it appears that mixing in royal circles is, for Rosetta and Zeno, so unexceptional that the Emperor's sister regards it as barely worth remarking upon.

Charlotte's correspondence now begins to move in disconcerting, rapid fashion between the domestic drama of the ailing Duke's battle to stave off death and a much larger stage: the tumultuous conflicts beginning to erupt among nations.

Hotel Marienbad,
Munich,
9 May 1914

> *The papers (of last night) brought bad news about the old Duke, and wish they were true, but my husband and self have heard nothing direct as usual, and feel he is pulling through once more. Can you see or feel anything? If so do tell me.*

Charlotte emerges from her preoccupation with the Duke's unwanted recovery to make the observation:

> *Politics look bad and strained, specially Albania! And feel as if serious trouble between Austria and Italy is growing!! And Russia as usual playing fool game.*

Zeno responds. He counsels forbearance. What else can he do? Charlotte is the least of his worries. He sleeps little, continues to be disturbed by the dreams that fill his mind once his eyes are closed, the ghastly images that even the small grains of opium he has begun to take do little to dispel.

> *Meiningen,*
> *20 May 1914*

> *Concerning the Duke, I wish indeed you were right; he arrives here on 29th, and [I] shall try again for another spell of patience, 'sweet patience' as you say, and 'it cannot be long'.*

Charlotte is writing from the royal family's estate. She complains that she is:

> *. . . surrounded by daily, never-ending worries and intrigues of all sorts and conditions. Lies I cannot clear or shake off. The enemies you felt months ago, with their tormenture and jealousy, are indeed a tidal wave, and don't feel getting ahead of it all; and these devilish creatures are beyond my comprehension! The Chinese method of killing enemies is charming!!! Pity we can't introduce it here.*

Politics, specially Albania, Austria and Italy's vile intrigues, look more grave than the powers seem to like to believe in; Albania is Mexico over again: bloodshed all round! And the Diplomats all more or less blind idiots.

Charlotte leaves Meiningen, its torments and intrigues, to return to the south of France.

Villa La Fôret,
Cannes,
3 June 1914

I saw the old Duke yesterday, found him feeble and aged . . .

Then the Princess writes:

. . . can't trust those Balkan states and the Albanian case is a hopeless one, in my eyes, and my nephew won't be lucky!

Charlotte is right. As events unfold, the future will hold little for her brother's son, Germany's young Crown Prince.

Grosses Palais,
Meiningen,
7 June 1914

I've seen the old Duke who looks very bad indeed, so small, shrunk, weak and pale, legs and feet swollen and such spasms at night, kept down by strong morphia injections. A few days ago I really thought at last the end had come: but tomorrow they drag the old gent to a watering place where a Dr. and friend of his promises to cure him! To me he looks like a dying man! What do you think? Or see and feel?

Again, politics intrude.

> *I'm looking forward to the big mess in Albania I'm expecting all along; Austria and Italy must have some fight as both are behaving badly and lying right and left.*

> *Meiningen,*
> *13 June 1914*

> *It seems too good to be true your saying 'cheer up, your dream will soon be realised': if it could but be so soon: matters stand too badly here and my husband gets more nervous and bitter daily . . .*
>
> *. . . fate is hard often and my husband is now the oldest of the whole generation, and the only one not reigning!! So use all your forces!!*

I imagine Zeno, turning to Rosetta with vexation, exclaiming, 'What exactly does she want me to do? "*Use all your forces*", she says – what, to cast a spell, to murder the old man by witchcraft? Is that what she wants?' Where once he might have smiled at the Princess's folly, now he is dismayed.

Then Charlotte remarks:

> *The terrible unrest of the whole world I quite see: but not that every country and city are threatened with danger . . . your tragic picture must be as true as you feel it by intuition I've learnt to believe in. Fire and slaughter daily take place already and Albania is closely nearing it now!*

The visions that he described at Torre Clementina in March, the same unwanted visions that visit him at night; Zeno cannot explain how it is that they come to him, but he believes what Charlotte still cannot accept. The world they know will be consumed by flames.

Meiningen,
22 June 1914

We are living in a terrible unrest ... Europe <u>must</u> fear danger in consequence arising between Austria and Italy, as they <u>misuse</u> my stupid nephew to profit by him. The idea of driving Albanians into submission is totally wrong and useless, and trust Germany will keep her fingers <u>out</u> of this mess: let <u>them</u> settle their things rightly themselves, as ... they can never become civilised.

Turkey and Greece are calming down again, and their warlike ideas seem too childish and wicked; bloodshed means nothing to them, but the unrest everywhere seems to continue.

On 25 June, the longed-for death has come: Charlotte's next letter is edged in a wide band of black. At last she has what she wants.

Meiningen,
1 July 1914

Now that the worst days are over the wretched, unkind, squabbling, fighting family have left, I am capable of thanking you so much ... Remembering what you said, I knew you would extend your thoughts and forces in my direction and help to overcome all the overwhelming difficulties ...

Next Charlotte refers to another death, about which, amazingly, Zeno appears to have warned her. This event will not have anything to do with natural causes. Its consequences will prove both grave and unimaginable.

The murder of the Austrian heir presumptive did <u>not</u> astonish me, after what you said ...

... and cruel as it may sound, it's a <u>blessing</u>, and may save Austria and <u>us</u> from war: 2 wicked, intriguing, false people less: but what will be next?

The first domino has fallen. The murder does not save anyone.

Archduke Franz Ferdinand, heir presumptive to the Austro-Hungarian throne, was killed by Gavrilo Princip, nineteen, in the Bosnian town of Sarajevo. On 28 June, this hitherto unknown, unremarkable young man was one of a group of assassins organised and armed by the Black Hand, a secret society devoted to Serbian unification. The Black Hand tried to kill the Archduke and his wife Sophie earlier that day but blundered. The bomb that had been thrown bounced off the archducal car.

Princip did not expect to see his quarry again. Quite by chance he was sitting in a cafe, gloomily contemplating this failure, when to his surprise he caught sight of the distinctive pale-green feathers of Franz Ferdinand's helmet only metres away. This was entirely unexpected; it seems the royal chauffeur had taken a wrong turning. The Black Hand would not miss its chance again. Princip walked over to the near-stationary car. He raised his pistol and shot twice. Within minutes the heir to the Austro-Hungarian throne and his wife were dead.

I wish I knew exactly what it was that Zeno said to Charlotte, the words that led her to respond to this murderous news without surprise.

As to her query '*what will be next?*', opinions varied. The day after Charlotte posed this question, the Austrian newspaper *Neue Freie Press* pronounced, 'The political consequences of this act are being greatly exaggerated.' Zeno did not share this optimistic view. He believed that evil would ensue.

Charlotte's final letter has another thick black border. It has been written just ten days after her brother, Kaiser Wilhelm, promises German support for Austria's revenge against the Serbian outrage.

Grosses Palais,
Meiningen, 1
5 July 1914

I am sorely disappointed to think you may not be able to come in 3 weeks time . . . I do so hope that your patients and work will be less and enable you after all to come, if but for a few days! Do try your best and come to give me strength for future happiness and life . . .

Despite Charlotte's pleas, Zeno will not come. Patients and work are but a ruse: he has no intention of leaving for Europe in three weeks' time. Indeed, he will not visit Paris, or the Riviera, and certainly not the palaces of Germany, for many years ahead.

On 28 July, Austria formally declares war on Serbia. This brings Russia into play.

In England, the *Daily Mail*'s headline of 31 July shouts 'Europe Drifting to Disaster'.

On 1 August, Germany declares war on its vast eastern neighbour. The following day, fifteen thousand people gather in London's Trafalgar Square. They stand in driving rain and call upon the British government to avoid entering the conflict. 'Think what war will cost!' their banners say.

The Cabinet is still grappling with its response. It is a 'moving situation', Britain's Lord Chancellor, Lord Haldane, remarks, 'like a huge cinematograph show, seen through a mist'.

Each day there is a new announcement. On 3 August, Germany declares war on France. The following day, its army invades neutral Belgium.

Britain can delay no longer. Alliances are invoked. At 7.00 pm the Prime Minister, Herbert Asquith, delivers a solemn statement to the House of Commons. An ultimatum is sent to Germany: withdraw your troops.

At 11.00 pm the ultimatum expires. Great Britain is at war. Kaiser Wilhelm II and his subjects are the enemy.

There will be no more letters from Charlotte.

THIRTY-NINE

LONDON, SEPTEMBER 1914

The two women are in Lilian's dressing room, trying on the purchases they have made for the new season. As they are quite alone they play at being ladies' maids, hooking up each other's delectable silken gowns of emerald and scarlet, sapphire and rose; it is an intimate indulgence. Lilian and Rosetta stand before the long double-sided mirror, admiring the images they see. They turn this way and that and, as they do so, exchange confidences. It is what women will do in circumstances like this.

Lilian bemoans her empty marriage. 'But what is my solution?' she laments, adding that she has no wish to participate in the casual arrangements so many bored, married women of her acquaintance make with the equally jaded men of their aristocratic set.

'Creeping down cold corridors on country house weekends … Rosetta, that is not for me!'

'Darling, stop. If we are going to talk about this properly you need to feel much more comfortable than this.'

Lilian stands, compliant, as Rosetta undoes the last dress, letting it fall around her friend in a shimmering heap. Next she unlaces Lilian's corset. The other woman remains motionless as Rosetta removes her fragile drawers. She has never seen her friend completely naked before. Really, she is terribly enticing. What is wrong with Arthur Pakenham?

Rosetta reaches forward and, as she does, allows the tips of her fingers to graze Lilian's breasts. Impulsively, she pinches each rosy nipple hard, feels them rise and stiffen.

Lilian tenses. Then, languidly, she stretches her arms out wide. A tiny shiver runs through her before she drops them back to her side. 'That was rather nice.' She smiles. 'If only Arthur would touch me like that.'

'What a cold fish that man is,' Rosetta says as she reaches for Lilian's loose white satin robe. 'Look, put this on and we'll sit on the chaise longue. I have an idea.'

'But are you sure, Rosie, really sure?' Lilian's blue eyes are open wide. 'You say that you won't mind. But how will you feel afterwards?'

'I will feel safe. Frankly, I will be thankful that I know where Zeno is. Most important, I will be relieved that the person with whom he is spending time is someone I trust above anybody else.'

Lilian looks a little flushed. Rosetta kisses her on the cheek.

'You both care for each other. Yes, it has never been in that particular way. But it could be. Dearest Lilian, just let him give you the pleasure that I know you need. All I ask is that you do not speak of it to anyone. Oh, and there is no need to speak of it to me.' Rising smoothly to her feet, she moves towards the brass bell on the wall beside the marble mantelpiece. 'Now, let us call for tea.'

Rosetta waits until late on Sunday afternoon. She and Zeno have returned to their mansion flat in exclusive Portman Square after a pleasant visit to that nearby temple of British culture, the Royal Academy in Piccadilly. Here, several happy hours have been whiled away, viewing a procession of commanding portraits by Gainsborough and Reynolds, some of Constable's bucolic landscapes and a number of J.M.W. Turner's more turbulent canvases. Zeno's interest in painting is as strong as ever. Sometimes he speaks of his wish to stop his ceaseless work and devote himself to art. 'One day,' he says, 'I really think I will.'

This particular Sunday has about it a warm, dreamy quality that makes it difficult for Zeno and Rosetta to believe they live in an era of such bloodshed and disarray. On a day like this, only the sight of so many khaki-clad men in the streets and tranquil parks signifies that dreadful things are taking place just across the Channel, that alarmingly narrow stretch of sea.

Once home, Rosetta wonders if she should make a pot of Lapsang Souchong tea but, on reflection, decides perhaps a fine malt whiskey might induce a more persuasive atmosphere. She begins to speak cautiously, does not make her intention clear. There is no reference to her fears, no mention of any liaisons in which Zeno might currently be involved. She speaks only of their vulnerability, observes that in these uncertain times there must be nothing in their behaviour that might lead them to be compromised.

'We have done well here,' Rosetta says to her husband. 'But despite your powers of prophecy,' she smiles, 'we don't know for how long this can continue. I am worried we might overreach ourselves. Oh, they can't seem to have enough of us now, but we must not forget that society is fickle. You have said it yourself. It will not last.'

Zeno, an intensely percipient man by nature, is on this occasion puzzled as to the direction that Rosetta's train of thought is taking.

'And there's the war,' she continues, adding, 'you are an admirer of Mr Churchill: for months now you have been reading what he's said in the Parliament and even heard him speak. In fact, sometimes I think it is Mr Churchill's incessant thundering that has been responsible for you imagining such gruesome things.

'Anyway, you both seem to think that this talk of the fighting being over in a few weeks or months is nonsense. Well, you have convinced me that you and he are right.'

Rosetta adds more whiskey to Zeno's crystal glass.

Then she speaks of Lilian, of how lonely and neglected her dear friend feels. 'All that Arthur Pakenham seems interested in is politics and soldiering,' she says. 'Do you know, Lilian told me she thinks he was secretly delighted that war broke out? He went straight away to Ulster, raised the 11th Royal Irish Rifles and took himself and his loyal Ulstermen off to fight on the Western Front. She'll never see him now, and I don't think she cares. Poor Lilian.'

'Yes, indeed,' Zeno says. He sips his drink and frowns, glances at his wife. 'You know how fond of her I am. It's a pity there's nothing I can do to help.'

'I think there is,' Rosetta replies. She looks into her husband's panther eyes. 'Go to her.'

Zeno is taken by surprise. 'And?'

'Make her happy, do those things you know how to do best.'

'Rose, you don't mean . . . ?'

'I do. I have always found her beautiful. After all this time you can hardly have failed to notice her appeal. It is what I want for her, for all of us.'

Zeno places his glass onto a side table with a slow deliberation that belies the impact of his wife's unexpected statement. 'Rosetta, really, you are the most astonishing woman. I never dreamt you would suggest such a thing.'

Rosetta takes a breath. 'I won't say more. Only this. I do not need to know when. I do not want you to speak about it. Only – go to her. I have already talked it over with Lilian. She is uncertain.'

'Well, if that is the case . . .'

'You will ensure she has no doubts.'

FORTY

AUSTRALIA, AUGUST 1914

The nation, obedient and united, follows Britain. Prime Minister Joseph Cook vows, 'If the Armageddon is to come, then you and I shall be in it ... if the old country is at war, so are we.' He makes a pledge to place the Commonwealth's vessels under the control of the British Admiralty and offers an initial force of twenty thousand men. He does not imagine that during the next four years four-hundred thousand more will serve; that sixty thousand of these soldiers will die on foreign soil so very far from home.

The response of Mr Andrew Fisher, Leader of the Opposition, is equally enthusiastic. Fisher declares that Australia will stand beside the Mother Country 'to the last man and the last shilling'. The statement strikes a resonant chord, wins him great support. By September this lion of the Labor Party is, for the third time, leading the government.

In Melbourne, two young men join the crowds that gather in the streets to sing patriotic songs. They are brothers. The elder, Hubert

Jacobs, is an honours graduate from an exclusive school, Wesley College. He is also *aide-de-camp* to Victoria's Lieutenant-Governor and in possession of a university scholarship. Though still a medical student, he is sent to Gallipoli in early 1915 where he does his best for soldiers who are wounded and dying. Frederick, four years younger than his brother, is eighteen when war breaks out. At twenty he enlists. He is not quite so talented as Hubert but a great deal more interested in the ladies. He sets sail for France.

One day Fred Jacobs will meet Rosetta's daughter, Frances Raphael, and make her his unhappy wife. One day they will have a child, my mother. Yet, lacking Zeno's professed powers to see into the future, neither can know that this will happen.

Frances remains at the convent, far from war, safe. In their small, closed world the girls speak French at breakfast overseen by the Paris-born Mère Angèle. They receive thin bread and butter and an apple. Frances knows she must cut and peel the fruit in the proper fashion, eat it with a knife and fork. Surprisingly, after this meagre meal, the girls are served good coffee. It is an indication of the nuns' French heritage.

There are not quite forty boarders at the school. Frances is well aware of the number because the girls are promised a holiday when the fortieth is enrolled. The holiday never comes. Perhaps it is the war.

At seven o'clock each morning Genazzano's students attend mass. There they are instructed to pray for the holy sisters and the children who suffer in the distant convents of Belgium and France. How fortunate they are to be so far away from bloodshed: the nuns remind them frequently. The girls are taught to knit khaki socks for the soldiers. Some organise raffles or plan small concerts to raise money. They try to do their bit.

There are dreadful days when the newspapers' black-edged casualty lists contain a name that one of the girls recognises.

Louis Raphael has not gone to war. He is too old. But many girls have fathers or brothers who have left to fight. Nobody knows when, or even if, they will return. The nuns counsel prayer; they must keep their hopes alive.

Frances doesn't understand this hoping. She learnt a long time ago to put hope aside.

FORTY-ONE

LONDON, OCTOBER 1914

The threat, when it arrives, comes not from a duchess but from a half-forgotten girl who has emerged from the shadows of the past.

'I suppose you don't remember me, do you?' she says.

It is late in the day and Zeno has left for his laboratory. The girl has just strolled through the waiting-room door in a manner that Rosetta's mother, Fanny, if she were there, would declare to be 'as bold as brass'. The girl is addressing Rosetta who, taken by surprise, looks at her quizzically from behind her pretty walnut desk.

'Let me explain. I used to work at Wonderland, one of the chorus girls Mr Anderson employed. I don't believe we ever met,' she says, a smirk upon her lips. 'Oh, there was one occasion when we got close to it, but you were in, well, let's say, something of a hurry at the time.

'You never really noticed me, did you?' The girl pauses, theatrically. 'But your husband did.

'My name's Mildred, by the way. I'm known as Marguerite these days – it's a lot more posh, you see. It was easy to make the change. But then you'd know more about that business than me.'

Rosetta realises, with rising consternation, exactly who has stepped back into her life. The memory remains, of the Palace of Illusions, of her husband in the half light embracing a figure wrapped in silver spangles ... Rosetta never saw the girl's face but recognises something in her posture, the way she arranges her limbs. Yes, she knows exactly who this intruder is.

Mildred is a pretty girl, even though her heavily applied powder has failed to hide her ginger freckles, and her thick, curly hair looks to Rosetta an unnatural shade of platinum. She has dressed up for the occasion; Rosetta observes her stylish suit, notes that here, too, something strikes a jarring note. 'Probably second-hand,' she thinks. 'Well cut, but obviously made for someone else.' Her eyes travel to the girl's shoes, a little worn, a little dusty. One of them is scarred by a scratch across the toe. 'She's fallen on hard times,' Rosetta thinks. 'This can only mean trouble.'

Then she speaks. 'Mildred.' Determined to regain the upper hand, Rosetta's brisk delivery masks the anxiety she feels. 'Exactly what is it that you want?'

'It is not a matter of what I *want*,' Mildred responds tartly, with a vermilion smile. 'It's really all about what you and your husband *need*.'

'Really? I can't imagine anything you have that either of us could possibly require.'

'Oh, but that's where you're wrong, Mrs Zeno. I do. Let's just call it ... protection, security.'

Rosetta's heart is thudding, but she remains absolutely still. She will not let Mildred see the rising panic that she feels.

'It's very simple, really. I came over here to find my fortune, thought I'd make a splash in one of the big shows. But it hasn't turned out quite as easy as I thought it'd be. I used nearly every penny I had to get here and now, as the Americans would say, I'm flat broke.

'You and Zeno, however, seem to have had some luck. Oh, I've hung about outside. I've seen the toffs line up.'

Rosetta, silent, waits.

'I read the illustrated papers every chance I've got. I can spot a title when I see one. The Duchess of Rutland, Lady Diana, the Countess of Glasgow and the rest of them. They all come here, don't they?

'Why, you must be making money hand over fist.'

Rosetta breaks her silence, though retains her cool hauteur. 'Mildred, perhaps you would be so good as to come to the point. I repeat, what exactly is it that you want?'

'I think you know, Mrs Zeno. But let me spell it out. It's simple, really. I want money and unless you give it to me, all this,' she gestures at the elegant room, the Persian rug, the delphiniums in their porcelain vase, 'will be gone. It'll disappear, a bit like ... yes, that's it,' she laughs, snaps her fingers. 'Like in a magic trick.

'I'll tell the papers who you two really are and where you're from. Just imagine the scandal! Wait till all your fancy patients find out. Ooh, I'd love to see their faces when they discover that their wonderful Japanese Professor is just a shabby little fairground fake who's been putting on a show.' Mildred laughs again; the sound is shrill and sharp.

Despite her fear, Rosetta maintains her composure. She knows what she must do.

'Mildred, my dear,' she smiles sweetly, 'I quite see what you mean. Life in London can be so expensive and I'm sure neither of us would want you to go without.

'Only we need to discuss this a little further, to decide on what is the best arrangement we can come to. Now, for the time being, as a demonstration of good faith, do you think that five pounds would do?'

Slowly, she counts out each note on the table. Mildred eyes the money, runs a pink, hungry tongue along her painted lips.

'And perhaps something to brighten up that lovely suit you are wearing?'

Rosetta unpins a small ruby and pearl brooch from her lapel, picks up the money and places both into Mildred's outstretched hand.

'Take this as well. I am quite certain that we can enter into a suitable agreement, but I really can't discuss it here; a patient might call in. Do you know the Gardenia Tea Rooms? They are not far away. Go there now and I'll meet you, just as soon as I can get away. I'll not be long.'

Rosetta watches Mildred leave, waits five minutes, then five minutes more. She strews the contents of her reticule across the floor, then pulls at the collar of her coat until it tears. Finally, she takes a pair of scissors from the drawer, leaves their gleaming blades open on the desk. Satisfied, she departs. Once outside the New Bond Street rooms, Rosetta walks a little way, then turns left. Yes, he is in his usual spot, close to the smart barber's shop.

Rosetta runs towards the thick-set policeman and, breathless, but with her most enchanting smile, cries out, 'Oh, I'm so very glad to see you, Constable Hall!'

He tips his tall hat. Mrs Zeno is a favourite of his; she and the Professor never fail to show their appreciation for keeping this expensive neighbourhood so safe. There is always a ham at Christmas for him and Mrs Hall. She's a good-looking woman too, a real stunner. Hall wonders what is wrong.

'Constable, a terrifying young woman just forced her way into the Professor's consulting rooms. I was there alone. She took money from my reticule and look –' Rosetta points towards her coat – 'she tore off my pearl and ruby brooch. She had sharp steel scissors – she threatened to cut my throat!

'Do hurry, Constable. She was raving; quite mad, you know.

'I was too frightened to follow. But I was able to watch her from the window. I think she went in the direction of the Gardenia Tea Rooms. Perhaps if you're quick, you'll catch her there now.'

As Constable Hall sets off at a clip Rosetta breathes a deep sigh. She has been lucky this time. But she knows it is a sign. Life cannot continue as it has been. Something is bound to come out soon. And what with Britain and Germany at war, and Zeno close to breaking point . . .

'We are on the wrong side of the world,' she thinks. 'It is time to go home.'

FORTY-TWO

NOVEMBER 1914

There are hurried goodbyes, frantic packing, a passage booked, a long sea voyage to be made. The many distinguished friends and patrons of Professor and Mrs Carl Zeno are very sorry to see them leave. Members of various royal families, a legion of lords and ladies and a number of outstanding representatives from the worlds of arts, letters and science all express their disappointment. Some of Professor Zeno's female patients shed tears. But in these most uncertain times, well, of course it is understood that, though the loss will be very great, the Professor and his wife must do what they think best. Mrs Zeno has relatives in distant Australia; it is only natural that she wishes to join them.

It is Lilian who suffers most. Rosetta says, 'Darling, you could come with us. We both want you to. Why not?' But her dearest friend is anxious and confused. She feels torn in two. There are her children. It is complicated.

~

The day before their ocean liner will set sail, Rosetta pays a final call. There is one matter to which she must attend that has so far remained undone.

She takes a cab from Portman Square to a smart Belgravia address. It is a white Georgian townhouse fortuitously located in a discreet side street. Rosetta had planned to wear her chic new navy Lucile suit, indeed, was already dressed when, suddenly, she changed her mind. Now, beneath her sombre coat, she wears a crimson garment that is considerably less restrained.

It is a dress in which to take a risk, a dress that can induce recklessness. Rosetta thinks of the last time she wore it, on Tamarama Beach, though so much has happened since then that the moonlit night seems less a recollection, more like an enchanting dream.

Rosetta knocks with her black suede-gloved hand upon the oak door. She hesitates. The person she has come to say goodbye to is probably not home. The wisest course would be to turn around and go.

Unexpectedly, the door swings open. 'Madame Zeno!' the striking young man before her exclaims. 'But I had no idea! Please, come in. Let me take your coat.'

It is clear that Alberto has not been expecting company. There are no servants and he looks unusually disordered in his attire. He is without either his jacket or a tie, and his high-collared shirt is unbuttoned and awry. She can see his throat, the outline of the muscles on his chest.

'I must apologise for the state of my undress.' He smiles ruefully. 'As you can see, I am leaving soon and have been busy sorting out my paintings and my books.'

'Alberto, really?' Rosetta's response is accompanied by a look of bemusement. 'And you didn't think to tell me? I am intrigued.'

He pushes back a lock of black hair, an expression of contrition on his handsome face. 'I am sorry I have caught you – what is it that you say? Yes, unawares. But everything has happened so suddenly,' he explains.

'With war declared, there is a great demand for wheat and beef. My father needs my assistance to run our estates in Argentina. I must return immediately.'

Alberto gestures with his hand. 'Everything I own is currently on the high seas, and I will soon set sail as well. All I have is a bed to sleep on and what little you see here.'

The only furniture remaining consists of two simple chairs and a small ebony table on which there is a gramophone. A record plays. It fills the bare room with music that Rosetta has come to know well. Pulsating, driving, it is unmistakably from the *barrios* of the Argentine.

'There is another reason I have to return. I am marrying.'

Rosetta looks up sharply.

'Yes, I see you are surprised. I am a little myself. Perhaps it was your husband's vision that changed my mind,' Alberto says with a droll look.

'The fact is, it is my father's wish. I have known Maria Louisa since I was a child. She is from a well-placed family. It is, what you would call, a very suitable alliance.' He shrugs his shoulders, gives an exaggerated sigh.

'In any case, there is only one woman I truly desire. Let me describe her to you. She is very beautiful, has hair the colour of the darkest wine and at the moment, she is looking quite enchanting in a very pretty red dress. Unfortunately, she has continued to reject me. What can I do?'

Alberto's stay in London has done nothing to lessen his easy charm.

'But I am forgetting myself. We can at least sit down. I still have brandy, or coffee if you prefer. Just don't ask me for some of your awful tea. That is one habit of the English I will honestly never understand.'

Rosetta shakes her head. 'Really, I only came to say farewell. Thank you, but there is nothing that I want.'

As the intoxicating music continues to pervade the room Alberto asks, 'Truly? Nothing?' Then he rises to his feet. 'Well, there is something I would like to ask of you, as we are quite alone. Just this once, while I still have the chance.'

Rosetta looks at Alberto, at the tanned skin of his chest, his white teeth and lazy smile. She feels her pulse begin to race, a slipping of her hard-won self-control.

Alberto reaches for Rosetta's hand. He looks at her and says with fierce intent, '*Donna Rosa*, you know what I want most in all the world.'

In the fading autumn light, in an empty house in Belgravia, they begin to dance.

PART THREE

AUSTRALIA

FORTY-THREE

SYDNEY, FEBRUARY 1940

She stands in her open doorway, her eyes half closed against the glare. The amber shards of light have an eerie quality, as if refracted by an alien sun in a strange galaxy.

'Bushfire season,' she whispers, blinking.

In valleys and gorges, thousands of eucalypts are burning in the Blue Mountains forty miles west of Sydney. As their silvery leaves and sap-filled limbs ignite, fiery clouds rise and billow, race towards the city. There, in Bronte, Rosetta lives by the sea, but even in this haven the air is thick and heavy. She can taste the acrid smoke; her tongue feels rough and gritty.

She looks up, startled by a chorus of screeching cries. A flock of ragged cockatoos are perched in the branches of an exhausted jacaranda. The birds throw back their sulphurous heads, flutter their pale, singed wings. 'At least,' she thinks, 'they have escaped the flames.' Her garden is a sanctuary.

Rosetta hurries across the parched lawn. She has seen the red-faced postman pause by her front gate and is impatient to discover what letters he might have.

'Hot enough for ya?' the man asks laconically when he sees her approaching. 'I reckon this summer'll be a record breaker,' he adds, wiping his face.

She gives him a quick smile of commiseration, then takes the mail and strides back to the welcome coolness of her house, filled with a sense of anticipation. One letter has captured her attention: it bears a distinctive crest with a frond-like curlicue at each side extending from an embossed crown at its centre. Quickly, she picks up a chased silver knife, slides it along the seam of the envelope and extricates the letter. Then she pauses. The printed address at the top of the watermarked page is Brook House, once the grand Park Lane mansion owned by the multimillionaire and intimate confidant of the late King Edward, Sir Ernest Cassel.

Apparently, the writer is not living in Brook House at this precarious time for underneath are typed the words of a different, even more illustrious residence, Kensington Palace. This is the grand London home of a dozen members of the British royal family. A glance at the foot of the letter confirms what Rosetta has suspected. The signature, written in a forceful hand and underlined, is that of Edwina Mountbatten.

The letter's date is 28 December 1939. An English winter, Rosetta thinks to herself, snow and ice, Christmas trees and sugared mice. She wonders how easy it has been to celebrate; while Australia's current inferno is the result of a natural conspiracy between heat and drought, in Europe a conflagration made by man has, once more, broken out.

Lord Louis Mountbatten, Edwina's husband and the cousin of the King, is captaining the destroyer HMS *Kelly*, though soon his drive, ambition and connections will propel him into a more elevated role. Edwina is busy doing other things.

For years regarded as among London's most glittering, albeit promiscuous, socialites, she has acquired an outrageous reputation.

In 1932 King George himself insisted that the Mountbattens sue for libel when it was suggested by *The People* that Edwina had been 'caught in compromising circumstances' with her lover (rumoured to be the black American actor Paul Robeson but in fact Leslie 'Hutch' Hutchinson, a West Indian cabaret singer). The King considered legal action to be the only way in which to mitigate the scandal's impact on the royal family.

Since then, Lady Mountbatten has undergone a remarkable change. Now she devotes her considerable energy and passion to the Red Cross and St John's Ambulance. Edwina works tirelessly. Lord Louis, filled with pride, says approvingly to his daughter Pamela that her mother has found her 'purpose in life'. Rosetta knows of these recent developments. She is aware that Lady Mountbatten will not wish an indelicate revelation to interfere with her new self-sacrificing status.

Rosetta skims the letter. She tries to swallow, finds her throat constricted. 'It is this hideous weather,' she tells herself and gulps a glass of water. Then she reads again, notes Edwina's sentiments, their careful wording. Edwina thanks Rosetta for her '*kind letter*' of 3 December and expresses gratitude for all Rosetta did for her aunt. Next, she thanks Rosetta for passing on '*various enclosures*'. Edwina then moves on to the matter of the grave and headstone: her nephew, Dermot Pakenham, and her nieces will more than likely reimburse Rosetta for her '*expenses*', she says.

Yes, Rosetta thinks, that is to be expected. She has not begrudged the fact of meeting the cost of Lilian's funeral expenses, not for a moment, but she sees the family's assumption of responsibility for this outlay is their equivalent of closing ranks. Far be it for a Mountbatten, an Ashley or a Pakenham to permit exposure of another scandal.

The 'war to end all wars' has not fulfilled its promise. Now, once more, it is a time for the defence not just of that island nation, but of those qualities that the people of her upper classes profess to hold so dear: decency, honourable family values. Lilian and her husband, Arthur, never divorced, nor formally separated. Their irregular relationship was not made public.

Edwina, however, is a woman of the world, and as such knows its ways better than do most. She fully appreciates the meaning of discretion at all costs, for others if not always for herself.

When she wrote her letter in December, Rosetta devoted considerable thought as to the wisdom of including one of the '*various enclosures*' to which Edwina refers. At last she decided to proceed, though with the addition of a pertinent question. Now Rosetta reads her correspondent's firm response.

Edwina writes that she is returning '*the one letter*' and agrees with Rosetta's suggestion that it not be forwarded to the children. In fact, she goes a step further and asks Rosetta to destroy it. After this, there comes a request for photographs, then additional expressions of gratitude and thanks. Nothing of particular consequence, unlike that brief, undated letter from Lilian that Edwina has returned. It shares a potential for damage similar to that of an incendiary device.

My Darling R,

I will be brief. It is enough to say that you have transported me to a realm which I had never imagined I might enter, yet now I revel in. Yes, I had a position in society, I had my husband and the children. I should feel guilt, I know, for casting all this aside, particularly those three innocents; I confess that I do not. I am shameless.

The depth of feeling I have for you is without parallel. Rosie, my sweet flower, I know you have never before expressed a wish to engage in particular activities, nor even for me to speak of certain matters pertaining to the man we both love dearly. But last night, when we three truly became one, I experienced an unsurpassable ecstasy. My lips are scalded from kisses given and received. Surely, it is worth forsaking the world for a night such as this!

The note is unsigned, save for the letter *L*.

Rosetta has a distant look in her dark gold eyes. Ah, dearest Lilian, she reflects, you were always artless, prone to emotional excess, and yet … she sighs, remembering how it was in those days when desire electrified their every thought and nothing seemed to matter more than each other's happiness. Then she does what Edwina wants. Rosetta strikes a match and in an instant there is no evidence that such rapture ever existed.

FORTY-FOUR

Ménage à trois.

A household of three. The phrase is French, of course. The French are so much better at expressing these things, the subtleties of human relationships.

I see it typed on a page. Just three words, though they make an impact, summing up the nature of the intimate relationship that my father deduced had existed between my great-grandmother, her best friend and my step-great-grandfather.

My father not only recorded his belief. He told me about it, more than twenty years ago. I remember entering his room on some small errand and he, looking up from the research scattered on his desk, declaring apropos of nothing in particular: 'A threesome, that's what your great-grandmother was in.'

A statement like that came as a surprise. It wasn't the kind of pronouncement I was expecting from my father, nor one I could easily forget. I think it might have been then that I first began to consciously consider the trajectory of my great-grandmother's rebellion, to wonder just how many taboos she was prepared to break.

Rosetta returned to Australia in early 1915, but whether in Australia or anywhere else in what was then referred to as 'the civilised world', women simply did not do the things Rosetta did. She was thirty-four years old. She had already left a husband, deserted a child, run away with a half-Chinese fortune-telling wizard. Now, having only just returned after completely reinventing herself on the other side of the world, bewitching European and British society and, in the process, creating considerable wealth, she embraced an entirely improper domestic arrangement. Was she a woman ahead of her time – a revolutionary, strong and extraordinarily brave – or simply selfish, wayward, mad? Rosetta did not just ignore convention, she tore at it.

My father didn't judge, at least as regards this latest development. It was the improbable conjunction that fascinated him, the unique melange of race, religion, class and sex; their incongruence.

Rosetta, Zeno and Lilian: the Jewish granddaughter of a convict who had acquired position and respect, the tradesman turned magician son of a goldfields Celestial from Canton, and the aristocratic Irish-born granddaughter of the Earl of Shaftesbury and aunt of the future Countess Mountbatten of Burma, Vicereine of India. Surely there could rarely have existed as unlikely a trio as this.

I remind myself that I must stop referring to my step-great-grandfather as Zeno. By now the name and the persona that went with it had transmogrified yet again. Just as was the case when, in an earlier incarnation, Zeno the Magnificent disappeared into a churning slipstream somewhere off Port Said, Professor Zeno, too, had gone. Vanishing: it was by now a practised conjuring trick. Once the Professor left the shores of Great Britain, Zeno simply ceased to exist.

The couple travelled via the United States. Rosetta had been claiming to be American; why not see the country of her invented birth? In any case, war-torn Europe and the Middle East were no longer safe. Travelling westward, towards the setting sun, was the wiser course. During the voyage from San Francisco on the SS *Sonoma* my great-grandmother's versatile husband reverted to his original name.

They passed through the wave-swept, sandstone cliffs of Sydney Heads on 11 January 1915. When they stepped ashore into the brilliant Antipodean sunshine it was not with the sea-induced stagger of other passengers but with the greatest ease: they had always been sure-footed, comfortable with self-belief. Husband and wife were, once more, officially Mr and Mrs William Norman, although the former professor continued to refer to himself as Carl. Rosetta followed suit: both found it difficult to break the habit.

In England, Lilian's confusion is soon at an end. Despite the existence of her children, her husband and the expectations that accompany her elevated social position, just a few short weeks after their departure, she sets out to follow her dear friends. At the age of thirty-eight, she realises that she cannot bear to live without them. Lilian sails to the other side of the world on the SS *Remuera*, though during the long voyage she begins to be plagued by doubt. Perhaps her decision was unduly precipitous; might she have been too rash? On sleepless, starlit nights, she paces the *Remuera*'s timber decks and, as she does so, wrestles with the wisdom of her choice.

The ship's first Australian port is Hobart, that same far settlement to which Abraham Rheuben was transported nearly a century ago. Hobart was the place where he married, raised a family, made his fortune. 'So this is where it all began,' thinks Lilian, as tugboats help the ship negotiate the Derwent

River's erratic currents and fickle winds. The landscape strikes her as primitive and dense, a wilderness, its wild beauty bleak and threatening. She feels the bitter edge of the Antarctic's icy air as she surveys the austere, windswept town. It leads her to consider the qualities possessed by Rosetta's grandfather. A man of such wretched circumstances – how was it that he thrived in such a place? She contemplates this question and, as she does so, gains a new understanding of Rosetta, her determination and resourcefulness.

Lilian leaves the *Remuera* after the ship reaches Melbourne. She has been awaiting this arrival with anticipation, anxious to rediscover the city in which she and her husband once lived, where he served an imperial governor and she hunted with a lord. But time has passed and the Melbourne that she knew in the year of 1900 seems very different now; the sounds in the street are sharper, more discordant, its smell has a new, metallic quality, the very rhythm of life has changed. 'Perhaps it is me,' she thinks. 'I am not the woman I once was.'

She finds she is relieved to board a locomotive at Flinders Street Station. Yet, strangely, the trip from Melbourne to Sydney, past dusty paddocks and small country towns, seems harder to endure than all the months at sea. After so much time, Lilian now feels a sense of urgency. She yearns for discovery, to determine if her agonising choice has been correct for, if not, she asks herself the question that has tormented her the most: 'What will become of me?'

As Lilian's train draws into Sydney's Central Station, that vast colonial tribute to late Victorian excess, she finds she is trembling. She has pictured this moment, many, many times, the way the platform would appear to rush towards her, how the flattering green dress she would be wearing might flutter as she descends; yes, that she had imagined, but not how she would feel, not this whirlpool of terror, hope and expectation, both perilous and thrilling.

Lilian smooths a tendril of dark-blonde hair. Then, struggling to place her quivering fingers into a pair of white kid gloves, thinks, 'Why have I been so unwise, so impetuous?'

The train stops. She sees her friend and lover, waiting. Rosetta, dressed in cornflower blue, is smiling. Carl, nearing forty now and as relaxed as ever, languidly raises his hat. Lilian alights. Amid the noise of porters calling, the throng of hurrying travellers arriving and departing, she steps uncertainly towards them. They reach for one another and, as the three of them embrace, Lilian discovers that her doubts have taken flight.

She will stay, always. Lilian Pakenham becomes the third apex of an intimate triangle though, for the sake of discretion, she maintains a separate address. All the same, it is a rather shocking arrangement.

Colonel Hercules Arthur Pakenham does not remain on the Western Front. He will fulfil a more clandestine duty. In 1917 he is appointed the British security service's man at the French War Ministry. By early 1918 he is head of MI5's Washington DC office and immersed in counter-espionage. Colonel Pakenham is not only good at keeping secrets: he is practised in the analysis of troubled situations. He doubts that, once the Great War has ended, he and Lilian will reunite.

The Colonel's judgement is correct: even after he returns home something of a hero, twice mentioned in despatches and the recipient, among other decorations, of the Legion d'Honneur from the French and the Distinguished Service Medal courtesy of the Americans, his wife chooses not to return. Nor, it seems, does Lilian reclaim her three children. They remain in Britain. When she leaves, Dermot is turning fourteen, Joan (known as Esther) is eleven and the youngest, little Beatrix, barely five.

Once more I contemplate what leads a woman to make such an immense and terrible decision. There are so many heartbreaking stories of mothers, Indigenous, unmarried, too poor or too young, who had their children torn from their arms and grieved bitterly. Yet, somehow, for Rosetta and for Lilian, relinquishment was necessary. Perhaps it was one of the elements that drew them to each other, this willingness to leave behind such precious things.

FORTY-FIVE

SYDNEY, 1918

War changes everything and nothing. After the fighting has ended and despite the senseless sacrifice of tens of thousands of young lives, Australia continues to be fiercely loyal to the British Crown. Though jobs are often hard to come by, most men don't want their wives to work; they think it shaming. The White Australia policy remains as well. The country may be part of a vast empire that includes the peoples of a number of African and Asian nations, but Australia's politicians continue, steadfastly, to turn all such individuals away. They are found lacking, unacceptable.

The Great War has not only deprived Australia of the flower of its manhood; among those who return home, damage is commonplace. More than one hundred and fifty thousand men have been injured or taken prisoner. Many are without a hand or arm, some have lost a leg or cannot see; the mines and mortars have maimed indiscriminately. Others, their lungs scarred by poisoned gas, struggle for each gasp of breath. Most terrible of all is the devastation that lies within, the wounds that no one sees but which impose savage consequences; the awful screaming in the night that wives and children hear but know not to remark upon; the sudden anger; the drinking that is done in a new, determined way that seeks only oblivion; the violence.

The war's horrors – worse, the appalling decisions that so often led to misfortune and disaster – are rarely acknowledged. Gallipoli, Gaba Tepe and Lone Pine, Fromelles, Villers-Bretonneux and Passchendaele; the men who come home from these places are changed forever. They have seen and done unimaginable things, had the unimaginable done to them in return. They do not speak of it. Their experience binds them to one another, separates them from their wives and children.

This war has also altered Carl. Communing with the dead no longer holds the same fascination as before. In fact, the practice fills him with distaste. He is well aware of the irony; now, more than ever, sweethearts, wives and mothers will do almost anything to establish contact with their lost lovers, husbands, sons. Carl considers this lucrative new market of grieving clients and finds that his heart is no longer in his old profession. There are too many unquiet spirits among the dead, too much sorrow among the living. It is unbearable.

Then there is the matter of his visions. The fire-filled, awful scenes of war that occupied his dreams still sometimes pass before his eyes. He wonders if perhaps it is the fault of opium. In London, faced with the prospect of another turbulent night, he frequently succumbed to the poppy's soporific spell. He thinks now that perhaps it may have done more harm than good; promising heaven, it has imposed a kind of hell.

Carl sits in his study late one evening and turns the matter over in his mind, then finds himself considering another substance, this one capable of undreamt-of effects. Once he claimed that radium had 'revolutionised the modern methods of healing'. But is it possible that the same material he had so enthusiastically endorsed has undiscovered properties that have contributed to his distressed mental and physical state? He doesn't know. No one does.

Most disturbing is the knowledge that his visions did not remain, as could reasonably be expected, merely the products of his fertile mind. Too many predictions came to pass. War of unparalleled scope and terror has waged across the world, just as he forecast. Sir Arthur Conan Doyle and Sir Oliver Lodge have both lost a son; he saw these things quite clearly.

The two distinguished men write to him and tell him of their tragedies. Briefly, he slips into the role of Professor Zeno once again. The famous author and the leading scientist are prepared to try anything, risk ridicule and humiliation, if there seems any prospect (no matter how absurd) of achieving contact with their beloved boys. In desperation, the two engage the services of seers and mediums. They beseech the Professor to return to England though, wisely, he declines their invitations.

Not so long ago, when alone with his Rosetta, Carl would have scoffed at those gullible souls who believed his visions and prognostications to be as true as the gospels. Since then, it has occurred to him that his own ability to separate illusion from delusion, imagination from reality, truth from fiction, is less certain. Even worse, Carl has the disturbing thought that, in calling forth his visions, he has been in some way instrumental in conjuring them into existence, making them concrete.

He doesn't tell Rosetta of his fears. She will not like it, will look at him with doubt flickering in her eyes. In any case, Carl knows that to travel down this path can bring nothing but torment, even madness. There can be only one way forward. He must put such thoughts aside and, with them, his long-standing practice of the art of magic.

Carl makes an exchange. The black arts for the black market. He has not told his wife about his fears; now he omits to confess the solution he's found. He makes sure that transactions are conducted discreetly, far from home. If Rosetta suspects, she doesn't say a word.

They are wealthy now; it's not a matter of the money, but of sensation. Spirits (though not the ethereal kind), cigarettes and, increasingly, art of unspecified provenance fly through his hands. Life is once more dangerous and thrilling. Yet, despite this promising beginning, the satisfaction doesn't last. When all is said and done, it's commerce. He misses sorcery.

Long ago, when Rosetta was still married to Louis, she'd claimed she visited Zeno's Swanston Street premises for instruction in watercolours. Much later, favourite clients were touched when he sent them small examples of his work. In a letter penned from her Cannes villa, La Fôret, on 20 December 1913, Princess Charlotte wrote:

> *My dear Professor*
>
> *I can't thank you enough for your . . . exactly pretty card just received, a proof that you are even an artist, for the roses are exactly painted, and I have put them on the mantelpiece, just behind the chair in which you sat, when I tried to learn from you during your alas! Far too short stay.*

Now he turns to these artistic pursuits with renewed pleasure. In the careful preparation of white surfaces and the blending of concentrated colours, in the dipping of his brush into singing oranges and yellows, deep blues and greens and brilliant reds and, finally, in the application of pigment onto canvas, his equilibrium is recovered. He paints his way back to tranquillity, to happiness.

Carl spends his time with those engaged in similar pursuits. Artists, writers and poets are much like seers and magicians. Unbothered by the unconventional, they accept not only his unusual domestic arrangements and his distinctly chequered past but seem not to mind his oriental origins. He finds he is at home with them.

~

My great-grandmother, at thirty-eight, finds fulfilment in other ways.

'You understand,' she tells her husband, 'I can't be confined. You have your painting and your artist friends, but I still need something more.'

Rosetta seeks adventure. Why not cross Russia one day, take the Trans-Siberian railway from frozen Vladivostok to Moscow? Or go to the floating lakeside palaces of Rajasthan, or the ancient temples of Peru? Perhaps she will. But first, she thinks, she'll sail for London.

Taking tea at The Ritz and drinking cocktails at The Savoy, viewing the paintings at the Royal Academy and watching Nellie Melba sing at the Albert Hall – Rosetta realises just how much she has missed these diverting pastimes. Paris, too, she must go there, see the divine new clothes designed by Jean Patou and Madame Paquin. Then there is racing at Longchamp and the ballet at the Palais Garnier before the quick dash to catch the train from Gare de Lyon and the journey south to the Riviera.

All these things remain, yet Rosetta knows that much else can never be the same. So many men, dashing and elegant, have perished on the battlefields and her dear friends, Baroness Stern, Princess Charlotte and the Empress Eugenie, are not long for this world. As for the Russian grand dukes and princes, there are no more sumptuous villas and winter palaces. In fact, she's heard that one of the late Czarina's godsons is now employed on the *Côte* as a hotel concierge. It seems incredible.

When Rosetta reflects upon the heady life she knew so well, the ravishing women wrapped in ermine and sable, the private railway carriages lined like jewel boxes in plush ruby velvet, the glittering balls attended by countesses who wore diamonds in their hair and, around their throats, ropes of glistening pearls; when she thinks back upon the sheer self-indulgence of an existence where each whim was treated by a fleet of servants with urgent diligence ... well, it might have been a fairytale, except that she was there and knows that, for a brief time at least, this fantastic, hedonistic world was real.

How much has changed, or disappeared? She's curious to know.

Florence and Winifred go to Sydney Cove and wave farewell to their glamorous sister. 'I don't know how she does it – and all alone,' one says to the other. 'How brave Rosetta is, how fearless.'

They see her, high above them on the great ocean liner, veiled by nets of coloured paper ribbons. Rosetta raises one hand, waves in return. With the other she holds on to her new summer hat, gay with blood-red poppies. Just for a moment, a single streamer becomes entangled with the blooms before a wanton gust of wind sends it spiralling into the sky. The sudden movement catches the eye of a fellow passenger. Gesturing, he says, 'I saw flowers like that in Flanders,' as the ship slips from its moorings, begins to pull away.

Rosetta travels widely. She has a taste for exploration, seeks out ships sailing for Bombay or Cairo or Rio de Janeiro. But, after each expedition comes to an end, she returns to her gabled Bronte home in Sydney.

Ever since her first visit in 1905, during the final, turbulent months of her marriage to Louis, Rosetta has been attracted to this inviting city. Her desire to stay near its sparkling waters remains a constant throughout her life, whether by the harbour where sailing boats and ferries are enveloped by soft azure serenity, or near the ocean and the rolling blue-green tides that rise and fall in endless, rhythmic waves.

An abundance of seductive physicality is not the only reason for the city's enduring appeal. War has come and gone, but Melbourne continues to be more self-consciously aware of origins, of what distinguishes a person and their family. Sydney remains a different kind of metropolis; perhaps it is to do with being a great sea port. It is more forgiving. In Sydney, reinvention – Rosetta and Zeno's stock in trade – is still a distinct possibility.

FORTY-SIX

Snapshots. It is in this way that Rosetta's four remaining decades are revealed. Her life does not present in a continuous, unfolding flow of events, but as fleeting images constructed from anecdotes and reminiscences, from possibilities and hints. My father continued to play the reporter's role, still chased leads and asked questions. On occasion, he recorded an opinion, sometimes he would speculate, or set down his dilemmas, perhaps write a brief vignette. Now it is these fragments that shape my understanding of the next forty years of my great-grandmother's life, together with my own memories. They are not of Rosetta, of course, but of my mother and grandmother, the lived experience of them.

Although Rosetta's child was named Frances Catherine at birth, for most of her life no one called her that. I remember Nana being very pretty, not tall but shapely, with that shape invariably enhanced by the wearing of a corset and a belt buckled at her waist. Perhaps it was a legacy of living in the convent: she was always particular about her appearance. In a way, I suppose that was how her change of name came about.

'I couldn't wait to have my hair bobbed after the Great War,' she told me once when I was in her sitting room and she was drinking brandy and soda. It must have been five o'clock, because you could set your watch by her nightly consumption of the cocktail. The procedure was unchanging, as much ritual as habit.

'It was the modern thing to do.'

My grandmother put her drink down and smiled, the coquette in her remembering, before she pursed her mouth into her customary 'O' and drew back on a cigarette. Nana would have been in her late sixties then and smoking had already etched deep lines that fanned out from her upper lip. Her flat reflected a liking for watercolours, pastel-coloured porcelain shepherdesses and other tasteful ornaments, though, such was her addiction to nicotine, the wallpaper always had a faintly sallow tint.

'This was when I lived at home in Melbourne, of course,' she said. 'I was stepping out with a young man and when he came to the house to collect me he had the biggest shock. I'll never forget it. He walked in, took one look at me and said, "You look just like a boy – I'm going to call you Billie!"'

In that carefree moment, her final link to her mother, the very name Rosetta gave her, was effaced. No one ever called her Frances again. She would be known as Billie for the rest of her life.

Billie marries my tall, blue-eyed grandfather Frederick Mitchell Jacobs on 30 December 1921. He has served his country. Now he is making his way in the commercial world. Fred's smile is disarming. Billie finds him charming.

He has no intention of keeping his wedding vows.

Fred is a complicated man. His mother (she requires him to call her 'Mater') has always doted on Hubert, his brilliant elder brother. Fred, the lesser, second son, is resentful. He has acquired a cruel streak, at least as far as women are concerned. Desperate for their attention and devotion, at the same time he seems to hate women, hate his needing of them.

Rosetta is not aware that her twenty-one-year-old daughter has married, that Frances Raphael is Billie Jacobs now. She doesn't know that her only, unhappy child has moved to Sydney, or what further misfortunes will befall her there.

My mother, Sybil, is born three years later, in 1924. After Billie brings her infant daughter home from hospital, Fred sets about seducing her nurse. But faithlessness is not Fred's only flaw.

'I have a memory.' My mother's voice catches. 'The picture in my mind is of my mother on her knees, my father's hands upon her, forcing her towards the floor.'

FORTY-SEVEN

Rosetta's mother, Fanny, may have cautioned 'only men can make their fortune' but, as has so often been the case, her daughter has not heeded this advice.

She has become deft at the conduct of business. Professor Zeno's fees provided her with the means to acquire property in Britain. For some time now, she has turned her attention to Sydney. The buying and selling of land and of the buildings that occupy that land; such speculation has been taking place ever since the establishment of the colony. It has long been a reliable way to attain wealth and, in that regard, nothing at all has changed.

Rosetta purchases a substantial number of properties. The flats and houses she has bought are rented out to tenants; it keeps her fully occupied. Indeed, she is so busy that sometimes it is difficult to keep track of exactly who her tenants are or to what purposes her properties are put. 'Well, as long as the rents are met,' she tells herself, 'why should I be concerned?' This blithe attitude remains until she discovers the disconcerting answer in unanticipated circumstances.

Like most citizens of Sydney, Rosetta has read about an infamous local madam with the name of Tilly Devine. Tilly is so successful in her chosen field that newspapers dub her the 'Queen of Vice'. One journalist, writing for *The Daily Telegraph*, describes her to his readers as 'a vicious, grasping, high priestess of savagery, venery, obscenity . . .'.

Matilda Twiss was born in 1900 in the crime-ridden London slums of Camberwell, where her family existed in a state of unforgiving poverty. She learnt quickly that the luxury of scruples would serve only to compromise her ability to survive.

Tilly's good looks, her halo of fair hair and voluptuous body allow her to enjoy a little more success than most girls whose livelihood depends on the patronage of eager men. She starts at age thirteen; at fifteen, for a girl from Camberwell, she is making a good income. Tilly might be a common street-walker, but the street in which she plies her trade is smart: London's fashionable Strand. Life changes when she meets James (Big Jim) Edward Devine, a gunner in the Australian army. Jim shares with Tilly a questionable moral code. He is both by nature and profession a criminal; a thief, drug dealer, pimp, gunman and vicious thug who will not hesitate to kill or maim.

They marry. When Jim returns to Australia in 1919, she soon follows him and then the fun, as Tilly would put it, really begins. Soon they set up house in the dangerous, gang-ridden district of Darlinghurst, described by the scandal sheet *Truth* as, variously, 'Razorhurst', 'Gunhurst', 'Dopehurst' and 'Bottlehurst' for reasons that are self-apparent. Pretty Tilly, just nineteen, is 'on the game' again: at ten shillings for a half-hour encounter she is doing well. But Tilly has her sights set higher. Why limit her income when there are so many hungry girls who have the capacity to make her rich? She adjusts. No longer solely a prostitute, young, quick-witted Tilly sets up a dozen houses of ill fame and puts a ruby light in the window of each one. She is successful, a born madam.

Tilly Devine becomes well known, indeed, infamous. Her notoriety derives not just from the fact that she supplies carnal services to a uniquely egalitarian range of many men, from Macquarie Street's black-suited politicians to tattooed dockworkers. Tilly is also known, feared, for her violence. At a time when razor gangs regularly battle for dominance, her willingness to wield a blade, to slash at a soft cheek, or ear, a nose or exposed throat, is singularly shocking.

There are many contretemps with members of the New South Wales constabulary, raids on her premises, inflammatory stories in newspapers and threats to close her down. Yet Tilly, who is clever and experienced in the ways of men's corruption, knows the power of favours given and what can be demanded in return, remains in business. A former New South Wales Police Commissioner named Norman Allan, no stranger to controversy himself (he will be accused of taking bribes from those responsible for some of the state's most nefarious activities), is heard to describe her as a 'villain' before adding, 'But who am I to judge?'

Tilly is irrepressible, buoyant as a cork. More than that, she thrives. The street-walker from Camberwell acquires a taste for luxury, for those things she considers constitute evidence of a successful life. When the Great Depression strikes, the starving wait their turn at soup kitchens for steaming bowls of paltry sustenance doled out by well-intentioned Salvation Army officers bent on saving souls. Tilly slows as she glides past in her Cadillac: she has come to find wives and mothers sufficiently desperate to consider her offer of some easy earnings. It is as simple as picking up bruised fruit. The women see the glint of diamonds on her fingers, fox furs around her neck and, despite the sound of hymns and tambourines ringing in their ears, find themselves tempted.

Tilly Devine is, then, a formidable woman. But so is her landlady, my great-grandmother.

I found my father's description of Rosetta and Tilly's unexpected nexus on one untitled piece of paper.

Rosetta, who was very jealous of her reputation, was shattered by unfounded rumours which came to her ears suggesting that she was a brothel keeper. This arose from the fact that two cottages that she owned in the inner City were being used as houses of ill-fame.

. . . what had happened was that the cottages were being rented on behalf of the notorious Sydney moll and associate of criminals, the infamous Tilly Devine. When Rosetta discovered what had happened she summarily locked the inhabitants out.

'That bloody woman's done what?' is Tilly's vociferous demand when Jim tells her the news.

She is not a woman it is safe to cross; her appetite for retribution is renowned.

'Jim, I reckon I'll take one of the boys with me and pay Mrs Norman a visit. Won't be 'ard to sort the bitch out.' Tilly's rouged mouth assumes a gleeful smirk.

'Easy does it, Til,' is Big Jim's response, though he is no stranger to savage violence. 'You've already done two years in Long Bay on account of your razor. I've got a new shipment of cocaine coming in any day now. It's worth a hell of a lot and I'd like to keep life nice and quiet. Bugger it, Til, I'll just nip down and fix things with me bolt cutters.'

Tilly Devine would have none of this.

'Yer bloody won't!' she cries. 'I'll sort it out meself.'

She kicked down the newly bolted doors to ensure that her girls could carry on business as usual.

In a moment of cool reflection following her initial impetuous action, Rosetta becomes aware that she has escaped lightly from a hazardous situation. She decides that she will not enlist the help of the police, or Carl, who knows a trick or two. Nor will she, in a potentially foolhardy act, go to treacherous Darlinghurst herself to confront Mrs Devine.

What Rosetta decides to do next demonstrates that she, too, is skilled in the art of survival. 'Carl, darling, about this unsavoury affair,' Rosetta says to her husband after she has collected her thoughts, 'I think it would be best to continue with the same arrangement we had before; you know, business as usual. In any case, one day that wretch will get what she deserves.' Her tone is philosophical.

'And until then, Rosie?' asks Carl. He knows his wife well enough to suspect that there is more.

'Strangely enough, I don't think it's going to take very long for Mrs Devine to discover that she is having considerable problems with the law.' Rosetta smiles enigmatically. Tilly is not the only woman in this city with favours upon which she can draw.

FORTY-EIGHT

For the first decade of her life my mother, Sybil, lives in a rambling, harbourside house in the fashionable suburb of Vaucluse. Directly opposite, the construction of the mighty Sydney Harbour Bridge begins in 1924, the same year she is born. As the years pass, she watches its two sides slowly creep across the sky, wonders if they will ever meet. And then, one day when she is aged eight, as if by magic they join together, a perfect fit.

Two years later, she is sent away. Her parents, unlike that great grey span, are not united; their marriage is in disarray.

Billie has been abandoned yet again, this time by her great love, the father of her child. She is but one of many women in Fred's life, now and in the future. They include not only several mistresses but three more wives.

And so, for Sybil, the pattern is repeated. Another only child, another little girl whose parents part amid trauma and who is deemed, like an awkward piece of furniture, to be in the way. This time the boarding school is in the Southern Highlands of New South Wales. During the freezing winters, desolation settles in her poisoned, chilblained hands.

She returns to live in Sydney after an absence of two years, though to considerably lesser circumstances than before. Mother and daughter have been obliged to move. The large waterfront house has gone. The Harbour Bridge has disappeared from view. Instead, their small apartment looks over a narrow passageway. The flat will do; it is far better, really, than many people have. But it isn't home, and they are no longer a family.

'After the divorce I used to see my father once a week,' my mother recalls. 'I remember one Saturday when we were at the Watson's Bay Hotel, eating fish. He and his latest girlfriend, Jo, started laughing about my mother. I think I was around twelve. I just stood up, walked out and got on the tram.'

I tell her she was brave.

'I had to learn to cope and did it in my own way,' she says.

'Which way was that?'

'I just let things go over my head. I was charming and amusing.'

'But not that time,' I say.

'No, not then.'

I am sitting on a comfortable wing-back chair, gazing at my ninety-year-old mother as she reminisces. She lies on her bed, a vision spun from sugar in her pink, lace-edged peignoir amid a cloud of frilled white pillows.

I see myself in memory gazing at her as I do now; the years liquesce. I am aged three or four. For the first time, I am aware of the way she looks. My mother is sitting at her dressing table, her back to me. I see her waved hair and long neck. She wears a dress that is green and smooth and gleaming like the surface of a leaf after the rain. The mirror has a hinged wing on each side so there are three images. She gazes straight ahead but I see more. I see her back before me, but as if by magic I see, too, the reflection of her face and each profile. She is like a jewel, her face carved in facets and each one luminous. I watch as she applies carmine lipstick. Inky mascara darkens lashes above opal eyes. She lifts her perfect face, puts on earrings and a necklace. I see four mothers doing this, all mine.

Now, despite the inevitable marks of age, the elegant harmony present in the line of her jaw, the curve of her cheek and the arch of her brow remains. Spread around her upon the bed are objects she can reach easily. Books, spectacles, the radio for news and a television guide. I see she has marked the classic films she wants to watch, the kind that star Lauren Bacall or Joan Crawford. Like them, she has a face that matters. It seems beyond the reach of time.

I turn my gaze away, look instead at the family photographs standing on the wide ledge beneath the window, closed and shuttered as it always is. Children, grandchildren, great-grandchildren; we are all there, captured at weddings and graduations and other celebrations. On the right there is a picture of my grandmother, Billie, in a silver frame. She must have been in her eighties when it was taken. She wears a smart dress and her hair has been carefully styled, but her expression is not happy. Some new, imagined slight seems to be playing on her mind. Of course, there are no photographs of Rosetta. Then my mother reaches behind one of her books and gives me a picture in a frame.

A figure, white as alabaster, in a dark, sylvan glade.

In the background, a pale aquamarine river, winding through a mysterious landscape. The figure, a woman, lies near the river bank beside the twisted, silver-grey limbs of trees. She glows with a pearly sheen; moonlight, I think. Her form is as devoid of colour as a classical sculpture but she is not quite nude and, in any case, she has a modern air. This woman doesn't have the cool remove, the Apollonian reserve admired by the Romans and the Greeks. She looks down with intensity at an object in her hand. It is difficult to tell what she is holding; something is laced through her fingers, trailing a long, looping cord.

The woman has thick chestnut hair, cropped short. She wears a brief garment, striped, that rides up high, stretched tight across her thighs. The intensity of her examination of the hidden object in her hand frees me to indulge in uninhibited scrutiny. I contemplate the woman's fleshy upper arm, then her torso until, finally, my eye travels along the full length of her slim, bare legs until it reaches a sudden, unexpected counterpoint: crimson slippers. They provide the only flare of colour in this otherwise monochromatic, sombre scene. Her body, though it reclines, appears tense to me, and if her legs are still for now, the brightly shod feet are flexed, which makes it seem as if at any moment they might spring away, lead her to dance like a river sprite underneath the shadowy canopy of leaves.

I see all this in a small watercolour, twenty-three centimetres long by eighteen centimetres high, executed on a piece of card. It is not an outstanding work, not by any means, but there is something about the woman's form, its whiteness against the dark, the absorbed expression on her face, the way her near-naked body is displayed and, above all, those insistent crimson slippers that makes it hard to look away.

It is Rosetta. Carl must have painted her. There is no title on the back of the painting, no signature on the front, but I recognise my great-grandmother's intense look. And the legs; I have seen those legs before.

There are several photographs of Rosetta which, similar to the painting, date from the 1920s. They show her striking insouciant poses, filled with confidence, aware of how well she looks in her smart clothes. Rosetta gazes out from underneath a cloche hat, worn fashionably low on her brow. She is wearing a fur-edged coat that ends just at the knee so I can easily take note of her limbs, which in this instance are encased by sheer black stockings and flattered by the addition of ankle-strapped high heels. She tips one foot back and bends her knee, then crosses the front leg over in order to display both legs advantageously, looks pleased. There are four of these photographs. Rosetta lounges by an immense motor car, its bonnet adorned by a small silver nymph, wings poised for flight. I can see that my great-grandmother is attended by a uniformed chauffeur in a peaked hat and long, polished boots. From the crenellated, neo-Gothic building behind her and the tree-filled gardens, it appears she is at Government House in Sydney, though I don't know what has brought her to this Vice-Regal residence.

I return to the little painting, look at the brushwork, hold it to the light. There is something not quite right. I think it has been painted over a photograph; in fact I can now see that the figure remains a photograph, though the face is tinted and those incongruous, deliciously red slippers have certainly benefited from a slick of paint. Carl always enjoyed illusion: I suppose it is only natural that his art would combine the real with the fanciful, aim to trick the eye.

FORTY-NINE

SYDNEY, 1922

Somebody (no one is sure if it was George Finey the cartoonist or handsome George Lambert the painter or, indeed, someone else entirely) has had the idea of reviving the annual Artists' Ball. There hasn't been one held in Sydney since before the war. These spectacular and, frankly, often decadent occasions are now all the rage in the bohemian circles of Paris, London and Berlin. Australians, too, are anxious to escape the tragedy of recent years. They want to be frivolous, seek abandonment, assert that life is there to be seized.

One of the Georges – the impish Finey, probably – is assigned to break down Carl's resistance. A few of the other artists are vaguely aware of their friend's past involvement in the world of prognostication, and the ball requires a fortune teller to complement an array of other acts. To date, Carl has not been enthusiastic.

'Come on, mate. Just do it, do it for me.' The cartoonist grins, runs his hand through his long, unruly hair, orders another round of drinks. The men stand at a bar in William Street, close to the tiny flats and disreputable old houses rented by the more impecunious artists.

'Well, if not for me, for the Red Cross. You know we're raising money for the wounded diggers. Four years on and a lot of the poor bastards are still struggling.

'You'll see. It'll be a laugh. You'll love it.'

After the consumption of a number of beers Carl's resistance begins to erode until finally, a celebratory whiskey in hand, he succumbs to Finey's blandishments. For one night only, the magician will return.

Early on the evening of 21 August 1922, Carl takes a sooty pencil once more and elongates his eyes. Next he dons a black silk robe with a rampant scarlet dragon emblazoned down one side. He catches sight of an image in the mirror, sees himself. The years melt away and, on this winter night, Zeno the Magnificent is restored to life.

Zeno strides into his Bronte sitting room only to stop, disorientated. The two women he expects to see have been replaced by Chinese courtesans. They wear white make-up, ruby lipstick and jet-black wigs. Each has on a long, vermilion cheongsam. The dresses both obscure and reveal: they have high collars but they cling to the women's breasts and buttocks and have deep slits on each side that reach nearly to their hips. The two wear elaborate sequinned masks that ensure their true identities cannot be ascertained.

With familiarity banished, Zeno finds the foreign appearance of the women to be intensely alluring. They present alien mirror images. For a moment even he cannot tell which woman is which. This uncertainty creates a frisson of excitement that he has of late been missing. He imagines the evening offering new, undreamt-of possibilities, as might his life.

~

Built in high Victorian style with sandstone arches, layered pediments and a striking clock tower, the Sydney Town Hall is one of the city's most ornate public edifices. A workplace for the Lord Mayor and his councillors, host to sedate receptions, concerts and memorial services, on this night of artistic merriment its dignified sobriety has been eradicated. The addition of towering three-metre-high grotesque figures and colourful friezes, strings of gleaming lights and a profusion of flowers has transformed this worthy civic building into a tiered pleasure palace of bohemian delight.

Two thousand guests make their way from busy George Street and climb the Town Hall's sweeping staircase. Each one wears fancy dress; there are several green-clad Robin Hoods and beribboned Marie Antoinettes, a number of pirate kings (one distinguished by the addition of a loquacious yellow parrot), and a small flock of flimsily attired fairy queens, their wings quivering gently in the breeze.

Underneath the Town Hall's lofty coffered ceilings, before its great gilded organ, Sydney's painters, models and muses, writers and cartoonists whirl about with members of the city's wealthy elite in uncharacteristic proximity.

The socialite Dora Walford, a fixture at more conventional balls and dances, enters wearing slave bangles and trailing iridescent scarves. With her drifting train borne by two small, wide-eyed boys, she makes her way to an alcove, takes up her position in a Persian garden tableau designed by George Lambert. George is rather pleased about her participation, considering that Dora's impossible husband, Leslie, recently vetoed his plan to paint her in the guise of the Madonna. Walter and Marion Burley Griffin, designers of the nation's capital, appear; they look like Aztec gods. Wild Bill Hickok dances with a milkmaid, a stout Napoleon twirls a veiled Salome and, behind a marble pillar, Cleopatra is observed embracing King Henry VIII.

Well before midnight, the unholy hour when someone (again,

nobody is sure whom) has decreed that identities must be revealed, masks begin to slip. The living portrait of a Renaissance beauty shimmying by turns out to be Rose, the artist Norman Lindsay's vivacious wife. The actress and energetic social doyenne Mrs T.H. Kelly can be glimpsed behind a black and gold Venetian mask; with her powdery white wig and strategically placed *mouche* she might have just slipped away from an eighteenth-century soiree in the Doge's Palace. Others court attention in more scandalous fashion. Even in this colourful crowd, the brief leopardskin worn by the otherwise naked writer Dulcie Deamer (dubbed by newspapers the 'Queen of Bohemia') is breathtaking. She shakes her long, dark curls, holds her bare arms high and spins around and around to the music, laughing beneath the lights.

A great deal of alcohol is consumed. Bottles of gin and whiskey circulate. As the night wears on, the combination of inebriation and disguise ensures that inhibitions evaporate. There is kissing in the darker corners and other forms of more intimate attention. Some men are seen to follow women into the ladies' conveniences and not emerge until much later. (The following week, in the Parliament, complaints will be made about 'licentious behaviour'.)

One level below the dancing, Zeno, reborn, is in his element. The Town Hall's basement has been converted into an imaginary carnival, filled with the sort of acts that might once have featured in Mr Anderson's splendid shows. There are fire eaters and contortionists and people who walk on stilts; a strong man called Reginald whose bulging, tattooed arms hoist enormous weights; Bea, a handsome, bearded lady in a pink faille gown; exciting rides to try and games of skill to play.

Half an hour before midnight a spotlight casts its beam across the room. A ripple of excitement runs through the crowd. It is more than just the sudden illumination. Zeno the Magnificent has appeared. Standing on an elevated dais, there is something about his poise, his showman's authority, that draws all eyes. Time seems to have stood still; he has lost none of his powers.

Napoleon, in fact one of the city's more self-important bankers, steps forward and is quickly mesmerised. He begins to sing a light operetta to general titters of amusement and surprise. Next, unwisely, a pirate king presents himself, assures his friends that, as a Crown solicitor, he has seen 'every trick in the book'. Consequently, he says, he will prove himself immune to the mesmerist's techniques. As popular rumour suggests that this respectable officer of the court is an enthusiastic patron of several illegal bookmakers, there are roars of laughter when, with a gesture from Zeno, he bares his teeth, paws the ground and whinnies like a horse. But these hypnotic feats, amusing as they might be, are but a modest prelude to Zeno's forte, magic and illusion.

The audience feels as if transported to another place and time. Afterwards, nobody can quite recall the details, or even decide on exactly what it was that occurred, though all agree that they have witnessed something extraordinary transpire. At some point in the performance a beautiful Chinese courtesan is introduced ... or is it two, or even four? It is impossible to tell: they seem to appear and disappear at will.

One of these exotic beauties steps into a mirrored wardrobe; in an instant she is gone. The wardrobe is opened a moment later and there are two of them, or is it more? Next, the courtesans appear to ascend calmly into the air. They hover in gorgeous defiance of gravity, their cheongsams softly fluttering, before they float serenely back down to earth. Finally, a single girl steps inside a large, black lacquered box: its door is closed and bolted. With a collective gasp the rapt spectators watch as, one by one, the magician drives six gleaming knives deep into its centre.

The other girl appears from left of stage and strolls into the spotlight – but where is her twin? The box is still there, the cruel blades remain, but there is no sign of Zeno. He has vanished.

The poor creature left alone in the glare struggles to unlock what has surely become a tomb; she starts to cry. The crowd shifts uncomfortably. This trick has gone seriously awry.

Suddenly, there is a clash of cymbals and a cheer as the missing girl, apparently emerging from thin air, flies gracefully across the room on a trapeze before landing, quite unscathed, on a soft pile of embroidered cushions conveniently placed at left of stage. The two seductive courtesans, reunited, hold hands and smile as a phosphorescent explosion ignites with a loud thunderclap of sound.

The air fills with golden, cinnamon-scented smoke. A shower of glittering stars rains down. White doves fly out of clouds which, by now, have mysteriously turned emerald green. Finally, out of this aromatic mist, Napoleon and the pirate king emerge with the victorious magician hoisted high upon their shoulders. From this vantage point Zeno raises an arm to salute his rapt audience.

Everybody agrees, it is a *tour de force*. They beg for more. But Zeno merely gestures for the light to be dimmed. Bows are taken. There are cries of 'Bravo!' and wild applause.

Lilian and Rosetta step behind a curtain and take off their masks. Rosetta is delighted that the acrobatic skills she acquired so long ago are still intact. As far as losing her nerve, that was never an issue; she knew she still had that.

The two remove their wigs and shake out their hair, anxious to be free and join the fun. Lilian is ready first. 'God, I'm parched,' she calls over her shoulder. 'I'll meet you upstairs at the bar.'

Rosetta, just before she follows, turns back to her husband in order to congratulate him. As she does, she sees his face turn ashen, sees him stagger back against a wall.

'Carl, what's wrong, what's the matter?' she cries urgently but he merely shakes his head.

Later, when he can speak, he tells Rosetta that at the very moment of his triumph his head was seized by a sharp, searing pain and an unspeakable vision passed before his eyes.

'Darling,' Rosetta says. 'It was a trick of the light, and the stress. It was all too much; you are simply not used to it.'

The magician is unconvinced. He saw death, though this time it was not that of others, but his own. Perhaps it was the light, the crowd, the heat, the hour; he is shaken, all the same. Later, a medical man says that he believes it was a minor cerebral incident, no cause for serious alarm.

It is enough. Zeno the Magnificent will not return again.

FIFTY

The masonic temple is the place to which Carl now turns for less demanding magic. Vulnerable, his health not what it was, the former sorcerer tells himself that the masons' harmless mysteries are safe, just what he needs.

A handwritten letter to my father from the Very Worshipful Brother Ern. W. McGregor, Secretary, states that Brother Norman was '*balloted for and accepted and initiated …*' into the First degree (Entered Apprentice) of the Ionic Lodge No. 181. He also advises that the event took place in the '*lodge room at Paddington Town Hall*'.

Occupying the highest point of a ridge line, the Paddington Town Hall dominates the landscape, its thrusting clock tower as emphatic as an exclamation mark. On the night of the initiation, the building's public visibility seems to Carl only to heighten the hidden nature of the rituals planned to take place within. He has a hazy idea of what lies in store. He knows a few scant details, but that is all.

Carl soon discovers that freemasonry's arcane rites are complex. Upon arrival, he is divested of a number of earthly possessions; he is asked to surrender his watch, his keys, his money. Next he is prepared in a peculiar manner; his left breast is bared, his right shirt sleeve rolled up, his left trouser leg folded back to a point above the knee. Finally, a noose is placed around Carl's neck and he is blindfolded. It is a position of uncommon vulnerability.

This procedure takes place outside the inner chamber, where he is attended by a tall, thick-set man known as the Tyler. The Tyler also plays the role of guard, barring entry to the sanctuary to anyone whose allegiance has not been adequately vouchsafed. When Carl is considered ready to proceed, the Tyler gives three distinctive knocks upon the door. A voice cries out, 'Whom have you there?'

'A poor candidate in a state of darkness,' is the answer.

There are several more questions and responses before the door is unlocked and Carl is led, yoked and half undressed, before the assembly. Due to the blindfold, he has no idea what the room looks like, nor who is present. Fifty pairs of eyes regard him, but he is unable to return the gaze of anyone.

At this point in the proceedings, it is usual for the prospective candidate, sightless and exposed, to feel alarm. It is a uniquely bizarre experience, after all, and even the most stout-hearted tend to be overwhelmed. Carl, however, undergoes not only this unorthodox introduction but the entire elaborate ritual with perfect equanimity. He occupies this esoteric world as naturally as a tiger might insinuate his way about the jungle or a falcon surmount the wind.

The lengthy ceremony is precisely choreographed. Carl makes vows of fidelity and swears to sacred obligations, he drops to his knees before the Worshipful Master and perambulates blindly across the chamber. At one stage, he feels the needle-like point of the long, knightly dagger, or *poignard*, being pressed against his naked breast. Even this threat fails to disconcert: Carl has long been aware that flirting with peril can be depended upon to produce a truly thrilling, theatrical effect.

Afterwards, he drinks brandy with Rosetta and, in what would be regarded by his new Brethren as a grave transgression, describes his curious evening. He tells her that final acceptance into the Lodge has required his solemn affirmation that, should he reveal the mason's secrets, 'My throat will be cut across and my tongue torn out. So you see, my love, I am risking a great deal for you.'

Rosetta smiles; these seem to her disproportionate penalties for divulging the name of King David's great-grandfather or the disclosure that the pressure of a fellow's thumb upon another's first joint might mean something to him. 'So much assiduous protection for such modest secrets,' she remarks with a grin.

It doesn't matter; Carl enjoys the fellowship. He also likes the drama. The showman in him appreciates the participants' performances, the appearance of their elaborate regalia. Carl discovers that, while Grand Masters might display ornate medals and embroidered collars, cuffs and gauntlets, Apprentices are presented with simpler stuff; a white lambskin apron, for purity; a twenty-four-inch gauge representing the division of a day into work, rest and assistance rendered; a common gavel symbolising conscience; and a chisel, for education.

Although he can't help but reflect that Professor Zeno had at his disposal a rather more potent arsenal, in the end, it doesn't matter. At this time in his complicated life of risk and adventure the medieval masons' tools of trade, the symbols of their craft, are enough for him.

The clandestine order to which Carl now subscribes is one in which concealed handshakes and words and signs are shared in a spirit of fraternity. It is a codified, sanctioned way of being. Not exactly a religion but not quite magic, either, freemasonry is not easy to define. Its members refer to it as 'a system of morality, veiled in allegory and illustrated by symbols'. Masons may aspire to do good works and live honourably, but approval is not universal. There are many, suspicious of what are rumoured to be ungodly practices, who look at them askance.

For Carl, freemasonry is neither wild nor dangerous. That is its appeal. It provides an orderly system of enchantment, brings into his life a new, fresh sense of trust and certainty.

Carl progresses through various stages of mystical enlightenment. He learns about the secret Sign of Horror and the Sign of Sympathy, the Sign of Joy and Exultation, the Sign of Grief and of Distress. He seems content with that.

FIFTY-ONE

In his correspondence with my father, Very Worshipful Brother McGregor sets out Carl's steady elevation; the passing to Second degree, Fellow Craft, and Third degree, Master Mason (Certificate No. 41612). Then he makes a note of Brother Norman's death, and his request for a masonic funeral. It is all there, written in McGregor's careful hand, on two single sheets of plain, lined paper.

Two notices are published in *The Sydney Morning Herald* on 31 August 1938. The first, placed by the undertaker W. Carter, advises relatives and friends that the interment of William Norman will occur at Botany Cemetery at 3.00 pm. The second, paid for by the Paddington Ionic Lodge No. 181, invites all Worshipful Brothers to attend. It refers to the late Brother Norman as 'esteemed' and advises 'Regalia at graveside'.

Carl has passed away just two days previously. According to Brother McGregor, he 'Died suddenly from Heart Attack'. It is not, then, a particularly dramatic end. As these things go, it is prosaic.

But what passed through Carl's mind during those final, painful moments? Despite all he had done to soothe his troubled soul, did he still see the blood-soaked trenches that used to torment him so, the young men lying cold and still, the mutilation? Was he there, with them?

It may be that Carl's end was more benign. Surrounded by that (much-reported) tunnel of transcendent white light, perhaps instead he glimpsed Princess Charlotte, ready to embrace him on the other side. If so, many other old friends and admirers were waiting, too: that fine physicist, Sir Oliver Lodge, was surely among this heavenly troop, delighted to be sharing the celestial ether with his old colleague Signor Marconi and the Honourable Beatrice, his first wife. It is likely that, to pass the time, the Empress Eugenie was quizzing Banjo Paterson on the subject of the Boers and that the Duchess of Rutland was discussing literature with Sir Arthur Conan Doyle. Although among the actresses and artists, duchesses and dukes, it is possible there were also a few who spent their lives engaged in vaguely criminal pursuits, in all it would have been a celebrated pantheon of the great and the good.

Dead then, and at only sixty-two: not very old. But, as Rosetta and Lilian agree, the man they knew lived more than one life during his allotted span. A tinsmith, fortune teller and seer, magician, Professor of Medicine, concocter of both medicines and spells, an illusionist and, finally, Artist and Master Mason. The women agree, it is a rare achievement.

That he has also been a husband, lover, companion and dear friend is not overlooked by them, nor in all honesty is the fact that, as Rosetta observes with a wry chuckle, 'He was, of course, a supreme charlatan.'

She and Lilian share a knowing look and laughter, the kind of strained merriment that turns into tears soon afterwards.

Grief assails the two women with a sharp intensity. Though Carl has not been well for some time, they find that anticipation of death is quite different to the fact of it. The official paperwork cites 'mitral regurgitation' and 'myocardial degeneration' as the cause; it is too brief, too clinical a description for the months of laboured breathing, the stabbing chest pains and fatigue. It does not capture the draining worry of the women who ministered to him throughout his illness, or what it was like to know that, no matter what they said or did, Carl was slipping away from them.

The graveside funeral is 'attended by [a] number of Brethren', reports Brother McGregor. Dressed in dark suits and black hats, white shirts and sober ties, the men also wear masonic aprons, black crepe bands above their left elbows and sprigs of acacia in their lapels. They remain huddled together in silent communion, a little apart from my great-grandmother's family and friends.

Beneath her flattering black-veiled hat, Rosetta is unusually composed; she does not weep. 'It is because I can't believe it, can't believe he's lying in that casket,' she confides in her sister Florence. 'I feel at any moment someone will tell me it is one of his illusions, that I will go home and there he'll be.'

It seems all too real to Lilian: she sheds silent, steady tears.

Lilian's estranged husband, Hercules Arthur Pakenham, CMG, Retired Colonel of Langford Lodge, Crumlin, County Antrim, Ireland, has died only a year earlier. Other than the fact that in 1895 he married a Miss Ashley in the Guard's Chapel, Hanover Square, his lengthy obituary in the *Belfast Telegraph* of 30 March 1937 has made no mention of her. The newspaper focused on Colonel Pakenham's political career, his stellar war record and illustrious relations. As far as his married life was concerned, the paper chose, discreetly, not to comment.

Lilian's reaction to the news of her husband's demise had been one of slight sentiment. She felt only a nebulous sadness, as if she had been informed of the death of someone who had once been married to a friend.

It is very different now that Carl has passed away. Sometimes she thinks that without Rosetta's force of will she will go mad with grief. Lilian is not well. She fears her life, too, may be coming to an end.

The Worshipful Master initiates proceedings by stepping forward and announcing, 'We have assembled in the character of Masons to offer a tribute of affection to the memory of our Brother; thereby demonstrating the sincerity of our esteem for him and our steady attachment to the principles of our Order.'

He then deposits Carl's white lambskin apron, 'an emblem of innocence', into his grave. 'This reminds us of the universal dominion of death,' the Master explains.

'The arm of friendship cannot interpose to prevent its coming; the wealth of the world cannot purchase our release; nor will the innocence of youth, or the charms of beauty propitiate its purpose.'

Next he takes the acacia sprig from his coat and holds it in his hand. He says it is 'the emblem of our faith in the immortality of the soul'.

'This plant is evergreen,' he declaims with quiet dignity. 'It symbolises dear Brother Norman's spiritual essence which, through our belief in the mercy of God, we confidently hope will continue to bloom in eternal spring.'

Rosetta thinks that perhaps it is the words, the theatre of it all, that make it so difficult to take in. 'This talk of spiritual essence and blooming in eternal spring,' she turns once more to Florence, 'it sounds so much like one of dear Carl's tricks.'

There is a brief pause before the Master carefully places his sprig of golden wattle into the grave. As he does, he solemnly intones, 'Alas, my Brother!'

The brethren follow in the footsteps of their Master. One by one every mason steps forward, deposits his own small stem of evergreen and utters the same refrain.

Only then does her beloved husband's death become real to Rosetta. Only when these three poignant words are spoken does she feel a wave of desolation.

'Alas, my Brother!' each man says, before he turns away.

Carl's grave is not difficult to find. Headed '*William Louis Norman*', constructed of red granite and flanked by decorative crosses, it is in the Anglican division, Section CC of Botany Cemetery. '*In loving memory*' has been carved on the tombstone and, beneath that, '*Never forgotten*'. More interesting is the placement given to an engraving of the masonic square and compasses; it surmounts everything.

Seeking illumination, I consult *Mackey's Revised Encyclopedia of Freemasonry, Volume 2*. There I learn that the square was used by medieval builders to verify that each building block of stone possessed a right angle that was straight and true. Integrity, balance and stability, firmness and resolve; these are the elements that masons say are essential to the formation of both sound structures and honest lives.

Compasses are used to create perfect circles, symbols of heaven and the immortal soul. Hence, this device invokes the boundaries that must be imposed in order that man's base desires are circumscribed and his carnal appetites curbed.

This restraint does not sound like something that Zeno the Magnificent would have been likely to adopt. It is a different question as to whether Brother Norman did, or not.

In his will William (Carl) Norman is described as 'Artist'. The statement is accurate, even if it leaves the impression that his talents were confined to the production of drawings and paintings. In fact, his artistry encompassed so much more than this; a master of invention, in truth it was his own life that was his greatest, most singular creation.

Carl left everything he had, 'all my property both real and personal whatsoever and wheresoever situate', to Rosetta. There is no mention of Lilian. He must have known that Rosetta would care for her until the end.

FIFTY-TWO

SEPTEMBER 1939

The women wait for news. They talk, though in a desultory fashion. At seven o'clock the two eat toast and boiled eggs. They are not hungry; the small tasks associated with the meal's preparation are a way to fill the time.

Lilian, now sixty-three, lives in Tara, a private hotel in Dudley Street near Coogee Beach. Her sitting room has pale-blue wall-paper and long windows that overlook the ocean. Lilian's health continues to deteriorate; she is too fragile to venture out. Alarmed, Rosetta sees the mauve-coloured shadows beneath her dear friend's eyes, hears the way that something in her throat seems to catch each time she inhales.

From time to time both women glance in the direction of the mantelpiece at the ticking clock. They wait, nervous and on edge, for an ultimatum to expire.

Far away in Europe and Great Britain events are taking place of awful consequence. Germany has annexed Austria. The

Czechoslovakian territory of Sudeten has been seized. Yet, last October, the British Prime Minister Neville Chamberlain had been so confident of the German Chancellor's probity that when Hitler promised there would be no more incursions he gleefully announced that 'peace in our time' had been achieved. In Australia, Prime Minister Joe Lyons was of the same mind. 'War has been averted,' he informed the nation, advising churches that a day of thanksgiving should be set aside.

Chamberlain and Lyons have been proven overly sanguine. Hitler's armies invaded the rest of Czechoslovakia in March. Tensions rose further when Germany and Italy signed a Pact of Steel. Then, two days ago, the final line was crossed. On 1 September (a year and a day after Rosetta buried her husband), Germany invaded Poland. Finally, Britain's hand was forced. Her government had no choice but to acknowledge that it must act.

Now, just two days later, it is Sunday, 3 September 1939. Time will soon run out. In Australia, though it happens to be Father's Day, few are in a festive mood. Many more congregants frequent church services than is usual, while attendances at football matches are noticeably poor. At 8.00 pm, Australian Eastern Standard Time, the country will know if it will once again be at war.

Lilian realises that if hostilities break out Dermot, her only son and an officer in the Grenadier Guards as was his father, will be thrust into the fighting. Though contact with her eldest child has been at best sporadic, as she looks out over the Pacific, so blue, so tranquil, she feels a cold, tight band of fear constrain her chest. She is afraid for him.

At such a time of crisis, Australia's vast distance from the Motherland imposes a special burden. International telephone calls are impossible. Nobody knows what is happening. Rosetta and Lilian share this equality of deficiency with their countrymen, including even the man who has, since Lyon's death in April, been the nation's new Prime Minister. Robert Menzies remains unaware that the United Kingdom has declared war on Germany until he, like everyone else, hears it on the radio. Only then does he receive a telegram from the British admiralty, formally requesting the dominion's assistance.

'Don't leave, Rose,' Lilian says. She feels frail and very tired. 'Stay here with me until we hear what Mr Menzies has to say.' Lilian turns and closes the window, shuts out a sudden wind. The ocean is no longer still. She sees rows of white-capped waves begin to surge and swell.

At 9.00 pm the Prime Minister makes a statement that is broadcast on every station. Menzies, grave and measured, speaks of his 'melancholy duty'. He announces that, as a result of Great Britain's declaration of war upon Germany, 'Australia is also at war.'

The Prime Minister continues, proclaiming, 'There can be no doubt that where Britain stands, there stand the people of the British world.' 'British': that is still the way not just Robert Menzies but most of Australia's seven million citizens regard themselves.

In a stirring conclusion, the Prime Minister affirms, 'I know that in spite of the emotions that we are feeling, Australia is ready to see it through. May God, in his mercy and compassion, grant that the world may soon be delivered from this agony.'

Rosetta and Lilian look at each other and wonder what this new calamity will bring.

My mother and grandmother are staying for a few days in the Blue Mountains in a clifftop hotel with panoramic bushland views, but any pleasure they may have taken in this brief holiday has fled. When Australia's participation in the Great War was announced there were widespread celebrations. But this time the atmosphere is sombre; there is no singing or dancing now. Billie, thirty-nine, remembers what it was like to be young and in the convent when one of her school friends, shocked and disbelieving, found the name of a father or a brother in the newspaper's black-bordered lists of casualties. That night she insists that they leave immediately and return home to their Sydney flat; she wants safety, some sense of security.

On 15 September, less than two weeks after war has been declared, Lilian dies in her bedroom at Tara. Rosetta must certify the death. Its cause is noted as 'chronic myocardial degeneration': like Carl, her heart has failed. Lilian has lived for just one year since he passed away. Perhaps, despite Rosetta's best efforts, the truth is she didn't wish to continue in a world without him.

The funeral takes place the next day at 11.15 am. The grave, numbered 120, is in the Anglican Section CC. The service is conducted by John Francis Gilbert Huthnance, Rector of St Matthew's, Botany.

The undertaker's records show that a hearse and one car are ordered. They also reveal that their account, for twenty pounds ten shillings, is paid by Mrs R. Norman.

Four decades later, my father went to the cemetery and recorded his impressions.

> *The grave of Lilian Pakenham, daughter of English nobility, in the Botany Cemetery on the far southern outskirts of Sydney, overlooks the Bay in which Captain Cook first landed on the coast of Eastern Australia in 1770.*
>
> *Now a bustling port feeding through a network of major roads a continuous stream of huge trucks and semi-trailers carrying containers from ports all around the world, it overlooks dozens of oil terminals. The winds from the south blow strongly . . .*
>
> *On the plain sandstone slab covering the grave the words chiselled in Gothic relief read,*

~

LILIAN

DAUGHTER OF

RIGHT HONOURABLE

EVELYN ASHLEY KG

AND GRANDDAUGHTER OF

ANTHONY ASHLEY

7TH EARL OF SHAFTESBURY KG

AND RUTH SAID 'INTREAT ME NOT TO LEAVE THEE OR TO RETURN FROM FOLLOWING AFTER THEE: FOR WHITHER THOU GOEST I WILL GO: AND WHERE THOU LODGEST, I WILL LODGE. THY PEOPLE SHALL BE MY PEOPLE AND THY GOD MY GOD: WHERE THOU DIEST WILL I DIE: AND THERE WILL I BE BURIED. THE LORD DO SO TO ME, AND MORE ALSO, IF OUGHT BUT DEATH PART THEE AND ME.'

Lilian is buried directly opposite Carl, their graves separated by only a narrow path. Rosetta has honoured the unorthodox relationship the two shared in life not only by the selection of Lilian's epitaph. She has ensured their proximity in death.

Life without Carl and Lilian is hard for Rosetta. This double blow strikes at her heart which, once the numbing anaesthesia of shock wears off, is filled with pain. Rosetta is distraught and, for the first time that she can remember, feels utterly alone. She wanders through her house, picks up an ornament, a book, a music box, puts them down again. Consumed with restlessness, she looks for something, some absent thing, but what?

It takes Rosetta many months to reconcile herself to the fact that both Carl and Lilian have gone forever, united in a place she cannot know, at least not yet. Over time, she learns to manage. Rosetta is accomplished at accommodating changing circumstances.

FIFTY-THREE

War continues for six more years. It will not be confined to Europe. When Japan becomes a combatant, the conflict spreads to the Hawaiian Islands and sweeps through Asia. Tropical Darwin, Australia's most northerly city, is bombed on Thursday, 19 February 1942. More than two hundred lives are lost and many more are wounded. The city is wrecked, with stores, buildings, port facilities and a large contingent of aircraft and ships destroyed. Then the unthinkable occurs: on Monday, 1 June, three midget Japanese submarines penetrate Sydney Harbour. Twenty-one sailors will be killed.

On the day of this small invasion, my mother is just seventeen. The combination of her arresting smile, long, dark hair and cornflower eyes means that, already, men lose their hearts to her. She is with my grandmother in their flat with her latest boyfriend, a blond American soldier called Ralph. They hear the sirens, fill the bath with water and fly to safety beneath the stairs. Then Ralph dashes back. 'I'm not going anywhere without my photos of you, honey,' he says. 'I'd rather risk my life than leave them behind.'

Ralph is flattering, if foolish. My mother declines his proposal of marriage and a life spent beside Lake Erie in Buffalo, USA.

Sydney is hosting an influx of these international servicemen. Mum enjoys the attention she receives, and her new position: secretary to Colonel Kennedy, a regular army officer based at historic Victoria Barracks near the Town Hall in Paddington. Her tone is matter-of-fact when she tells me how it came about. 'The Colonel inspected a line of girls, then announced I had the job.'

When I ask her what the Colonel had thought of her shorthand and typing skills, she says blithely, 'He didn't seem particularly interested.'

Apparently, the Colonel had been obliged to share his office with his secretary and, as my mother observes, 'He must have wanted something attractive to look at.'

She hasn't met my father yet: he is out of the country. Dad, now thirty years of age, serves in Papua New Guinea and then the Philippines. He is a naval officer, seconded to the staff of the charismatic Supreme Commander of the South West Pacific, General Douglas MacArthur.

When we were young Dad delighted my brother and me with his stories. He said the Americans had fought with their stomachs filled with 'hot rolls and ice cream'; that they had flown an entire orchestra into the Tacloban jungle 'for one show only' so the troops could hear Ravel's *Bolero* the night before the major thrust to liberate Manila.

We heard how General MacArthur would stride down a beach under enemy fire, seemingly both oblivious to and immune from the bullets that flew past him, and about Commander Branson, the 'Pirate King' of Milne Bay, who conducted military operations half naked, wearing a sarong. Dad told us about sharing a small shack made from palm leaves with a python, about drinking watery soup with a young impoverished lieutenant, Prince Philip of Greece (later the Duke of Edinburgh), and about the way he had distracted himself as he rode a warship into battle by reading poems by Shelley and watching the flying fish spin.

My father had a knack for storytelling. He made war sound not like the hell it was but rather a kind of Boys' Own adventure set on foreign beaches and gentle southern seas.

FIFTY-FOUR

SYDNEY, 15 AUGUST 1945

At 9.30 on a Wednesday morning Rosetta is dressing for a trip to town. She has an appointment at the bank to discuss some future plans. She selects a suit, a blouse, a hat and gloves (wartime has limited the choice); the radio is on. That is the moment, so ordinary, so everyday, when the longed-for announcement comes. Rosetta hears the Prime Minister, Ben Chifley, say that the Second World War is at an end. He tells the nation that hostilities with Japan have ceased. 'Let us offer thanks to God,' he says. Rosetta drops her gloves and gives a small, involuntary scream.

Sirens rend the air and crowds gather across the country to cheer and celebrate. When Rosetta arrives in Sydney's Martin Place she is soon swept up in the elation. There are thousands crammed together in a spontaneous outpouring of joy. People of all ages run and shout to each other, they sing and embrace. One man kicks his legs up and begins an exuberant dance; another kisses Rosetta full on the mouth. From city offices high above, a blizzard of hastily torn up paper floats down in billowing white clouds onto hats and hair and blissful, upturned faces.

At the same time, clouds of a more lethal kind continue to discharge their deadly vapours upon Hiroshima and Nagasaki: the release of atomic bombs on the 6th and 9th of August have led to the conflict's cataclysmic termination. Few Australians contemplate this new menace; they are too relieved that their own travails are at an end. What matters is that the boys, those who have survived, are safe. They will come home again.

Lord and Lady Louis Mountbatten have had not so much a good as a triumphant war. Handsome, clever Lord Louis is now the Supreme Allied Commander of South-East Asia; his elevation has been both showy and rapid. Edwina, widely applauded for her selfless work among the sick and wounded, still contrives to look chic even while wearing her army uniform. (The hand-stitched ensemble has been made to measure by one of Savile Row's finest bespoke tailors; even Edwina's shoes have been created just for her.)

Not long after the war has ended, the Mountbattens arrive in Australia. *The Sydney Morning Herald* of Saturday, 30 March 1946, reports that their plane, en route from Melbourne, landed the day before at 11.55 am. Next, according to the paper, Lord and Lady Louis 'drove straight to Admiralty House to visit the Duke and Duchess of Gloucester'.

HRH Prince Henry William Frederick Albert, Duke of Gloucester, Earl of Ulster, Baron Culloden, third son of the King and Mountbatten's cousin, has been Australia's Governor-General since his arrival on 28 January 1945. The decision was not without controversy. This had nothing to do with the secret mistress for whom he maintained a suite in London's Grosvenor Hotel, nor the illegitimate child thought to have resulted from the affair, nor even that Queen Mary is said, once an incriminating letter was revealed, to have bought the woman's silence for one million pounds; all these details emerged much later.

It is Prince Henry's excessive partiality to strong drink that drove the Labor Party's new Minister for Immigration, Arthur Calwell, to question his reputation. The then Prime Minister John Curtin, though no stranger to the difficulties associated with the immoderate ingestion of alcohol himself, was not persuaded. The royal appointment went ahead.

Nobody really knows whether the Duke wanted the position. He was obliged to take it on in the most unfortunate of circumstances when the first choice, his younger brother the Duke of Kent, died in an aviation crash in Scotland. But he applies himself to the task, and if the official residence in rural, fly-blown Canberra is not to his taste, who can blame him? Much better that his rich and glamorous relations join him at Admiralty House, his official Sydney residence.

The *Herald* sets out their crowded schedule on its front page. The newspaper notes that the couple will both attend a Lord Mayoral reception, go to dinner at Government House, visit Canterbury Park races and the Returned Soldiers League at Anzac House. The itinerary also states that 'at 1.00pm, Lord Louis will lunch with the Premier, Mr. McKell'.

Then, almost as an afterthought, the paper adds, 'Lady Louis will remain at Admiralty House.'

This welcome respite from official duties provides the perfect opportunity for Edwina to engage in private conversation with her late Aunt Lilian's dear friend, Mrs Norman.

In a brief note my father wrote:

> *Edwina invited Rosetta to visit her in Sydney ... so that they might discuss Lilian Pakenham's affairs and recompense her for the funeral, so apparently Dermot did not receive [the invoice for] the expenses.*

Tragically, on 2 April 1940, just six months after Rosetta and Edwina Mountbatten's initial correspondence, Lilian's son succumbed, according to *Debrett's*, to 'wounds received in action'. He had been on patrol in West Flanders when he was shot by a lone German sniper.

The magnificent Vice-Regal car is despatched. It creates something of an impact when it pulls up in suburban Murray Street and its liveried chauffeur steps out. One neighbour, not normally given to the expression of emotion, is heard to emit a low whistle and mutter, 'Crikey, look at that.'

Conscious of Lady Louis' reputation for modish style, Rosetta has dressed carefully. She has chosen a fine chocolate-brown and white checked linen suit, so well cut you would never suspect it was crafted from the meagre lengths of fabric permitted by the ration book. A small hat, its brim turned up on one side with a single rust-speckled feather to add panache, completes the outfit. It is not showy but elegant, in good taste. It will give the desired effect.

As Rosetta is driven northward, across the commanding gun-metal span of the Sydney Harbour Bridge, she withdraws into a world of private thought. Ferries, sailing boats and tankers, tugs and ocean liners, all ply the pellucid waterway she rides above, yet she hardly notices these craft. She doesn't see the tiny island of Fort Denison, its golden sandstone walls and iron cannons, nor the many looping coves and bays that indent the harbour. Instead, Rosetta thinks about a distant Melbourne day when she first gazed into Lilian's eyes, blue as pieces of the sky. She reflects on all they did and shared together since then, and who they loved. For a moment, she is filled with longing for the way it was.

Rosetta's reverie is interrupted by her arrival at Admiralty House. Like most Sydney-siders she is familiar with the appearance of this graceful mansion; it stands, surrounded by verdant lawns, poised on the city's northern foreshore in an eye-catching position. Now Rosetta crosses its distinctive wide veranda beneath the vaulting arches of a white colonnade. Just before she passes through the entrance she turns, takes a moment to admire the sweeping, sun-drenched scene laid out before her; water shading from malachite to aquamarine, land that dips and curves, and city buildings pressing hard against the sky.

Rosetta is met by Lady Louis' private secretary, a thin woman with the keen expression of a fox, who briskly ushers her past the elaborate staircase and into an informal reception room. Despite its handsome timber wainscots and commodious proportions, Rosetta notes the modest furnishings; there are landscapes on the walls of an uneven quality, a number of tired, chintz-covered couches and some woven rugs, rather threadbare in places. She expects it is the result of wartime stringency. Rosetta sees that someone, no doubt for the benefit of the illustrious English visitors, has arranged a vase of native Australian flowers; there are spiky banksias, red kangaroo paws and Sturt's desert peas. There, on the mantelpiece, amid these polite, indifferent surroundings, the blooms strike her as out of place; they look too wild, too primitive.

Lady Mountbatten enters, soignée in navy and white coin-spotted silk. While extending conventional greetings, she evaluates her guest, ponders strengths and weaknesses.

A moment later she gives one of her famously dazzling smiles and says, 'Mrs Norman, I do believe I can be quite frank.'

Rosetta has passed an invisible test; she can be trusted. Edwina pours tea and offers sandwiches, tiny triangles filled with pink slivers of smoked salmon and frills of lettuce. Then the two women speak about Lilian, and the past, and what it meant.

FIFTY-FIVE

It was 1991, the year after my child had died, the year my second daughter was born. Impaled between grief and joy, I paid scant attention to the preoccupations that held my father in their thrall.

Now, I read the results of that year of his research with intense fascination. He left the transcripts of five interviews behind, all but one conducted during what was for me a transcendent twelve months of change. Reading my father's words brings forth the sensation that I am walking in his footsteps. Type, like footprints, fades of course, but not the words themselves, they retain their clarity. Words keep their capacity for surprise.

It is through the transcripts that I learn the way in which my great-grandmother met her third and final husband. His name is Thomas Reginald Rufus Tait, otherwise known as Tom Tait.

Rosetta's last husband is not like Zeno the Magnificent. He is not a magician, nor a seer, not a healer nor a black marketeer. Tom does not amaze. He is a painter, though not an artist. He paints more prosaic things – fences, doors, the window frames of houses; he is a regular sort of man. But, as has so often been the case in Rosetta's life, all is not as it seems. There is, in fact, something remarkable about Tom, after all. At just thirty-three years old, he is half Rosetta's age.

My great-grandmother has managed to astonish me once again. If I had any thought that, nearing seventy, her defiance of convention might be diminishing, I now know how mistaken I have been.

When news reaches them of her impending nuptials, the family – Rosetta's five sisters, Florence, Ivy, Winifred, Daisy and Evelyn, and their husbands, her much younger brother, Clifford, his wife and all their children – are aghast. There is ample speculation as to young Tom's motives. They speak of dark purposes.

'He doesn't love her. It's the money, can't you see?' One of Rosetta's nephews puts voice to the family's worst suspicions. 'Just look at what she has. Houses and flats everywhere, in Bondi, Bronte, Tamarama. Plus she owns half of Bondi Junction. There are probably fifty, maybe sixty places. Why wouldn't he want to marry Auntie Rose?'

Though not so extensive as her nephew would like to believe, Rosetta's portfolio is by now impressive. She has even bought cottages in Wonderland Avenue, a street named after the old amusement park that, in another lifetime, she used to know so well. It amuses her, this proof of how far she has come. Once a mere dependent young wife, trapped by an ill-fated marriage, now she has the deeds to many properties. Rosetta has not just remade herself. She has created her own version of Wonderland.

It is the Yellow Peril that brings Tom and Rosetta together. Ironic, really, considering this is the unpleasant, xenophobic way that Australians describe an imagined Asian threat. When Rosetta's neighbours laugh and throw this term about, they carelessly ignore the fact that her late husband was half Chinese. Nine years have passed since his death; perhaps they never knew the man. In any case, it isn't Carl Norman they are referring to. It is Rosetta's enormous twelve-cylinder vintage Packard motor car, coloured just as brightly as the yolk of an egg.

Rosetta acquired a taste for the finer things in life a long time ago and Packards, with their smooth leather upholstery, their gleaming finish of rich paint and shining chrome, have a reputation for unparalleled American opulence. The King of Yugoslavia, the Queen of Spain, the Shah of Iran and the Aga Khan had all bought them. The Emperor of Japan was rumoured to own ten of these glamorous vehicles while, prior to the Russian revolution, the Czar selected a Packard for his luxurious imperial state limousine. Now, it is in this eye-catching brand of automobile that Rosetta alarms her staid neighbourhood, hence the sobriquet. Rosetta is still drawn to danger, remains partial both to speed and risk. She is mad about fast motor cars. The Yellow Peril is her pride and joy.

By now, Rosetta is increasingly volatile: 'the epitome of stormy', as Tom Tait will later remark. The temper she had as a young woman, the flare of annoyance that over the years she has contained, is starting to become unchecked. People who know her say she 'flies off the handle'. She lacks restraint.

'Wretched, wretched thing!' Rosetta is shouting when Tom, all taut muscles and thick sandy hair, first catches sight of her. He has been occupied painting a large house in Murray Street, opposite her own. As it is a big job and the work has made Tom hot, he decided to take his lunch over to Rosetta's shady garage, just across the road. But it is not his sitting there, eating ham sandwiches and drinking tea in a place in which he has no right to be, that ignites Rosetta's ire. She's having trouble with the Packard. 'This damn car won't start!' she cries. Her eyes flash and her hands fly to her hips.

Tom watches as she floods the engine. He is a self-confessed erratic driver. Nevertheless, he offers his assistance. Tom starts the Packard up and, as he put it to my father more than forty years after this propitious intervention, 'She thinks I am a miracle man.'

As the car roars into life so, too, does the marvel of this new relationship.

FIFTY-SIX

Rosetta and Tom appear to have little in common, save for their religious persuasion, though this faith is not the same one into which my great-grandmother was born. During her life with Zeno Rosetta traversed the furthest reaches of a plethora of Eastern creeds, became familiar with the gods of ancient Egypt, Hindu philosophy, the sayings of Buddha and the principles of Zen. At various stages theosophy and, of course, spiritualism were all encountered and embraced. Of late, however, Rosetta has adopted a new set of heavenly beliefs. She is devoted to the Roman Catholic faith. Though Rosetta does not formally convert, she brings to this most recent set of religious convictions a passionate zeal.

It began after Carl died in 1938 when, as had so often been the case, a new man entered my great-grandmother's life. She was lonely when she first met Father Martin Riley yet, even after Tom became a fixture, their relationship would endure. Father Riley has the black hair and emerald eyes of Ireland's sons. His female parishioners agree that he is really far too handsome for his ecclesiastical vocation.

As for Rosetta, she has never lost her allure. Though in the year of Carl's death she turned fifty-eight, there was something about her, beyond her full figure and the dark gold in her eyes, some inner, carnal appeal still capable of tempting even a man of God. Despite the fact that Father Riley had long been a member of the Order of the Sacred Heart, had vowed to maintain a state of chastity in thought and deed, he was entranced.

Rosetta now visits this good-looking man at least once a week. It has continued for four years; Tom discovers that Rosetta 'won't make a move without consulting him'. She no longer has a fortune teller by her side. Perhaps she thinks that Father Riley has unnatural powers; that with his Celt's eyes he can see into the future just as Zeno the Magnificent once did.

Despite her ardour, Rosetta is not truly a member of the Catholic faith. All the same, she wants to enter into the sanctity of the confessional: Martin Riley might be persuaded to make an exception in her case. Perhaps not in church, but in a less formal place. It is interesting to speculate on what version of the truth she might have decided to reveal, or what penance would have been required.

Something gnaws, it needles. Rosetta does not acknowledge, even to herself, what could be the cause of her disquiet. Whatever it is, she decides that it might help to do some good during her life. On a warm spring day scented with gardenias, in that tranquil moment which so often follows one of their intimate exchanges, she asks her spiritual guide, 'Is there anything I can do, perhaps, for one of your charities?'

'Why of course, my dear.' Father Riley smiles, relieved that there is a way for him to expiate such feelings of disturbing guilt as might arise. He covers her hand with his own and says, 'I know St Catherine's would welcome your help.'

St Catherine's is an orphanage for girls. Situated north of Sydney in the tiny hamlet of Brooklyn, it occupies a narrow stretch of land by the peaceful waters of the Hawkesbury River. Surrounded by dense bushland, the setting is idyllic, though life within the orphanage itself is desolate. This is not unusual. It is the way the disenfranchised live.

The home was established in unlikely circumstances: a member of the Sisters of Mercy inherited the old Brooklyn Hotel. As a result of the Great Depression, there was a pressing need for a place for children who had been left. Opened in 1931, where once men yarned, smoked, fought and, above all, imbibed, now the Sisters reign. The girls consigned to St Catherine's arrive as a result of their parents' death, or poverty, or clandestine relationships, universally condemned. They are told that they are lucky the Lord has provided them with a roof above their heads. This does nothing to mitigate their feelings of abandonment.

At St Catherine's, as in most institutions of the time, the view is widely held that good character is forged only in the iron cauldron of discipline. Many years later, when former residents of the home make submissions to a Senate Inquiry, they allege that they received regular beatings inflicted on them by nuns with canes. It is not an isolated complaint.

But all Rosetta knows is that she now donates substantial funds to a place for unwanted girls. That it is called St Catherine's, the second name of her own forsaken child, is not the only irony.

FIFTY-SEVEN

Rosetta marries Tom according to the holy rites of the Roman Catholic Church on 31 July 1947. She has insisted that only St Mary's, Sydney's pre-eminent cathedral, will suffice. The cathedral's majestic size, soaring nave, the fine French oil paintings of the Stations of the Cross, all meet her current requirements: a fitting stage for an occasion of personal triumph. Father Riley, green eyes or not, does not conduct the ceremony. That task is assigned to Rosetta's local priest, Father Peter Gilligan, a man she barely knows since he is newly appointed as minister to St Patrick's and St Anne's in the parish of Bondi, close to where she lives.

My father spoke to Peter Gilligan. He found him living peacefully in the southern suburb of Sans Souci. Four decades after the then inexperienced, freshly ordained priest first met Rosetta, the impression that she made was lasting. Father Gilligan said she was 'an artistic type of lady', if somehow 'strange'. Did he mean Rosetta had a love of art, or that she was daring, individual, unlike other women of that time? Probably both, I think.

Then the ageing priest told my father something that was unexpected. He said how attractive she was. Father Gilligan would have been a young man in his twenties when he first saw Rosetta, who was many decades older than he. Yet, even after all this time had passed, the priest still remembered just how appealing she could be.

'Thank God for Christian Dior,' Rosetta says to her sister Florence, as she contemplatively sips from a crystal glass filled with champagne.

In a curious reprise of the past, once more she stands before a mirror on another wedding day. The eighteen-year-old bride that she was has, of course, long been eclipsed. Now the face reflected in the glass belongs to a mature woman. It bears evidence of experience; the dark eyes are more calculating and there are fine lines beside her full, curved mouth, the expression on that arresting face is infinitely more knowing – she has seen and done so much!

The fact is, nearly half a century has passed since the unfortunate day on which she married Louis Raphael, father of her lost child. During that time Rosetta has had another, infinitely more exotic husband, travelled the world and acquired the freedom that comes with wealth. She has known well-born, clever, rich and famous men and women, grown used to their devotion and desire. For Rosetta, in her seventh decade, the word 'enough' has no resonance. Her appetite for life and love has not waned. She still craves adventure, wants more, more of everything.

Tom Tait may not have the attributes of the other men she has known, but he has the special beauty only youth bestows. She has defied so many things, why not time as well? Tom is like a magical elixir. The banality of advancing years is vanquished by the very fact of him.

'I do adore the New Look, don't you?'

On this matter, if not on the subject of her intended, Rosetta and her sister are in perfect accord. Fortunately for this bride-to-be, half a year ago in a freshly painted Parisian salon on the

Avenue Montaigne, a previously unknown designer unveiled a revolutionary style. As the fashion writer Georgina Howell later observed, 'Each dress and suit was an orgy of all things feminine and forbidden.'

Christian Dior's New Look caused an international sensation, rendering wartime's spare, broad-shouldered clothes – never flattering to Rosetta's lush figure – indisputably *démodé*. With a Gallic shrug Monsieur Dior simply remarked, 'I brought back the neglected art of pleasing.'

For Rosetta, the timing could not have been better. Her wedding present from Helena Rubinstein is the Dior dress she now admires. Wrapped in a cloud of tissue paper, placed inside a white box tied with trailing tendrils of soft grey ribbon and shipped from Paris, it is a flawless example of the couturier's art.

'Quite divine,' Rosetta murmurs. Helena, herself a Dior devotee, has always known the fashions that will best serve to enhance the striking looks of her old friend.

Remarkably, when Rosetta enters splendid St Mary's Cathedral, she has an ageless quality. Her deep reservoir of self-belief, combined with that Dior dress, has woven a silken spell and made her not just beautiful but young, again.

The pale *café au lait* shade flatters Rosetta's complexion and her hair, especially as it is no longer the dark wine it used to be but, thanks to artifice, a rather brighter red. The shoulders of the dress are neat, which serves to emphasise Rosetta's breasts, as does the waist, nipped in and defined by the addition of two creamy roses held by a jewelled pin. Best of all is the skirt. In a length called ballerina, it swoops down to a point just between calf and ankle, and consists of a sinful profusion of silk taffeta and rustling petticoats. Australian women continue to wear skimpy outfits, the unhappy result of rationing. Rosetta's attire, by contrast, speaks of voluptuous luxury. It signifies something else, as well: a vision of the future, of how abundant it can be.

~

There is another echo from the past. St Mary's Cathedral is directly opposite the Macquarie Street site of Rosetta's civil marriage to her second husband, the magnificent Zeno. Like the Registry Office, this grand church is built of blocks of golden stone. Its style is Gothic, too, but there the similarity ends. St Mary's is a place of sanctity, not the government-sanctioned transactions that take place between women and men.

Father John Therry, Sydney's first officially recognised Catholic priest, imagined a mighty church with two spires that would pierce the heavens like the very sword of God. William Wardell, St Mary's architect (and, coincidentally, that of Genazzano, Frances' school, as well), has brought Father Therry's vision to life, though not the spires. These thrusting symbols of faith must wait until Australia marks a new millennium. Even so, the building's carved doors and pointed windows, its flying buttresses, steeply pitched slate roof, domes, towers and gables constitute an impressive hymn to God.

When a Catholic wishes to marry an unbaptised person, it is first necessary for a bishop to provide what is known as a 'dispensation from disparity of cult'; the church authorities dislike it when one of their flock marries out of the faith, but at least this device permits them to maintain some control over the nuptial proceedings. Although Rosetta has embraced many cults, she is successful in attaining the dispensation. It does not mean, however, that her marriage to Tom may be conducted before the high altar with its carved relief of Christ. They are consigned to a small chapel just behind the dais.

Here, Tom and Rosetta kneel side by side. Late winter sunshine streams in through the stained-glass windows, washing the pair in coloured light: sapphire, ruby and topaz. Beneath the elevated red cedar roof, watched over by chiselled saints, the wedding ceremony takes place.

Rosetta promises to both love her husband and obey. Obedience might be unlikely, but she does love Tom. Not in the way she has loved before, but in the way a woman loves a much younger man when he holds her in his strong, lean arms during the night.

'I do,' Rosetta says, in the correct place, and so does Tom.

There is now no duty left for Father Gilligan to perform save for declaring the newlyweds man and wife. He might look askance at their disparity not just of cult but, more pertinently, of age, but wisely makes no remark. 'You may kiss the bride,' he says, instead.

And then, as St Mary's fine set of eight bronze bells rings out, that most unlikely couple, Mr and Mrs Thomas Tait, leave the Cathedral and begin their wedded life.

FIFTY-EIGHT

Tom knows when he marries Rosetta that she is an older woman – how can he not? He does not realise how much older.

Rosetta has her own Holy Bible. It is covered in rich maroon leather, the colour of ox blood, and the type is etched in gold. The birthday of each member of her family is set down on a separate page of its own. Tom has already noticed that the page recording the details of Rosetta's birth has been ripped from the binding. There is nothing to indicate when she was born. I imagine her conducting this excision; she tears the page and then she tears and tears again until she has nothing but a small pile of shredded paper that resembles ash.

It is not enough. She must go further in order to eliminate the past. And so once more she sets about a process of re-creation. Rosetta changes her date of birth; she ensures that the new date is officially recorded. Her third marriage certificate states that Tom was born in 1914. This is correct. He is thirty-three. But in Rosetta's case, the year of her birth, 1880, becomes 1890. She is no longer a woman who will turn sixty-seven in two weeks' time. She is a decade younger. Simply by deciding it is so, ten years vanish.

My great-grandmother is skilled in more than the art of fabrication. She is expert in extinguishment. Sometimes it is facts, sometimes events. And, as has long been her practice, people, too, disappear when they no longer suit.

'I never even knew she existed, my cousin Frances,' Rosetta's nephew, Frank, tells my father on the telephone (his real name, like that of my grandmother and her grandmother – though with the spelling customarily adopted for males – was Francis). Frank's father, Clifford, was the last of Rosetta's siblings. Born in March 1900, he was twenty years younger than she was, a different generation. In fact, Clifford was born just weeks after the birth of Rosetta's own child: he was almost exactly the same age as his niece, Frances Catherine. But Clifford never mentioned this other child to his son Frank. Perhaps he had forgotten she ever lived.

Rosetta's sister Florence, known as Florrie, did not banish her memories of the little girl. Florence spoke of her to Lionel, her son.

'Frankie, they used to call her,' Lionel says to Dad, his words captured in one more transcript. 'Of course, we children of the other sisters never saw Frankie, even as a child.'

This is the way I learn that my grandmother, Frances, who I called Nana Billie, had another nickname altogether. 'Frankie': it sounds so familiar, so affectionate, yet she was banished from their midst.

I turn back to Clifford's son, Frank, who reveals a rich stream of memories about his aunt. They are recounted in a conversation with my father dated 23 February 1993, later than the rest. Frank says Rosetta became eccentric. Her flamboyance, her tantrums, her hair – now dyed a flaming red – all these things are recalled. Frank remembers his childhood, the way he mowed Rosetta's lawn when he was still a boy and in return she always offered him a drink.

'What would you like, Frank? Banana or pineapple flavour or what?'

Invariably, Frank chose banana, though it wasn't cordial but a more potent brew. The boy drank deeply from a cup of sweet, golden liqueur.

Accessing the recollections of unknown relatives (all save Frank, now dead) has reignited my struggle to understand the act that was to affect the next three generations of women concluding, finally, with me. They have brought Rosetta into sharper focus but also evoked disturbing emotions. I find my objectivity beginning to evaporate. In his conversation with Dad, Frank says, 'I was one of Rosie's favourites.' How nice for you, I think.

The next transcript I come to does little to assuage these unruly feelings. In 1991, my father discovered that Tom Tait was still alive. But he didn't contact him directly. The first conversation that took place was between Tom and the resourceful Jan Worthington, Dad's principal research assistant.

My father kept a record of his own subsequent conversation with Jan, who begins by telling him that Tom claimed Rosetta 'never talked about her daughter'. Later, it becomes apparent that this wasn't true. Tom was holding something back.

'He did come back to the daughter,' I read Jan saying. Unfairly, I take umbrage. Why did Jan refer to her like that, 'the daughter'? She had a name; it was Frances or, if not Frances, Billie. She was my grandmother. I realise how raw this evisceration of the past has made me feel.

Next, Jan reports, 'I said to Tom that it was a bit sad there was a child who had no contact with her mother.'

'A bit sad': the words seem too small, too slight to encompass a life of grief.

'I was told something about that,' Tom replies. 'I don't know whether I should tell you or not.'

Tom is wary. He is right to be. Some part of him knows that, once said, the searing words that he might utter next can never be taken back.

Tom puts his doubts aside. Jan recounts, 'He decided it wasn't going to do any harm at this late stage.' I feel my stomach lurch and keep on reading.

'The reason Rosetta never had anything to do with the child was because she had been raped by Louis Raphael on her wedding night.

'She hated the child who had been born of it.'

There is more, but I am too stunned to go on. My great-grandmother hated her child. Hated her. I am wounded and enraged. The words might have been spoken more than two decades ago but their power remains.

I had persuaded myself that Rosetta believed giving up her daughter was a necessary sacrifice. Perhaps it was the only way for her to keep her sanity. Now I discover that I am quite wrong. All my explanations, the carefully constructed arguments, have been nullified. Rape is unforgivable. But what justification could there be for visiting the sins of the father, if that is what they were, upon the child?

A sense of disturbing synchronicity comes upon me, the feeling when, across time, two terrible worlds collide. I turned five the year Rosetta died, the same age that my grandmother, Frances, was when she was left behind. Now the turbulent emotions of that five-year-old stir within me. Rosetta chose not to know me, too. I never saw her, never knew her name. But, somehow I can't help wondering, would she have wished me away as well?

Later, in a calmer, more meditative moment, I come to suspect that my turmoil and self-doubt might have less to do with Rosetta than I had originally thought. I think these feelings have become entangled with my own, separate loss. It seems that grief cannot be readily apportioned; it is boundless.

I consider love and hate, two states that share the same white-hot intensity. Surely, to move from profound love to mere dislike is rare – there is no equivalence. Maybe the terrible emotion that filled Rosetta's heart was the way she reconciled a love she found impossible to have. I don't believe one's children can be easily escaped.

The next transcript is no easier to read than the last. This time it reveals a telephone conversation between my father and Tom. My father starts: 'I hope you don't find me presumptuous.'

It is not just good manners. Dad has been a professional seeker of the truth and knows the most effective way to finesse retrieval of the facts. He continues, 'Did she ever refer to her daughter at all, apart from the story that she'd had a bad experience on her wedding night?'

'That was the only time. The only time she ever spoke of her, I'm sorry to say this, was disparagingly. She did not like her at all.'

'But she had never seen her.'

'That's it.'

'She left the child ...'

'That's right, and anyone who'd ever mention it, she'd get up in arms about it and say, "I don't want to know."'

I don't want to know. Those five words glide before my eyes; they take their toll.

My father decides that he wants to meet Tom and that he is going to bring my mother with him. Tom, white-haired now, is seventy-seven. He is living in a substantial house on a man-made canal supplied with water from a lagoon, also man-made, named, in one of life's small ironies, Lake Wonderland. The address is

21 Bight Court, Mermaid Waters. The neighbourhood lies inland immediately behind Mermaid Beach; it is called after *The Mermaid*, a cutter ship that brought the surveyor John Oxley to the region in 1823. Today it forms a part of Queensland's famous Gold Coast, a place for holidaymakers attracted by a certain hard-edged glamour and retirees like Tom who crave the sun.

My father takes photographs. In one of them Tom wears beige slacks, a crisp shirt and a deep blue cardigan. He looks genial, relaxed; a man at ease, in comfortable circumstances and enjoying a good life. In others I see Tom's house. It is a modern, light-coloured, two-storey brick home with a red-tiled roof, a television aerial as tall as a ship's mast and, at the front, a wide, paved pathway leading to a double garage. Inside there are shiny-skinned reclining chairs, wood-veneer shelves and angular aluminium lamps. The terrace features plastic chairs. There is also a row of white planter boxes in which there are no plants.

My father takes the lead. Unusually, Mum has little to say; she sizes up the room, looks at Tom. Despite the fact that she sits before the man who shared the last eleven years of her unknown grandmother's life, she is detached. She waits to see what will happen.

Tom hasn't much to add to what he has already told Jan and my father earlier. The visit seems to be something of an anti-climax; an agreeable morning tea, that's all. They chat amiably as northern sunshine streams in through the window. It is strange to imagine my parents sitting, talking to Tom about a chain of events that commenced when Rosetta was eighteen years old and Queen Victoria still occupied the throne. In that tidy, contemporary house, with its gleaming white refrigerator, chlorinated swimming pool and ubiquitous TV, it provokes an odd feeling, as if time might be more elastic than one thinks.

Tom serves tea and opens a packet of biscuits. My mother notices that just one item stands out in this unexceptional house. It is the tea cups. They are beautiful, of fine china, a pleasing shape and have an oriental pattern. My mother exclaims, 'These are exquisite.'

Tom says, ‘Those were your grandmother’s.’

How does she feel? Mum struggles for the right word and settles on ‘unusual’ to sum up the uncommon emotion evoked by holding in her hand something precious that was once pressed against the lips of the grandmother she never knew.

‘I would have liked one of those cups,’ my mother, wistful, said to me years later. But she hadn’t asked, and Tom hadn’t offered, so she remained disappointed. He did, however, send many other things. It was Tom who despatched Lilian’s riding crop, Tom who forwarded the contents of a small child’s suitcase that had remained untouched and overlooked for years in one of the sunny rooms that lay next to that man-made Gold Coast canal. Inside were the rare, century-old letters and telegrams written to Zeno and Rosetta by their crowned and titled friends and clients from both Britain and Europe. But as to who that little case might have originally belonged to, Tom never said.

He did reveal that he knew Rosetta’s granddaughter had married my father. He claimed that it was ‘common knowledge’ between them, that he and Rosetta had been aware of it ‘for years’. By the 1950s Dad was a member of the Parliament of New South Wales. He had a profile, Mum was a beauty and, as a consequence, their photographs were in the papers from time to time. But how did Rosetta become aware that Sybil Jacobs, as my mother was, had married him? How had she found out that Sybil was her daughter, Frances’ child? All of which leads me to ponder just how much about her daughter and her granddaughter Rosetta had really known.

FIFTY-NINE

'I couldn't see her. That made no difference. She was a disturbing presence in my life.'

I was talking to a fine woman called Nancy. Both her husband, Hal, and his brother, Col, were dear friends of my father's for more than half a century. When, near the end of his days, my father's ill health meant he had to be admitted to a nursing home, Col came not just to visit Dad. He took a razor in his hands and shaved the silver stubble on my father's cheeks, a rare act of intimacy between men.

Nancy is the only person I have met who also knew Rosetta, the single thread from my life that connects directly to my great-grandmother, though even this strand is flimsy and distinctly strange in type. Indeed, 'knew' is probably not the right choice of word to describe their relationship. It could, perhaps, be more properly said that Nancy 'experienced' my great-grandmother.

It was my mother who discovered that, in a remarkable coincidence, Nancy lived adjacent to Rosetta's Murray Street house when she was a girl. Intensely curious, I telephoned her late one afternoon and asked what it was like.

'She existed somewhere behind us,' Nancy recalled. 'I didn't know who she was, but I couldn't ignore her; she was too loud, too volatile.

'Her language could be shocking. I remember the churned-up feeling I'd have in my stomach once she'd start.

'I don't remember ever seeing your great-grandmother.

'She was just a very upsetting voice, a sound.'

Afterwards, thinking over what Nancy said, I imagined it was like dwelling in the shadow of a disembodied phantom whose fearful curses and unholy spells spread alarm each time they floated over the fence and across the lawn.

Sometimes Rosetta is as gay and charming as she used to be. Her house which, in a rare, nostalgic nod to her past and the irresistible charms of Alberto, she has named *Donna Rosa*, still reflects her refined taste. The furnishings and art are elegant and so is she. But she is increasingly erratic, can surrender to inexplicable, appalling rage.

One night Rosetta and Tom have a fiery argument. 'Unfaithful, untrustworthy, disloyal!' she shouts angrily. Accusations fly: Tom might have returned home late, perhaps Rosetta found his stumbling explanations to be inadequate. The following morning he rises early, goes to collect the milk and newspapers. He is a tolerant sort of chap, knows that Rosetta, tempestuous by nature, is becoming eccentric. As Tom walks across the lawn he passes the lavish granite cross, engraved in gold, that Rosetta has had installed above the grave of her champion Pekingese, Chu-Chu, and smiles indulgently.

The matter of Chu-Chu's demise attracted some small notoriety. Even the *Newcastle Herald* carried an account. The paper noted the way in which the prize-winning dog lay in state in 'a pale blue coffin at a Waverley mortuary chapel' before being interred next to his half-sister, Trinket, on the front lawn of Rosetta's house. Apparently, she had invited the Archbishop of Sydney, Cardinal Gilroy, to conduct the funeral rites.

The story concluded with the information that '... since Chu-Chu's death, [Mrs Tait] had received more than 100 phone calls and letters from strangers offering her sympathy'.

Then the *Herald* quoted Rosetta stating, 'It was just like losing a child. Their condolences were a great comfort to me.'

It was just like losing a child. No, it is not possible. I tell myself that the newspaper must have made a mistake. Rosetta could not have made this statement – it is outrageous. And yet, once more I succumb to doubt. I can't decide whether she was utterly callous, which renders the sentiment monstrous, or whether, as Freud might speculate, it was but the expression of a long-denied well of pain, hidden deep within the realms of her troubled mind.

Tom wonders not for the first time at the unique woman who is his wife. 'Ah, Rosetta,' he thinks, and shakes his head. He breathes deeply of the dewy air but then stops abruptly, his musing at an end. A surge of shocked disbelief comes upon him as he discovers that, where his carefully nurtured rosebushes once stood, there is now a scene of fierce butchery.

Tom sees that, in what must have been a frenzy of revenge, Rosetta has slashed and hacked with savage shears until not a single flower has been left intact. The ground is covered with bruised petals and jagged stems, all that remain after this nocturnal attack. He scoops up some of the damaged blooms before, with a certain rueful resignation, he spreads his fingers and lets them slowly fall from his hand.

Rosetta's tempests escalate. When she becomes ill, it is not hard for Tom to locate a facility that will accept her. But it is impossible to find one in which she can stay. Rosetta is too difficult, demands too much attention. Finally, she is admitted to a nursing home attached to St Vincent's Hospital in Darlinghurst. Not long afterwards Tom receives a phone call from one of the staff. The caller is polite but firm. 'Mr Tait, we would appreciate it if you could kindly take Mrs Tait home.' She is too trying even for the inexhaustible patience of the Sisters of Charity.

The Restorium Private Hospital in Sir Thomas Mitchell Road at Bondi will be Rosetta's last residence. The old hospital is not there anymore. It has been replaced by a modern, blond-brick block of flats. In an effort to evade the thumping beat of the rap music pouring from the top floor, I escape to the small park below, to sit beneath a sycamore and think.

I consider a book that I read only recently, in which the author, Elena Ferrante, wrote of a woman who 'knew how to go beyond the limit without ever really suffering the consequences'. At the time I found these words uncanny, felt that the author could have been describing my great-grandmother. Now, this certainty has faded. I find myself wondering if, at the end, Rosetta was consumed, depressed, dismayed by what she had done. Maybe a lifetime of repression and unacknowledged love and hate and guilt had exerted a final, dreadful penalty. Those with a more mystical inclination – a Madame Stern comes to mind – might call it 'the torment of the damned'.

But perhaps all this rumination is but a fruitless search for meaning, a doomed attempt to comprehend this most complex of women. I suspect I am once more endeavouring to make sense of something where there is no sense to be made. Being in such close proximity to the place where Rosetta drew her last breath seems to have unbalanced me, so I stand up and turn away.

Later, I seek out my psychiatrist friend again. Robert provides a more detached, medical point of view, reminding me that many people become chaotic, even violent during their advancing years. 'It can be because of senility, Alzheimer's, schizophrenia or disease,' he says as he takes off his glasses and polishes them. 'As to your great-grandmother's disturbed state of mind; that remains open to interpretation.'

Robert concludes that, in her absence, no one can ever be certain of what demons drove Rosetta to act in the manner that she did. (Now that I recall this conversation, he might have said 'factors' rather than 'demons' – I rather think the latter word is mine.)

The date is 28 July 1958, a cold, mid-winter day. Rosetta is very ill. She lies in one of the Restorium's beds, not far from where the splendid fantasy that was Wonderland once stood. As she slips in and out of consciousness, she dreams about the Imperial Menagerie of Wild Beasts and the Palace of Illusions, about Alice the elephant and of the way that once she danced with an almond-eyed sorcerer in the moonlight by the sea.

In less than a week I will turn five. Somehow, I can already read, though I don't know how I acquired this precious skill; it seemed to descend upon me as if by magic. Rather disappointingly, save for the initial thrill whereby marks upon a page turned into words with meaning, this pastime has not proven as diverting as I'd hoped. So far, the only books I have had access to are my elder brother's, the kind where Sue and Peter throw the ball to Spot the dog. Today promises something much more than that. Joining the mobile library is a sort of early birthday present, a mark of my transition from being a little child at home to one who is about to start school.

My small arm shoots up at an angle so that my mother can keep hold of my hand in her own. My legs are small as well. I struggle to keep up with her as she walks away from our house in Pleasant Avenue, East Lindfield, and up the hill. I try to match my mother's far wider strides by executing a kind of half-skipping hop, to no avail. No matter how far I stretch my limbs and flatten out my scabby knees I realise that I will never be in step with Mum.

As I trot jerkily along I am vaguely aware of houses with neat front gardens, letterboxes and painted fences. They pass me by in a suburban blur but mostly I keep my eyes down, focusing on my black lace-up shoes, their shuffle.

By the time I arrive at the asphalt strip in front of the scatter of local shops, the combination of anticipation and exertion has made me light-headed. Perhaps that is why the large green truck with the caravan attached seems so enchanting. In the middle of this metal wagon is an open door and descending from that door is a retractable set of painted steps. I don't know where they lead but I sense there might be treasure there.

A moment later Mum and I are inside a room of wonders. I look around and there are books everywhere – fat and thin volumes stand in enticing lines, books of different colours from red to green and blue and gold, all with writing down the spines, all waiting for discovery.

I look up at Mum and smile. She smiles back. I have entered her realm now and we are fellow travellers. It is her gift to me.

That night, Rosetta lies in Tom's arms and sighs as she departs this world for the next.

SIXTY

30 JULY 1958

In death, Rosetta has left behind another version of herself, shed it as easily, as naturally as a snake sheds its unneeded skin. Her Catholic faith has been set aside and, after many years, she reverts to the religion of her convict grandfather, Abraham Rheuben. Rosetta has declared herself Jewish once again. Yet even now, when she is cold and still, she challenges convention. Her final rebellion is against the ancient rituals of death that have existed for a millennium.

Rosetta's funeral is held just two days after she has passed away. Until that time, her body is never left alone. The Jewish burial society, the Chevra Kadisha, ensures that a *shomer*, or watcher, does not leave her side. The *shomer* is not there to observe; he is her guardian. He neither eats nor drinks but spends his time reciting psalms. It is important. In earlier times it was believed that death released ghosts from their unearthly realm: the watcher's holy recitations protected the departed against the evil that these unruly spirits might unleash. But what would Sir Oliver Lodge believe, or Sir Arthur Conan Doyle or Princess Charlotte? Would they think the spirits could be so easily vanquished?

It doesn't matter who you are, Jewish funerals are all the same. There is a unique equality in death. The Book of Proverbs says it is in this state that 'The rich and the poor meet together': whether wealthy or impoverished, of high station or low, untainted or sinful, all must be treated equally before God. In accordance with this requirement, after Rosetta's body has been bathed it is wrapped in a simple linen cloth; white, for purity. There are no pockets in her shroud, for unlike the ancient Egyptians, who filled their burial chambers with golden plate and jewels and fruit and grain, no material possessions are permitted to accompany the dead on their final journey to another realm.

But not all traditions are observed; there is one last act of defiance. 'For dust thou art and unto dust shalt thou return' is a holy command contained within the Book of Genesis. It is for this reason that Jews are interred in boxes of plain pine. Metal is forbidden; even the coffin's handles must be made of rope. The Rabbinical authorities claim that observance of these strictures ensures 'the soul rises to God, but the physical shelter, the … elements that clothe the soul, sink into the vast reservoir of nature'.

Rosetta didn't care what either God or his rabbis might decree. She would not be despoiled by those small creatures that live beneath the earth. Somehow, contrary to every tenet of the faith, she persuaded the Chief Rabbi of Sydney, Dr Israel Porush, to intervene. Rosetta had her way; he gave his consent.

Now Rosetta's body rests in a lead-lined coffin of polished wood. It is unheard of. The casket is so heavy that ten pallbearers are needed to carry it, and still they stagger beneath its weight.

~

When my father was a little boy and living in Enmore, his parents made certain that he regularly attended the Newtown Synagogue Sunday School. He must have managed to suppress his natural exuberance, for I am holding *The Authorised Daily Prayer Book* in my hands that he was awarded in 1920 at the age of eight. Produced by His Majesty's Printers, Eyre and Spottiswoode of London, it was the Conduct Prize.

It is in this near century-old black book that I turn to 'The Burial Service' and find the same words that would have been spoken at Rosetta's funeral. This takes place in an unadorned red-brick chapel abutting the main thoroughfare of Oxford Street in the Sydney suburb of Woollahra.

It is a locality filled with memories. The building is directly opposite the broad lawns of Centennial Park, that same park where, in the year following the birth of Rosetta's only child, the Federation of Australia was declared by the Governor-General Lord Hopetoun. Nearby stands the terrace house in which Rosetta lived during the years that Zeno the Magnificent performed his spell-binding feats at Mr Anderson's Wonderland City and, further down Oxford Street, is Paddington Town Hall, the place he went to find succour for his unquiet mind and troubled soul.

Forty, perhaps fifty people come to pay Rosetta their respects. Her brother and his wife, her sisters, their husbands and their children, all in black dresses, suits, coats and hats, attend. But not her own child, not her granddaughter or great-grandchildren. We remain unenlightened.

Reverend David Krass of The Great Synagogue officiates. A bearded bear of a man, he has recited the necessary holy words in his sonorous, Russian-accented voice many, many times, yet they never fail to elicit his compassion. The Reverend composes himself, then intones, 'As for man, his days are as grass; as the flower of the field, so he flourisheth. For the wind passeth over it, and it is gone; and the place thereof shall know it no more.

'O Lord, who art full of compassion, who dwellest on high – God of forgiveness, who art merciful, slow to anger and abounding in loving kindness, grant pardon of transgressions, nearness of salvation, and perfect rest …'

The service is brief. Afterwards, mourners shake hands or embrace. They wish one another, as is customary at Jewish funerals, 'a long life'. Florence and her sisters weep and wipe their eyes. Rosetta, clever and determined, vibrant and resolute: she was the eldest, always daring and different. What will they do without her now?

Tom is lost in thought. He has spent more than a decade with Rosetta, yet never fathomed the secrets she carried in her heart. They were known only by one mesmerising man with a haunting, low voice, coal-black hair and panther eyes. Tom is an easygoing sort of chap and philosophical about her loss. Rosetta, always a challenging woman, has in her last years presented him with many difficulties. Some part of him must surely feel relief.

He is only forty-four. Should he wish to do so, there is ample time for him to marry once more.

'Come on, come with me,' says Florence. She takes Tom's arm, turns towards the funeral car, which waits behind the hearse. There are no flowers lying on Rosetta's casket to mitigate or soften the harsh fact of her demise. There is no sense of celebration; this is not Judaism's way in which to mark a death.

The moment when burial takes place is the time when the irrevocable nature of mortality, its brutal certainty, is most keenly felt. Rosetta's sisters are in tears again; their husbands, affecting a manly stoicism, purse their mouths and look grim. Some of the younger family members, Rosetta's nieces and nephews, are shocked by the sight of the freshly dug, yawning pit. They are unused to the raw confrontation of interment. The young men catch one another's eyes then look away, too ill at ease even for a half-hearted attempt at nonchalance.

Tom, who held Rosetta in his arms just two days previously, watched as she drew her last breath, is unexpectedly stricken. The loss is naked now. He knows that he will never meet another woman possessed of such bewitching, thrilling force. He shivers, conscious for the first time of the meaning of Rosetta's death. Standing by his wife's grave under a grey winter sky, he feels cold and dispirited.

Reverend Krass steps forward, leads the distressed band of mourners in their prayers to God.

'Thou sustainest the living with loving kindness, quickenest the dead with great mercy, supportest the falling, healest the sick, loosest the bound, and keepest thy faith to them that sleep in the dust.'

Slowly, with straining muscles and trembling arms, the pall-bearers lower the casket, heavy as the most wretched heart.

'May she rest in peace,' the Reverend says, as the first damp clod of earth is cast.

SIXTY-ONE

Randwick Cemetery, a small hillside necropolis surrounded by neat, red-brick houses and suburban streets, is Rosetta's final resting place. My father went there to investigate. More than two decades later, I follow him. At the time of my visit, admittedly mid-week and on a day of harsh, dry heat, there is not another soul in sight. There are no grieving mourners, no curious members of the public, nor even a caretaker to help find the right grave. It is not so much an eerie place as desolate, filled with dry weeds and bleached stone, barren in the blazing light.

Dad discovered that there were three graves in a row, for here lies my great, great-grandmother Fanny and great, great-grandfather Lewis, as well. According to the records Dad unearthed, this triple burial site, located in Section A, cost one pound ten shillings. Towards the very end of the trusty blue folder, he included one sheet of paper on which were typed his observations.

> *Although not an ostentatious grave, it [reflects] considerable expenditure for the times. A broad expanse of burnished*

brown tiles, three headstones of a similar design and all . . . executed in conformity with a pre-determined pattern.

He also noted that there were few Jewish graves, and those that did exist were surrounded by hundreds more from other religious persuasions. I think Rosetta, an aficionado of so many faiths, would have enjoyed being at the centre of this ecumenical assembly of the departed.

My great-grandmother's grave is broken and battered. I peer at the words on the tombstone, for weathering has blurred their edges, but they contain no revelations. Indeed, particularly when one considers her vivid character and the remarkable life she led, the inscription is dull and formulaic. '*In loving memory of Rosetta Tait*' is all it says.

After my father recorded these nondescript words he wrote, 'No more, no less.'

Like him, I am struck by the inadequacy of the epithet.

I turn to go, then turn back, filled with the strangest feeling. I realise that, at this stage in my journey of discovery, my great-grandmother has become like a story-book character to me. She might have inhabited the pages of the myths and legends that I used to read as a child in the East Lindfield mobile library. Rosetta is transcendent, fantastic; a creature from a dream.

Yet here I am, and there can be few things more tangible than a grave in a cemetery. After all, what is a grave but proof, should proof be needed, of existence?

Something shifts. I drop to my knees, run my fingers over the cracked tiles and whisper, 'Once, you lived.'

Rosetta drew up her Last Will and Testament on 12 August 1957, a year before she died. The Union Trustee Company of Australia Ltd has been appointed sole executor and trustee. Immediately after the funeral Rosetta's adviser, a fellow Tom has never met, comes up to him and says, 'I want to see you at nine o'clock tomorrow in my office, 2 O'Connell Street.' It seems a bit abrupt, but all the same, he presents himself.

Rosetta's family is there as well, assembled in a dark, wood-panelled room for the reading of the will. There is consternation in the office of the Union Trustee Company when Mr B.C. Menzies, the company officer responsible for Rosetta's affairs, announces her bequests. Rosetta's sisters Ivy and Evelyn each receive two hundred and fifty pounds. Florence is given two still-life paintings of fruit and flowers by the fashionable Edwardian artist Giovanni Barbaro; they had originally belonged to Lilian.

Father Riley is bequeathed fifty pounds.

Then Clause 5 of Rosetta's will is read:

> *I give and bequeath all the rest and residue of my personal Estate and devise all my Real Estate of or to which I may be … possessed or entitled or over which I shall then have any power of testamentary disposition unto my husband Thomas Reginald Rufus Tait absolutely …*

All the land, the houses and the flats, everything goes to Rosetta's young husband.

Tom, conscious of the strained atmosphere, protests: he didn't know until then that the property would be left to him. (Many years later, when talking to my father, he will claim, 'I had no idea,' before confiding, 'the sisters were pretty upset.')

Rosetta's family, unhappy with this outcome, tries to accept. The contents of the will are, after all, but a reflection of what they had both long feared and half come to expect. Tom is Rosetta's heir and that is that. With a wry half grin Frank says, 'Well, he pulled it off. Good luck to him.'

Tom does not care to remain alone. He marries again in the year following.

~

My grandmother's existence is noted on Rosetta's Death Certificate. Next to the space marked 'Issue in order of birth (living and deceased)' is written just one word, *Frances*, and then *age unknown*. That seems heart-wrenching to me, the not knowing.

Nobody thinks to tell Rosetta's only child that her wayward, beautiful mother with the curving smile is now truly lost to her forever. There is not a soul who murmurs to her how it was when the woman who gave birth to her drew her last breath and ceased to live.

SIXTY-TWO

Rosetta lived in the same city as her daughter for more than forty years, yet they never met.

For her part, Billie, or Frances as Rosetta would have known her, made no attempt to find her mother. That painful part of her life would not be revisited. Having been rejected when a little child and suffered bitterly, she could not countenance the possibility that she might be wounded once again.

Billie waited, instead. She waited in vain: there was no message, no phone call, nor a letter. It was as if her mother were already in her grave among the spirits of the dead.

My grandmother, my mother, myself: each one of us had been marked by Rosetta's absence, in different ways and to varying extents.

But, for me, the story hadn't finished yet.

I see the address on her Last Will and Testament, learn with numbing shock that, until 1958, during the final six years of Rosetta's life, mother and daughter lived only minutes apart. That my grandmother Billie should have been in such close proximity to her lost mother and yet known nothing of this seems to me to be the final, cruel twist in this extraordinary tale.

I begin to imagine the two of them, unknowingly, passing each other in the street. Perhaps they are at a bus stop, or in the post office, or a shop. Like an inner film rewinding in rapid time, a vast jumble of vivid images rushes through my mind. I wonder if during just such a fleeting encounter there might have been some small thing – a look, a gesture, the way a head is turned or a pair of eyes narrows in the light – that ever leads one of them to experience a brief flutter of unconscious recognition, a faint, unacknowledged rapport.

In the early 1950s Rosetta moved away from *Donna Rosa*, the home in Murray Street, Bronte, where Tom first brought her silent yellow Packard back to life. Now in her seventies, maintaining the house had become onerous. My great-grandmother was the proprietor of an elegant block of six apartments situated at 34 Salisbury Road, Rose Bay, and so, after one of her tenants decided to vacate, it seemed natural that she and Tom would take his place.

She left behind her beloved Pekingese, Chu-Chu, buried under his lavish headstone alongside Trinket, sold most of her fine furnishings and incinerated many of her more personal possessions. Numerous letters and photographs were burnt. 'She was a beggar for destroying things,' Tom said. The fact is, Rosetta was never one to be burdened by the past. Somehow, the child's suitcase containing the precious evidence of her glamorous life abroad escaped this inferno. She preserved a few of her paintings, a sculpture. And, of course, the tea cups with their fine oriental markings; they were kept.

I have an old black and white photograph of the building, but I go there anyway to see for myself what it is like, this place so close to the modest flat in which Billie lived, the one with the china shepherdesses and the wallpaper with the stains of nicotine.

Though Melton Hall's open balconies have been enclosed and a flourishing rainforest garden of staghorns and tree ferns has been planted in the front, it is still easy to recognise. Painted a pale buttermilk and shaded by spreading trees, it has retained the original Georgian-style portico with the white tapered columns standing to attention at each side. Rosetta and Tom lived in the top right-hand apartment, so I tilt my head back and, in order to have a better look, squint at it through a crosshatching of branches and leaves. I don't attempt to enter. It is enough to know it's there.

Rose Bay is a gorgeous cove, sweeping in a voluptuous arc between the promontories of exclusive Point Piper and Vaucluse. Its cerulean waters are crowded with expensive craft and there is a small island in the middle called Shark, so perfectly positioned it looks as if it were placed there by an especially artful god. The sun is shining in a sky licked by a hot blue glaze and so I decide I will stroll, as Rosetta never did, to the flat where her daughter, my grandmother, lived at Midlothian, 2a Victoria Road, Bellevue Hill. It is not very far; just down the road. Nana is not there now, of course; she died in 1988. The journey would be merely minutes by car, but I wish to know how long it takes to walk and, more importantly, how it feels. I want the sense of the thing.

As I make my way under that bright sky from one flat to the other I become lost in a conjurer's dream.

It is a day just like this: hard-edged, hot and clear. Only a few insubstantial white wisps interrupt the expanse of cobalt sky. My brother, Michael, is at school. We live in a suburb still so undeveloped that he makes his way there by trudging through the bush. Children do that in the 1950s. They walk everywhere by themselves, even if they're only five or six.

I am four years old, too young for school, but I recognise the shapes made by 207 and 324. These are the numbers on front of the two green buses Mum and I need to catch so that we can visit my grandmother way over on the other side of the Sydney

Harbour Bridge. We live in the verdant north and she, in the cosmopolitan east.

Usually, we alight at the stop opposite her block of flats, but this day will be different. My mother and I stay on a little longer until we reach Rose Bay and a long footpath that curves around the shore. This is where we plan to meet my grandmother, watch the fishermen and feed the sea birds.

It really is very warm; my cotton dress is sticking to my back. We have not gone far when Nana announces she has had enough, she wants to stop and rest beneath a tree. 'But you go on,' she says. My mother and I walk further and then pause to watch some pelicans search for aquatic treats. With their enormous, greedy beaks they appear faintly menacing until, suddenly, the birds take flight and as they do acquire a grace and beauty that is transformative.

There is a noise. Not the sound of the birds' insistent cries nor their beating wings, but something else. It is a woman, a striking old lady with cardinal-red hair. This woman talks in a loud voice, though I don't know who she can be speaking to as she is sitting on a bench, quite alone. She is not frightening, just very strange.

I leave my mother's side, run over and ask her the only thing that comes into my mind. 'Are you lost?' I say. She stops shouting, studies me with toffee-coloured eyes and says, quite lucidly, 'I'm no more lost than those birds you see up in the sky.'

She stands and turns, not shouting now but muttering all the while. The way her hair looks as it catches the sun reminds me of fireworks, all blazing sparks and flame. I watch her as she moves past me, then my mother, until finally, in the distance, she passes my grandmother waiting in the shade.

A quick glance at my watch tells me that the walk from Rosetta's flat to her daughter's takes just fifteen minutes, but time's dance is rarely a reliable entity. The journey might have been as brief as the blink of an eye or, then again, as lengthy as eternity.

POSTSCRIPT

Truth is always strange;
Stranger than fiction.

Lord Byron, 1823
Don Juan Canto xiv, Stanza 101

Fact and fiction, truth and fabrication, the incongruous nature of reality and yet the utter believability of that which is untrue – when real events seem impossible and fantasy all too likely, separating the two is challenging.

That historic material and personal reminiscences are rarely in perfect accord adds another layer of complexity. Determining accuracy is particularly difficult when the principal protagonists are, themselves, notoriously unreliable sources. For these reasons, in the writing of Rosetta's story, allowance has been made for both the vagaries of memory and imagination's caprice.

With regard to the latter, it occurs to me that at least a little of my great-grandmother's penchant for invention might have been inherited.

Notwithstanding the above, it should be noted that all the legal records, newspaper reports, journals, my father's typed accounts, transcribed interviews, the list of patrons, Professor Zeno's pamphlet and the astonishing letters, postcards and telegrams from which extracts have been drawn exist.

The sole exceptions are the two letters from Lilian. The first letter was, by necessity, invented. Re-creation of the second was required as the original correspondence was destroyed at the insistence of Edwina Mountbatten.

PEOPLE AND EVENTS

The images of Zeno and Rosetta that appear in this book are all drawn from the collection that was discovered in the small child's suitcase and subsequently despatched from Mermaid Waters by Tom Tait.

The name of Rosetta's father, my great, great-grandfather, Lewis, appears in the family tree in parentheses, next to his given name of Louis. The former designation has been utilised in order to eliminate confusion with Rosetta's first husband who, coincidentally, was also named Louis.

The name of Lilian's son reflects a number of different spellings, depending on the source. Although recorded as Dermott in both Lilian's death certificate and in Edwina Mountbatten's letter to Rosetta, his will, together with that inarguable authority, *Debrett's Illustrated Peerage*, states that it is Dermot. Accordingly, this is the spelling that has been adopted.

The identity of the priest with whom my great-grandmother shared a long relationship has been disguised.

Although the names of all the ships on which Zeno, Rosetta and Lilian voyaged are correct, it has not been possible to determine the name of the particular ocean liner that carried Rosetta and Zeno to London. As the SS *Omrah* sailed to and from Australia during this period, in the absence of the relevant maritime records the name of this vessel has been utilised.

A few minor characters are fictitious. These include Ivy, the young woman who provided Rosetta with domestic assistance, Constable Hall, the helpful English bobby, and the showgirl, Mildred.

Alberto Rivero is an amalgam of several of the young Argentinians who brought tango to London.

All of the other characters in the book, from Empress Eugenie to Princess Charlotte and Baroness Stern, are real: the circumstances of their lives are true, even if, on occasion, this might seem unlikely.

For instance, few people are aware that Helena Rubinstein founded her cosmetics empire in Melbourne. Although in this case there is no proof that she and Rosetta met, given their personalities, plus the fact that the two young women lived in close proximity to each other, during a similar period of time, it is not unlikely that they might have developed a friendship.

Likewise, I have no evidence that William Norman and Banjo Paterson ever shared a drink, though both men did reside in Queen Street, Woollahra, concurrently.

Finally, I do not know if Sir Arthur Conan Doyle was ever introduced to my great-grandparents or not. Nevertheless, as he was a friend of their patron, the great physicist Sir Oliver Lodge, and a passionate fellow spiritualist, it seems well within the realms of possibility.

It might be observed that, rather like Rosetta and Zeno, Sir Arthur Conan Doyle, Banjo Paterson and Helena Rubinstein were all, albeit each in his or her own way, superb masters of invention. In that regard, their presence in Rosetta's story seemed to me to be entirely congruent.

The activities described at Wonderland City, from the restaging of Ned Kelly's siege at Glenrowan to the blazing house-fire tableau and the perilous shipwrecks, really occurred. As Zeno worked as a clairvoyant at Wonderland prior to leaving for London, it can be assumed that, given his and Rosetta's singular talents, they would have participated in many of these hazardous events.

The description of the 1922 Artists' Ball is largely a conflation of the incidents that transpired at this and several subsequent revelries.

PLACES

At the time of Rosetta's marriage to Louis Raphael in 1899, the Hotel Windsor was called the Grand Hotel. The name by which this establishment has most commonly been known during the great majority of its one hundred and thirty-two year history has been used in order to avoid confusion.

The hotel's address in Melbourne's Spring Street is unchanged. Indeed, the address of every location referred to in this book, be it public edifice or private dwelling, is both precise and correct, from the Raphael family home, Frances Villa, in Faraday Street, Carlton, and Rosetta's Queen Street, Woollahra, residence, to Professor Zeno's New Bond Street rooms in London and Baroness Stern's Cap Martin villa.

In appearance, most buildings remain more or less intact, although several, including Zeno's laboratory in the Edgware Road, London, and the Restorium Private Hospital at Bondi, have been demolished in favour of more contemporary developments.

Sadly, save for several information panels that have been strategically placed by Waverley Municipal Council along the approaches to Tamarama Beach, virtually no trace of Mr Anderson's fantastic amusement park, Wonderland City, remains.

Nevertheless, I have been told that, if you happen to be strolling on the cliffs late at night when the wind sweeps in from the south and the tide is running high, you might hear a certain, indistinct sound carried on the breeze. I believe it is a kind of faint trumpeting, strangely like the cry of a distant beast, a pachyderm.

A.J.

ACKNOWLEDGEMENTS

There are many extremely generous people who made this book possible. First and foremost among them are my mother, who never hesitated to share her memories even though this could not always have been either easy or comfortable; and my father, without whose rare combination of skill, curiosity and determination much of the research that informs *Rosetta* would have been unavailable.

Among the substantial number of institutions and individuals who rendered invaluable assistance are: Julianne Barlow, Archivist, and Sarah Salter, former Alumni Manager, Genazzano; Elizabeth Brown, Library and Research Officer, Australian Racing Museum; David Dale; Silvana Ferraris, Open Space Booking Officer, Randwick City Council; Jane de Teliga; Faber Academy; Dr Robert Fisher; Nancy Goldstein; Martin Indyk; Michael Joel; Evelyn Juers; David Kent; Philip Krass; Patti Miller; Judy Morgan; Gloria Parry; Frank Solomon; the NSW Government Office of Environment and Heritage; the NSW Registry of Births, Deaths and Marriages; the Chinese Museum, Melbourne; the Museum of Sydney; the National Library of Australia; the State Library of New South Wales; the State Library of Victoria; and Waverley Municipal Library.

I would like to express particular appreciation to my friend and trusted reader, Susan Williams, for her enthusiasm and encouragement.

A special debt of gratitude is owed to Mr Frederick Koch for inviting me to Villa Torre Clementina at Cap Martin, France, and to Mr Koch's property manager, Mark Ryan.

I am also grateful to Jan Worthington, my father's principal researcher. Sadly, many of the people who were interviewed by either Jan or my father, or who helped in other ways, have now passed away. I remain, as was my father, very thankful for their contribution.

I have been especially fortunate to have the support of my agent, Catherine Drayton, my inspiring editor, Fiona Daniels, and the exceptional Random House team, including commissioning editor Sophie Ambrose and publishing director Nikki Christer. Designer Sandy Cull created the cover of my dreams. All brought to *Rosetta* the best possible combination of passion and dedication.

When one writes a book the people closest to the author have a great deal with which to contend. My children, Bennett and Arabella, were unfailingly supportive, as was my husband, Philip Mason. Philip also provided much practical assistance, enabling me to both embark upon far-flung research forays and, indeed, continue to write *Rosetta* without losing my way.

PROFESSOR CARL ZENO'S LIST OF PATRONS

Lady Archibald Campbell (the Duke of Argyll's daughter-in-law and subject of a famously controversial portrait by Whistler); the Princess of Pless (the former Daisy Cornwallis-West, wife of the extraordinarily wealthy Hans Heinrich XV of Germany); Lord Victor Paget (heir to the Marquis of Anglesey); Prince Min of Korea (ministerial plenipotentiary); Lady Lilian Bagot (Baltimore-born daughter of a US Congressman, wife of Conservative politician the 4th Baron Bagot); Sir Edgar Vincent (art collector, politician, diplomat and author, 12th Baronet of Stoke d'Abernon); Her Grace the Duchess of Rutland (Lady Violet Manners, artist and prominent member of the literary salon The Souls); Lady Diana Manners (actress, daughter of the Duchess of Rutland, later social identity Lady Diana Cooper); The Right Hon. Diana Lister (daughter of the 4th Baron Ribblesdale, became the wife of Chanel's former lover Boy Capel and later married the Earl of Westmorland); Her Grace the Duchess of Westminster (the former Constance [Shelagh] Cornwallis-West, sister of the Princess of Pless); Lady Juliet Duff (daughter of the 4th Earl of Lonsdale and the Marchioness of Ripon, patron of the arts, notable supporter of the Ballets Russes); Lady Bathurst (daughter of Baron Glenesk, owner of *The Daily Telegraph*); Sir Fitzwilliam (Eric Spencer Wentworth-Fitzwilliam, 9th Earl, army officer); The Right Hon. the Countess of Glasgow (wife of the former Governor of New Zealand); Lady Anna Rosslyn (Countess Rosslyn, previously Minneapolis chorus girl Anna Robinson); Sir John (former Australian politician and Chief Justice of Tasmania) and Lady Dodds; Vice Admiral Charles

Windham (naval hero and Gentleman Usher to the King); Colonel Smith; Captain Parker; Lady Parker; Major Simpson; Thomas Beecham (renowned conductor, founder of the London Philharmonic and Royal Philharmonic orchestras); Sir Oliver Lodge (winner of the Royal Society's Rumford Medal, first Principal of the University of Birmingham); Miss Gertie Miller (actress and singer, married the Earl of Dudley, 4th Governor General of Australia and great-grandfather of Australian actress/director Rachel Ward); Miss Thelma Raye (Brazilian-born performer, later the wife of English screen legend Ronald Colman); Miss Gabrielle Ray (musical comedy star, included Alfred Vanderbilt and King Manuel of Portugal among her admirers); Captain Higson (Master of the Hunt, served with the 14th Hussars); Mrs Marconi (wife of the Nobel Prize-winning inventor Guglielmo Marconi, formerly the Hon. Beatrice O'Brien, daughter of the 14th Baron Inchiquin, and later the Marquise di Montecorona); The Right Hon. Earl of Sandwich (author, spiritualist, Conservative Member of Parliament); Madame Ernesta Stern (authoress, famous saloniste, widow of the French banker Baron Louis Stern); Lady Miller.

BIBLIOGRAPHY

A number of publications have provided me with invaluable information. These include:

Ackroyd, P., *London: The Biography*, Vintage, London, 2001

Barnes, J., *Arthur & George*, Jonathan Cape, London, 2005

Bell, M. (Editor), *And The Spirit Lingers . . .*, Genazzano College History Committee, Burwood, 1988

Betcherman, L., *The Riviera Set: From Queen Victoria to Princess Grace*, Bev Editions, Smashwords, 2010

Farris Thompson, R., *Tango: The Art History of Love*, Vintage, 2006

Freyd, J., *Betrayal Trauma: The Logic of Forgetting Childhood Abuse*, Harvard University Press, Massachusetts, 1998

Hoss de le Comte, M.G., *The Tango*, Maizal, Buenos Aires, 2000

Howell, G., *In Vogue*, Penguin, London, 1978

Kolatch, A., *The Jewish Book of Why*, Jonathan David, New York, 1981

Lindsay, N., *Bohemians of the Bulletin*, Angus and Robertson, Sydney, 1965

McKernan, M., *Australians at Home, World War I*, The Five Mile Press, Scoresby, 2014

Penglase, J., *Orphans of the Living: Growing Up in 'Care' in Twentieth-Century Australia*, Fremantle Press, Perth, 2010

Twopeny, R., *Town Life in Australia*, Sydney University Press, Sydney, 1973 (first published London, 1883)

Van der Kiste, J., *Charlotte and Feodora*, Amazon KDP, 2012

Woodhead, L., *War Paint: Miss Elizabeth Arden and Madame Helena Rubinstein*, Virago Press, London, 2003

Writer, L., *Tilly Devine, Kate Leigh and the Razor Gangs*, Macmillan, Sydney, 2001

Ziegler, P., *Diana Cooper*, Penguin Books, Harmondsworth, 1983

Ziegler, P., *Mountbatten: The Official Biography*, Collins, London, 1985